OUTDOOR
SCHOOL

An imprint of Macmillan Publishing Group, LLC
120 Broadway, New York, NY 10271
OddDot.com

Library of Congress Control Number: 2020021757
ISBN 978-1-250-23065-2

OUTDOOR SCHOOL LOGO DESIGNER Tae Won Yu
COVER DESIGNER Tae Won Yu & Tim Hall
INTERIOR DESIGNER Tim Hall
EDITOR Justin Krasner
ILLUSTRATOR John D. Dawson

Art from *Golden Guides: Birds* by James Gordon Irving.
Art from *Golden Guides: Rocks, Gems, Minerals* and *Golden Guides: Fossils* by Raymond Perlman. Art from *Golden Guides: Seashells of North America* by George Sandstrom. Art from *Golden Guides: Dinosaurs* by John D. Dawson.
Golden Guides are published by Macmillan Publishing Group, LLC.
Maps, charts, and cover images used under license from Shutterstock.com

Our books may be purchased in bulk for promotional, educational, or business use. Please contact your local bookseller or the Macmillan Corporate and Premium Sales Department at (800) 221-7945 ext. 5442 or by email at MacmillanSpecialMarkets@macmillan.com.

Printed in China by 1010 Printing International Limited,
North Point, Hong Kong

First edition, 2021
5 7 9 10 8 6

ROCK, FOSSIL, AND SHELL HUNTING

JENNIFER SWANSON

ILLUSTRATED BY
JOHN D. DAWSON

Odd Dot New York

OPEN YOUR DOOR.
STEP OUTSIDE.
YOU'VE JUST WALKED INTO
OUTDOOR SCHOOL.

Whether you're entering an urban wilderness or a remote forest, at Outdoor School we have only four guidelines.

- → **BE AN EXPLORER, A RESEARCHER, AND—MOST OF ALL—A LEADER.**
- → **TAKE CHANCES AND SOLVE PROBLEMS AFTER CONSIDERING ANY RISKS.**
- → **FORGE A RESPECTFUL RELATIONSHIP WITH NATURE AND YOURSELF.**
- → **BE FREE, BE WILD, AND BE BRAVE.**

We believe that people learn best through doing. So we not only give you information about the wild, but we also include three kinds of activities:

TRY IT → **Read about the topic and experience it right away.**

TRACK IT ↘ **Observe and interact with nature, and reflect on your experiences right in this book.**

TAKE IT TO THE NEXT LEVEL ↗ **Progress to advanced techniques and master a skill.**

Completed any of these activities? Awesome! Check off your accomplishment and write in the date.

This book is the guide to the adventures you've been waiting for. We hope you'll do something outside your comfort zone—but we're not telling you to go out of your way to find danger. If something seems unsafe, don't do it.

And don't forget: This book is **YOURS**, so use it. Write in it, draw in it, make notes about your favorite rocks, fossil finds, unique shells, whatever! The purpose of Outdoor School is to help you learn about your world, help you learn about yourself, and—best of all—help you have an epic adventure.

So now that you have everything you need—keep going. Take another step. And another. And never stop.

Yours in adventure,

THE **OUTDOOR SCHOOL** TEAM

CONTENTS

PART II: FOSSILS 204

PART III: SHELLS 320

PART I

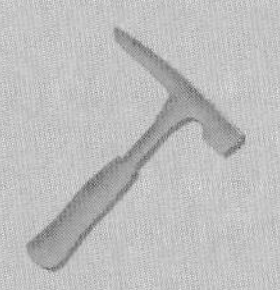

ROCKS & MINERALS

What would YOU do?

You're hiking through the woods.

It's a beautiful, sunny day, and the trail ahead of you is clear. As you hike, you stop to pick up rocks along the way. That smooth oval one looks good. Oooh—there's a white one with a lot of black spots on it! Rocks are all over the place. All you have to do is look. One next to the trunk of a tree. Another near the edge of the lake. Two that you dig out of the rocky trail itself.

Hold on. What's that shiny thing sparkling in the bottom of the stream? You reach your hand in, immediately soaking your sleeve. Grasping the rock, you pull it out of the water. Gold! Or a diamond or other precious gemstone! Well, maybe. But how can you tell? And should you take it home or chuck it back into the stream? What would you do?

ROCK & MINERAL HUNTING

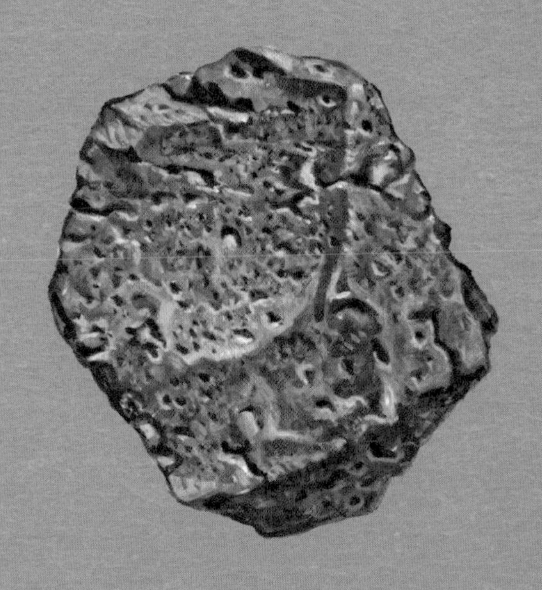

CHAPTER 1

Rocks & Minerals & Where You Can Find Them

Bink!

That rock you just kicked down the street, it's history. Not like the "it's gone" sort of history, but the "hundreds of thousands of years old" type of history. That's right. Rocks tell us a lot about our planet. They give us clues to how our planet works, from our earliest beginnings to today. And tomorrow, too. Just by walking out your front door (or your back door, for that matter) you could learn about your world.

Are you outside right now? If not, what are you waiting for? Get out there and look around! Do you see any rocks? Be sure to look up, down, and all around you because rocks are everywhere! You will find them on the ground you walk on, the mountains you climb, and deep under the ocean. (You might need your scuba gear for that last one, though.)

Pick up a rock. Close your fist around it. Now think about this: You are holding a bit of the planet in your hand!

(And you thought all rocks were good for was kicking down the street or skipping across the lake. Just wait!)

What Is a Rock and a Mineral?

Rocks are solid, natural objects. That means that they are made by nature. The ocean, land, sun, wind, and rain all play a part in making rocks. Most rocks are made up of a mix of chemicals known as minerals.

Can you see the minerals in the rock? Sometimes. If you look closely at a rock, you will see specks, or grains, that make up the rock. Those are the minerals. Minerals are formed from nonliving things, like the earth's crust—the outermost part of the planet, the thing we walk on every day. Minerals from the crust are solid and, like rocks, are made by nature.

Sounds like rocks and minerals are the same things. Not exactly.

Five Characteristics of a Mineral

1. NATURALLY OCCURRING Not man-made.

2. INORGANIC Not derived from living organisms.

3. SOLID Not a liquid or a gas.

4. ORDERED INTERNAL STRUCTURE Its atoms are arranged in a repeating pattern that forms crystals.

5. SPECIFIC CHEMICAL COMPOSITION All specimens are made up of the same atoms in the same amounts, with very little variation.

If one of these characteristics is missing, the substance is not a mineral.

How are rocks and minerals different? Unlike rocks, minerals have a specific composition. They are all composed of chemicals, or elements, that cannot be broken down any further. These elements are found in the periodic table.

PERIODIC TABLE OF ELEMENTS

Atomic Number → 1; Symbol → H; Name → Hydrogen; Atomic Weight → 1.008

1 IA	2 IIA	3 IIIB	4 IVB	5 VB	6 VIB	7 VIIB	8 VIIIB	9 VIIIB	10 VIIIB	11 IB	12 IIB	13 IIIA	14 IVA	15 VA	16 VIA	17 VIIA	18 VIIIA
1 H Hydrogen 1.008																	2 He Helium 4.002602
3 Li Lithium 6.94	4 Be Beryllium 9.0121831											5 B Boron 10.81	6 C Carbon 12.011	7 N Nitrogen 14.007	8 O Oxygen 15.999	9 F Fluorine 18.998403163	10 Ne Neon 20.1797
11 Na Sodium 22.98976928	12 Mg Magnesium 24.305											13 Al Aluminium 26.9815385	14 Si Silicon 28.085	15 P Phosphorus 30.973761998	16 S Sulfur 32.06	17 Cl Chlorine 35.45	18 Ar Argon 39.948
19 K Potassium 39.0983	20 Ca Calcium 40.078	21 Sc Scandium 44.955908	22 Ti Titanium 47.867	23 V Vanadium 50.9415	24 Cr Chromium 51.9961	25 Mn Manganese 54.938044	26 Fe Iron 55.845	27 Co Cobalt 58.933194	28 Ni Nickel 58.6934	29 Cu Copper 63.546	30 Zn Zinc 65.38	31 Ga Gallium 69.723	32 Ge Germanium 72.630	33 As Arsenic 74.921595	34 Se Selenium 78.971	35 Br Bromine 79.904	36 Kr Krypton 83.798
37 Rb Rubidium 85.4678	38 Sr Strontium 87.62	39 Y Yttrium 88.90584	40 Zr Zirconium 91.224	41 Nb Niobium 92.90637	42 Mo Molybdenum 95.95	43 Tc Technetium (98)	44 Ru Ruthenium 101.07	45 Rh Rhodium 102.90550	46 Pd Palladium 106.42	47 Ag Silver 107.8682	48 Cd Cadmium 112.414	49 In Indium 114.818	50 Sn Tin 118.710	51 Sb Antimony 121.760	52 Te Tellurium 127.60	53 I Iodine 126.90447	54 Xe Xenon 131.293
55 Cs Caesium 132.90545196	56 Ba Barium 137.327	57 - 71 Lanthanoids	72 Hf Hafnium 178.49	73 Ta Tantalum 180.94788	74 W Tungsten 183.84	75 Re Rhenium 186.207	76 Os Osmium 190.23	77 Ir Iridium 192.217	78 Pt Platinum 195.084	79 Au Gold 196.966569	80 Hg Mercury 200.592	81 Tl Thallium 204.38	82 Pb Lead 207.2	83 Bi Bismuth 208.98040	84 Po Polonium (209)	85 At Astatine (210)	86 Rn Radon (222)
87 Fr Francium (223)	88 Ra Radium (226)	89 - 103 Actinoids	104 Rf Rutherfordium (267)	105 Db Dubnium (268)	106 Sg Seaborgium (269)	107 Bh Bohrium (270)	108 Hs Hassium (269)	109 Mt Meitnerium (278)	110 Ds Darmstadtium (281)	111 Rg Roentgenium (282)	112 Cn Copernicium (285)	113 Nh Nihonium (286)	114 Fl Flerovium (289)	115 Mc Moscovium (289)	116 Lv Livermorium (293)	117 Ts Tennessine (294)	118 Og Oganesson (294)

57 La Lanthanum 138.90547	58 Ce Cerium 140.116	59 Pr Praseodymium 140.90766	60 Nd Neodymium 144.242	61 Pm Promethium (145)	62 Sm Samarium 150.36	63 Eu Europium 151.964	64 Gd Gadolinium 157.25	65 Tb Terbium 158.92535	66 Dy Dysprosium 162.500	67 Ho Holmium 164.93033	68 Er Erbium 167.259	69 Tm Thulium 168.93422	70 Yb Ytterbium 173.045	71 Lu Lutetium 174.9668
89 Ac Actinium (227)	90 Th Thorium 232.0377	91 Pa Protactinium 231.03588	92 U Uranium 238.02891	93 Np Neptunium (237)	94 Pu Plutonium (244)	95 Am Americium (243)	96 Cm Curium (247)	97 Bk Berkelium (247)	98 Cf Californium (251)	99 Es Einsteinium (252)	100 Fm Fermium (257)	101 Md Mendelevium (258)	102 No Nobelium (259)	103 Lr Lawrencium (266)

Take the mineral quartz, for example. It is made up of two elements: silicon and oxygen. Quartz needs one atom of silicon and two atoms of oxygen to form silicon dioxide, SiO_2, aka silica. That's it. But to form quartz, those silica atoms must also come together in a specific, repeating pattern.

A Common Mineral You Might Know

Quartz is one of the most widespread minerals on earth because oxygen and silicon are the two most common elements in the earth's crust. Quartz crystals can be found in rocks like granite, sandstone, and shale, and make up much of the sand in the world. That's right, visit just about any beach and you'll discover quartz crystals!

MAJOR VARIETIES OF QUARTZ

Each mineral has an ordered internal structure based on the pattern of its atoms. The pattern repeats, forming a three-dimensional crystal. The shape of the crystal, including the number of sides and position of its angles, is determined by the atoms' pattern, so every mineral has its own unique crystalline structure. You can tell whether two minerals are the same by comparing their crystals.

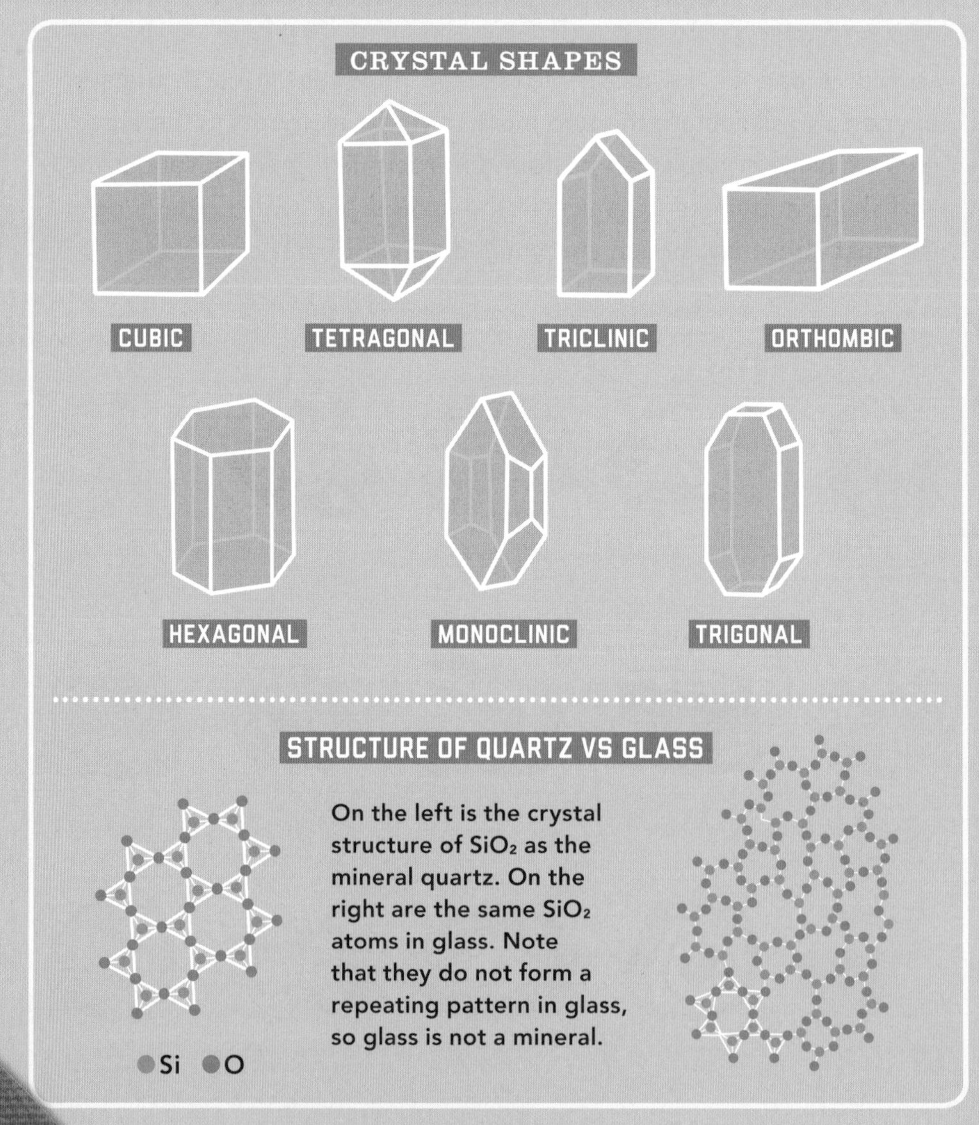

Want to see crystals right now? Go outside and pick up a ball of snow or open your freezer and take a closer look at an ice cube!

Just remember this—rocks and minerals are *not* the same. A mineral is made up of one substance. A rock is made up of more than one substance. Minerals have a specific chemical composition and crystalline structure. Rocks are mixtures of *at least* two minerals, but can contain many types of chemicals and don't have to have a crystalline structure. Unlike minerals, rocks can contain organic substances, material derived from living things. Coal, for example, is a rock made mostly of carbon, but it formed from plants that died in swamps millions of years ago. Amber is a rock made of tree sap that hardened over millions of years. Coquina is made completely from shell debris that cemented together.

COAL

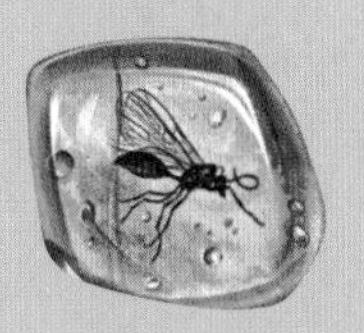

AMBER

Types of Minerals

There are more than five thousand different minerals on the earth, and they can be split up into the following categories:

NATIVE ELEMENTS Made of only one chemical element on the periodic table. This can be a metal like copper or gold, a metalloid or semimetal like arsenic or antimony, or a nonmetal like sulfur or carbon. These elements can be found anywhere on the planet.

SULFIDES Made of sulfur plus a metal or semimetal. It is common to find multiple sulfide minerals in the same location. These can be found everywhere in nature and may be found deep underground in mines near hydrothermal vents.

SULFOSALTS Made of sulfur plus a semimetal and one or more metals. These minerals are rare and are usually found near sulfide minerals.

OXIDES Made of oxygen bonded to one or more metals. Most oxide minerals are found in soil. Oxides are everywhere. They make up the ten most abundant compounds in the earth's crust.

HALIDES Contain either fluorine, chlorine, bromine, or iodine, four elements that make salts. Many are water soluble and can be found where water has evaporated, such as dried-up rivers, lakes, and seabeds. These minerals can also have four elements that bond to a metal.

CARBONATES Made of one or more metals plus a carbon atom bonded to three oxygen atoms. These may be found in shallow and warm seas as well as mountainous regions.

BORATES Made of one or more metals plus two boron atoms bonded to three oxygen atoms. These may be found in desert regions.

SILICATES Contain silicon bonded to oxygen. These constitute about 95 percent of the earth's crust and upper mantle. Since silicates make up so much of the earth's crust, they can be found most anywhere on the planet, and on the moon and in meteorites.

HYDROXIDES Made of one or more metals plus hydroxyl, a compound of one hydrogen atom bonded to one oxygen atom. These may be found wherever water has weathered rocks, such as in mountain ranges.

PHOSPHATES, NITRATES, AND TUNGSTATES These are very rare minerals to find on the earth, thus we have not included them here.

PRO TIP

Note to the rock hound: Rocks move! And many rocks contain more than one mineral, so it is possible to find rocks with these minerals practically anywhere. These are suggestions of where you *might* find these rocks, but really, look all around you. It could be possible that you find some of these in your own backyard.

* Rock Hound is a fun term that is used to mean someone who loves geology, or is an amateur rock collector. HINT: That's *you*!

What's an Ore?

IRON ORES

As you read this book, you will come across the term *ore* as in "this rock is the primary aluminum ore" or "this mineral is a great iron ore." What does that mean? An ore is rock that contains certain valuable minerals, like gold, lead, or iron, that can be extracted from it. In other words, rock that is "a great iron ore" is one that can have iron pulled from it. That iron is then used to make certain products, like steel.

Most Common Minerals

There is a long list of minerals in the rock and mineral identification guide on pages 94–203, but many rocks are made out of the minerals listed here:

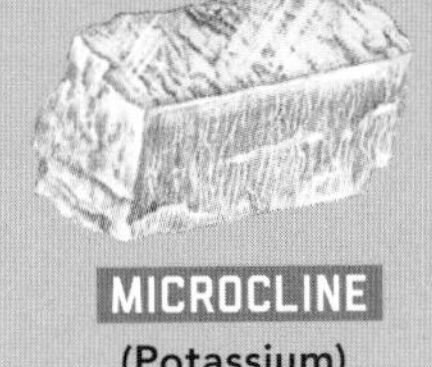

MICROCLINE (Potassium)

FELDSPARS Closely related minerals made of aluminum and silica. Together they make up more than half of the earth's crust. Feldspars are classified as potassium or plagioclase (containing calcium or sodium or both). Potassium feldspar is pink or cream. Plagioclase is white or gray. (Found in igneous, sedimentary, and metamorphic rocks.)

ALBITE (Plagioclase)

QUARTZ Made of silicon dioxide silica. It's colorless when pure, but trace amounts of other chemicals can make it purple, pink, yellowish green, or gray. (Found in igneous, sedimentary, and metamorphic rocks.)

MILKY QUARTZ

ROSY QUARTZ

PYROXENES Silicate minerals that generally contain sodium, calcium, magnesium, iron, or aluminum. They typically form short, stubby crystals, and colors range from dark green, brown, or black to light green or white. (Found in igneous and metamorphic rocks.)

DIOPSIDE

AMPHIBOLES Closely related to the pyroxenes, with the same chemical elements, plus hydroxyl. They form needlelike crystals that are dark colored, like green or black. (Found in igneous and metamorphic rocks.)

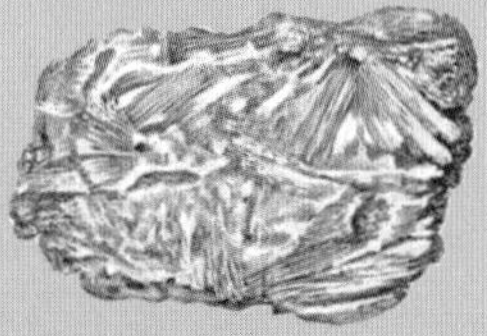

ACTINOLITE

MICAS Silicate minerals generally made of potassium and aluminum plus hydroxyl, along with other chemicals such as iron, magnesium, or lithium. They readily peel into thin sheets and can be many different colors: purple, rose, silver, gray, dark green, brown, or black. (Found in igneous, sedimentary, and metamorphic rocks.)

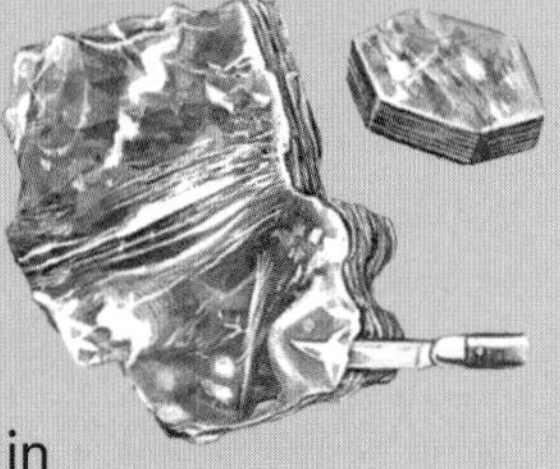

MUSCOVITE

OLIVINES Silicate minerals containing iron, magnesium, or both. They can be green, light gray, or brown and are shiny like glass. (Found in igneous and metamorphic rocks.)

OLIVINE

CALCITE Made of calcium carbonate. It can be colorless, white, or light colored. (Found in igneous, sedimentary, and metamorphic rocks.)

TRAVERTINE

Know Before You Collect!

If you plan to do your rock collecting in a park, especially a state-owned one, please be sure to observe their rules for removing rocks. Many may not allow this. Instead take a picture of it. If you are able to do some rock collecting, here are a few tips:

- Use good judgement.
- Wear gloves to protect your hands from sharp rocks.

- Don't inhale any of the dust on top or near a rock.
- Be aware of your surroundings. Don't go near high drop-offs or cliffs. Do not enter tunnels, mines, or wade into unfamiliar bodies of water. Avoid roads and bike paths.
- Be safe! Depending on where you decide to venture, go with a friend. Take a cell phone, compass, bottle of water, snacks, sunscreen, and maybe a whistle to blow if you get lost.

TRACK IT ↘ Make a Rock-Hunting Map

Now that you know more about rocks and minerals, let's take this rock-hunting mission on the move. You are headed out to collect your *own* rocks! Pick a safe place to explore. It could be a local park, rocky trail, mountain, stream, lake, or even your own backyard. Most important, you'll need a rock-hunting map to mark where you find everything. This will help you figure out what types of rocks and minerals you've collected later on. You can draw your own map, trace your path on an existing map of a park or trail, or find one using a program like Google Maps and print it out and paste it on page 17.

Using a Compass

While you may just pull out your phone and use your GPS, it's always a great idea to know how to use a compass, too.

- Hold the compass flat in your hand at chest level. Point the arrow of direction (the red one on the holder) in the direction that you are facing.

- You will notice different letters around the compass. N = north, S = south, W = west, E = east, NE = northeast, SE = southeast, SW = southwest, NW = northwest

- The arrow in the middle of the compass might be split into half-red, half-black (like the one on the facing page) or the arrow can be all one color. If it's split the red side of the arrow points towards the direction you are facing.

- Get a feel for the compass by moving your hand from side to side. For example, in this image, you are facing slightly northeast.

- Keep track of your distance as you walk forward. But watch where you are going! Don't be so focused on the compass that you trip.

If you're drawing your own map, follow these instructions:

WHAT YOU'LL NEED

- A pen or pencil, a piece of paper or this book, and a compass.

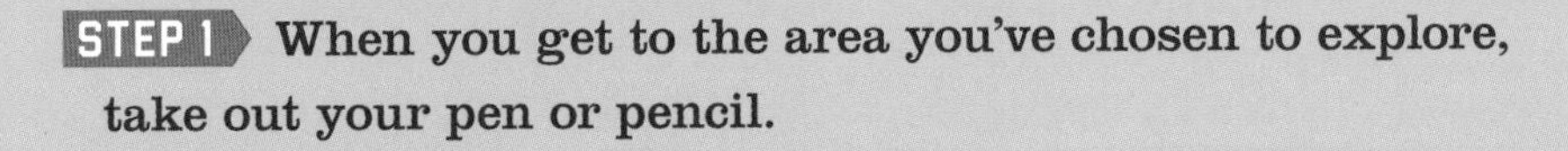

STEP 1 When you get to the area you've chosen to explore, take out your pen or pencil.

STEP 2 In the corner of a piece of paper, or on page 17, draw a short line pointing north and south, and cross it with another short line that points west and east. Label each point with an initial (N, S, W, E). This is your compass rose.

STEP 3 Position the map so the north arrow points north. You may need to use your compass. Draw a small **X** in the middle of your map. This is where you are standing.

STEP 4 Look around and note what you see on the map. This could be the outline of the trail or trees, mountains, a lake, etc. If there's a boulder on your right, draw it to the right of the **X**. Keep drawing the map as you walk around looking for rocks.

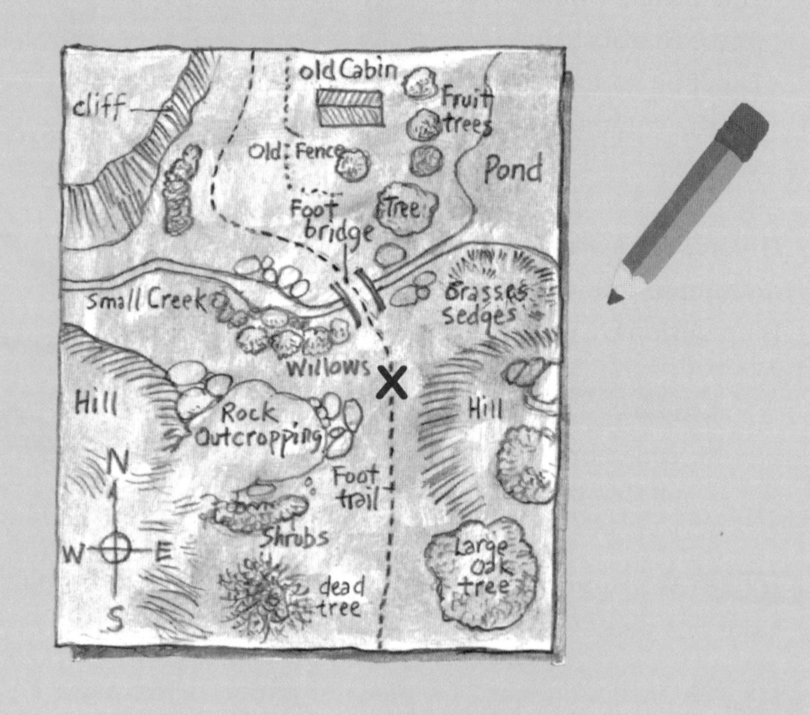

TRY IT → Your First Rock Hunt!

It's time to start your first rock collection! Be sure to pick your rocks carefully and keep them in a safe place because you'll be using this collection for all the activities in this part of the book.

WHAT YOU'LL NEED

- A dry day, a strong backpack, twelve bags or containers that close easily or an empty egg carton, a permanent marker and a roll of masking tape to make labels, a water bottle and a snack (rock hunting can make you hungry!), a small shovel and gloves, safety goggles or glasses, your rock-hunting map, a compass (even if you have a smartphone with GPS), and a camera.

STEP 1 Put your gloves on and let's go! Walk along the trail looking for rocks. You don't want to pick up every one you see (your pack will get very heavy), just the ones that catch your eye.

PRO TIP Don't just look for rocks along the trail. Look all around you—by trees, near the lake, in the streams (but not too deep!), even on the side of a big rock mountain (but not too close to the edge!). You want to gather as many different types of rocks as you can. If some rocks are tough to get, use your shovel. Remember, you are a Rock Hound on the hunt!

STEP 2 When you pick a rock, put it in its own bag or container. Take your marker and masking tape and number the bag or container. If you're using the egg carton, you can put the number on the inside top of the cup.

STEP 3 Now look at your map. Mark on the map where you picked up the rock, using the same number that you put on the bag or egg container cup with that rock.

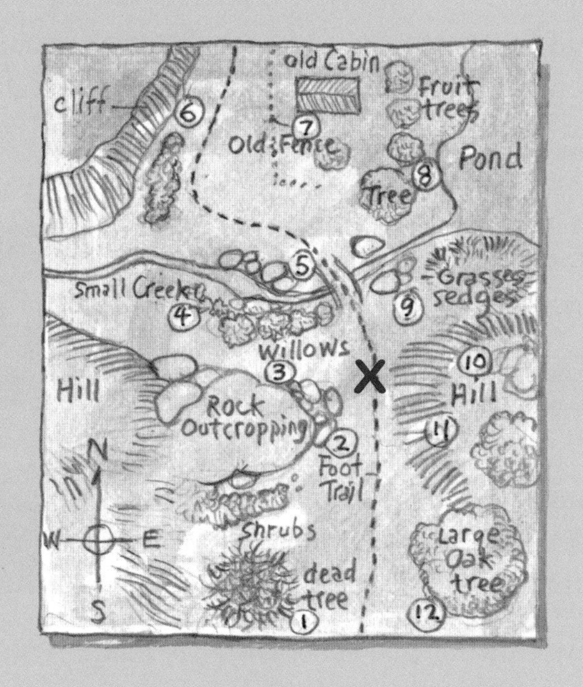

TRY IT → Hammer It Out

Did you find a rock that you really want to collect, but it's stuck inside a larger piece? You don't need to bring the whole gigantic rock home. Just bring a piece of it.

WHAT YOU'LL NEED

- Hammer and chisel; small, clean paintbrush (to brush dirt off rocks); safety goggles or glasses.

STEP 1 Find a part of the rock that might be partially sticking out or is on an edge that looks crumbly and unstable.

STEP 2 Put on your safety goggles or glasses.

STEP 3 Take your chisel and place it at an angle on the edge of the rock.

STEP 4 Hold the chisel firmly in one hand. With your other hand strike the top of the chisel with the hammer. Be careful! Make sure you hit the chisel and not your hand (ouch).

STEP 5 Keep hitting the chisel with the hammer until you break through the rock. You may need to move the chisel around to other parts of the rock to "free" it from the bigger section of rock. This can take a little while, depending on the toughness of the rock.

STEP 6 Use the brush to sweep away the debris as you go so you can see your progress.

TRY IT → Wading for Treasure

See a bunch of rocks in the bottom of a shallow stream? Maybe there is gold in there! The only way to find out is to wade in! Be sure to take your sieve.

WHAT YOU'LL NEED

- Sieve with a handle, clothes you can get wet (or roll up), a towel, and a bucket.

STEP 1 Roll up your pants and push up your sleeves. Try to stay as dry as you can, unless you really want to get wet.

STEP 2 Either crouch down on the edge of the water or wade in. If you wade in, be sure that the water is no higher than your ankles and is not fast flowing. Be careful as you bend over to scoop rocks off the bottom.

STEP 3 Take the sieve and gently skim the top layer of the stream bed (the layer of sand or dirt at the bottom). You don't want to dig deep; that will just give you a lot of sand or dirt.

STEP 4 Lift the sieve and let the water flow out of it. Then shake it back and forth to get the bits of sand and dirt to fall through the tiny holes. Keep sifting until most of the sand and dirt is gone. What is left will be a few (hopefully) exciting rocks that you can add to your collection. Don't worry if you don't recognize them now. You will identify them later. Just make a note in your chart where you found them.

Describe Your Rock-Hunting Field

Write a few notes here about the area where you found each rock. Was it flat, mountainous, wet, dry? Did you have to dig your rock out? Was it found in a running stream or a still lake?

ROCK #

DESCRIBE THE AREA AROUND THE ROCK #

ROCK #	DESCRIBE THE AREA AROUND THE ROCK #

> If you collect more rocks than this chart can hold, photocopy the page and extend your chart. Staple it inside this book to keep everything in one place!

Clean Up Your New Collection

Once you return from your rock-hunting trip, it's time to give your rocks a nice good clean. Removing any dirt and debris that might be attached to the rock will make it easier to identify later.

WHAT YOU'LL NEED

- Some old newspaper to lay out on the floor or table where you will work, a bowl or pan filled with water, paper towels or an old towel, and a small scrub brush or toothbrush that's okay to use on the rocks.

STEP 1 Remove each rock from its container one at a time and wash it. If the outside isn't too bad, you can use the wet paper towel to just wipe it off. If it's really dirty, give it a good scrub with the brush.

STEP 2 Use the towel to polish up your rock.

STEP 3 Be sure to put the rock back into its correct container *before* you move on to the next rock.

STEP 4 When all rocks are clean, find a place in your home where you can temporarily store them. Pick a place that can remain undisturbed for a while. (Hint: Not on your floor or the top of your bed. You don't want to trip over them or, worse, have the rocks fall on your head. Ouch!) A corner of your desk or a shelf will work.

CHAPTER 2

Investigating Your Rock & Mineral Collection

You have some great rock samples. Now it's time to analyze them! Do you feel a little bit like you are looking at buried treasure? You should. These rocks all contain tiny bits of history. (And possibly *actual* treasure!) Maybe they came from the bottom of an ancient lake or were washed down from the top of a tall mountain. Perhaps they once oozed out of a volcano, or were part of a beautiful landscape, like the Grand Canyon or an arch in Arches National Park.

Wherever they came from, these rocks are part of our planet. And like any good rock scientist, or geologist, you need to organize your collection so that you can analyze it and figure out exactly what treasure you have! But where do you start? The first thing to do is to set up a field journal.

Your field journal will be this book! Here you will draw or take a picture of your rocks. Then, describe the rocks' characteristics: Is your rock smooth? Bumpy? Sharp? It is soft or hard? Does it break easily? Pretty much any observation you make is important.

TRACK IT ↘ Inspecting Your Rocks

Go through each of your rocks and follow the steps below to describe these four characteristics:

WHAT YOU'LL NEED

- A pencil or pen and a ruler that measures in inches or centimeters.

TEXTURE (How does it feel?)

COLOR (Gray? Brown? Black spotted?)

DIAMETER (Get out your ruler for this one.)

SHAPE (Is it square, rectangular, triangular, circular, spiral, cone-shaped, or something else?)

STEP 1 Take out each rock one at a time. Turn it over and over in your hand, looking very closely at it.

STEP 2 Record what you see in the charts on pages 27–28. Be specific. If the rock is dark gray, say that. Or if it's very rough, slightly bumpy, or quite smooth, say that. Of course, there are many ways to describe rocks. Feel free to add your own observations in the notes section.

STEP 3 Place your ruler in the center of your rock and measure the length from one end to the other. This gives you its diameter.

DIAMETER

STEP 4 Once you have finished describing the rock's physical properties, put it back into its container before going on to the next rock.

STEP 5 Repeat steps 1–4 for each rock that you have.

SAFETY NOTE! *Do not* put the rocks in your mouth or try to taste them. That is not recommended. (Unless you are a burrowing sea urchin: Sea urchins burrowing through rocks will be able to tell which of the rocks are crunchy and which ones are chewy.)

ROCK #

TEXTURE

COLOR

SHAPE

DIAMETER

NOTES

IMAGE OF ROCK

WHERE I FOUND IT

ROCK #

TEXTURE

COLOR

SHAPE

DIAMETER

NOTES

IMAGE OF ROCK

WHERE I FOUND IT

ROCK #

TEXTURE

COLOR

SHAPE

DIAMETER

NOTES

IMAGE OF ROCK

WHERE I FOUND IT

ROCK #

TEXTURE

COLOR

SHAPE

DIAMETER

NOTES

IMAGE OF ROCK

WHERE I FOUND IT

ROCK #

TEXTURE

COLOR

SHAPE

DIAMETER

NOTES

IMAGE OF ROCK

WHERE I FOUND IT

ROCK #

TEXTURE

COLOR

SHAPE

DIAMETER

NOTES

IMAGE OF ROCK

WHERE I FOUND IT

I DID IT!

DATE:

TAKE IT TO THE NEXT LEVEL ↗

Making Rock Connections

Go back over your notes and ask yourself a couple of questions:

- Do the rocks that were found in similar places have similar textures? Are they about the same size, color, and shape?
- Are the rocks that were found in different places actually different, or are they similar?

Add these observations under the notes section. Use a highlighter to signal connections you see between rocks. (Highlight just the rock numbers with the same color.)

I DID IT! DATE:

Geodes: A Rock with a Surprise Inside

You have just gone through all your rocks. And while you haven't started identifying them yet, perhaps a few look familiar to you. The big question is, do you have a rock that looks like this?

Yes, this rock does look rather ordinary. The only difference is that it might feel a bit lighter in your hand as you hold it. But really, it's just a rock. No big deal, right? Actually, this rock has a surprise. This rock is a geode, and the space inside the rock contains beautiful, three-dimensional crystals.

How do geodes form? Like any rock, over millions of years. Scientists believe that geodes form when minerals are deposited in hollow spaces in rocks. These cavities could be from bubbles of volcanic gas that were trapped when lava cooled and hardened. Or they could have been created by a burrowing animal or a tree root growing in sediment. The sediment formed into rock, and the organic material decayed away, leaving a cavity.

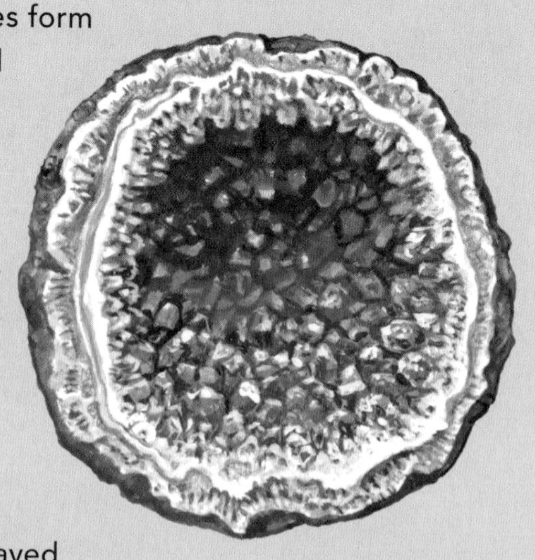

In both cases, mineral-rich water seeps into the empty space and then evaporates, leaving behind minerals such as quartz and calcite. The warm, empty space inside the rock is perfect for growing crystals over millions of years as water deposits layer after layer of minerals.

The crystals inside geodes are usually brown or white, but depending on which minerals are present, they can be blue, green, pink, purple, yellow, or orange. The outside of a geode is typically brown or gray and bumpy, with a rounded shape.

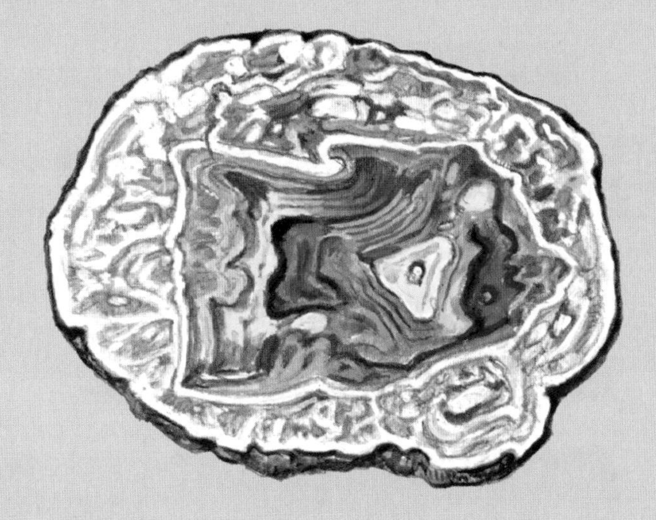

Geodes that have crystals that fill the entire inside of the rock are called nodules.

Where can you find geodes? Pretty much anywhere in the world where there is volcanic rock and ash or limestone. In the United States, that generally means the deserts of the Southwest, and parts of the Midwest and Southeast. Because the outer layer of a geode is harder than the rock it formed in, geodes are left intact when the surrounding rock erodes away. You can find them washed into streams and riverbeds. The state of Iowa has a lot of geodes. In fact, the geode is their state rock.

Take a good look. Do any of your rocks look like they might be a geode? If so, let's take a look inside.

Geode Geology!

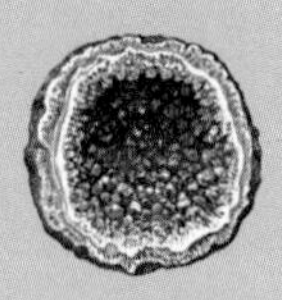

WHAT YOU'LL NEED

- Small hammer and chisel, safety goggles or glasses, old newspaper or paper bags to cover your work area, gloves, and a large cardboard box (optional).

STEP 1 Use the flowchart to see whether your rock could be a geode. If so, follow steps 2 through 4 to break it open.

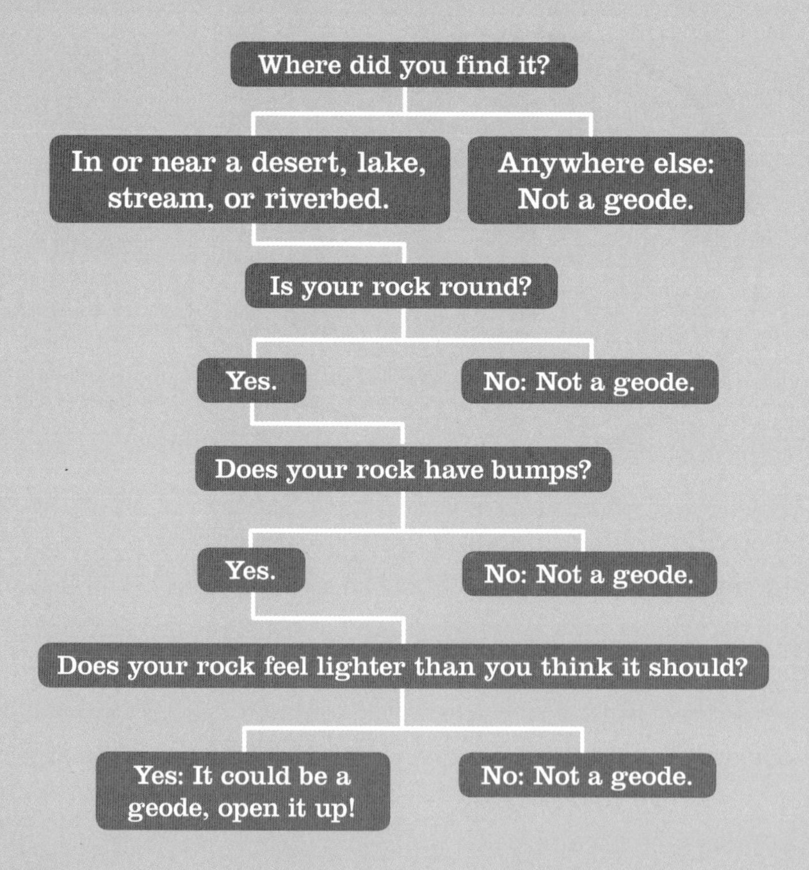

STEP 2 To open up your rock, go outside and find a safe place to work with a flat, stable surface.

STEP 3 Cover your work area with newspapers and place your rock on top. Or to be extra safe, place your rock in a large box first, so pieces won't fly everywhere. Put on your safety goggles and gloves.

STEP 4 Hold the sharp end of the chisel at an angle on top of the rock. Carefully strike the chisel with the hammer. Continue doing so until the rock breaks open. Take a look inside.

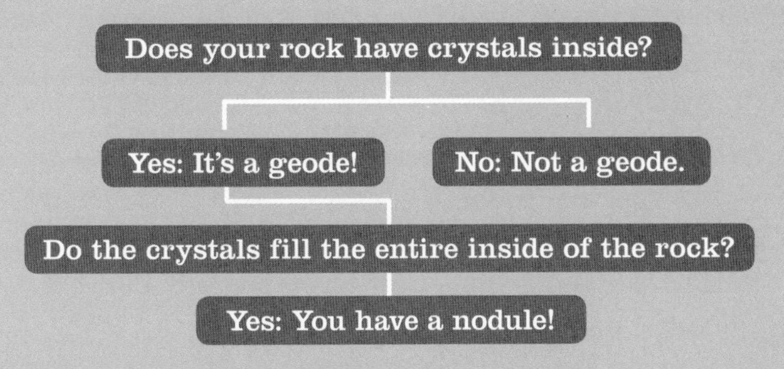

Describe (and draw) what you see below:

TRY IT → DIY Display Case!

Now that you have a rock collection, it's time to keep it organized! Create a display case box with different compartments for each rock. Then label each rock with the original number you gave it when you first picked it up. It is important to keep the same rock number throughout.

WHAT YOU'LL NEED

- A cardboard box or shoe box (depending on how big your collection is!), extra pieces of cardboard that you can cut up, a ruler or measuring tape, a pair of scissors, a marker, tape, and a bag of cotton balls.

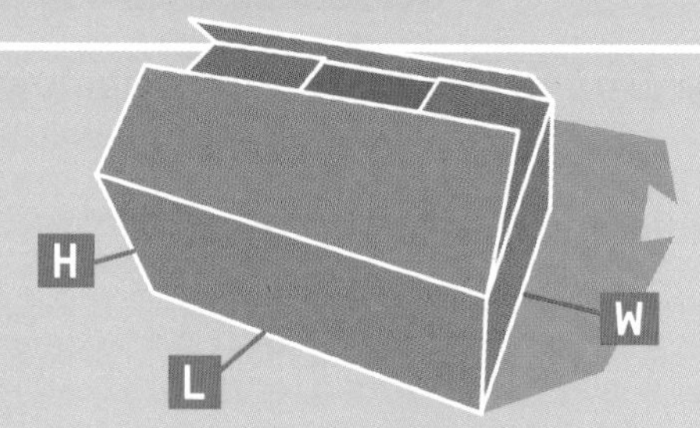

STEP 1 Measure your box and write down the height, width, and length.

Height: ______ Width: ______ Length: ______

STEP 2 To determine the size of the compartments, measure the diameter of the biggest rock you plan to store in the box. (If the biggest rock is much bigger than the all the rest, measure an average rock and pull out extra dividers to make room for it.)

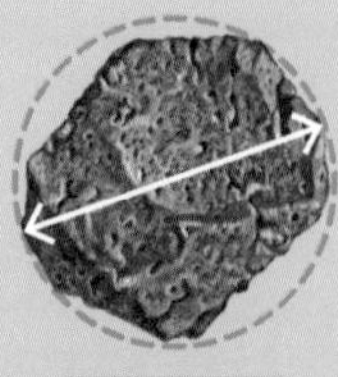

STEP 3 Trim box flaps to make dividers or measure extra cardboard to fit L and W of box.

STEP 4 Measure and cut notches halfway down dividers.

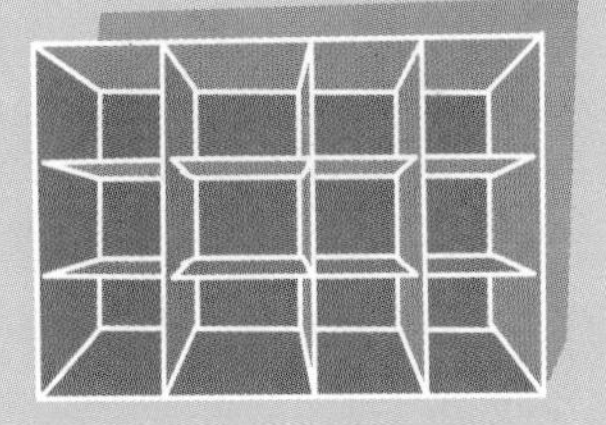

STEP 5 Fit dividers together inside box.

STEP 6 Add cotton balls for padding and labels for each compartment.

Here are some suggestions for other ways to store your rock collection:

- fishing tackle box
- art supply box
- tiny reusable containers
- collection of mason jars

Whatever you decide, be sure to label everything!

TRY IT → Make Them Shine!

Cleaning your rocks might have given you a better look at their characteristics, but if you want them to sparkle in your display case, you need to give them a good polish. This is especially useful if you have any gemstones in your rock pile. The minerals in jewelry have been highly polished to a bright shine. Want your rock to look the same? Get polishing!

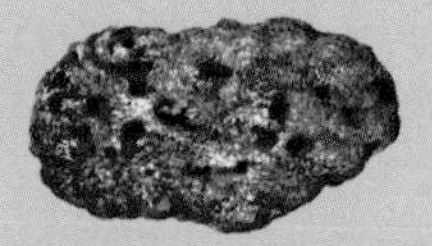

ROUGH AGATE

CUT AGATE

SHAPED & POLISHED

WHAT YOU'LL NEED

- Gloves, safety glasses, sandpaper or a wire brush, a soft cloth or towel (one that it's okay to get really dirty), some old newspaper or paper towels to cover your work area, your rock collection, and a bucket of clean water.

STEP 1 This is going to be a bit messy so it's best to head outside if possible. Find a space that's open to the air and where it's okay to create some rock dust.

STEP 2 Put on your gloves and safety glasses.

STEP 3 Remove one rock from your collection. Take one piece of sandpaper or your wire brush and give the rock a good scrubbing. It's okay if tiny bits of rock and debris fall off.

You are trying to expose everything that might be in it: the lines, the grains, the colors. Scrub the rock well, but not too hard; you don't want to break it apart (not yet anyway).

STEP 4 Once you've scrubbed enough so that the rock feels a bit smoother, dunk the rock into the water to rinse it clean.

STEP 5 Dry it with the soft cloth or paper towel. Then put it back into its place. Repeat for all your rocks.

I DID IT! DATE:

TAKE IT TO THE NEXT LEVEL

Give Them a Polish

If you happen to have a rock polisher, now is the time to use it. You can purchase one at a local hardware store or an online retailer. Follow the directions, but be sure to polish only one rock at a time. You don't want to mix them up! You need to know the correct number of each rock when it comes time to identify them. Also, you don't want your rocks to be too smooth and polished; just take the rough edges off.

CHAPTER 3

Hunting Igneous Rocks

You've collected, cleaned, inspected, and stored your rocks. Now it's time to *identify* them! The best way to identify your rocks is to put them into a category. A good way to start is to write down exactly where you found your rock. Luckily, you've already done this! The location of the rock can help you determine its identity. But location doesn't tell you everything. You need more characteristics to figure out just what type of rock you have. Thankfully, to make identification even easier, geologists have created three basic rock categories: igneous, sedimentary, and metamorphic.

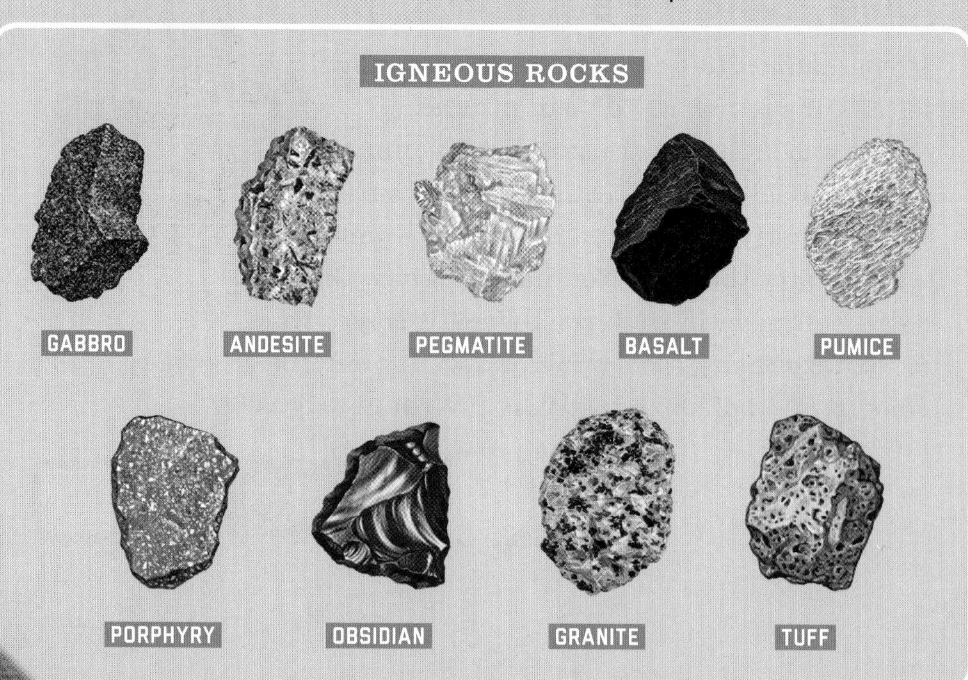

Igneous rocks are formed when magma cools and hardens. Magma is a mix of superhot liquid rock and chunks of partially liquefied rock that forms under the earth's crust. Think of it sort of like lumpy breakfast oatmeal, but *really* hot! Magma contains many different kinds of minerals and dissolved gases like water, carbon dioxide (you know, the stuff you exhale when you breathe), and sulfur (that's the rotten egg smell).

What keeps the magma from solidifying? High temperatures—1,300°F to 2,400°F (704°C to 1,315°C)—and reduced pressure, plus water vapor, which lowers the melting point. Let's face it. At those temperatures, rocks melt easily. (Hint: You would, too.) Below the earth's crust, inside the mantle, the weight of all that rock creates extreme pressure that keeps everything solid. But in spots where the pressure is reduced or water is introduced (like a crack in the crust), the superhot rocks melt.

Liquid Rock Lingo

Magma and lava are *not* the same thing, even though people often think they are. After all, both words describe really hot, liquefied rock. Magma is found *under* the earth's surface, deep in the crust and upper mantle. Lava is found *on* the earth's surface. It is magma that has risen through the crust and oozed onto the surface. You will probably recognize lava when you see it. It is usually flowing down the side of a volcano. Safety note: Please watch lava from afar!

Occasionally, the lava leaves tunnels in its wake. These lava tubes happen when the outside of the lava cools and hardens while the inside still flows. Take a look at this lava tube at El Malpais National Monument, New Mexico.

Lava tubes can be found in Hawaii—obviously, since the islands were created by volcanoes!—and in western states, including Washington, California, Oregon, Nevada, Idaho, New Mexico, Utah, and Arizona. Volcanic regions all around the world have them: the Canary Islands, Galapagos Islands, Italy, Japan, Korea, Kenya, Mexico. Search the internet for "lava tubes" to see whether any are located near you. Then go visit one!

Magma rises through the earth's crust because as a liquid it is less dense than the surrounding rock. It pushes up, melting some of the surrounding rock, until the downward pressure from the rock above exceeds its upward pressure. Stopped here, the magma may simply cool over millions of years into new igneous rock. But if the magma continues to rise, the dissolved gases in it will come back together and form bubbles. The bubbles expand as they rise, and eventually the pressure from the expanding gas cracks the rock, allowing the magma to reach the surface and become lava.

Intrusive or Extrusive?

Magma hardens into igneous rocks in two basic ways—either below the surface of the earth very slowly, or on the earth's surface much more quickly. So that magma that never reached the earth's surface and basically just intruded on older rocks' space for millions of years? It formed intrusive rocks. And the magma that managed to exit the earth's hot interior and get some air? It formed extrusive rocks.

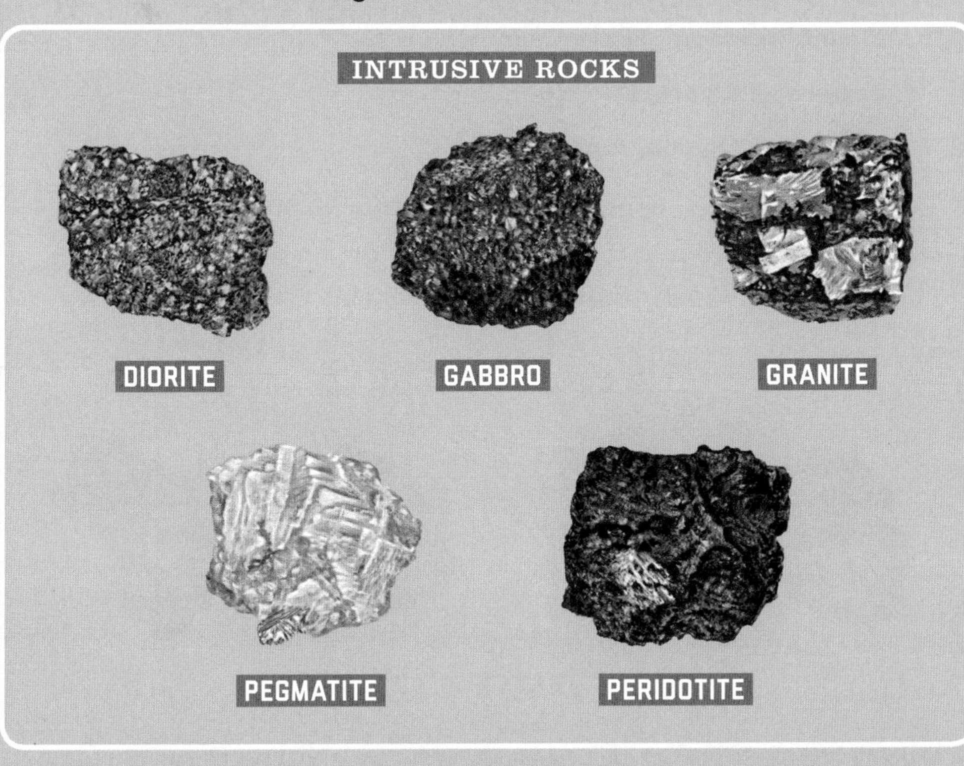

Take a good look at the images of these intrusive rocks. What do you first notice about them? Probably their spots. Those spots are the mineral crystals, the grains. The crystals have grown larger because the magma took so long to cool deep underground.

Look at your rock collection. Can you identify any that might be intrusive igneous rocks?

Intrusive Rocks in the Wild!

Wish you could see intrusive igneous rocks out in the real world? You can! Go visit one of these places:

- **Acadia National Park, Maine, USA**
- **Yosemite National Park, California, USA**
- **Joshua Tree National Park, California, USA**
- **Mount Rushmore, South Dakota, USA**
- **Bowerman's Nose, Dartmoor, England**
- **Wave Rock, Hyden, Australia**

Of course there are many more, but these are a few to start with. Take this book with you to compare the grains of the rocks. See? They are big, just like intrusive rocks should be.

Take a good look at the images of these extrusive rocks. What do you first notice about them? Although some of them do appear at first to have spots like the intrusive rocks, look closer and you'll see that these "spots" are actually holes. These holes come from gas bubbles trapped in the lava as it cooled. You might notice, too, that you can't even see mineral grains in some of the rocks without a magnifying glass or microscope, and if you can, they're much smaller than the ones in the intrusive rocks.

Look at your rock collection. Can you identify any that might be extrusive igneous rocks?

Extrusive Rocks in the Wild!

Wish you could see extrusive igneous rocks out in the real world? You can! Go visit one of these places:

- **Hawaii Volcanoes National Park, Hawaii, USA**
- **Sunset Crater Volcano National Monument, Arizona, USA**
- **Crater Lake National Park, Oregon, USA**

Of course there are many more, but these are a few to start with. Take this book with you to compare the grains of the rocks. See? They are small, just like extrusive rocks should be.

Let's Talk Texture (aka Grain Size)

When you hear the word *texture* to describe something, you probably think that means how the object feels. In the case of rocks, the word *texture* means how the rock *looks*. Texture specifically describes the shape, arrangement, and distribution of the grains in the rock. (In geology, a grain generally refers to the particles that make up a rock; with igneous rocks, that means mineral crystals.)

Igneous rocks typically have four different textures.

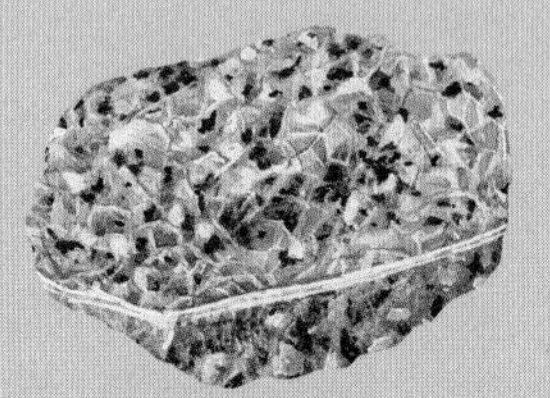

COARSE

Intrusive rocks with large crystals are coarse grained.

FINE

Extrusive rocks with small crystals are fine grained.

PORPHYRITIC

Igneous rocks with large crystals surrounded by small crystals are porphyritic. (They can be extrusive or intrusive.)

GLASSY

Extrusive rocks with no grains are glassy.

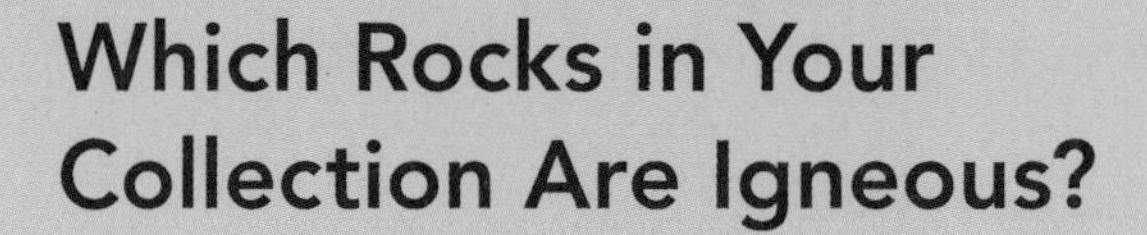

Which Rocks in Your Collection Are Igneous?

Can you really tell which rocks in your collection are igneous? Yes! Just compare them against the rock and mineral identification guide in this book. But before you do that, let's see whether you can guess which ones are igneous by checking for these characteristics:

STEP 1 Igneous rocks are strong. That means they can't be broken easily. Pick up each of your rocks one at a time and see whether you can break off a piece of it with your hands (even a little corner counts). Don't use a tool yet; we will try that later. Record the numbers of the rocks that you could break on the appropriate line below.

Rocks that you couldn't break:

Rocks that you could break:

STEP 2 Igneous rocks are made mostly of minerals. That means their colors are typically black, white, or gray. If they have color, it appears faded. Evaluate the color of each rock individually and record the numbers in the appropriate line below:

Rocks that are gray, white, black, or faded in color:

Rocks that are other colors:

STEP 3 Igneous rocks might have holes or large crystals that you can see. Examine each of your rocks for this characteristic and record the numbers in the appropriate line below:

Rocks that have holes or large crystals:

Rocks that don't have holes or large crystals:

STEP 4 Now look at your lists above. Ask yourself these questions:

- Do any rocks have all three characteristics outlined in Steps 1–3? List them here:
- Do any rocks have two characteristics? List them here:

These are the rocks that are more likely to be igneous.

CHAPTER 4

Hunting Sedimentary Rocks

Sedimentary rocks are common on the surface of our planet and can be found pretty much everywhere—from the bottom of the ocean, to the desert, to the layers in a mountain. They are formed from rocks and organic matter that have been broken down by the forces of nature.

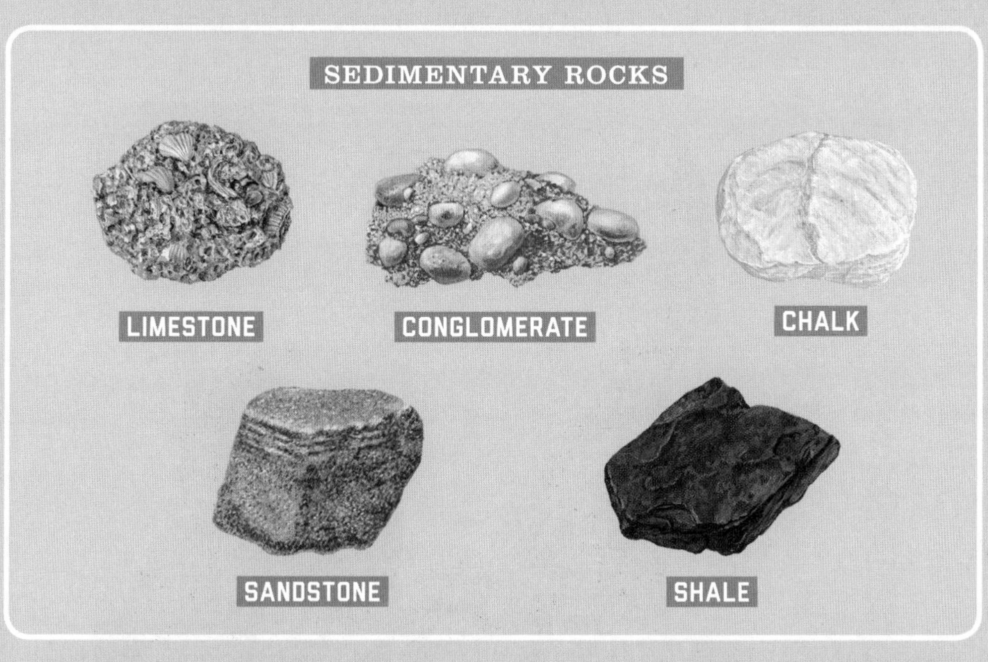

Rocks break down through weathering and erosion. Weathering breaks down rocks where they sit. This can happen when tree roots grow into a rock. Or when water seeps in and freezes, causing cracks that get wider and wider with every freeze until a great big chunk falls off. Or when water dissolves minerals in a rock. Erosion happens when the forces of nature carry away the bits and chunks of weathered rock, which in turn scrape against other rocks, breaking off more bits and pieces. Exposed to weathering and erosion for thousands of years, the bits and pieces can become quite small.

As you might have guessed, water is a primary cause of all this wearing away. Rain falls and flows over rock into streams and rivers, carrying lots of particles that carve away more rock. Or water forms glaciers that move slowly downhill, picking up everything in their path as they sculpt mountains and valleys. Wind plays a powerful role, too, especially in dry areas. Wind constantly picks up tiny particles and blows them from one place to another. When wind and water finally slow down, the particles drop out. That's what we call sediment.

Balanced Rock in Utah did not always look like this. At one time, this sedimentary rock was much larger and most likely more rectangular. Weathering and erosion over hundreds of thousands of years created the appearance of a large rock balanced on a pile of smaller rocks. On your next rock hunt, be on the lookout for similarly weathered and eroded rocks.

Clastic or Chemical?

Sedimentary rocks can be classified as clastic or chemical. The difference has to do with the type of sediment and how it came together to form rocks.

Sediment made of broken bits of rock is called clastic. Clastic sediment can be deposited anywhere, but you'll naturally find a lot of it in deserts, at the bottom of hills or mountains, around the mouths of rivers, in lake bottoms, and on beaches. Clastic sediment can sit undisturbed for many, many years. As it sits, water and wind cover it with more and more layers of sediment. Over hundreds of thousands of years, the weight of all that material creates enough pressure to compact and cement the layers into rock.

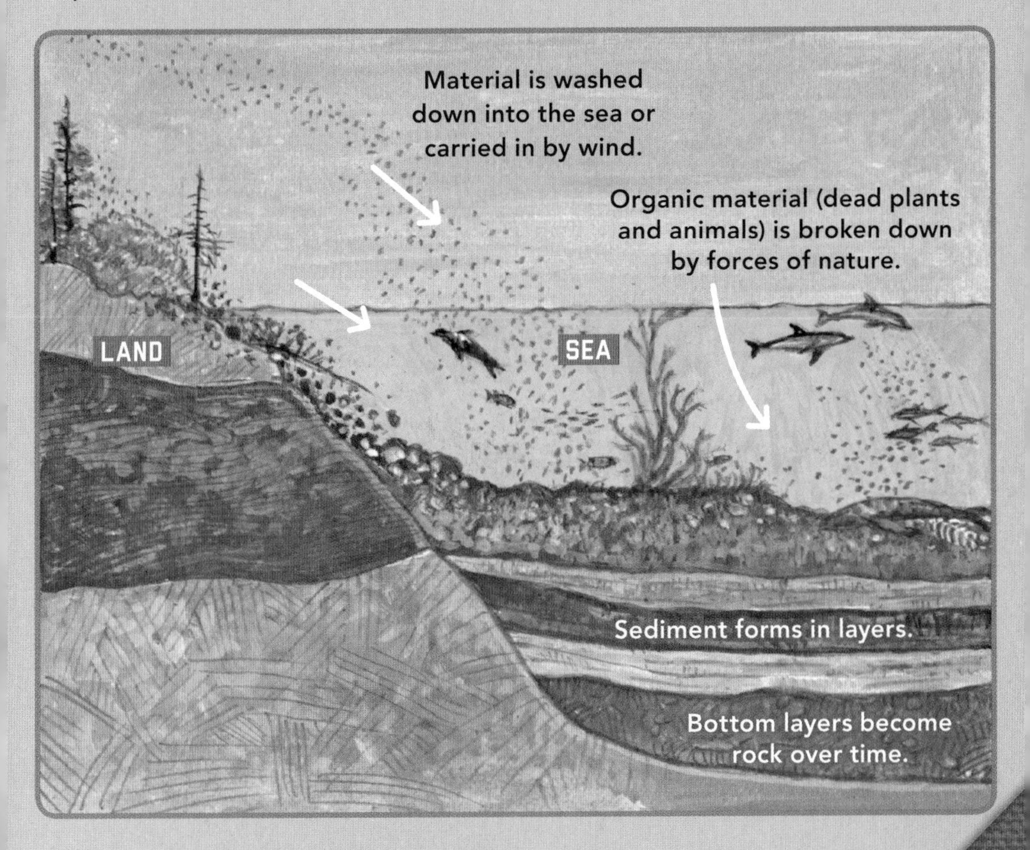

Look at your rock collection. Can you identify any that might be clastic sedimentary rocks?

QUARTZ BRECCIA

See the big fragments in this breccia rock? Those are fragments of quartz.

Clastic Sedimentary Rocks in the Wild!

Want to get a good look at clastic sedimentary rocks in nature? Check out some of these famous rocks:

- **Arches National Park, Utah, USA**
- **Grand Canyon National Park, Arizona, USA**
- **Bryce Canyon National Park, Utah, USA**
- **Zion National Park, Utah, USA**
- **Flatiron Mountains, Boulder, Colorado, USA**
- **Table Mountain, Cape Town, South Africa**
- **Songliao Basin, northeast China**
- **Los Mallos de Riglos, Spain**

Of course there are many more, but these are a few to start with.

With chemical sedimentary rocks, the sediment is actually chemicals that were dissolved in the water. (Remember the periodic table on page 6? Chemical sediments are atoms of those elements, so they are much, much, much smaller than clastic sediment.) The chemicals come from rocks or living organisms. Water picks up chemicals because the hydrogen and oxygen in it react with elements in the environment. The dissolved chemicals crystalize into minerals when the water's temperature or acidity changes or when the water evaporates.

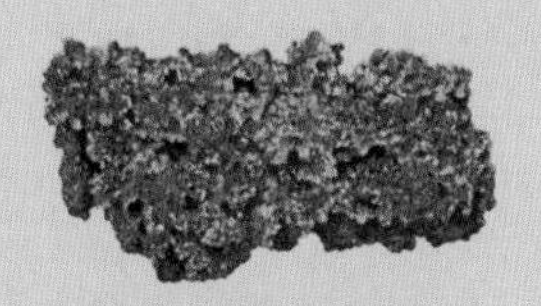
BOG IRON ORE

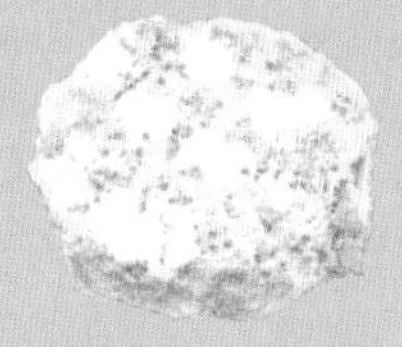
DIATOMITE

Chemical sediments can crystallize into a new a rock, change an existing rock into a different rock, and cement together organic matter or other pieces of rock. (Hint: Clastic rocks contain small amounts of chemical sediments.) Chemical sedimentary rocks often have a crystalline texture because they are formed from crystals (like igneous rocks) and generally contain only one mineral.

Look at your rock collection. Do any look like they might be chemical sedimentary rocks?

Chemical Sedimentary Rocks in the Wild!

Looking for examples of chemical sedimentary rocks in the world? You might try visiting these places:

- **Oregon Caves National Monument, Oregon, USA**
- **Carlsbad Caverns National Park, New Mexico, USA**
- **White Sands National Monument, New Mexico, USA**
- **Biscayne National Park, Florida, USA**
- **Guadalupe Mountains National Park, Texas, USA**
- **Dolomites, northern Italy**
- **Percé Rock, Quebec, Canada**

Of course there are many more, but these are a few to start with.

Water containing dissolved magnesium changes limestone into dolomite rock. Why should rock collectors like you care about these two types of sedimentary rock? Because determining what type of sediment formed the rock you've found will help you identify it—and possibly tell you something about the environment it came from. If you know you have a rock made of chemical sediment, for example, you know your rock was formed in an area where there was once water.

DOLOMITE

In clastic rocks, grain size and shape give you clues about how the sediment was transported and for how long. The more rounded the grains, the more they've been moved around. Angular grains did not travel far. If a rock contains grains of different sizes, the sediments were deposited quickly, often close to their source rock, perhaps by a flood or mudslide. Uniform grains indicate the sediments were transported for a long time or by a constant force, like ocean waves. Because it takes more energy to move larger sediments, generally the larger the grain size, the shorter the distance the sediment traveled from its source rock.

TRACK IT ↘

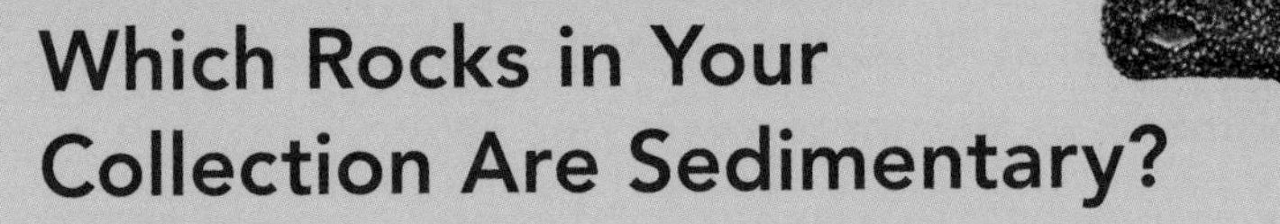

Which Rocks in Your Collection Are Sedimentary?

Can you really tell which rocks in your collection are sedimentary? Yes! Just compare them against the identification guide in this book. But first, let's see whether you can guess which ones are sedimentary by checking for these characteristics.

STEP 1 Sedimentary rocks are usually soft. That means they can be broken easily. Pick up each of your rocks one at a time and see whether you can break off a piece of it with your hands. Don't use a tool; we will try that later. Record each rock's number on the appropriate line:

Rocks that you could break:

Rocks that you couldn't break:

STEP 2 Sedimentary rocks might have grains that you can see. Take a close look at each rock. Do you see any black or brown specks? Or maybe bits of other rocks inside ? Those are also grains, just really large ones. Record the numbers on the appropriate line below:

Rocks with grains:

Rocks without:

STEP 3 Sedimentary rocks sometimes have layers. Or maybe even bits of shells or a tiny fossil. This is because stuff gets trapped in the sediment. Examine each of your rocks and record the numbers in the appropriate line below:

Rocks with layers, shells, or fossils:

Rocks without:

STEP 4 Now look at your lists above, and ask yourself these questions:

- Do any rocks have all three characteristics outlined in Steps 1–3? List them here:

- Do any rocks have two? List them here:

These are the rocks that are more likely to be sedimentary.

CHAPTER 5

Hunting Metamorphic Rocks

There is one more type of rock for you to discover. Are you outside? If not, head out there now. You want to see whether you can discover a metamorphic rock. The best place is in a volcano (but hopefully you don't have one of those in your backyard). Still, if you have mountains near where you live, there's a good chance that you will find metamorphic rocks nearby.

Of course, they most likely won't be lying on the ground. Metamorphic rocks are formed deep in the earth and only come to the surface when pushed upward (like in a volcano). Or they form in a mountain as the pressure and heat change the igneous or sedimentary rock into metamorphic ones.

That's right. Metamorphic rocks were once another rock. Originally, they were either a sedimentary, igneous, or even a different metamorphic rock. What happened to them? Heat and pressure changed the minerals inside the rocks.

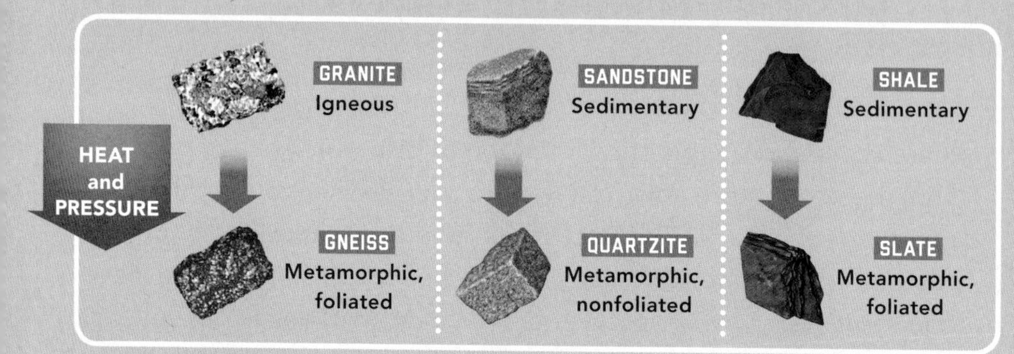

Where does this metamorphosis take place? Deep under the earth's surface, especially where two pieces of the earth's crust meet.

The hard outer shell of the earth, the lithosphere, is broken up into a bunch of pieces. These pieces, called tectonic plates, all fit together like a puzzle. For the most part, the plates sit tightly up against each other. After all, if they didn't, there would be big gaps in the earth's surface. (Gaps that would be filled by magma from rocks melting due to the decreased pressure.)

LITHOSPHERE

The thing is, these plates are constantly moving. (It's so slow that you can't see it, only a few inches a year, but once in a while you might feel it. Hint: That's an earthquake.) As the plates move over millions of years, their edges slip under, slide over, and scrape against one another. And all that pressure squishes, smears, folds, and *sq-eee-zzz-es* the rocks there.

The earth's lithosphere has twelve major tectonic plates, plus several smaller ones, which move slowly over time. Seven of these plates make up the seven different continents.

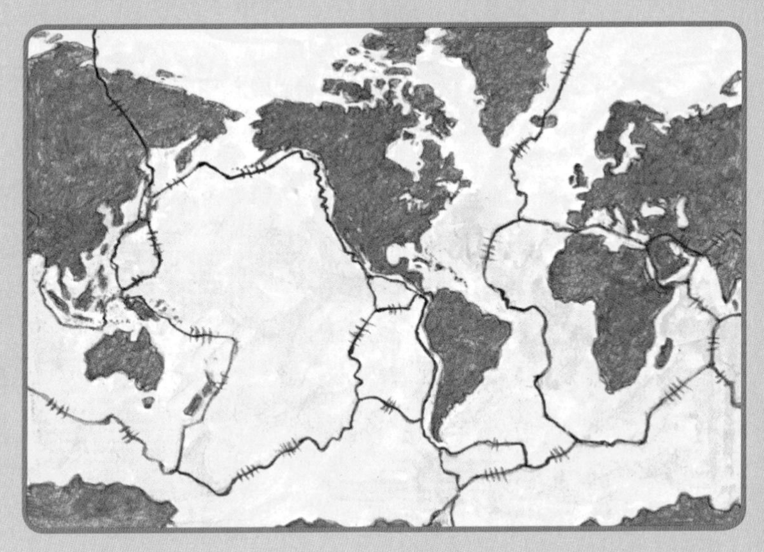

The great pressure rearranges the atoms inside the rocks, forcing them closer together. This makes the rocks denser and forms new minerals, and therefore different rocks. Sometimes it's just great heat that rearranges a rock's atoms, like when magma intrudes on older rocks and partially melts them. (They don't melt much. If they did, they would be igneous rocks.) Often it's a combination of heat and pressure. However they re-form over time, metamorphic rocks end up with a different color, texture, and mineral makeup from their original rocks.

Foliated or Nonfoliated?

Metamorphic rocks can be classified as either foliated or nonfoliated. Put simply, the foliated rocks have lines throughout them. They look as if they were stretched flat or folded over.

Think of a long ribbon that is folded back and forth on top of itself. If you squish the folds together and look at them the from the side, you'll see lines. That's what happens in a foliated rock. Take a look!

Foliated Rocks in the Wild!

Want to get a good look at foliated rocks? Check out some of these places:

Gneiss is a foliated metamorphic rock

- **Morton Outcrops Scientific and Natural Area, Minnesota, USA**
- **Funeral Mountains, Death Valley National Park, California, USA**
- **Grand Teton National Park, Wyoming, USA**
- **Chesapeake and Ohio Canal, West Virginia, Maryland, and Washington, DC, USA**
- **Great Pillars, Black Canyon of the Gunnison National Park, Colorado, USA**

Of course there are many more, but these are a few to start with.

Nonfoliated Rocks in the Wild!

Want to get a good look at nonfoliated rocks? Check out some of these places:

Hornfels is a nonfoliated metamorphic rock

- **Rock Creek Park, Washington, DC, USA**
- **City of Rocks National Reserve, Idaho, USA**
- **Palisades, New Jersey and New York**
- **Marble Caves, General Carrera Lake, Chile**

Of course there are many more, but these are a few to start with.

TRACK IT ↘

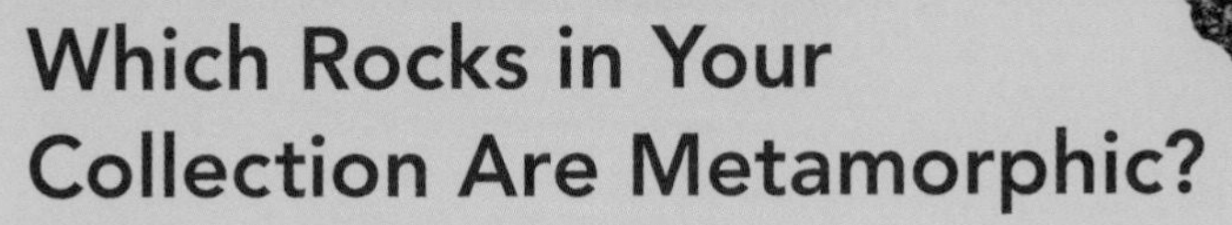

Which Rocks in Your Collection Are Metamorphic?

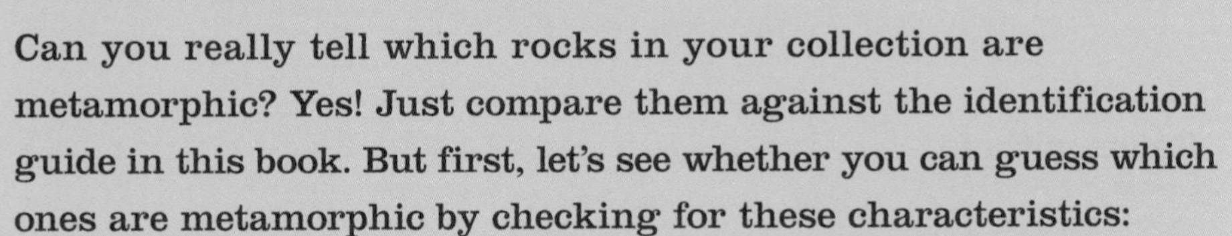

Can you really tell which rocks in your collection are metamorphic? Yes! Just compare them against the identification guide in this book. But first, let's see whether you can guess which ones are metamorphic by checking for these characteristics:

STEP 1 Metamorphic rocks are really strong. They are definitely stronger than sedimentary rocks. They can be even stronger than igneous rocks. That means they can't be broken easily. Pick up each of your rocks one at a time and see whether you can break it with your hands. Don't use a tool; we will try that later. Record the numbers on the appropriate line:

Rocks that you could break:

Rocks that you couldn't break:

STEP 2 Metamorphic rocks can have layers that look like stripes. (Think of a folded ribbon or a stack of papers.) Examine each rock for evidence of layers. Record the numbers:

Rocks with layers:

Rocks without:

STEP 3 Metamorphic rocks might have grains that you can see. Examine each rock for grains of any color and record the numbers:

Rocks with grains:

Rocks without:

STEP 4 Now look at your lists above. Ask yourself these questions:

- Do any rocks have all three characteristics outlined in Steps 1–3? List them here:

- Do any rocks have two? List them here:

These are the rocks that are more likely to be metamorphic. Now go to the rock guide to check your guesses.

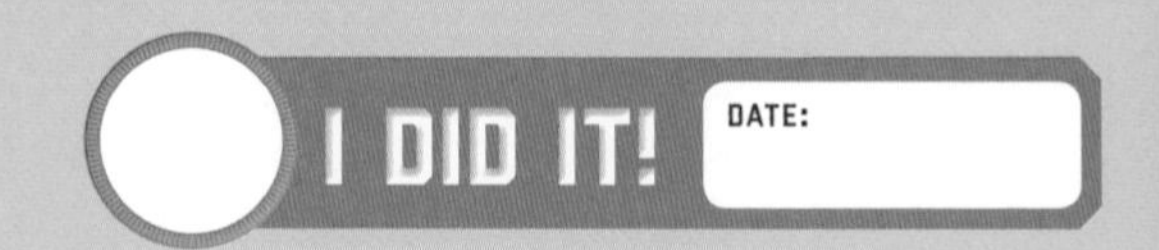

The Rock Cycle

The one thing you've probably figured out as you've gone through your collection is that you have a mix of many different kinds of rocks. How is that possible? As was mentioned before, rocks don't always stay the same. They can be broken down, pulverized, mixed with other things, heated, melted, put under great pressure and re-form. Over and over throughout time, rocks can change from one type to another. This process is called the rock cycle.

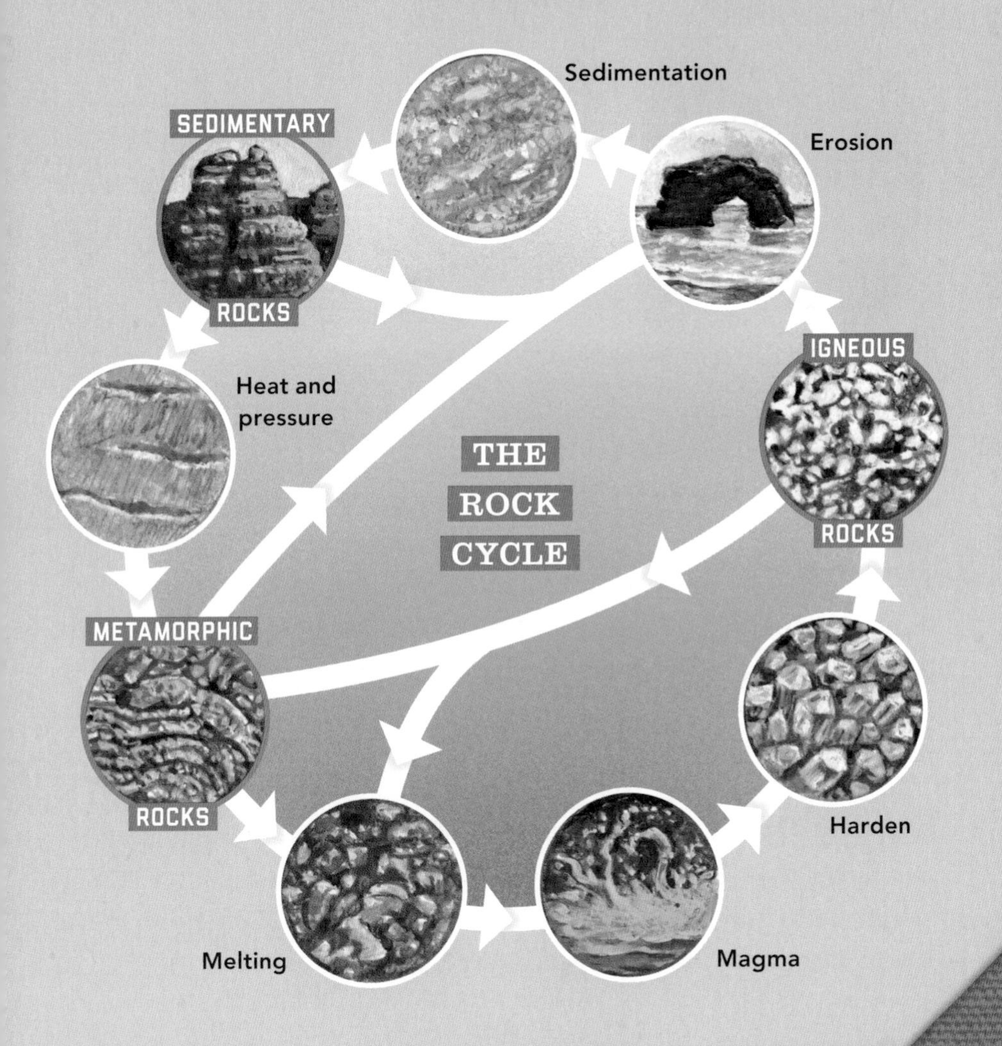

To better understand how the rock cycle works, let's take a step back and look at rocks on a global scale. Let's look at the entire earth! The earth is basically one huge rock. It can be divided into four layers—three solid, and one liquid:

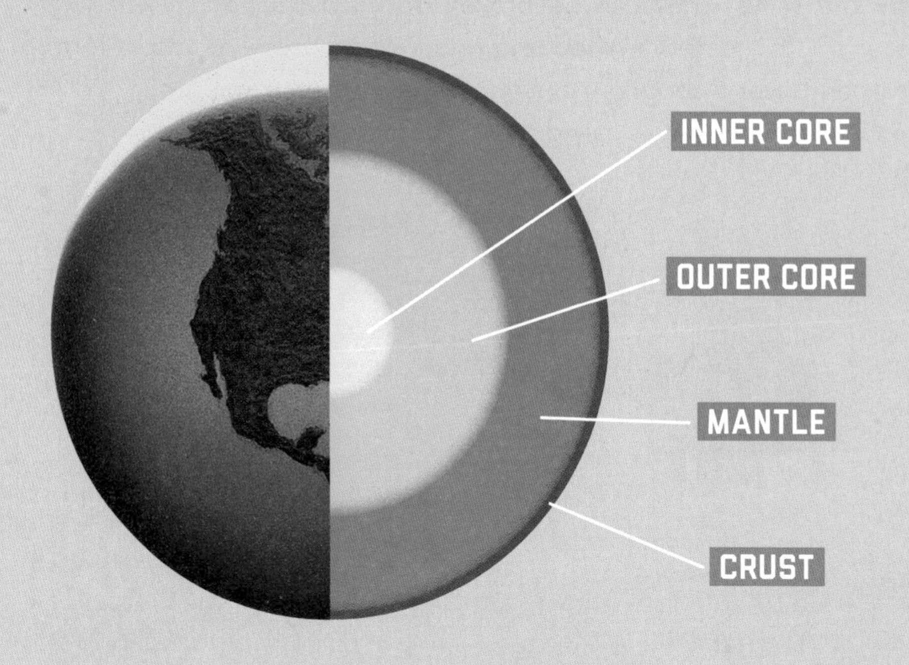

INNER CORE A dense solid ball of mostly iron. It is *extremely* hot here! Between 8,500°F and 12,100°F (4,700°C and 6,700°C), which is as hot as the surface of the sun. The metal is solid because of the ultrahigh pressure created by the weight of all the layers on top of it.

OUTER CORE A fourteen-hundred-mile-thick layer of liquid iron and nickel that rotates around the inner core. Although it's a little cooler here, only 7,200°F to 9,000°F (4,000°C to 5,000°C), the metal is liquid because the pressure is lower.

MANTLE Solid rock made of silicates, about eighteen hundred miles thick. (That's as long as the drive from Washington, DC, to Albuquerque, New Mexico.) Temperatures here drop from 6,700°F (3,700°C) near the outer core to 1,800°F (1,000°C) near the crust. Pressure keeps the mantle solid, but the rock is soft and moldable, kind of like Silly Putty, which allows the plates in the crust to move over millions of years.

CRUST This is the outermost layer of the earth, where we live. It is made of hard, brittle rock, about 95 percent igneous and metamorphic, and 5 percent sedimentary. It's only about three to six miles thick under the oceans and averages about twenty-five miles thick on the continents. Think of the earth's crust like the skin of an apple. It's very thin compared with what's inside.

How is the earth involved in the rock cycle? Let's break down the parts of it one at a time:

MANTLE This is where igneous rocks come from. The solid mantle melts in spots and forms magma, which rises into the earth's crust and eventually cools and hardens into new rock. This happens either at or below the earth's surface.

CRUST This is where rocks get pushed around when tectonic plates collide. Some are pushed deep below the surface, where heat and pressure alter their makeup and transform them into new metamorphic rocks. Some may melt and become magma. Other rocks are pushed up onto the surface, exposing them to wind and water.

ON THE EARTH'S SURFACE This is where rocks weather and erode away, creating sediment that is deposited somewhere else. Over time the sediments cement into new sedimentary rock.

Weathered and eroded rocks create sediment

Rocks exposed to erosion and weathering

EARTH'S SURFACE

Rising magma cools and hardens into rock

Melting mantle forms magma

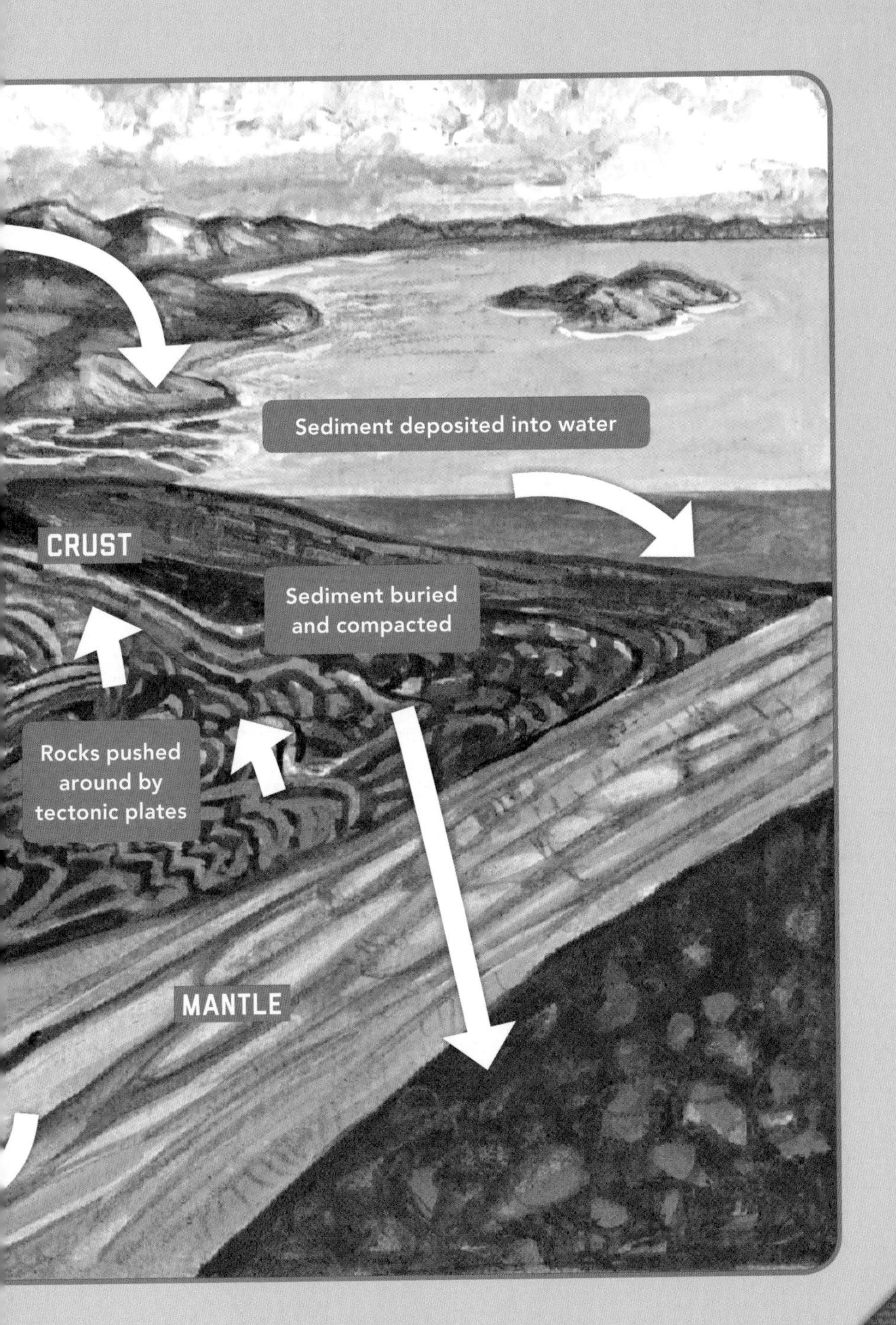
Sediment deposited into water
CRUST
Sediment buried and compacted
Rocks pushed around by tectonic plates
MANTLE

TRY IT → Plan Your Next Rock Hunt!

Time to expand your collection. We're going on a hike again! Choose a place where you can see different types of landforms than the ones you saw on you first rock hunt. If that isn't possible, go for a walk in a different direction from where you went previously. Preferably, the new place you explore will have one or more of these features:

- mountain
- riverbank
- creek
- valley
- hill
- lots of trees
- flat area like a meadow or prairie
- ocean shore

Here are a few types of rocks you might see, depending on your location:

- On a beach you are more likely to find hard rocks, like igneous and metamorphic. These type of rocks will most likely be smoother because they've been tossed about in the surf.
- Rocks near a river delta or a wide, slow-moving river might be sedimentary because the water drops sediments in the riverbed.
- Rocks in a mountain can be any type. If you see lines in the mountain, it can mean sedimentary or metamorphic rocks.
- Rocks in a valley might be more sedimentary since sediments fall from the mountain. Or they could be metamorphic if the valley was formed by movement of tectonic plates.
- Rocks in a forest might be sedimentary if they were formed by an ancient river. Or the rocks could be granite, which is an igneous rock that forms much of the earth's crust.

TRACK IT ↘

Make a Rock-Hunting Map

WHAT YOU'LL NEED

- A pen or pencil and a piece of paper or this book.

Before you start exploring, you'll need to create a rock-hunting map or paste an existing map of your location below. (Follow the instructions on pages 14–16 if you need a refresher.) When you get to your location, record the different areas you see on the map, particularly the landforms you checked earlier.

I DID IT! DATE:

TRY IT → Your Next Rock Hunt!

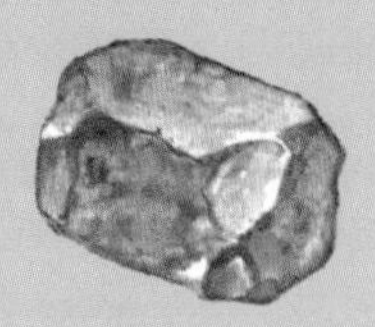

WHAT YOU'LL NEED

- A dry day, a strong backpack, twelve bags or containers that close easily or an empty egg carton, a permanent marker and a roll of masking tape to make labels, a water bottle and a snack (rock hunting can make you hungry!), a small shovel and gloves, safety goggles or glasses, your rock-hunting map, a compass (even if you have a smartphone with GPS), camera, hammer and chisel, sieve with a handle, small clean paintbrush (to brush dirt off rocks), binoculars (if you are looking at mountains from far away), sunglasses, and sunscreen.

STEP 1 Put your gloves on and let's go! Walk along the trail looking for rocks. Look up, down, and all around you as you search for rocks on the different land formations.

STEP 2 When you pick up a rock, put it in its own bag or container. Take your marker and masking tape and number the bag or the container. If you're using an egg carton, you can put the number on the inside top of the cup.

STEP 3 Now mark on the map where you found the rock with the same number that you put on the bag or container.

I DID IT! DATE:

TRACK IT ↘

Describe Your Rock-Hunting Field

Write a few notes on the next page about the area where you found each rock.

ROCK #

DESCRIBE THE AREA AROUND THE ROCK #

I DID IT!

DATE:

TRACK IT ↘ Inspecting Your Rocks

Go through the rocks you have collected and describe them below.

ROCK # ADD IMAGE OF ROCK	LOCATION WHERE YOU FOUND IT	COLOR

➢ Did you find a type of rock that you didn't expect in your environment? Remember, rocks move via the rock cycle. Animals and humans move rocks around, too. So it is completely possible that you might find a rock in a certain environment that looks nothing like the rocks around it.

SIZE DIAMETER	SHAPE	TEXTURE ROUGH OR SMOOTH	WHAT TYPE OF ROCK?

I DID IT! DATE:

CHAPTER 6

Identifying Your Rock & Mineral Collection

By now you probably have a ton of rocks in your collection. And you probably want to find out *exactly* what they are (beyond just igneous, sedimentary, or metamorphic)! You will find a handy rock and mineral identification guide on pages 94–203, but there are other ways of uncovering the mysteries of your collection. Identifying a rock is a process. There are many different things you can check to determine what it is or isn't. Of course, none of these are foolproof. You can misidentify a rock. It happens. Even geologists do it on occasion.

Location, Location

It might help to know where you could possibly find your rock in the world. Although, that's not as easy as it sounds. After all, rocks are recycled. They can be physically moved from place to place as they travel through the rock cycle. A rock that once started at the bottom of the ocean could end up on top of a mountain or even your own backyard. Rocks are also moved about by animals and yes, people. Have you ever collected a rock while on vacation and taken it home? That rock may not normally be found in your area, but it is now.

Rocks found at the peak of Mount Everest originally came from an ancient sea that flowed more than four hundred million years ago! And they didn't even have to train for the climb.

Rocks Where You Live

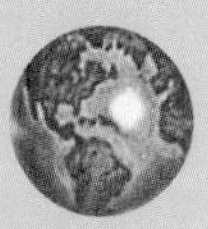

If you are curious about what rocks might be in your area, check out local sources like natural history museums, college or university geology departments, or consider joining a local geology or rock-hunting group. Perhaps other people out there love rocks as much as you do. If there isn't a geology group or club, start your own! You can probably find other kids at your school who like rocks and maybe even collect them. Get together and help each other identify your rocks.

Visit local parks and nature centers to see whether they have any information about the rocks in your area. They may have pamphlets or fact sheets on the local geology. And you can always do an internet search. Put in your state and area and "rock types" to see what comes up. If all else fails, ask an adult to ask a geologist on Twitter by using the hashtag #AskaGeologist.

Break It Down

Crash! Bang! Crunch! Sometimes the easiest way to identify a rock is to smash it. When you break up a rock, you can see whether there is something cool inside. Perhaps it has lines or maybe spots or even a bunch of crystals.

Whatever you find—or don't find—tells you something about the rock. How? Geologists use the following characteristics to classify rocks and the minerals that are in them. Of course, these tests will just give you an idea of the types of minerals that can be found in your rock. If your rock has more than one mineral, you may get mixed results. Still, you can use these tests as a guideline to help you determine the minerals that might be in your rock, and that might help you identify it.

Color

Minerals can be pretty much any color of the rainbow. Take a look at the guide on pages 94–203 for the colors of specific rocks and minerals.

The Rainbow Mountains in the Zhangye Danxia Landform Geological Park in China display layers of different colored sandstone and minerals.

Hardness

This is exactly what it sounds like—a measure of how hard the mineral (or minerals) inside the rock is. The hardness of a rock indicates its structure and what minerals were used to make it. Geologists use the Mohs scale shown below to attach a number to the hardness of a mineral. One is soft, ten is very hard. A mineral that is a ten will be able to scratch any minerals under it. Minerals that are on the lower end of the scale will fall apart if they are rubbed together. If you want to compare a mineral to some common items you might have around your house, use the Mohs hardness scale of common objects.

SCALE #	Indicator Mineral
1	talc
2	gypsum
3	calcite
4	fluorite
5	apatite
6	orthoclase
7	quartz
8	topaz
9	corundum
10	diamond

COMMON OBJECTS	
fingernail	**(2 to 2.5)**
copper penny	**(3 to 3.5)**
glass or pocketknife blade	**(5 to 6.5)**
steel file or nail	**(6.5)**
masonry drill bit	**(8.5)**

Streak

The streak is the color of the mark that is left behind when a rock is rubbed against a piece of white porcelain tile. This only works for rocks with minerals that have a Mohs number less than seven. A really hard mineral (more than eight on the Mohs scale) will just scratch the porcelain and not leave a color. Each mineral in the identification guide has a streak color that helps you to identify it.

Luster

Luster refers to how an object reflects light. A particular luster clues geologists in to which minerals may be present in the rock. The rock itself may appear dull and earthy, but the minerals inside can be sparkly. Before checking luster, be sure that your rock is clean and polished. That might help you determine if it has any shine to it.

ADAMANTINE Sparkly and transparent or translucent

DULL Not reflective

EARTHY Dull and grainy

GREASY Shiny but blurry, as if coated with thin layer of oil

METALLIC Like metal

PEARLY Like pearls or inside of mollusk shell

RESINOUS Like honey or tree sap

SILKY Like soft, shiny fibers

VITREOUS Glassy

WAXY Like candle wax or beeswax, translucent to opaque

METALLIC

RESINOUS

VITREOUS

Cleavage

This is a measure of *how* the minerals inside a rock breaks. If a rock breaks along one or more flat surfaces, that is, if you break the rock and it is flat, not jagged, then it has cleavage. Not all rocks and minerals display cleavage. Quartz and pyrite do not.

TYPES OF MINERAL CLEAVAGE

CUBIC

OCTOHEDRAL

PERFECT

TRY IT →

Look for Color, Streak, Luster, Hardness, and Cleavage

Now that you know what to look for to help identify the rocks and minerals in your collection, let's put your knowledge—and strength—to the test. Time to break up your rocks.

WHAT YOU'LL NEED

- Safety goggles or glasses, gloves, mask, a hammer, an empty cardboard box (to keep rock pieces from flying everywhere) about 9 x 11 in (23 x 28 cm), tongs with rubber ends (to hold the rock as you hit it), a piece of white porcelain tile, an old towel or shirt (to wipe off the tile), your rock collection, and a pen or pencil.

PLEASE NOTE Be sure to wear your mask when breaking apart your rocks. This will create dust, which you do not want to inhale. Use your gloves, too, to keep your hands safe from dust. Throw away or clean gloves afterward. Be sure to wash your hands thoroughly when you are done.

STEP 1 Get your rock-smashing space ready by finding an open area outdoors approved by an adult. It could be a patio, the backyard, or maybe a nearby park.

STEP 2 Set up your cardboard box and place your hammer, tongs, safety goggles, and gloves alongside. Be sure that all people and pets are at least six feet away.

STEP 3 Pick up one of your rocks and note its number in the Rock # column on the chart on the following page. Use the chart for the remaining steps.

ROCK #	COLOR	STREAK	LUSTER	HARDNESS MOHS NUMBER	CLEAVAGE

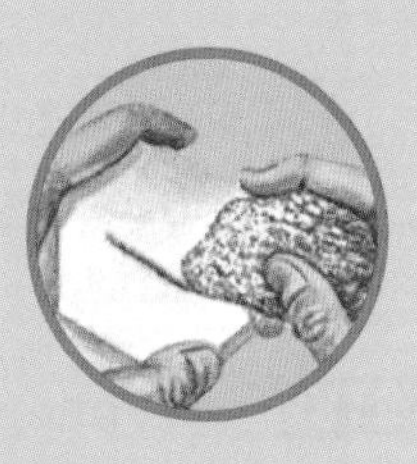

STEP 4 Note its color in the next column.

STEP 5 Scratch the rock across the porcelain tile. Write down what color streak (if any) was left behind.

STEP 6 Hold the rock up to the sunlight to determine if you can see its luster as the light reflects off of the minerals inside. Write your observation.

STEP 7 Now determine the Mohs hardness level of your rock:

a. First, put on your safety goggles and gloves.

b. Hold the rock in your hand and scratch it with your fingernail.

c. Did you see any kind of indentation on the rock? Use your fingernail to feel for it. (Sometimes the mark is so slight that you can't see it very well.)

d. Continue to scratch your rock with any of the Mohs common objects from page 75 that you might have around the house, increasing in hardness levels.

e. The hardest object (the one with the highest number) that *did not leave a scratch* gives you the approximate Mohs hardness. Record this number in the chart.

STEP 8 Time to test the cleavage of your rock. Keep in mind that while hitting rocks is fun, you don't want to pulverize all the rocks you worked hard to collect. They're so cool—plus, you will need them for more tests later! Follow these steps:

a. Put the rock into the cardboard box and hit the rock with the hammer.

b. Keep hitting it until the rock breaks.

c. Look at your rock. Did it break with a flat plane like the cleavage pictures on page 76? If so, note that in the final column of the chart on page 78. If the rock did not break with a flat plane, note that, too.

STEP 9 Once you are done testing your rock, scoop up the pieces and put them back in the rock's numbered bag or container.

Repeat these steps for as many rocks as you like.

CHAPTER 7

Rock & Mineral Testing

Hopefully, you did not go wild with the rock smashing and you still have samples left to test. The next tests don't involve smashing, but they do involve using water and chemicals, so they are also best done outside.

What will you be looking for? Minerals, which will help identify the rock.

- Specific gravity will help you figure out which minerals are in your rock.
- An acid test will determine whether your rock contains a carbonate mineral.

- A magnetic test will determine whether your rock contains iron.

Specific Gravity

Specific gravity is used is to determine the density of your rocks so you can compare them. Why can't you just weigh the rocks? Because weight alone, or rather mass, tells you very little about what's inside the rock. Density, however, tells you how tightly the rock's atoms are packed, which can give you some idea of the minerals inside.

MASS Mass tells you how much matter an object contains, and it is the same no matter where an object is. Weight is the pull of gravity on that mass, and it varies. On Earth, mass and weight are essentially the same since the strength of Earth's gravity is almost constant. But on the moon, which has much less mass than Earth,

ON THE EARTH: 100 POUNDS

ON THE MOON: 16.5 POUNDS

gravity is weaker—only 16.5 percent of the earth's force. So objects weigh a lot less on the moon than on Earth.

DENSITY Density tells you how tightly packed the molecules are inside the object. It is calculated by dividing the mass of the object by its volume, or the amount of space the object occupies. Think of two cubes of the same size, one solid lead, the other Styrofoam. They both take up the same amount of space, but as you can imagine, the lead cube weighs significantly more than the Styrofoam cube. That's because the lead has more molecules packed into that cube than the Styrofoam, so the lead has greater density. Because density is a ratio, you find it by dividing the mass by the volume:

Density = Mass ÷ Volume, or $\mathbf{D = \frac{M}{V}}$

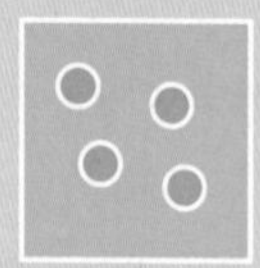
LOWER DENSITY

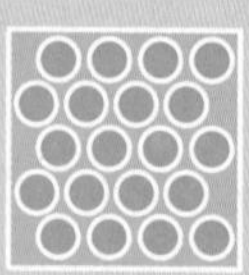
HIGHER DENSITY

Specific gravity compares a rock's density to the density of water. This ratio is what geologists use to help identify minerals within rocks since it is a known number for all minerals.

Got it? Give it a try along with these others tests for identifying the minerals within your rocks.

TRY IT → Finding Density and Specific Gravity

WHAT YOU'LL NEED

- A graduated cylinder or a transparent measuring cup, water, scale that can weigh both small and large rocks in grams, and a pen or pencil.

STEP 1 Choose a rock from your collection. Record its number in the chart on page 85.

STEP 2 Place your rock on the scale. Record the mass in grams in the chart.

STEP 3 Fill your graduated cylinder with ten milliliters of water. Record the number under initial volume.

READING A MENISCUS

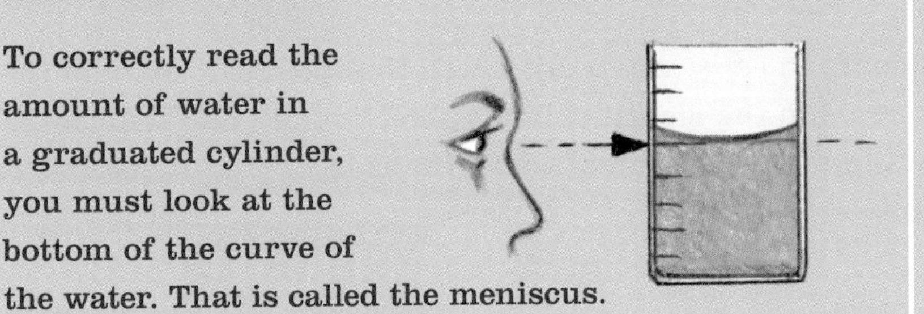

To correctly read the amount of water in a graduated cylinder, you must look at the bottom of the curve of the water. That is called the meniscus.

STEP 4 Add your rock to the graduated cylinder. How high did the water go up? Record the number under final volume.

STEP 5 Subtract the initial volume from the final volume to get the change in volume. Record the number in the chart.

FINDING THE CHANGE IN VOLUME

Example: If your initial volume was ten milliliters and your final volume after adding the rock was sixteen milliliters, then it's

16 mL – 10 mL = 6 mL

Your change in volume is six milliliters.

STEP 6 Take the mass and divide it by the change in volume to get the density of your rock. Record the number in the chart.

STEP 7 Calculate the specific gravity. Since you are using water, that's easy. The specific gravity of water is 1.0. So you take the number in the density column and divide by one *or* just copy over your density number to the specific gravity column and be done with it!

Compare the specific gravity with the specific gravity of the minerals in the identification guide. You are one step closer to finding out what kind of rock you have!

ROCK #	MASS IN GRAMS	INITIAL VOLUME IN mL	FINAL VOLUME IN mL	CHANGE IN VOLUME	DENSITY $\frac{M}{V}$	SPECIFIC GRAVITY

TRY IT → Acid Test

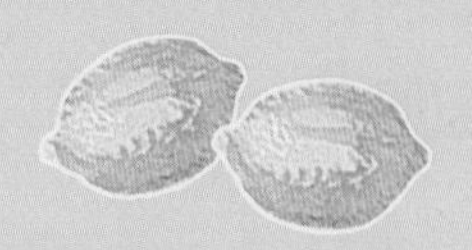

Another method that geologists use to identify minerals in a rock is an acid test. A rock that bubbles when exposed to acid contains carbonate. Geologists perform this test with diluted hydrochloric acid and carry bottles of it when they go rock hunting. But hydrochloric acid is a very corrosive, hazardous liquid. For our purposes, we'll use lemon juice and vinegar. This experiment will let you know whether your rock contains a carbonate mineral, most likely calcium carbonate, one of the most common rock-building minerals.

WHAT YOU'LL NEED

- One glass or plastic bowl (not metal), a cloth or a roll of paper towels, 1–2 cups lemon juice, 1–2 cups vinegar, small spoon or a medicine dropper, a hammer (to crush rock if needed), safety glasses, a place to dump the lemon juice and vinegar when you are done, a magnifying glass if possible, and a pen or pencil.

STEP 1 Place one of your rocks into a bowl. Be sure to record the rock's number in the chart on the next page.

STEP 2 Put on your safety glasses. Use the medicine dropper or small spoon to put a few drops of lemon juice on the rock.

STEP 3 Watch to see what happens. Use the magnifying glass if necessary. Note what you see in the following chart. (Hint: You are looking for bubbles or any type of fizzing.)

STEP 4 Wipe off your rock with a cloth or paper towel. Now take the medicine dropper or spoon and put a few drops of vinegar on the rock. Look for fizzing. Note in the chart. If you saw fizzing after applying either the lemon juice, vinegar, or both this is most likely a rock that has carbonate in it.

ROCK #	LEMON JUICE REACTED X FOR YES	VINEGAR REACTED X FOR YES	CONTAINS CARBONATE YES / NO

I DID IT! DATE:

TRY IT → Magnetic Test

A final way to help identify your rocks is to see whether they contain iron. How do you do this? With a magnet. Iron has magnetic qualities. Have you ever held a magnet over a paper clip? What happens? The paper clip jumps to the magnet. That is magnetic attraction.

Rocks that contain iron will also be attracted to a magnet. Sometimes the attraction will be strong. Other times, it will be slight. Let's give it a try.

WHAT YOU'LL NEED

- A small magnet (one off your refrigerator will work best), a pen or pencil.

STEP 1 Choose a rock from your collection.

STEP 2 Start by holding the magnet in one hand and the rock in the other hand. Keep the magnet still and slowly bring the rock toward the magnet. Do you feel a pull from the rock as it tries to get closer to the magnet? If so, that rock might contain iron. If you don't feel any pull at all between the rock and the magnet, then this rock is not attracted to a magnet and doesn't contain iron.

STEP 3 Do this test for all your rocks and record your results below.

PRO TIP Rocks that are attracted to a magnet may contain magnetite, a common iron oxide that is the most abundant magnetic mineral on earth. However, some magnetic rocks are a bit more spacey, and can actually be out of this world!

ROCK #	MAGNETIC ATTRACTION X FOR YES	NO MAGNETIC ATTRACTION X FOR YES	CONTAINS IRON YES / NO

I DID IT!

DATE:

TAKE IT TO THE NEXT LEVEL ↗

Did You Find a Meteorite?

Rocks that are slightly magnetic may actually be meteorites. Finding a meteorite is not common, but it is possible, especially if you found your rock in a warm, dry place, such as a desert or a dried-up lake bed. (Meteorites are less likely to wear away in warm, dry areas.) You might have a meteorite if your rock gets a yes on all these questions:

- Is it magnetic?
- Is the rock very dense? Does it feel heavier than a normal rock? (Check the rock's density on page 85 and compare it with your other rocks.)
- Does the rock have a metallic shine to it?
- Is it black or brown? Meteorites are burned by the high temperatures in the atmosphere as they fall through it.
- Does it have small rounded stones on its outside?
- Does it have dents on the surface that might look like fingerprints?

I DID IT! DATE:

Space Rock Terminology

Do you ever get confused about what to call a rock that flies through space? Is it a comet? An asteroid? Meteor? Meteoroid? Or maybe a meteorite? Well, have no fear, if you use these definitions, you'll get it right every time. (And sound really smart!)

COMETS A comet starts out as a small body of frozen gases, rocks, and dust that orbits the sun. When its orbit brings the comet close to the sun, the heat expands the gases into a giant glowing ball bigger than most planets, trailing a tail of dust and gases millions of miles long.

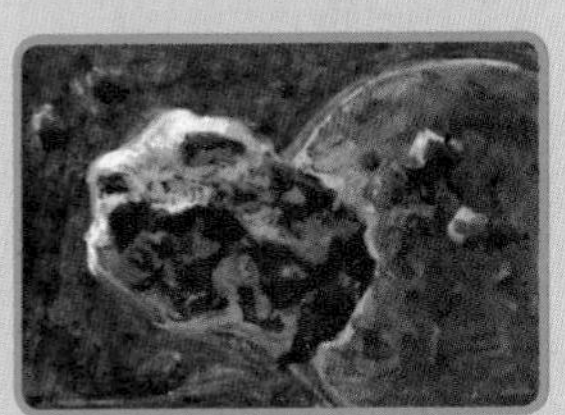

ASTEROIDS An asteroid is a rocky body that orbits the sun. They are found mostly in the asteroid belt between Jupiter and Mars. They range in size from 33 feet (10 meters) to 329 miles (529 kilometers) in diameter and have no atmosphere.

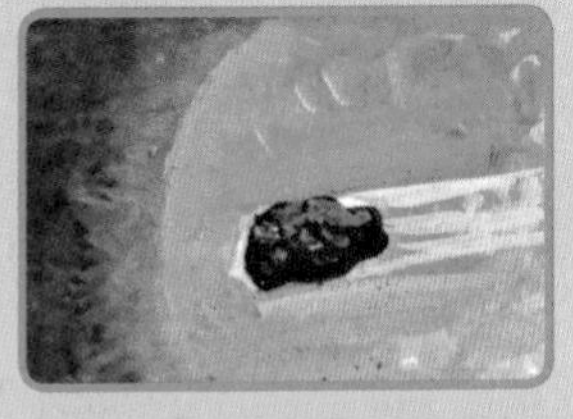

METEOROIDS A meteoroid is any small object that orbits the sun, from a bit of dust to a small asteroid. They're often called space rocks.

METEORS Meteors are meteoroids that enter the earth's atmosphere and burn up completely. We call these brilliant fireballs shooting stars. (Have you ever seen one?)

METEORITES Meteorites are meteoroids that make it all the way through the atmosphere and land on earth. Scientists estimate that around five hundred meteorites hit the earth every year. They are not easy to find, but they do exist, so keep your eyes out for them.

TRACK IT ↘ Final Answer

You have gathered a lot of information about the rocks in your collection. Like a geologist, you have analyzed them, tested them, compared them to others, and yes, even broken them apart to see what was inside. Now, with all the data you've collected in this book and the help of the identification guide, it's time to come up with a final answer. What type of rocks have you found?

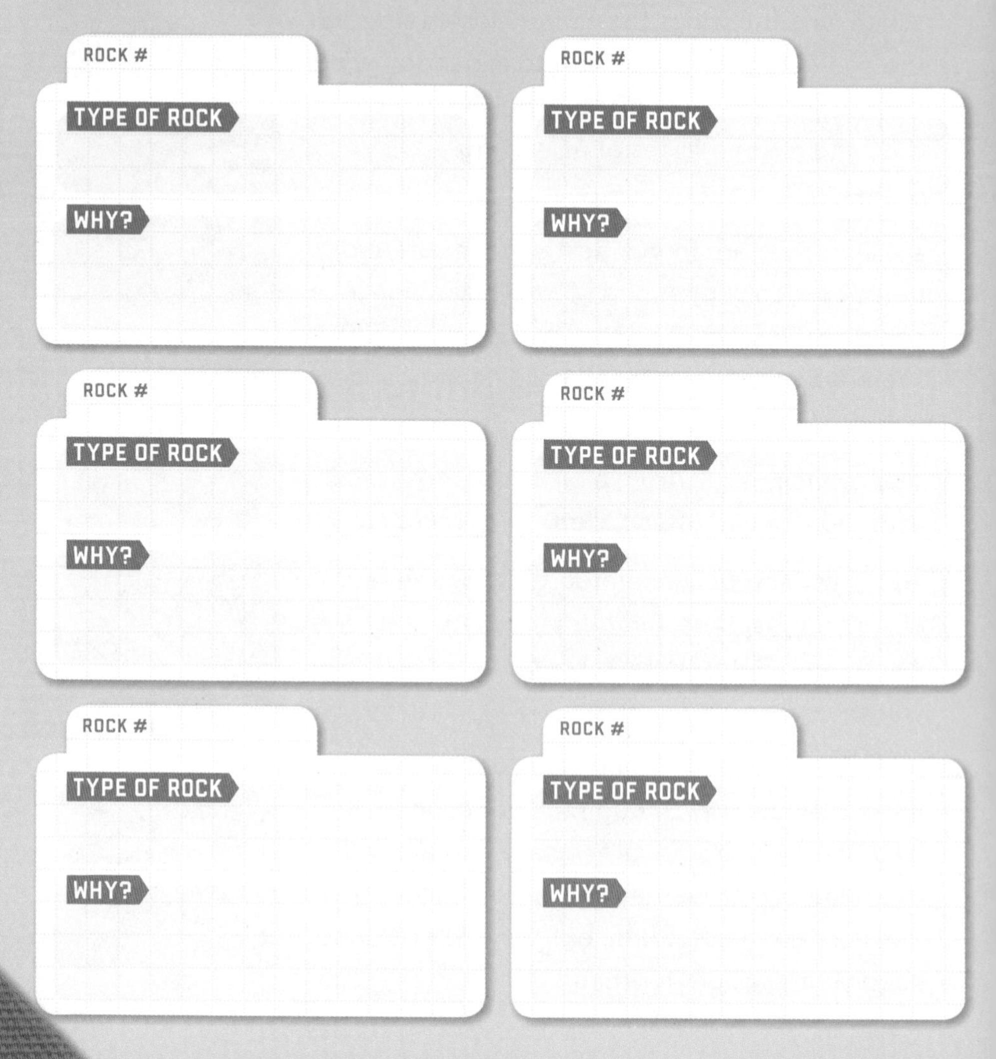

ROCK #

TYPE OF ROCK

WHY?

ROCK #

TYPE OF ROCK

WHY?

ROCK #

TYPE OF ROCK

WHY?

ROCK #

TYPE OF ROCK

WHY?

ROCK #

TYPE OF ROCK

WHY?

ROCK #

TYPE OF ROCK

WHY?

ROCK #

TYPE OF ROCK

WHY?

ROCK #

TYPE OF ROCK

WHY?

I DID IT!

DATE:

ROCK & MINERAL IDENTIFICATION

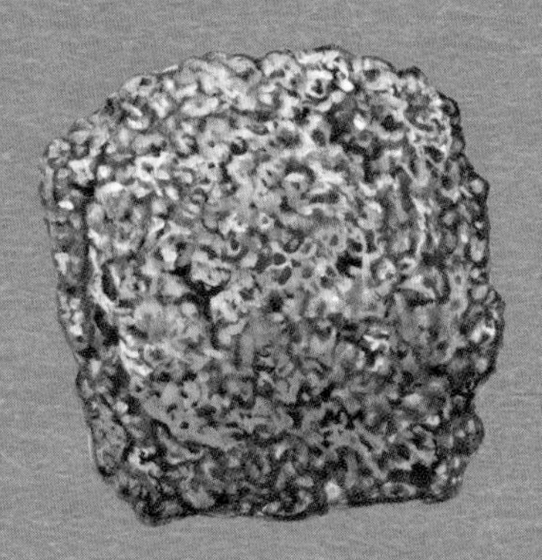

The pages here will give you details about various rocks and minerals, where they might be found, and pictures to help you identify the specimens in your collection. Remember, the rock cycle moves rocks all over the planet, so it's not always easy to say specifically where you will find a certain rock or mineral. The places listed in this guide are the most likely places to find this rock or mineral, *but* that doesn't mean that you will find them there or that you won't find them elsewhere. Think of your rock search as a hunt for treasure. You may end up with something that's really special, and you'll have no idea how it got there. So pick up a specimen from your collection and start comparing!

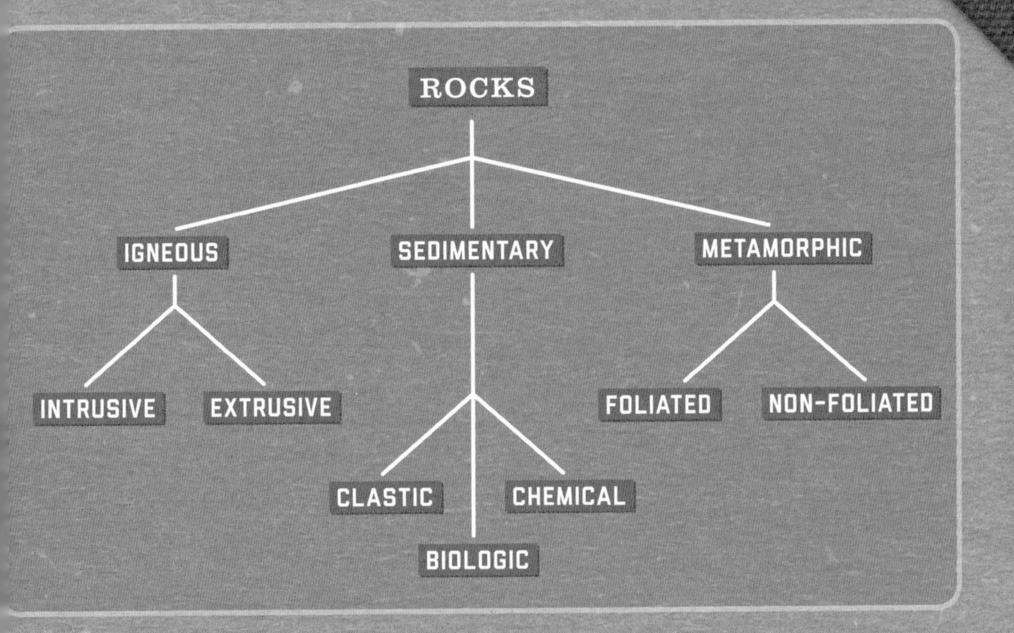

MINERALS

NATIVE ELEMENTS

BORATES

HALIDES

SULFIDES

OXIDES

SULFATES

CARBONATES

HYDROXIDES

SILICATES

(This only includes the mineral categories present in the following pages.)

NOTE Always be careful when handling rocks and minerals as they can contain harmful substances. Wash your hands after handling your rocks and never put a rock into your mouth.

IGNEOUS ROCKS

Andesite

Extrusive

NAME After the Andes Mountains in South America, where andesite is common.

MINERALS Plagioclase feldspar, also may contain biotite, pyroxene, or amphibole

COLOR Light to dark gray, reddish pink, brown if weathered

TEXTURE Fine grained

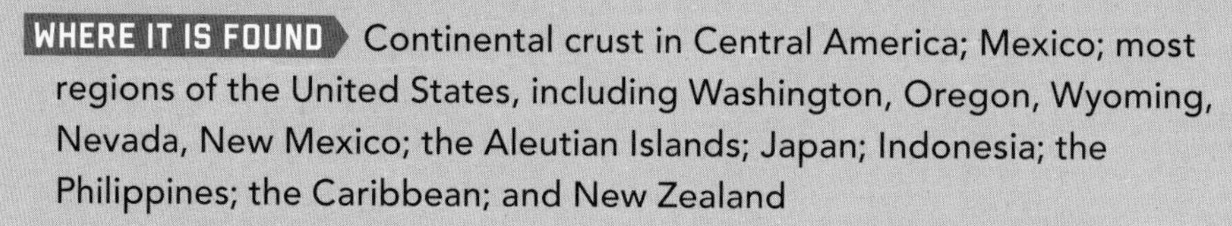

WHERE IT IS FOUND Continental crust in Central America; Mexico; most regions of the United States, including Washington, Oregon, Wyoming, Nevada, New Mexico; the Aleutian Islands; Japan; Indonesia; the Philippines; the Caribbean; and New Zealand

RELATED TO ANOTHER ROCK? Yes. It forms from the same magma as diorite.

WHAT IT IS USED FOR Decoration, crushed as fill for construction projects.

POINT OF FACT It forms when andesite lava erupts from a volcano and cools quickly.

FOUND IT!

WHEN

DATE

WHERE

SPECIFIC PLACE AND SURROUNDINGS

NOTES

IGNEOUS ROCKS

Basalt

Extrusive

NAME From Latin *basaltes*, based on Greek *basanitēs*, from *basanos*, "touchstone."

MINERALS Plagioclase feldspars, pyroxene, olivine, magnetite

COLOR Dark gray to black

TEXTURE Fine grained

WHERE IT IS FOUND A very abundant rock on earth, it is found mostly on the ocean floor and most regions of the United States.

RELATED TO ANOTHER ROCK? Yes. It forms from the same magma as gabbro and diabase.

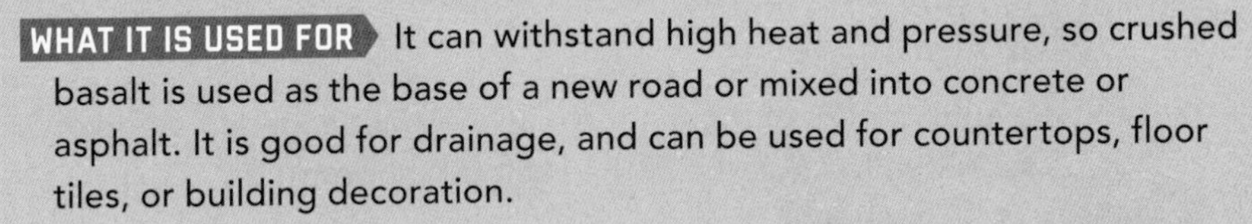

WHAT IT IS USED FOR It can withstand high heat and pressure, so crushed basalt is used as the base of a new road or mixed into concrete or asphalt. It is good for drainage, and can be used for countertops, floor tiles, or building decoration.

POINT OF FACT Basalt is one of the most abundant rocks on the moon and makes up the largest volcano on Mars, which is also the largest volcano in our solar system.

FOUND IT!

WHEN

DATE

WHERE

SPECIFIC PLACE AND SURROUNDINGS

NOTES

IGNEOUS ROCKS

Diabase

Intrusive

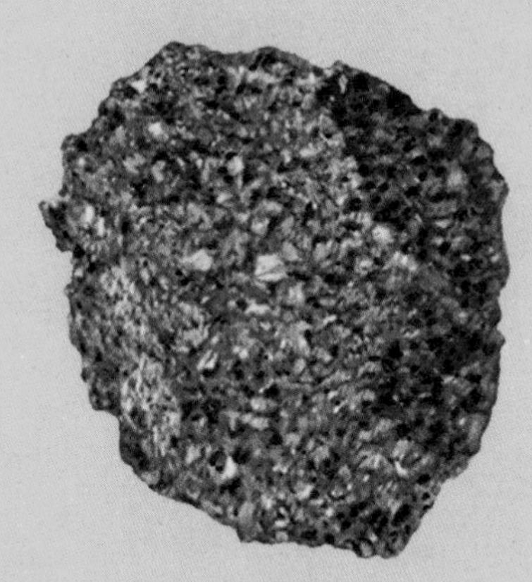

NAME From Greek *diabasis*, "act of crossing over."

MINERALS Pyroxene, plagioclase feldspar

COLOR Dark gray to black or grayish white

TEXTURE Fine grained

WHERE IT IS FOUND Most regions of the United States, Britain, Australia

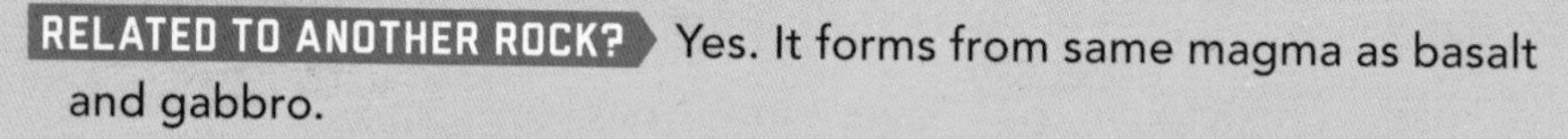

RELATED TO ANOTHER ROCK? Yes. It forms from same magma as basalt and gabbro.

WHAT IT IS USED FOR Mostly mined for use in construction.

POINTS OF FACT

- More than eighty blocks of the inner circle at Stonehenge are made of diabase, which is called dolerite in the United Kingdom.
- The Palisades in New York and New Jersey are made of diabase.

FOUND IT!

WHEN

DATE

WHERE

SPECIFIC PLACE AND SURROUNDINGS

NOTES

IGNEOUS ROCKS

Diorite

Intrusive

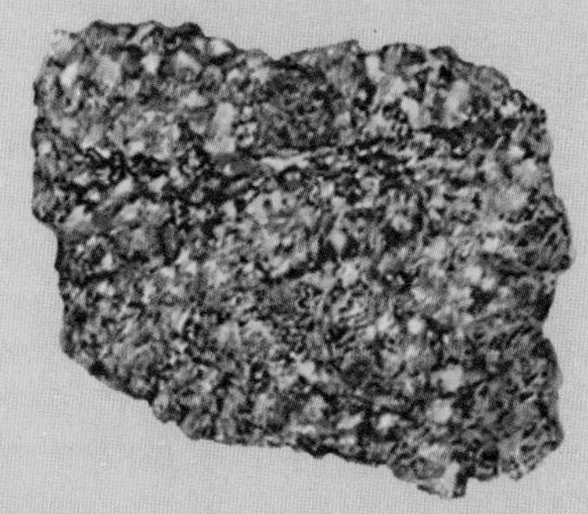

NAME From Greek *diorizein*, "to distinguish," because hornblende is easily distinguishable from other minerals.

MINERALS Sodium-rich plagioclase feldspar, with hornblende and biotite

COLOR Black and white mineral grains, lots of spots, but darker than granite, green

TEXTURE Coarse grained

WHERE IT IS FOUND Continental crust in Central America, Mexico, most regions of the United States, the Aleutian Islands, Japan, Indonesia, the Philippines, the Caribbean, New Zealand, and the Middle East.

RELATED TO ANOTHER ROCK? Yes. It forms from same magma as andesite.

WHAT IT IS USED FOR Crushed as the base for roads and buildings. Excellent for drainage and erosion control.

POINT OF FACT It's a very hard rock, so it's difficult to carve. But once you do, the sculpture lasts for thousands of years.

FOUND IT!

WHEN
DATE

WHERE
SPECIFIC PLACE AND SURROUNDINGS

NOTES

IGNEOUS ROCKS

Dunite

Intrusive

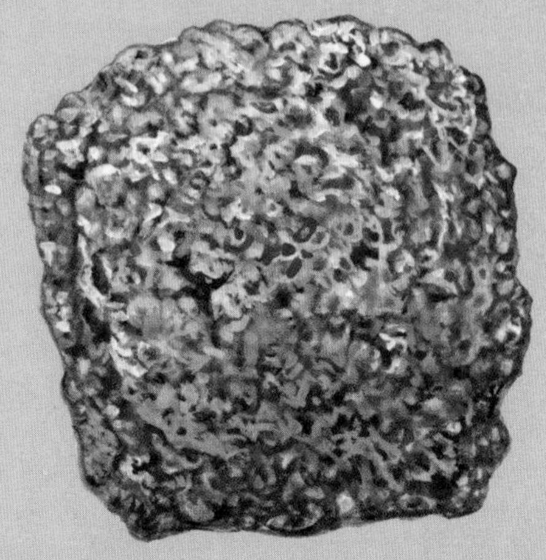

NAME After Dun Mountain, New Zealand, where it was first recorded.

MINERALS 90 percent olivine with some chromite

COLOR Yellowish green

TEXTURE Coarse grained

WHERE IT IS FOUND Maryland, Vermont, Washington, New Zealand, Norway, Sweden, South Africa, Brazil, China

RELATED TO ANOTHER ROCK? Yes. It is a type of peridotite.

WHAT IT IS USED FOR Important source of chromium, which is added to other metals to increase strength and resistance to corrosion.

POINT OF FACT The Twin Sisters Mountains in Washington are a huge block of dunite thrust up from the earth's mantle.

FOUND IT!

WHEN

DATE

WHERE

SPECIFIC PLACE AND SURROUNDINGS

NOTES

IGNEOUS ROCKS

Gabbro

Intrusive

NAME After a tiny town in Italy where the rock was first described by the Italian naturalist Giovanni Targioni Tozzetti in 1751.

MINERALS Plagioclase feldspar, augite, pyroxene, olivine

COLOR Black, black and white, or dark green

TEXTURE Coarse grained

WHERE IT IS FOUND It is found under ancient lava flows, so it is deep below the ocean floor, at the base of volcanic mountains such as the Apennines in Italy and the Deccan Traps of India, and most regions of the United States. If you happen to be walking along the Columbia River in Washington and Oregon, you might see gabbro there.

RELATED TO ANOTHER ROCK? Yes. It forms from same magma as basalt.

WHAT IT IS USED FOR Countertops, floor tiles, grave markers, as well as crushed for base of roads and buildings.

POINT OF FACT Gabbro can be found on Mars, the moon, and many large asteroids.

FOUND IT!

WHEN

DATE

WHERE

SPECIFIC PLACE AND SURROUNDINGS

NOTES

IGNEOUS ROCKS

Granite

Intrusive

NAME From Latin *granum*, "grain." The first thing you notice about granite is its large mineral grains.

MINERALS Quartz and feldspar with small amounts of mica, hornblende, amphiboles

COLOR Red, pink, gray, white, with dark spots

TEXTURE Coarse grained

WHERE IT IS FOUND It's the most common igneous rock on the planet. And is found on every continent in the world, and most regions of the United States. After all, it's part of the earth's continental crust

RELATED TO ANOTHER ROCK? Yes. It forms from same magma as rhyolite, except rhyolite has much finer crystals.

WHAT IT IS USED FOR Granite is used widely in construction, for buildings, countertops, floor tiles, pavers, and cemetery headstones. You might have granite countertops in your house!

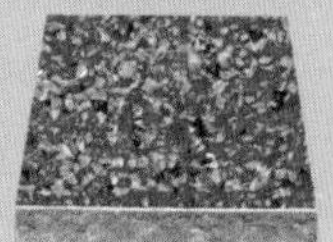

POINT OF FACT Granite can be billions of years old. (That's right! You are holding history in your hand.)

FOUND IT!

WHEN

DATE

WHERE

SPECIFIC PLACE AND SURROUNDINGS

NOTES

IGNEOUS ROCKS

Imperial Porphyry

Intrusive

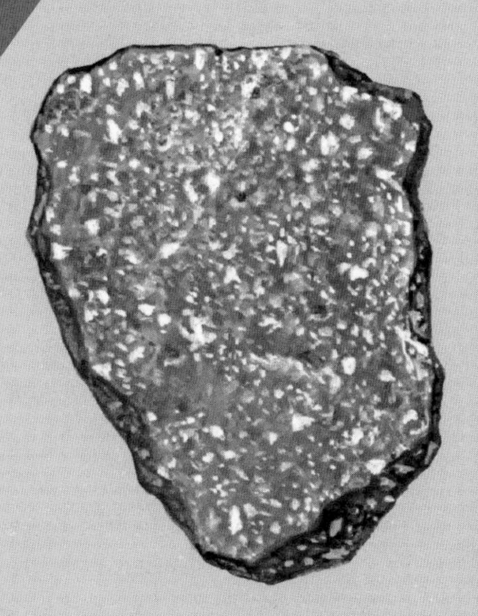

NAME From ancient Greek *porphyra*, "purple."

MINERALS Plagioclase and potassium feldspars, quartz, hematite, amphibole

COLOR Purple

TEXTURE Large coarse grains surrounded by fine grains

WHERE IT IS FOUND Egypt

RELATED TO ANOTHER ROCK? Yes, but in name only. Any igneous rock of any composition with a similar texture is called porphyry, so there are granite and diorite porphyries, for example.

WHAT IT IS USED FOR Nothing today since it comes from only one ancient quarry.

POINT OF FACT In ancient Rome the stone was used only in art and buildings created for the imperial court.

FOUND IT!

WHEN
DATE

WHERE
SPECIFIC PLACE AND SURROUNDINGS

NOTES

Kimberlite

Intrusive

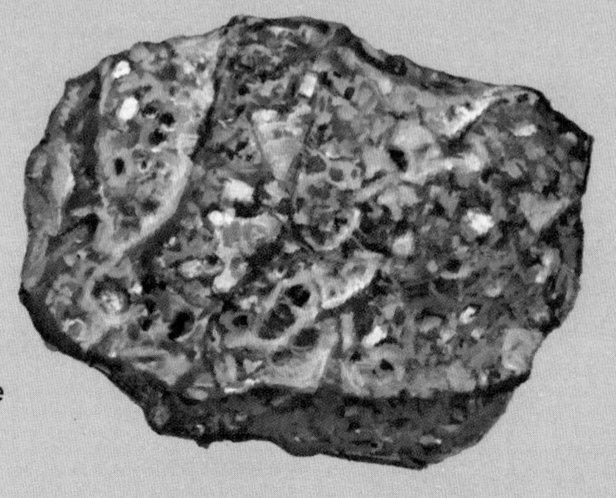

NAME After Kimberley, South Africa, the center of the diamond industry.

MINERALS Olivine, carbonates, pyroxene, mica, garnet, diopside

COLOR Dark gray

TEXTURE Large, coarse grains surrounded by fine grains

WHERE IT IS FOUND Continental crust around the world, including New York, Pennsylvania, Kansas, Missouri, Wyoming, Russia, India, South Africa (where it is prevalent), Australia.

RELATED TO ANOTHER ROCK? Yes. It is a type of peridotite.

WHAT IT IS USED FOR Major source of gem-quality diamonds.

POINTS OF FACT

- The largest gem diamond ever found, at 3,106 carats uncut, came from a South African kimberlite mine in 1905. That diamond weighed more than a pound!
- Kimberlite magma can form nearly vertical solid pipes in the earth's crust.

FOUND IT!

WHEN

DATE

WHERE

SPECIFIC PLACE AND SURROUNDINGS

NOTES

IGNEOUS ROCKS

Obsidian

Extrusive

NAME From Latin *obsidianus*, misspelling of *obsianus*, "of Obsius," after a Roman who discovered a similar stone.

MINERALS Mostly silica but it can have crystals of cristobalite

COLOR Black often with a swirl of brown, also brown, tan, or green, rarely blue, red, orange, or yellow, can have white spots

TEXTURE Glassy, with practically no visible grains

WHERE IT IS FOUND Don't look for it east of the Mississippi River in the United States. Obsidian is only found around recently active volcanoes. You can find it in the western US, most notably around Paulina Lake, within the caldera of Newberry Volcano in Oregon. While it hasn't erupted in 1,300 years, it still has active lava flows today.

RELATED TO ANOTHER ROCK? Yes. It forms from same magma as granite, pumice, and rhyolite.

WHAT IT IS USED FOR Gemstones, surgical blades, sculpture.

POINT OF FACT Humans have used tools made of obsidian (arrowheads, spear points, knife blades) as far back as the Stone Age.

FOUND IT!

WHEN

DATE

WHERE

SPECIFIC PLACE AND SURROUNDINGS

NOTES

IGNEOUS ROCKS

Pegmatite

Intrusive

NAME From Greek *pēgma*, "thing joined together."

MINERALS Quartz, mica, and feldspar

COLOR White, sometimes pink, with black lines or spots

TEXTURE Coarse grained, with very large crystals of at least one centimeter

WHERE IT IS FOUND Western and Eastern United States and around most of the world

RELATED TO ANOTHER ROCK? Yes. It forms during last stages of magma crystallization, so its composition can be like any igneous rock, but most often granite, with or without minerals.

WHAT IT IS USED FOR Gemstones, ore

POINTS OF FACT

- This valuable rock sometimes contains ores of lithium and beryllium.
- Some of the world's best gemstones are found in pegmatite: tourmaline, aquamarine, and topaz

FOUND IT!

WHEN

DATE

WHERE

SPECIFIC PLACE AND SURROUNDINGS

NOTES

IGNEOUS ROCKS

Peridotite

Intrusive

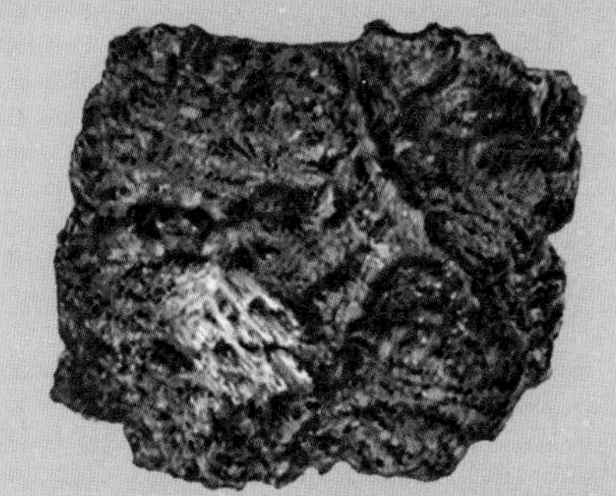

NAME After the gemstone peridot.

MINERALS Olivine, plus various other minerals

COLOR Dark green to black

TEXTURE Coarse grained

WHERE IT IS FOUND Most regions of the United States, New Zealand, South Africa, and all over the world.

RELATED TO ANOTHER ROCK? Yes. Peridotite is a generic name for any intrusive igneous rock that consists mainly of olivine.

WHAT IT IS USED FOR Source of valuable ores and minerals, including chromite, platinum, nickel, and precious garnet.

POINTS OF FACT

- Peridotites are thought to be the main rock of the earth's mantle.
- The olivine in peridotites reacts with carbon dioxide to form silica and magnesite, so the rocks could be a great help in pulling the greenhouse gas out of our atmosphere.

WHEN

DATE

WHERE

SPECIFIC PLACE AND SURROUNDINGS

NOTES

IGNEOUS ROCKS

Pumice

Extrusive

NAME From Latin *pumex*, "foam," since pumice looks kind of like a sponge.

MINERALS Similar composition to rhyolite, it may contain tiny crystals of feldspar, augite, hornblende, and zircon

COLOR White, light gray, tan, black

TEXTURE Glassy and very holey

WHERE IT IS FOUND California (Cascade Volcanic Field), Washington, Oregon, New Mexico, Idaho

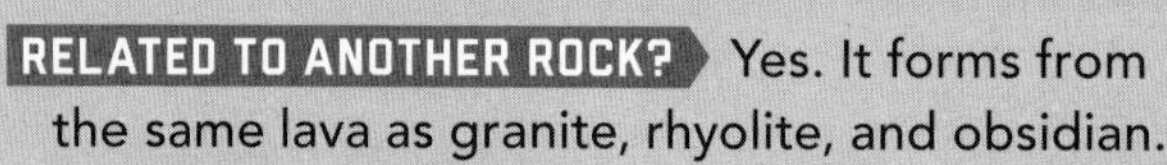

RELATED TO ANOTHER ROCK? Yes. It forms from the same lava as granite, rhyolite, and obsidian.

WHAT IT IS USED FOR Landscape decoration, lightweight concrete, abrasives

POINT OF FACT It floats in water because it has so many air pockets. Air pockets are formed when gas bubbles are trapped inside lava that cools very quickly.

FOUND IT!

WHEN

DATE

WHERE

SPECIFIC PLACE AND SURROUNDINGS

NOTES

IGNEOUS ROCKS

Rhyolite

Extrusive

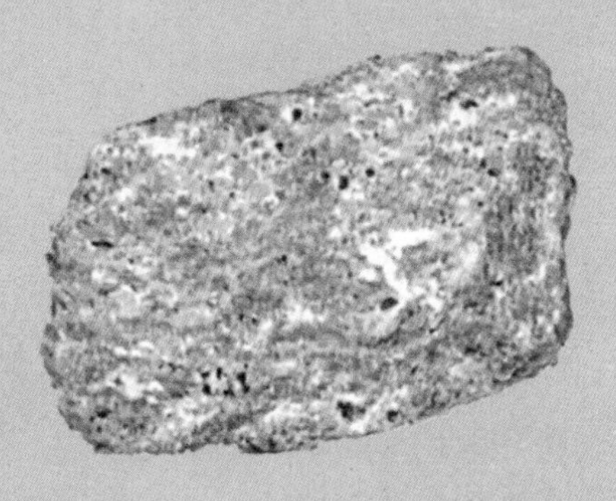

NAME From German *Rhyolith*, from Greek *rhyax*, "lava stream."

MINERALS Quartz, potassium and plagioclase feldspars, with small amounts of hornblende and biotite

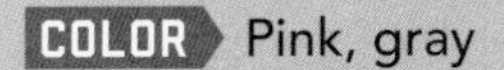

COLOR Pink, gray

TEXTURE Very fine grained

WHERE IT IS FOUND Edges of lava flow or near an active volcano on land, most regions of the United States.

RELATED TO ANOTHER ROCK? Yes. It forms from same magma as granite, obsidian, and pumice.

WHAT IT IS USED FOR Not much because it is easy to break apart. Sometimes it is used as crushed stone in road construction.

POINT OF FACT Many gems are found in rhyolite because thick lava traps gases that leave holes in the rock, allowing crystallized minerals from groundwater to fill the space.

FOUND IT!

WHEN
DATE

WHERE
SPECIFIC PLACE AND SURROUNDINGS

NOTES

IGNEOUS ROCKS

Scoria

Extrusive

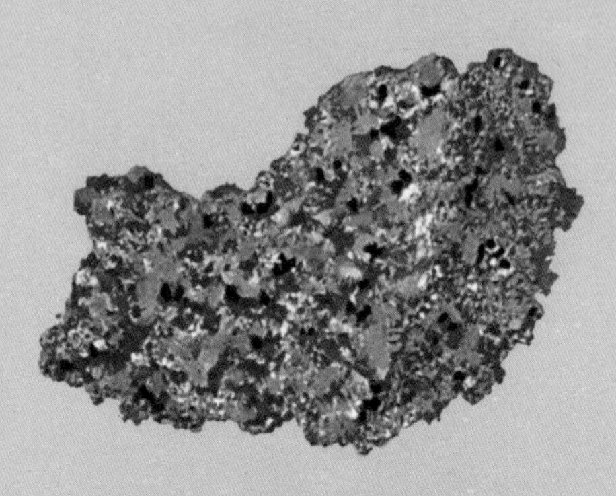

NAME From Greek *skōria*, "trash," from *skōr*, "dung."

MINERALS Similar composition to andesite or basalt

COLOR Black, red, dark brown

TEXTURE Very holey

WHERE IT IS FOUND Around cinder cone volcanoes, including Hawaii, California, Oregon, Arizona, Italy, the Canary Islands.

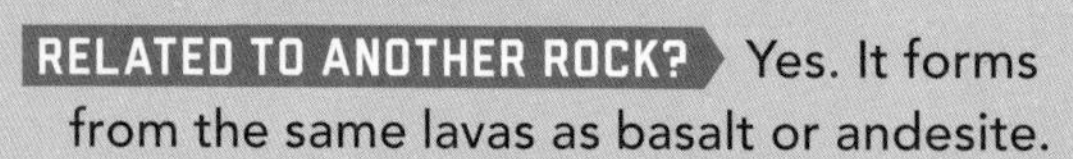

RELATED TO ANOTHER ROCK? Yes. It forms from the same lavas as basalt or andesite.

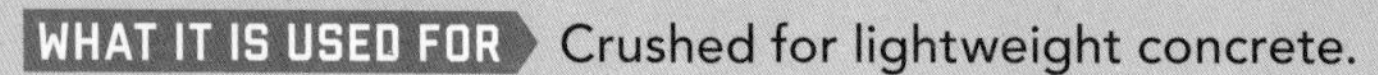

WHAT IT IS USED FOR Crushed for lightweight concrete.

POINTS OF FACT

- The iron in scoria rusts, changing its color to medium brown.
- Although scoria is foamy and contains air pockets like pumice, it is much denser so it sinks in water.

FOUND IT!

WHEN

DATE

WHERE

SPECIFIC PLACE AND SURROUNDINGS

NOTES

IGNEOUS ROCKS

Syenite

Intrusive

NAME After Syene, Egypt (ancient Greek name of Aswân).

MINERALS Potassium and plagioclase feldspars

COLOR Gray, pink, red

TEXTURE Coarse grained

WHERE IT IS FOUND Most regions of the United States, Egypt, and New Zealand.

RELATED TO ANOTHER ROCK? Yes. It is a type of granite that contains very little quartz; it is similar in composition to extrusive rock trachyte.

WHAT IT IS USED FOR Construction in buildings or floors

POINT OF FACT Even though it's named after Syene, the monuments in Syene are not built of syenite, but rather a dark granite.

FOUND IT!

WHEN

DATE

WHERE

SPECIFIC PLACE AND SURROUNDINGS

NOTES

IGNEOUS ROCKS

Tuff

Extrusive

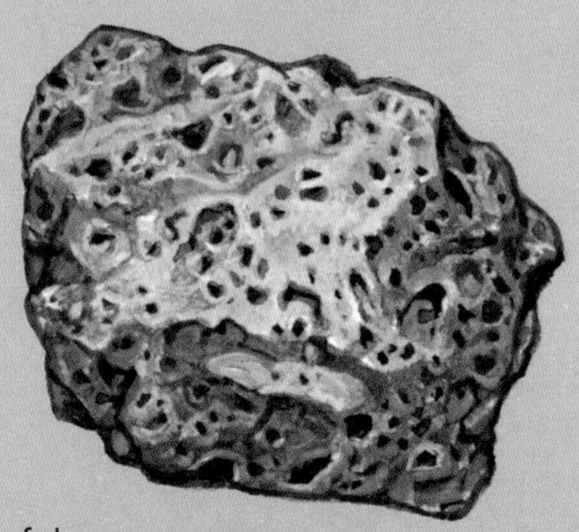

NAME From Latin *tofus*, "porous rock."

MINERALS Varies depending on type of lava

COLOR Light to dark brown

TEXTURE Varies depending on proximity to volcano vent

WHERE IT IS FOUND Most regions of the United States and wherever there have been explosive volcanic eruptions, like Mount Saint Helens in Washington, La Garita Caldera in Colorado, Yellowstone Caldera in Wyoming.

RELATED TO ANOTHER ROCK? Yes. It is basically consolidated volcanic ash, the igneous equivalent of sandstone.

WHAT IT IS USED FOR Building stone since it's easy to cut.

POINT OF FACT The famous statues on Easter Island were carved out of tuff.

FOUND IT!

WHEN

DATE

WHERE

SPECIFIC PLACE AND SURROUNDINGS

NOTES

SEDIMENTARY ROCKS

Breccia

Clastic

NAME Italian for gravel.

MINERALS Varies depending on rock fragments

COLOR Varies

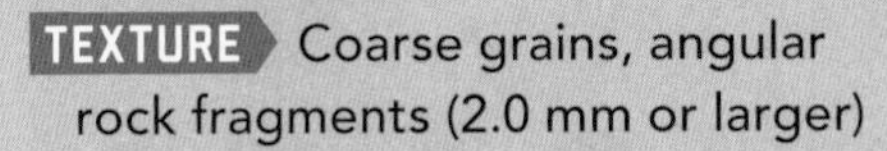

TEXTURE Coarse grains, angular rock fragments (2.0 mm or larger)

WHERE IT IS FOUND Worldwide, wherever rock debris collects, like at the base of cliffs, including in California, Texas, Illinois, Michigan, Virginia, Washington, and Massachusetts.

HOW IT IS FORMED Rock fragments that have not been transported very far by wind or water are cemented together.

WHAT IT IS USED FOR Not much. Crushed for road fill, polished to make jewelry.

POINT OF FACT The meteorite Black Beauty is breccia from Mars.

FOUND IT!

WHEN

DATE

WHERE

SPECIFIC PLACE AND SURROUNDINGS

NOTES

SEDIMENTARY ROCKS

Coal

Organic

NAME From Old English *col*, "glowing ember" or "charred remnant."

COMPOSITION Mostly carbon from decayed plants

COLOR Black or brownish black

TEXTURE Coarse grained, feels rough

WHERE IT IS FOUND Worldwide, including most regions of the United States

HOW IT IS FORMED From plants that died in swampy areas and only partially decayed in the mud. Over time the layers of mud and plant debris compacted into rock.

WHAT IT IS USED FOR Fossil fuel for energy production.

POINTS OF FACT

- The most abundant fossil fuel on earth, coal produces a large percent of the world's energy.
- Coal takes millions of years to create. It is a nonrenewable energy source.

FOUND IT!

WHEN

DATE

WHERE

SPECIFIC PLACE AND SURROUNDINGS

NOTES

SEDIMENTARY ROCKS

Conglomerate

Clastic

NAME From Latin *conglomerare*, "to roll together."

MINERALS Varies depending on rock fragments

COLOR Varies

TEXTURE Coarse grained, rounded rock fragments (2.0 mm or larger)

WHERE IT IS FOUND Worldwide, including most regions of the United States, and near swiftly flowing streams or beaches with hard waves.

HOW IT IS FORMED Strong currents carry away larger pieces of rock, tumbling and rounding them over some distance. After they are deposited, finer sand fills the spaces in between, and chemical sediment cements it all together.

WHAT IT IS USED FOR Not much. Crushed for road fill if nothing else is available.

POINTS OF FACT

- Conglomerate was found on Mars by the Mars rover in 2012. It is strong evidence that water may have once flowed on the planet.
- Glaciers deposit lots of large rounded sediments that become conglomerate.

FOUND IT!

WHEN

DATE

WHERE

SPECIFIC PLACE AND SURROUNDINGS

NOTES

SEDIMENTARY ROCKS

Dolomite

Chemical

NAME After French geologist Déodat de Dolomieu, who first described it.

MINERALS Dolomite

COLOR White, gray, light brown, pink, green

TEXTURE Coarse grained, feels rough like sandpaper

WHERE IT IS FOUND Mostly in Europe and most regions of the United States

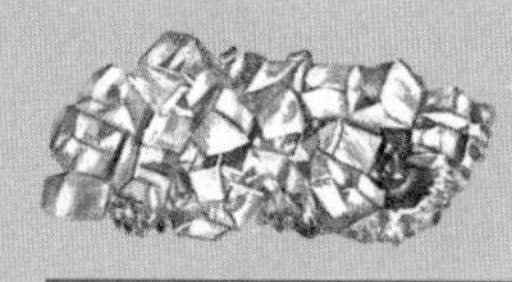

DOLOMITE CRYSTAL

HOW IT IS FORMED Magnesium-rich groundwater alters chemical composition of lime mud and limestone.

WHAT IT IS USED FOR Building stone, crushed for fill and concrete, steel and glass production, soil conditioner, feed additive for livestock.

POINTS OF FACT

- The Dolomite Mountains in Italy are predominantly dolomite rock.
- Adding dolomite to soil reduces its acidity, which is especially good for growing asparagus, but also for peas, broccoli, carrots, and spinach.

FOUND IT!

WHEN

DATE

WHERE

SPECIFIC PLACE AND SURROUNDINGS

NOTES

SEDIMENTARY ROCKS

Iron Ore

Chemical

NAME From Old English *īren.*

MINERALS Hematite, magnetite, goethite, siderite

COLOR Dark gray, bright yellow, purple, dark red

TEXTURE Coarse grained, feels rough

WHERE IT IS FOUND Worldwide, Arizona, Maine, Michigan, Minnesota, New Hampshire, South Dakota, Wisconsin.

HOW IT IS FORMED Dissolved iron in Earth's early oceans reacted with oxygen produced by tiny cyanobacteria and crystallized into minerals on the seafloor.

WHAT IT IS USED FOR Almost every iron or steel object, from paper clips to steel building supports.

POINTS OF FACT

- Most iron ore was formed over 1.8 billion years ago.
- Humans have been using iron for over five thousand years to make jewelry, cooking utensils, and weapons.

FOUND IT!

WHEN

DATE

WHERE

SPECIFIC PLACE AND SURROUNDINGS

NOTES

SEDIMENTARY ROCKS

Limestone

Chemical or Organic

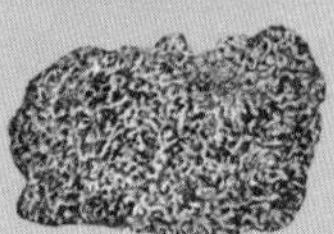

NAME From Old English *līm*, "sticky substance" or "mortar."

MINERALS Calcite (calcium carbonate), with small amounts of other minerals

COLOR White, gray, light brown, pink

TEXTURE Coarse, feels smooth

WHERE IT IS FOUND Areas underlain with sedimentary rocks, on all continents except Africa and Antarctica, all regions of the United States.

HOW IT IS FORMED One of three ways:

- Marine organisms in warm, shallow water excrete calcium carbonate to make their shells, and when they die, their remains form sediment on the seafloor. Calcium carbonate crystallizes out of the water in the spaces around the sediments and cements them.
- Calcium carbonate that crystallizes when the water's temperature or acidity changes.
- When water evaporates, especially in caves, leaving deposits of calcite that build up over time, like stalactites and stalagmites.

WHAT IT IS USED FOR Building stone, but mostly crushed for a wide variety of uses.

POINT OF FACT Limestone is used as a mild abrasive and filler in toothpaste.

FOUND IT!

WHEN

DATE

WHERE

SPECIFIC PLACE AND SURROUNDINGS

NOTES

SEDIMENTARY ROCKS

Sandstone

Clastic

NAME After its sand-sized grains.

MINERALS Quartz or feldspar

COLOR Tan, brown, yellow, red, gray, white

TEXTURE Medium grains (0.1–2 mm)

WHERE IT IS FOUND Worldwide, including most regions of the United States

HOW IT IS FORMED Grains of sand cemented together by silica, calcium carbonate, or iron oxide.

WHAT IT IS USED FOR Construction, pavers, glassmaking

POINTS OF FACT

- Sandstone made of quartz and cemented by silica is resistant to weathering and can last for thousands of years.
- Sandstone is the official state rock of Nevada.

FOUND IT!

WHEN

DATE

WHERE

SPECIFIC PLACE AND SURROUNDINGS

NOTES

SEDIMENTARY ROCKS

Shale

Clastic

NAME Probably from German *Schale*, "bowl."

MINERALS Clay minerals such as illite, kaolinite, and smectite, often with clay-size particles of silica, feldspar

COLOR Black, gray, green, red, brown, yellow

TEXTURE Fine grains in thin layers

WHERE IT IS FOUND Worldwide, including most regions of the United States.

HOW IT IS FORMED From the compaction of silt and clay-size particles that we call mud.

WHAT IT IS USED FOR Ground shale makes clay for plant pots, roof tiles, and bricks. It is also mixed with limestone and heated to make cement.

POINTS OF FACT

- Black shale is a source of many oil and natural gas deposits. When the layers of mud were buried and warmed underground, organic matter in the mud turned into natural gas or oil.
- Shale accounts for 70 percent of the sedimentary rocks on earth, making it the most abundant of the sedimentary rocks.

FOUND IT!

WHEN

DATE

WHERE

SPECIFIC PLACE AND SURROUNDINGS

NOTES

METAMORPHIC ROCKS

Amphibolite

Nonfoliated

NAME From Latin *amphibolus*, "ambiguous," from Greek root *amphi-* "on both sides."

MINERALS Amphibole and plagioclase feldspar

COLOR Green, black, brown

TEXTURE Coarse grained

WHERE IT IS FOUND Appalachian states including Alabama, Georgia, North Carolina, Tennessee, Virginia, and West Virginia, along with southwestern states Arizona and Nevada.

HOW IT IS FORMED From igneous rocks basalt and gabbro, or from clay-rich sedimentary rocks.

WHAT IT IS USED FOR Architectural stone, countertops, crushed for road base.

POINT OF FACT Some amphibolite deposits contain garnet, a red gemstone.

FOUND IT!

WHEN

DATE

WHERE

SPECIFIC PLACE AND SURROUNDINGS

NOTES

METAMORPHIC ROCKS

Gneiss

Foliated

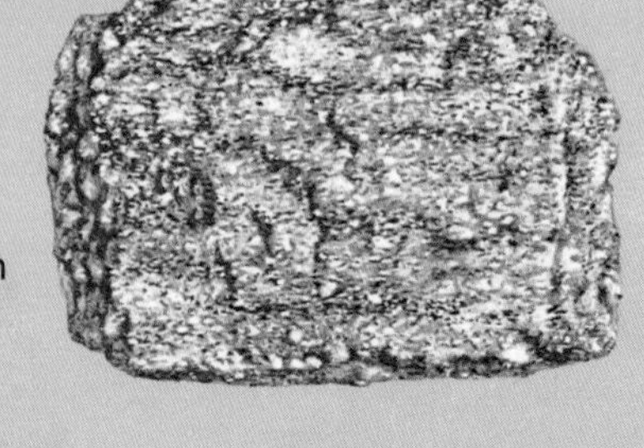

NAME Pronounced "nice." From Old High German *gneisto*, "spark," because the rock is sparkly.

MINERALS Feldspar and quartz

COLOR Gray, pink, or white with dark gray or black lines ("salt and pepper" banding)

TEXTURE Coarse grained

WHERE IT IS FOUND Most regions of the United States and worldwide in the earth's crust and on the surface of the earth in Canada and Scandinavia.

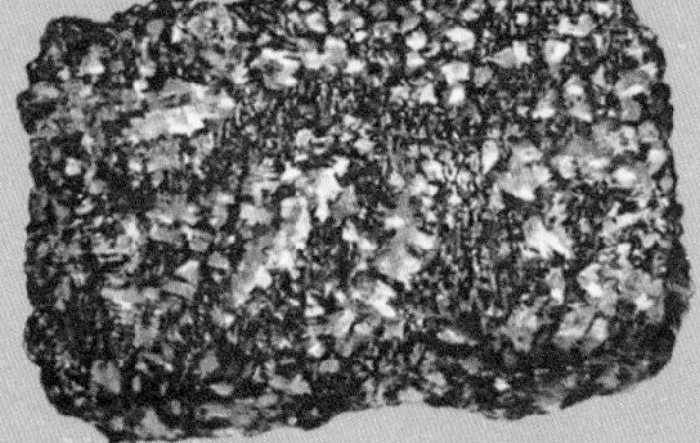

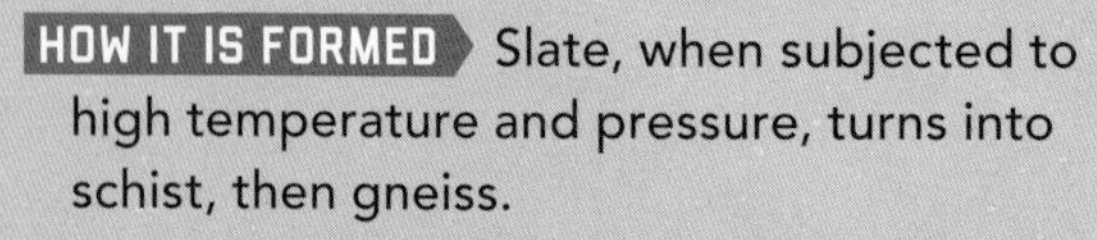

HOW IT IS FORMED Slate, when subjected to high temperature and pressure, turns into schist, then gneiss.

WHAT IT IS USED FOR Architectural stone, pavers, countertops, headstones, crushed for roads and construction.

POINT OF FACT Some of the oldest rocks ever found are gneiss.

FOUND IT!

WHEN

DATE

WHERE

SPECIFIC PLACE AND SURROUNDINGS

NOTES

METAMORPHIC ROCKS

Hornfels

Nonfoliated

NAME German for "horn rock," because its texture is similar to animal horns.

MINERALS Varies depending on parent rock

COLOR Black, gray, brown, reddish, green

TEXTURE Fine grained

WHERE IT IS FOUND California, Texas, New Jersey, Washington, Georgia, Arizona, North Carolina, Idaho, Vermont, Alaska, Africa, Australia, and New Zealand.

HOW IT IS FORMED From sedimentary shale, siltstone, sandstone, limestone, and dolomite. From igneous basalt, gabbro, rhyolite, granite, and andesite. From metamorphic schist and gneiss.

WHAT IT IS USED FOR Crushed rock in roads and concrete.

POINTS OF FACT

- Hornfels rings like a bell when it's struck.
- Early humans used hornfels to make tools six hundred thousand years ago.

FOUND IT!

WHEN

DATE

WHERE

SPECIFIC PLACE AND SURROUNDINGS

NOTES

METAMORPHIC ROCKS

Marble

Nonfoliated

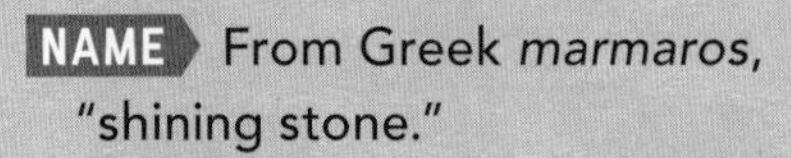

NAME From Greek *marmaros*, "shining stone."

MINERALS Calcite, micas, quartz, pyrite, iron oxides, graphite

COLOR Mostly white, although it can have bits of other colors such as green, blue, gray, pink, yellow, or black

TEXTURE Fine grained

WHERE IT IS FOUND Most regions of the United States, Italy, Ireland, Spain, Greece, Russia, Romania, Sweden, Germany, and Asia.

HOW IT IS FORMED From sedimentary dolomite or limestone.

WHAT IT IS USED FOR Architectural stone, sculpture, gravestones, countertops, interior decoration, whitener, abrasives, soil conditioner, acid neutralizer, calcium supplement for chickens and cows.

POINTS OF FACT

- The Taj Mahal is built of marble. As the light passes over the Taj Mahal, it appears to have different colors throughout the day.
- Very pure marble is ground into a calcium carbonate powder and used in antacids to treat heartburn and acid indigestion.

FOUND IT!

WHEN

DATE

WHERE

SPECIFIC PLACE AND SURROUNDINGS

NOTES

METAMORPHIC ROCKS

Phyllite

Foliated

NAME From Greek *phyllon*, "leaf."

MINERALS Quartz and small amounts of feldspar, chlorite, mica, graphite

COLOR Gray or dark green

TEXTURE Fine grained, slight sheen

WHERE IT IS FOUND Most regions of the United States, Asia, Africa, Europe.

HOW IT IS FORMED From sedimentary shale or pelite.

WHAT IT IS USED FOR Not much, occasionally for landscape, paving, or sidewalks.

POINT OF FACT Phyllite tells geologists a lot about the conditions where it formed. It undergoes a low grade of metamorphosis, which means the heat and pressure were not as great as they were for higher grade metamorphic rocks.

FOUND IT!

WHEN
DATE

WHERE
SPECIFIC PLACE AND SURROUNDINGS

NOTES

METAMORPHIC ROCKS

Quartzite

Nonfoliated

NAME After its quartz composition.

MINERALS Quartz

COLOR Varies

TEXTURE Large, coarse grains surrounded by fine grains

WHERE IT IS FOUND Most regions of the United States, Norway, Ireland.

HOW IT IS FORMED From sedimentary sandstone.

WHAT IT IS USED FOR Architecture, tools, crushed rock

POINTS OF FACT

- Humans' ancestors used quartzite to make cutting tools more than one million years ago because it breaks into very sharp flakes.
- Quartzite is so hard (seven on the Mohs scale) that hammer blows usually bounce off it. Be very careful if you try to break it and don't forget your safety gear!

FOUND IT!

WHEN

DATE

WHERE

SPECIFIC PLACE AND SURROUNDINGS

NOTES

METAMORPHIC ROCKS

Schist

Foliated

NAME From Greek *skhistos*, "split," from the base of *skhizein*, "cleave."

MINERALS Mica minerals chlorite, muscovite, or biotite, with quartz and feldspar

COLOR Black, brown, blue, red, green, gray

TEXTURE Fine to medium grained (easily visible crystals)

WHERE IT IS FOUND Most regions of the United States, Scotland, Brazil, Ireland.

HOW IT IS FORMED From sedimentary shale.

WHAT IT IS USED FOR Not much. It breaks too easily, but it is a great place to find valuable gems like garnet, kyanite, zoisite, emerald, andalusite, titanite, sapphire, ruby, scapolite, iolite, chrysoberyl.

POINTS OF FACT

- Schist breaks into thin slabs or layers. This is due to its "schistosity," the parallel arrangement of its platy or stretched out minerals.
- Schist forms at plate boundaries, where moderate pressure and temperature force the parent minerals into lines.

FOUND IT!

WHEN

DATE

WHERE

SPECIFIC PLACE AND SURROUNDINGS

NOTES

METAMORPHIC ROCKS

Slate

Foliated

NAME From Anglo-French *esclater*, "to splinter, break off."

MINERALS Mainly clay and micas, with quartz and small amounts of other minerals

COLOR Dark to light gray, sometimes green, red, black, purple, and brown

TEXTURE Fine grained, dull

WHERE IT IS FOUND Most regions of the United States, Asia, Belgium, France, Germany, Italy, Norway, Portugal, Spain, United Kingdom.

HOW IT IS FORMED From sedimentary shale.

WHAT IT IS USED FOR Roofing material, siding, floors, landscaping.

POINTS OF FACT

- Slate looks similar to shale, but they are not the same rock. Slate is metamorphic and shale is sedimentary. You can tell the difference by hitting slate with a hammer. If it makes a ringing sound, it is slate. Shale does not make any sound.
- Some pool tables use cloth-covered slate as a playing surface because it stays smooth and doesn't warp like wood.

FOUND IT!

WHEN

DATE

WHERE

SPECIFIC PLACE AND SURROUNDINGS

NOTES

MINERALS

Arsenic

Native Elements

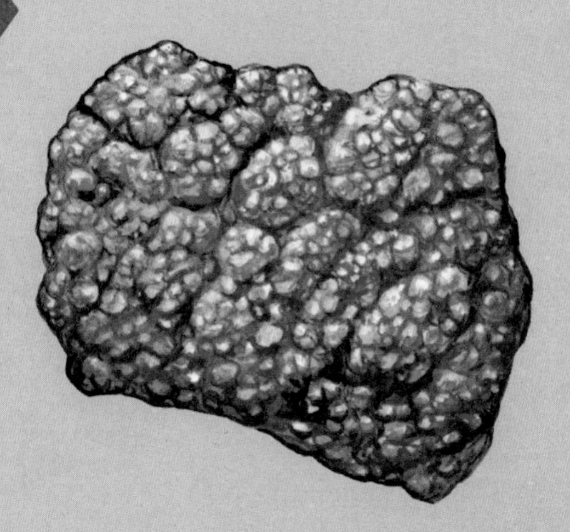

CHEMICAL FORMULA As

COLOR Steel gray to silver white

CLEAVAGE Perfect

STREAK White

HARDNESS 5.5 to 6 on the Mohs scale

LUSTER Metallic

SPECIFIC GRAVITY 5.7

WHAT IT IS USED FOR Poison, transistors, fireworks, lasers

POINT OF FACT Because it kills bacteria, arsenic was used to preserve dead bodies until it was banned as a hazard to the living people who worked with it.

WARNING: DO NOT COLLECT ARSENIC

Do not touch arsenic and do not inhale the dust. Arsenic is poisonous to humans.

FOUND IT!

WHEN

DATE

WHERE

SPECIFIC PLACE AND SURROUNDINGS

NOTES

MINERALS

Bismuth

Native Elements

CHEMICAL FORMULA Bi

COLOR Silver white

CLEAVAGE Perfect

STREAK Lead gray

HARDNESS 2 to 4.5 on the Mohs scale

LUSTER Metallic

SPECIFIC GRAVITY 9.7 to 9.8

WHAT IT IS USED FOR Added to other metals to lower their melting point

POINT OF FACT Bismuth is twice as abundant as gold in the Earth's crust.

FOUND IT!

WHEN
DATE

WHERE
SPECIFIC PLACE AND SURROUNDINGS

NOTES

MINERALS

Copper

Native Elements

CHEMICAL FORMULA Cu

COLOR Light rose or brown (turns green or black over time)

CLEAVAGE None

STREAK Light rose color

HARDNESS 2.5 to 3 on the Mohs scale

LUSTER Metallic

SPECIFIC GRAVITY 8.9

WHAT IT IS USED FOR Copper pipes and wire

POINT OF FACT People during the Stone Age first used copper as a stone substitute.

FOUND IT!

WHEN

DATE

WHERE

SPECIFIC PLACE AND SURROUNDINGS

NOTES

MINERALS

Gold

Native Elements

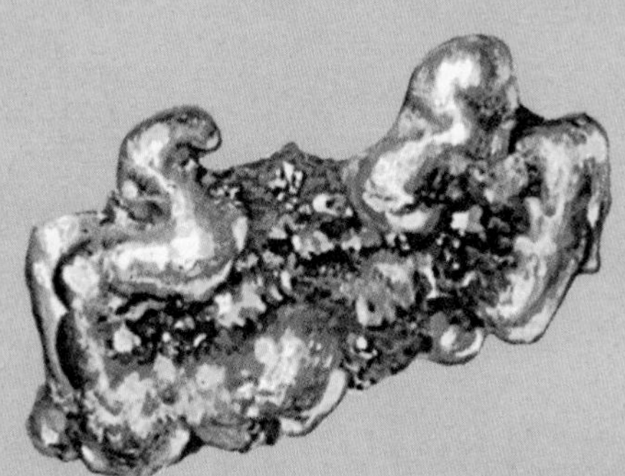

CHEMICAL FORMULA Au

COLOR Shiny yellow

CLEAVAGE None

STREAK Shiny yellow

HARDNESS 2.5 to 3 on the Mohs scale

LUSTER Metallic

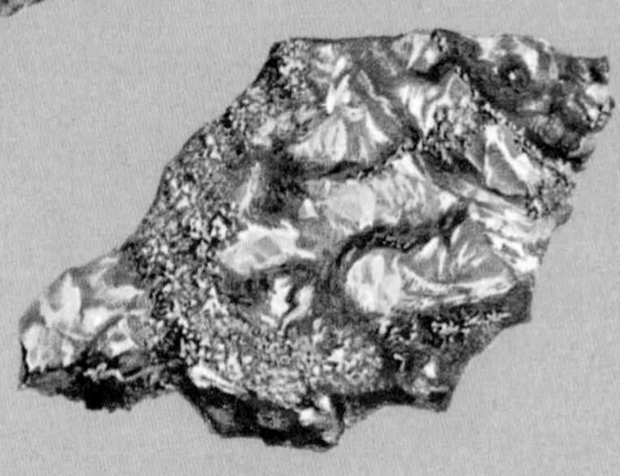

SPECIFIC GRAVITY 19.3

WHAT IT IS USED FOR Precious metal, jewelry, money, electronics

POINT OF FACT Gold is ductile, which means it can be stretched into thin wire or thread. One ounce of gold can be stretched into fifty miles of wire five microns thick. That's one twentieth the thickness of a single human hair, so thin you can't see it without a microscope!

FOUND IT!

WHEN

DATE

WHERE

SPECIFIC PLACE AND SURROUNDINGS

NOTES

MINERALS

Graphite

Native Elements

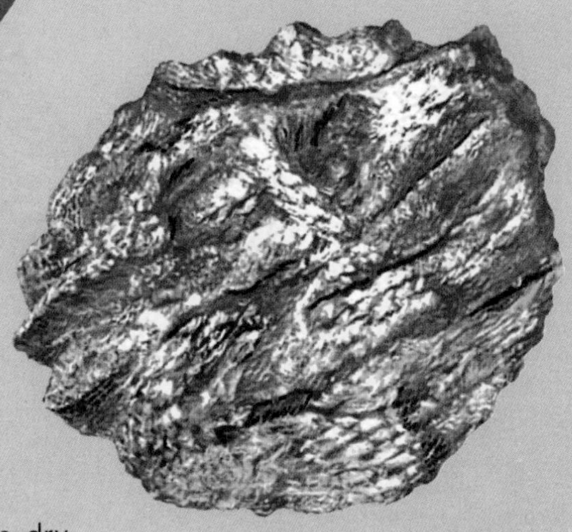

CHEMICAL FORMULA C

COLOR Black to steel gray

CLEAVAGE Single sheet

STREAK Black

HARDNESS 1 to 2 on the Mohs scale

LUSTER Metallic or dull

SPECIFIC GRAVITY 2.2

WHAT IT IS USED FOR Pencils, dry powder lubricant for machines

POINT OF FACT Graphite is a form of carbon. Pencils use graphite rather than lead for writing.

FOUND IT!

WHEN

DATE

WHERE

SPECIFIC PLACE AND SURROUNDINGS

NOTES

MINERALS

Iron

Native Elements

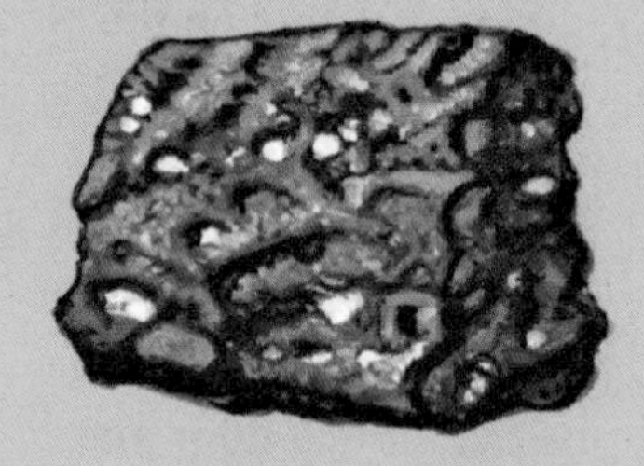

CHEMICAL FORMULA Fe

COLOR Metallic gray, dull to bright red

CLEAVAGE One layer

STREAK Red or black

HARDNESS 4 to 4.5 on the Mohs scale

LUSTER Metallic

SPECIFIC GRAVITY 7.3 to 7.9

WHAT IT IS USED FOR To make steel, which is an alloy of iron and carbon

POINT OF FACT The most abundant metal in the universe, iron makes up about 35 percent of the entire earth. It's found in the sun and other stars, as well as your own blood.

FOUND IT!

WHEN

DATE

WHERE

SPECIFIC PLACE AND SURROUNDINGS

NOTES

MINERALS

Platinum

Native Elements

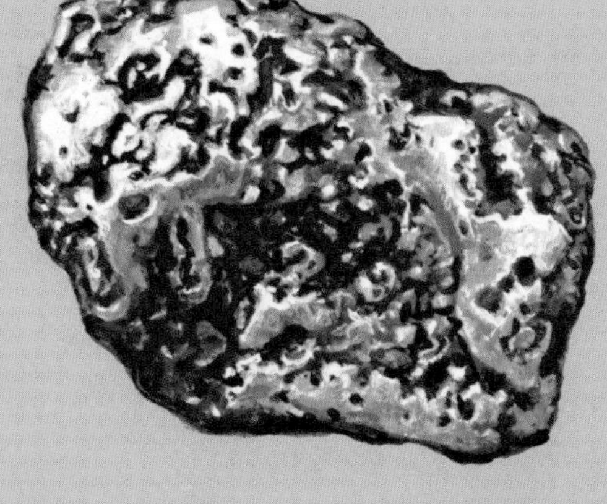

CHEMICAL FORMULA Pt

COLOR Dark gray, whitish gray

CLEAVAGE None

STREAK Grayish white

HARDNESS 4 to 4.5 on the Mohs scale

LUSTER Metallic

SPECIFIC GRAVITY 14 to 19

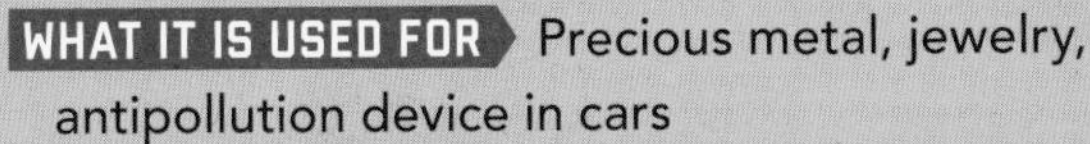

WHAT IT IS USED FOR Precious metal, jewelry, antipollution device in cars

POINT OF FACT The first Spaniards who saw this mineral in South America in the 1500s named it *platina* for its resemblance to silver.

FOUND IT!

WHEN

DATE

WHERE

SPECIFIC PLACE AND SURROUNDINGS

NOTES

MINERALS

Silver

Native Elements

CHEMICAL FORMULA Ag

COLOR Silver, but can be weathered to dark gray or black

CLEAVAGE None

STREAK Silver white

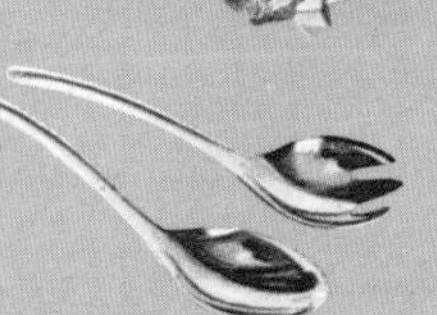

HARDNESS 2.5 to 3 on the Mohs scale

LUSTER Metallic

SPECIFIC GRAVITY 10.1 to 11.1

WHAT IT IS USED FOR Precious metal, electronics, coins, jewelry, silverware

POINT OF FACT Of all the metals, silver is the best conductor of electricity and heat, which makes it great for solar panels.

FOUND IT!

WHEN

DATE

WHERE

SPECIFIC PLACE AND SURROUNDINGS

NOTES

MINERALS

Sulfur

Native Elements

CHEMICAL FORMULA S

COLOR Bright yellow to brown

CLEAVAGE None

STREAK White

HARDNESS 1.5 to 2 on the Mohs scale

LUSTER Dull

SPECIFIC GRAVITY 2.1

WHAT IT IS USED FOR Rubber, gunpowder, sulfuric acid for batteries and fertilizers

POINT OF FACT Pure sulfur has no smell, but combined with hydrogen, it sure stinks. That potent combo is responsible for the smell of rotten eggs and skunks' spray.

WHEN

DATE

WHERE

SPECIFIC PLACE AND SURROUNDINGS

NOTES

MINERALS

Chalcocite

Sulfides

CHEMICAL FORMULA Cu_2S (copper sulfide)

COLOR Gray to black, possibly with a bluish tinge

CLEAVAGE Indistinct

STREAK Blackish lead gray

HARDNESS 2.5 to 3 on the Mohs scale

LUSTER Metallic

SPECIFIC GRAVITY 5.5 to 5.8

WHAT IT IS USED FOR Important copper ore

POINT OF FACT Collectors prize chalcocite crystals, especially if they come from the Cornwall area of England, which has an ancient deposit mined since the Bronze Age.

FOUND IT!

WHEN

DATE

WHERE

SPECIFIC PLACE AND SURROUNDINGS

NOTES

MINERALS

Chalcopyrite

Sulfides

CHEMICAL FORMULA $CuFeS_2$ (copper iron sulfide)

COLOR Brassy yellow, iridescent tarnish

CLEAVAGE Distinct

STREAK Green black

HARDNESS 3.5 to 4 on the Mohs scale

LUSTER Metallic

SPECIFIC GRAVITY 4.2

WHAT IT IS USED FOR Main copper ore

POINT OF FACT Often what's sold in stores as "peacock ore" is actually chalcopyrite treated with acid to produce unusually bright colors.

FOUND IT!

WHEN

DATE

WHERE

SPECIFIC PLACE AND SURROUNDINGS

NOTES

Galena

Sulfides

CHEMICAL FORMULA PbS (lead sulfide)

COLOR Steel gray

CLEAVAGE Perfect

STREAK Lead gray

HARDNESS 2.5 on the Mohs scale

LUSTER Metallic

SPECIFIC GRAVITY 7.6

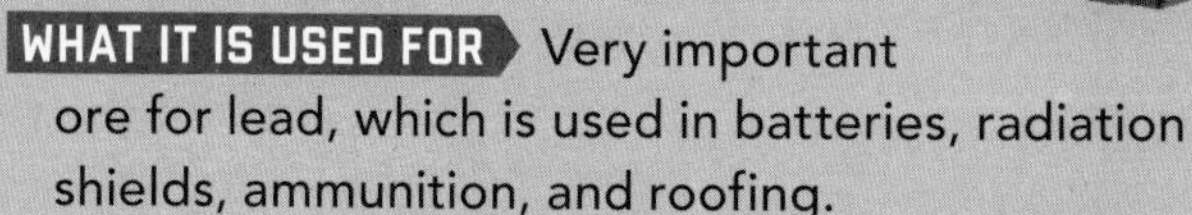

WHAT IT IS USED FOR Very important ore for lead, which is used in batteries, radiation shields, ammunition, and roofing.

POINT OF FACT Galena has been melted down to extract lead for several thousand years.

WARNING:
DO NOT SCRAPE AND DO NOT INHALE DUST
Contains lead. While not immediately toxic, be careful handling galena and always wear gloves. The lead content is poisonous to humans.

FOUND IT!

WHEN

DATE

WHERE

SPECIFIC PLACE AND SURROUNDINGS

NOTES

MINERALS

Molybdenite

Sulfides

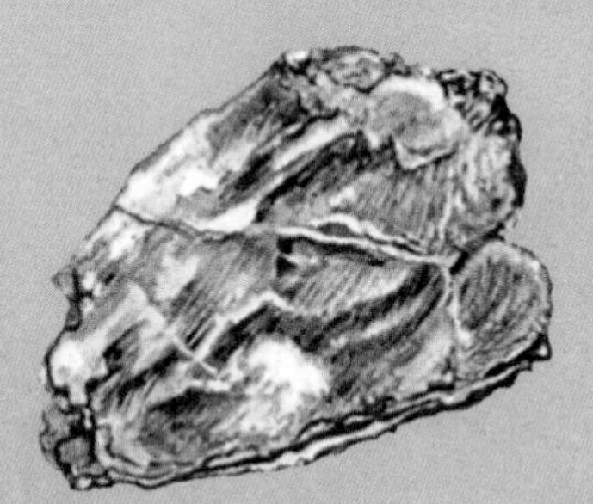

CHEMICAL FORMULA MoS_2 (molybdenum disulfide)

COLOR Black, lead gray, gray

CLEAVAGE Perfect

STREAK Greenish or bluish gray

HARDNESS 1 to 1.5 on the Mohs scale

LUSTER Metallic

SPECIFIC GRAVITY 4.7

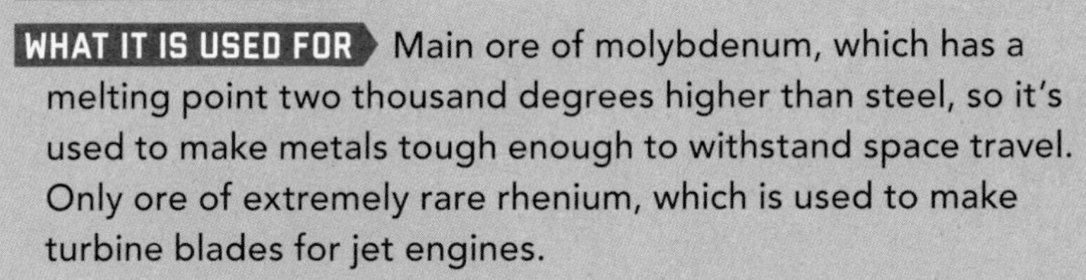

WHAT IT IS USED FOR Main ore of molybdenum, which has a melting point two thousand degrees higher than steel, so it's used to make metals tough enough to withstand space travel. Only ore of extremely rare rhenium, which is used to make turbine blades for jet engines.

POINT OF FACT Most of the molybdenum in the earth's mantle comes from the outer solar system, brought here 4.4 billion years ago by the protoplanet Theia, which collided with the earth and created the moon.

FOUND IT!

WHEN

DATE

WHERE

SPECIFIC PLACE AND SURROUNDINGS

NOTES

MINERALS

Pyrite

Sulfides

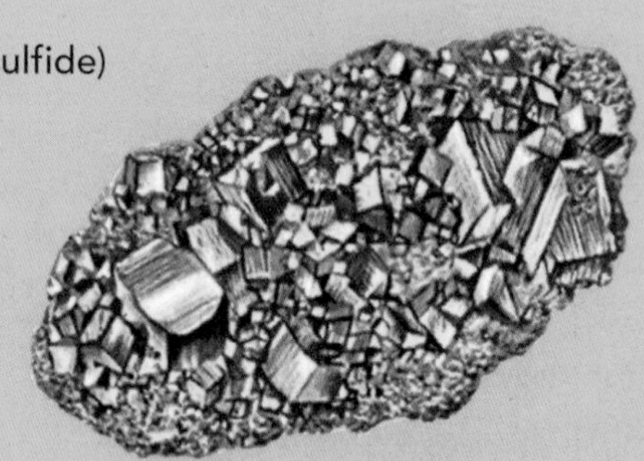

CHEMICAL FORMULA FeS_2 (iron sulfide)

COLOR Pale, brass yellow

CLEAVAGE None

STREAK Greenish black to brownish black

HARDNESS 6 to 6.5 on the Mohs scale

LUSTER Metallic

SPECIFIC GRAVITY 5.0

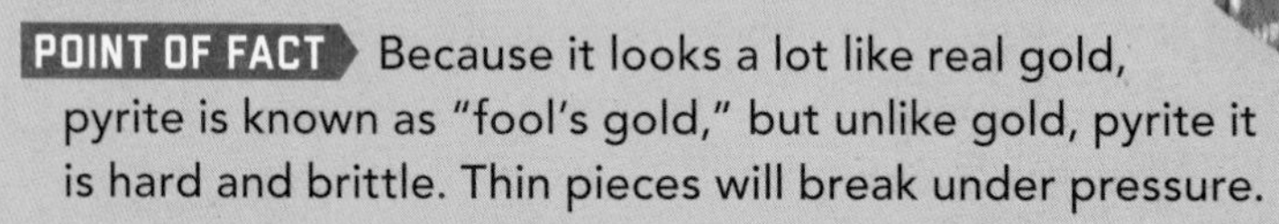

WHAT IT IS USED FOR Good source of sulfur and iron

POINT OF FACT Because it looks a lot like real gold, pyrite is known as "fool's gold," but unlike gold, pyrite it is hard and brittle. Thin pieces will break under pressure.

(Hint: Gold will bend or dent, so that's how you know it's real gold.)

FOUND IT!

WHEN

DATE

WHERE

SPECIFIC PLACE AND SURROUNDINGS

NOTES

MINERALS

Sphalerite

Sulfides

CHEMICAL FORMULA ZnS (zinc sulfide)

COLOR Black, brown, red, orange, yellow, green, gray

CLEAVAGE Perfect—in six directions

STREAK Brown to light yellow

HARDNESS 3.5 to 4 on the Mohs scale

LUSTER Adamantine, metallic, or resinous

SPECIFIC GRAVITY 3.9 to 4.1

WHAT IT IS USED FOR Major ore of zinc, which is used in brass, batteries, galvanized steel.

POINT OF FACT Its name comes from Greek *sphaleros*, "deceptive," because it was often mistaken for galena, a very valuable lead ore.

FOUND IT!

WHEN

DATE

WHERE

SPECIFIC PLACE AND SURROUNDINGS

NOTES

MINERALS

Aragonite

Carbonates

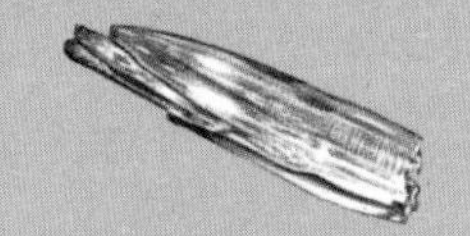

CHEMICAL FORMULA $CaCO_3$ (calcium carbonate)

COLOR Colorless to white gray, sometimes blue, green, red, yellow, violet

CLEAVAGE Good

STREAK White

HARDNESS 3.5 to 4 on the Mohs scale

LUSTER Vitreous, resinous, dull

SPECIFIC GRAVITY 2.95

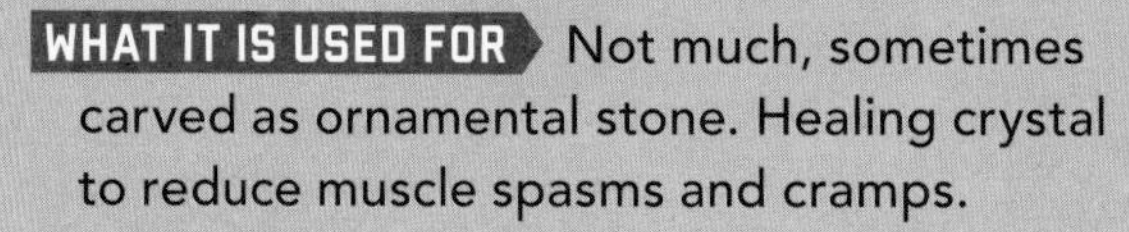

WHAT IT IS USED FOR Not much, sometimes carved as ornamental stone. Healing crystal to reduce muscle spasms and cramps.

POINT OF FACT Sometimes forms banded mounds near mineral-rich hot springs.

FOUND IT!

WHEN

DATE

WHERE

SPECIFIC PLACE AND SURROUNDINGS

NOTES

MINERALS

Azurite

Carbonates

CHEMICAL FORMULA $Cu_3(CO_3)_2(OH)_2$ (copper carbonate)

COLOR Light to dark blue

CLEAVAGE Perfect

STREAK Blue

HARDNESS 3.5 to 4 on the Mohs scale

LUSTER Vitreous or dull

SPECIFIC GRAVITY 3.8

WHAT IT IS USED FOR Copper ore, paint pigment, gemstone, ornamental stone

POINT OF FACT It is believed to have properties that boost your energy and memory, and it almost always occurs with green malachite.

FOUND IT!

WHEN
DATE

WHERE
SPECIFIC PLACE AND SURROUNDINGS

NOTES

MINERALS

Calcite

Carbonates

CHEMICAL FORMULA $CaCO_3$ (calcium carbonate)

COLOR White, yellow, red, orange, blue, green, brown, gray

CLEAVAGE Perfect

STREAK White

HARDNESS 3 on the Mohs scale

LUSTER Vitreous

SPECIFIC GRAVITY 2.7

WHAT IT IS USED FOR Primary ore of calcium. It's also used to make chalk, and is the primary mineral of sedimentary rock limestone and metamporphic rock marble.

POINT OF FACT Calcite is used to make dog food and other animal feeds.

FOUND IT!

WHEN
DATE

WHERE
SPECIFIC PLACE AND SURROUNDINGS

NOTES

MINERALS

Cerussite

Carbonates

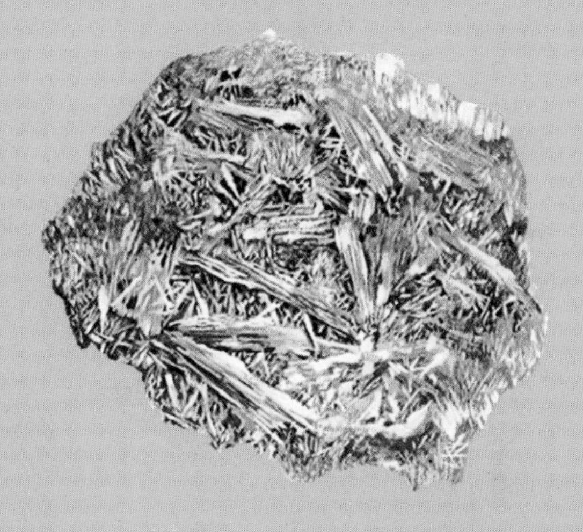

CHEMICAL FORMULA $PbCO_3$ (lead carbonate)

COLOR White, gray, pink, light red, brown, colorless

CLEAVAGE Distinct

STREAK White

HARDNESS 3 to 3.5 on the Mohs scale

LUSTER Vitreous

SPECIFIC GRAVITY 6.5

WHAT IT IS USED FOR Lead ore

POINT OF FACT The crystals of this mineral often "twin," grow together in a symmetrical fashion, forming shapes like stars, hearts, even snowflakes, which makes them highly sought after.

WARNING: DO NOT SCRAPE AND DO NOT INHALE DUST
Contains lead. While not immediately toxic, be careful handling cerussite and always wear gloves. The lead content is poisonous to humans.

FOUND IT!

WHEN

DATE

WHERE

SPECIFIC PLACE AND SURROUNDINGS

NOTES

MINERALS

Dolomite

Carbonates

CHEMICAL FORMULA $CaMg(CO_3)_2$ (calcium magnesium carbonate)

COLOR White, gray, pink, light red, brown, colorless

CLEAVAGE Perfect

STREAK White

HARDNESS 3.5 to 4 on the Mohs scale

LUSTER Vitreous

SPECIFIC GRAVITY 2.8 to 2.9

WHAT IT IS USED FOR To make magnesia, an acid neutralizer. It's also a source of magnesium for livestock and a filler in paints, detergents, and ceramics.

POINT OF FACT The Dolomites in Italy were the first mountains named after a mineral; usually it's the other way around, with minerals named after locations.

FOUND IT!

WHEN

DATE

WHERE

SPECIFIC PLACE AND SURROUNDINGS

NOTES

MINERALS

Magnesite

Carbonates

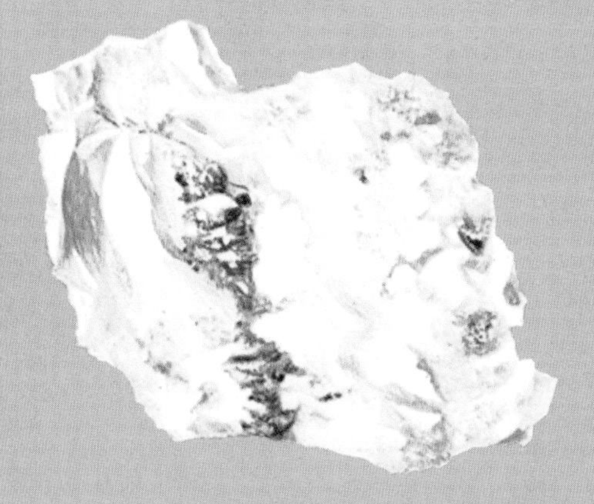

CHEMICAL FORMULA $MgCO_3$ (magnesium carbonate)

COLOR White, gray, brown, colorless

CLEAVAGE Perfect

STREAK White

HARDNESS 3.5 to 4.5 on the Mohs scale

LUSTER Dull and chalky

SPECIFIC GRAVITY 3.0

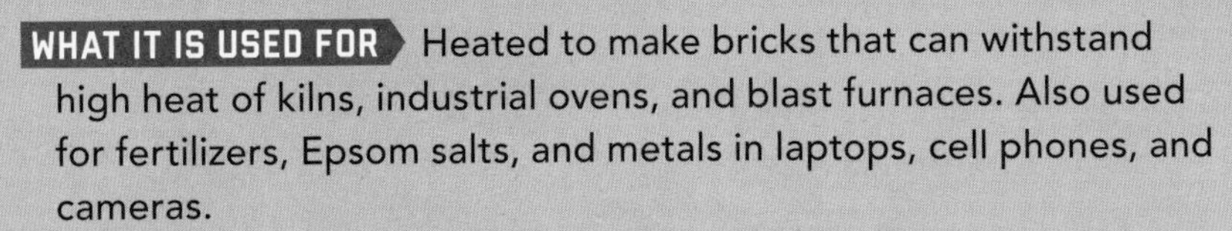

WHAT IT IS USED FOR Heated to make bricks that can withstand high heat of kilns, industrial ovens, and blast furnaces. Also used for fertilizers, Epsom salts, and metals in laptops, cell phones, and cameras.

POINT OF FACT White magnesite is porous and can be dyed to produce fake turquoise and lapis lazuli.

FOUND IT!

WHEN

DATE

WHERE

SPECIFIC PLACE AND SURROUNDINGS

NOTES

MINERALS

Malachite

Carbonates

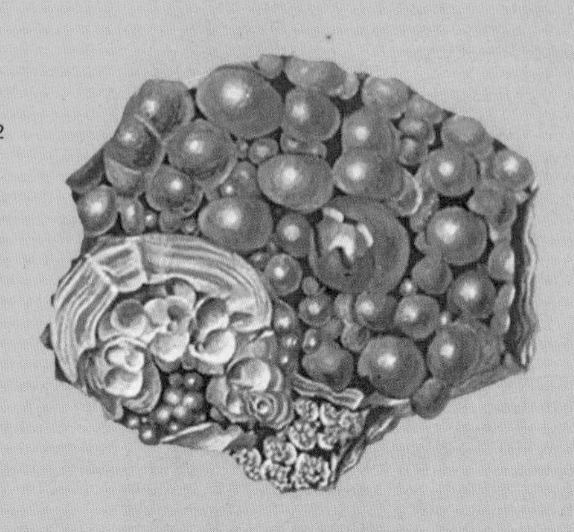

CHEMICAL FORMULA $Cu_2(CO_3)(OH)_2$ (copper carbonate)

COLOR Light to dark green

CLEAVAGE Perfect

STREAK Pale green

HARDNESS 3.5 to 4 on the Mohs scale

LUSTER Adamantine

SPECIFIC GRAVITY 3.9 to 4

WHAT IT IS USED FOR Copper ore, pigment, gemstone, sculpture

POINT OF FACT The ancient Egyptians used malachite to produce copper.

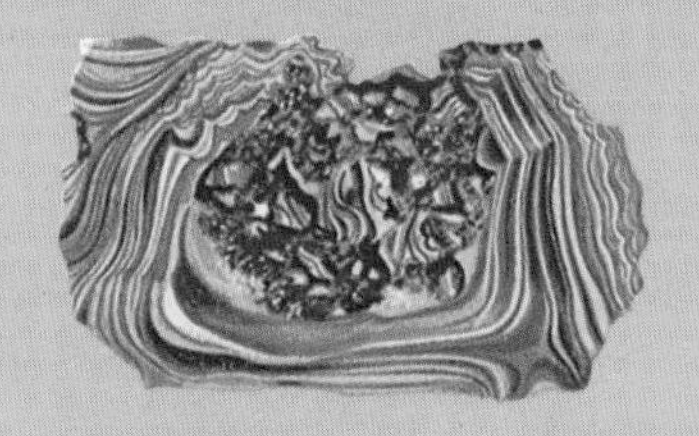

FOUND IT!

WHEN

DATE

WHERE

SPECIFIC PLACE AND SURROUNDINGS

NOTES

Siderite

Carbonates

CHEMICAL FORMULA $FeCO_3$ (iron carbonate)

COLOR Brown, gray, white

CLEAVAGE Perfect

STREAK White

HARDNESS 3.5 to 4 on the Mohs scale

LUSTER Vitreous to pearly

SPECIFIC GRAVITY 3.9

WHAT IT IS USED FOR Iron ore, paint pigment

POINT OF FACT It may be found in sedimentary iron ore from the Precambrian era, around the time the earth was formed.

FOUND IT!

WHEN

DATE

WHERE

SPECIFIC PLACE AND SURROUNDINGS

NOTES

MINERALS

Borax

Borates

CHEMICAL FORMULA
$Na_2[B_4O_5(OH)_4] \cdot 8H_2O$
(hydrous sodium borate)

COLOR Colorless, gray, white, sometimes bluish, greenish

CLEAVAGE Perfect

STREAK White

HARDNESS 2 to 2.5 on the Mohs scale

LUSTER Vitreous, resinous, earthy

SPECIFIC GRAVITY 1.7

WHAT IT IS USED FOR Detergent, pottery glaze, welding, fiberglass, water softener, insecticide, herbicide, disinfectant

POINTS OF FACT

- Borax has been used as a pottery glaze since the Middle Ages.
- The Mojave Desert in the United States is one of the biggest sources of borax.

FOUND IT!

WHEN
DATE

WHERE
SPECIFIC PLACE AND SURROUNDINGS

NOTES

MINERALS

Colemanite

Borates

CHEMICAL FORMULA $CaB_3O_4(OH)_3 \cdot H_2O$ (hydrous calcium borate)

COLOR Colorless, white, gray, yellowish

CLEAVAGE Perfect

STREAK White

HARDNESS 4.0 to 4.5 on the Mohs scale

LUSTER Vitreous to adamantine

SPECIFIC GRAVITY 2.4

WHAT IT IS USED FOR Significant ore of boron, which is used in glassmaking, semiconductors, tank armor, bullet-proof vests, and green fireworks.

POINT OF FACT It is pyroelectric, generating an electric charge when the temperature goes up or down. Scientists have no idea why this happens.

FOUND IT!

WHEN
DATE

WHERE
SPECIFIC PLACE AND SURROUNDINGS

NOTES

Cassiterite

Oxides

CHEMICAL FORMULA SnO_2 (tin oxide)

COLOR Red, yellow, black, brown

CLEAVAGE Indistinct

STREAK White, gray, brown

HARDNESS 6 to 7 on the Mohs scale

LUSTER Adamantine to greasy

SPECIFIC GRAVITY 7.0

WHAT IT IS USED FOR Most important ore of tin, which is used to coat other metals to prevent corrosion. Tin cans are actually tin-coated steel.

POINT OF FACT Cassiterite can be found in igneous and metamorphic rocks. It resists weathering, so much of what we use today comes from sediments deposited along shorelines and stream valleys.

FOUND IT!

WHEN

DATE

WHERE

SPECIFIC PLACE AND SURROUNDINGS

NOTES

MINERALS

Chromite

Oxides

CHEMICAL FORMULA $FeCr_2O_4$ (iron chromium oxide)

COLOR Black or dark brown

CLEAVAGE None

STREAK Brown

HARDNESS 5.5 on the Mohs scale

LUSTER Submetallic

SPECIFIC GRAVITY 4.5 to 4.8

WHAT IT IS USED FOR Only ore of chromium, used to make stainless steel

POINT OF FACT Trace amounts of chromium are responsible for the red of rubies and the green of emeralds, and chromium is in many pigments today.

FOUND IT!

WHEN

DATE

WHERE

SPECIFIC PLACE AND SURROUNDINGS

NOTES

Chrysoberyl

Oxides

CHEMICAL FORMULA $BeAl_2O_4$ (beryllium aluminum oxide)

COLOR Yellow, yellow green, green, brown

CLEAVAGE Distinct

STREAK Colorless

HARDNESS 8.5 on the Mohs scale

LUSTER Vitreous

SPECIFIC GRAVITY 3.7

WHAT IT IS USED FOR Gemstones

POINT OF FACT Chrysoberyl is one of several minerals that make "cat's eye" gems. If you turn this gemstone from side to side, you will see a band of reflected light move across the surface.

WHEN

DATE

WHERE

SPECIFIC PLACE AND SURROUNDINGS

NOTES

MINERALS

Cuprite

Oxides

CHEMICAL FORMULA Cu_2O (copper oxide)

COLOR Dark red, dark gray

CLEAVAGE Distinct

STREAK Brownish red

HARDNESS 3.5 to 4 on the Mohs scale

LUSTER Adamantine

SPECIFIC GRAVITY 6.1

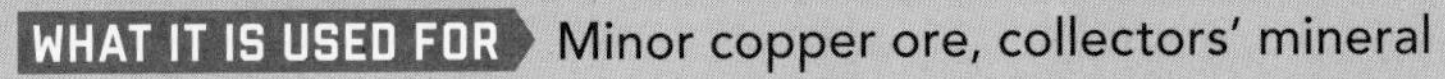

WHAT IT IS USED FOR Minor copper ore, collectors' mineral

POINT OF FACT Found in the southwestern United States, it is a soft, heavy mineral that some people believe has the ability to strengthen your willpower.

FOUND IT!

WHEN

DATE

WHERE

SPECIFIC PLACE AND SURROUNDINGS

NOTES

MINERALS

Hematite

Oxides

CHEMICAL FORMULA Fe_2O_3 (iron oxide)

COLOR Dark gray to black as a crystal, can contain red

CLEAVAGE None

STREAK Brownish red or cherry red

HARDNESS 5 to 6 on the Mohs scale

LUSTER Earthy to metallic

SPECIFIC GRAVITY 5.3

WHAT IT IS USED FOR Important iron ore, red pigment, radiation shields

POINT OF FACT The official state mineral of Alabama, its name comes from Greek *haimatitēs*, "bloodlike."

FOUND IT!

WHEN

DATE

WHERE

SPECIFIC PLACE AND SURROUNDINGS

NOTES

MINERALS

Magnetite

Oxides

CHEMICAL FORMULA $Fe^{2+}Fe^{3+}{}_2O_4$ (iron oxide)

COLOR Dark gray to black

CLEAVAGE None

STREAK Black

HARDNESS 5.5 to 6.5 on the Mohs scale

LUSTER Metallic

SPECIFIC GRAVITY 5.2

WHAT IT IS USED FOR Important iron ore

POINT OF FACT Magnetite is one of the few minerals attracted to a magnet. The Chinese used a naturally magnetic form of magnetite, lodestone, as a compass in the fourth century BCE.

FOUND IT!

WHEN
DATE

WHERE
SPECIFIC PLACE AND SURROUNDINGS

NOTES

MINERALS

Rutile

Oxides

CHEMICAL FORMULA TiO_2 (titanium dioxide)

COLOR Black, red, brownish yellow, gray

CLEAVAGE Good

STREAK White

HARDNESS 6 to 6.5 on the Mohs scale

LUSTER Adamantine, metallic

SPECIFIC GRAVITY 4.2

WHAT IT IS USED FOR Sunscreen, white pigment, ceramic glaze. Important ore of titanium, which makes super strong, lightweight materials like airplane frames and hip implants.

POINT OF FACT Titanium is as strong as steel, but is lighter by half.

FOUND IT!

WHEN

DATE

WHERE

SPECIFIC PLACE AND SURROUNDINGS

NOTES

MINERALS

Zincite

Oxides

CHEMICAL FORMULA ZnO (zinc oxide)

COLOR Red, orange, yellow, green

CLEAVAGE Perfect

STREAK Orange yellow

HARDNESS 4 on the Mohs scale

LUSTER Resinous

SPECIFIC GRAVITY 5.7

WHAT IT IS USED FOR Zinc ore, collectors' mineral

POINT OF FACT Powdered zinc oxide is used in sunblock, calamine lotion, and cosmetics.

FOUND IT!

WHEN
DATE

WHERE
SPECIFIC PLACE AND SURROUNDINGS

NOTES

MINERALS

Bauxite

Hydroxides

CHEMICAL FORMULA $Al_2(OH)_3$ plus extra Al and OH (groups of aluminum hydroxides)

COLOR Red brown, brown, orange, yellow

CLEAVAGE None

STREAK White

HARDNESS 1 to 3 on the Mohs scale

LUSTER Earthy

SPECIFIC GRAVITY 2.3 to 2.7

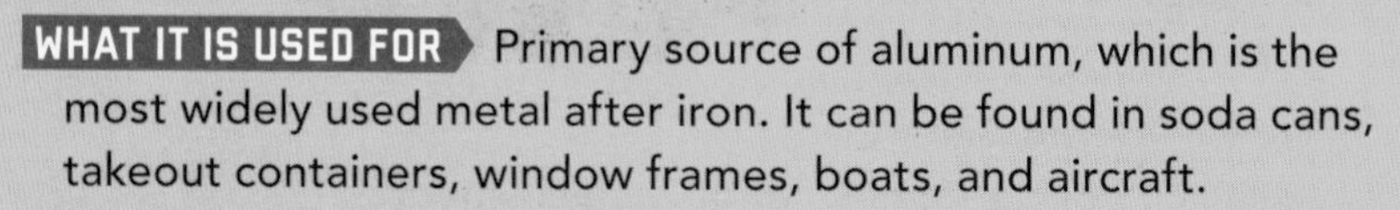

WHAT IT IS USED FOR Primary source of aluminum, which is the most widely used metal after iron. It can be found in soda cans, takeout containers, window frames, boats, and aircraft.

POINT OF FACT Aluminum is the most abundant metal in the crust, and the third most abundant element, behind oxygen and silicon. (Bauxite is not technically a mineral but an ore containing three aluminum hydroxide minerals: gibbsite, boehmite, and diaspore.)

FOUND IT!

WHEN

DATE

WHERE

SPECIFIC PLACE AND SURROUNDINGS

NOTES

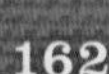

MINERALS

Cryolite

Halides

CHEMICAL FORMULA Na_3AlF_6 (sodium aluminum fluoride)

COLOR White, brown, gray, colorless

CLEAVAGE None

STREAK White

HARDNESS 2.5 on the Mohs scale

LUSTER Vitreous or greasy

SPECIFIC GRAVITY 3

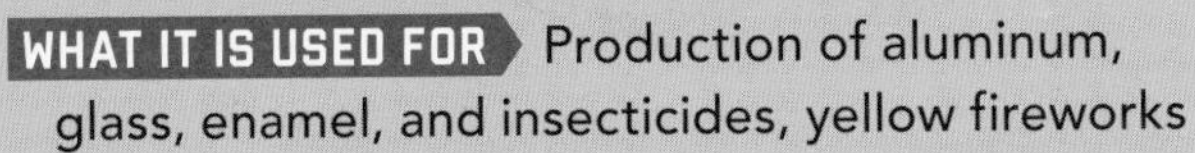

WHAT IT IS USED FOR Production of aluminum, glass, enamel, and insecticides, yellow fireworks

POINT OF FACT Today, it's artificially made from fluorite, since natural cryolite is rare. The one large deposit in the world, in Ivigtût on the west coast of Greenland, was used up in 1987, but there are other smaller deposits, including one in Colorado.

FOUND IT!

WHEN

DATE

WHERE

SPECIFIC PLACE AND SURROUNDINGS

NOTES

MINERALS

Fluorite

Halides

CHEMICAL FORMULA CaF_2 (calcium fluoride)

COLOR Purple, yellow, green, colorless, blue, pink, brown

CLEAVAGE Perfect

STREAK White

HARDNESS 4 on the Mohs scale

LUSTER Vitreous

SPECIFIC GRAVITY 3 to 3.3

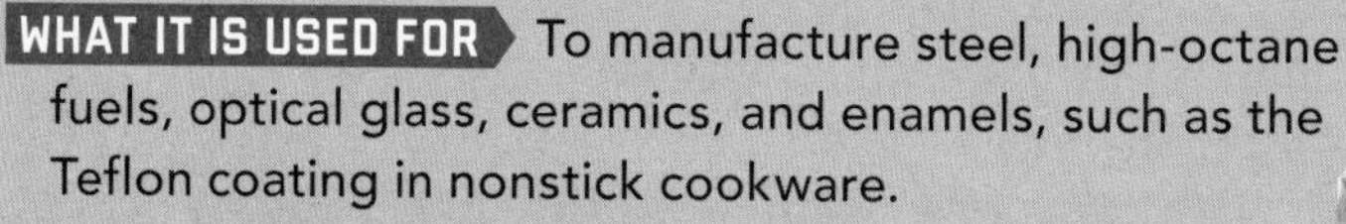

WHAT IT IS USED FOR To manufacture steel, high-octane fuels, optical glass, ceramics, and enamels, such as the Teflon coating in nonstick cookware.

POINT OF FACT Fluorite often glows blue under ultraviolet light. The scientist who discovered this phenomenon named it "fluorescence" after the mineral.

FOUND IT!

WHEN

DATE

WHERE

SPECIFIC PLACE AND SURROUNDINGS

NOTES

MINERALS

Halite

Halides

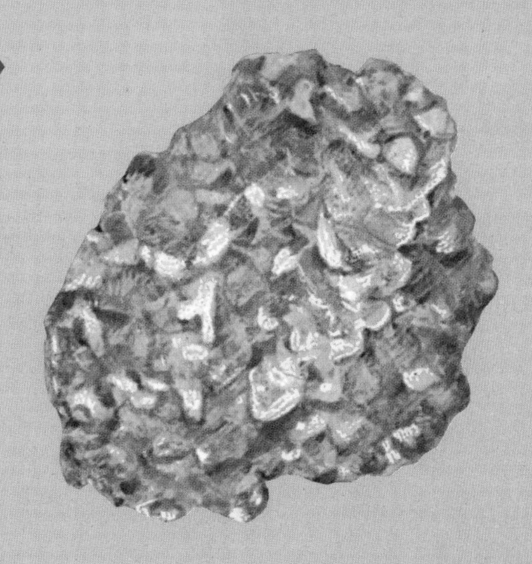

CHEMICAL FORMULA NaCl (sodium chloride)

COLOR White, yellow, red, purple, blue, orange

CLEAVAGE Perfect

STREAK White

HARDNESS 2.5 on the Mohs scale

LUSTER Vitreous

SPECIFIC GRAVITY 2.1 to 2.6

WHAT IT IS USED FOR Common table salt that you put on your food.

POINT OF FACT Why is it called halite? Because the Greek word for salt is *hals*.

FOUND IT!

WHEN

DATE

WHERE

SPECIFIC PLACE AND SURROUNDINGS

NOTES

MINERALS

Barite

Sulfates

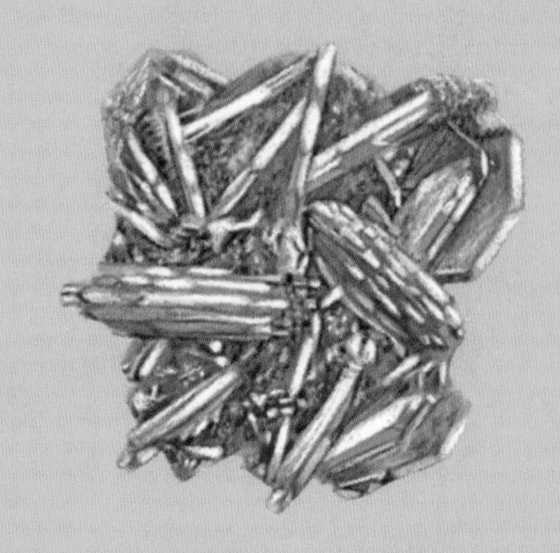

CHEMICAL FORMULA $BaSO_4$ (barium sulfate)

COLOR Colorless, white, light blue, light yellow, light red, light green

CLEAVAGE Perfect

STREAK White

HARDNESS 2.5 to 3.5 on the Mohs scale

LUSTER Vitreous to pearly

SPECIFIC GRAVITY 1.3 to 4.6

WHAT IT IS USED FOR Its weight makes it useful in oil and gas drilling and as a filler for rubber, cloth, and paper, in particular playing cards. It absorbs radiation so it used in X-rays of the digestive tract and radiation shields. It is also used in brake pads for cars and trucks. It is the main ore of barium.

POINT OF FACT Its name comes from Greek *barys*, "heavy," and the element barium was named after the mineral.

FOUND IT!

WHEN

DATE

WHERE

SPECIFIC PLACE AND SURROUNDINGS

NOTES

Glauberite

Sulfates

CHEMICAL FORMULA $Na_2Ca(SO_4)_2$ (sodium calcium sulfate)

COLOR Gray, yellowish, colorless

CLEAVAGE Perfect

STREAK White

HARDNESS 2.5 on the Mohs scale

LUSTER Greasy, vitreous, dull

SPECIFIC GRAVITY 2.75 to 2.85

WHAT IT IS USED FOR Source of glauber's salt, which is used to make paper and glass and stomach medications

POINT OF FACT This stone will dissolve in water.

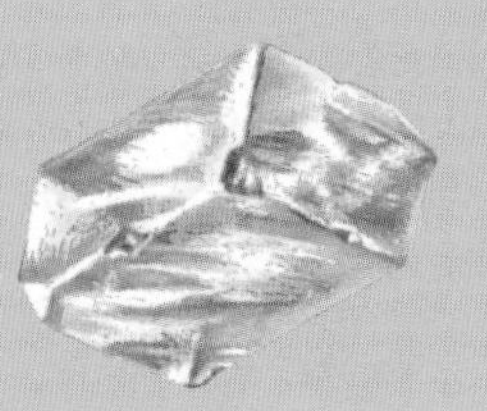

FOUND IT!

WHEN

DATE

WHERE

SPECIFIC PLACE AND SURROUNDINGS

NOTES

MINERALS

Gypsum

Sulfates

CHEMICAL FORMULA $CaSO_4\ 2H_2O$ (hydrous calcium sulfate)

COLOR White, pinkish, yellowish, gray

CLEAVAGE Perfect

STREAK White

HARDNESS 2 on the Mohs scale

LUSTER Vitreous, silky

SPECIFIC GRAVITY 2.3

WHAT IT IS USED FOR Plaster, wallboard, joint compound

POINT OF FACT The Mesopotamians were using powdered gypsum as a plaster to cover walls as early as seven thousand years ago.

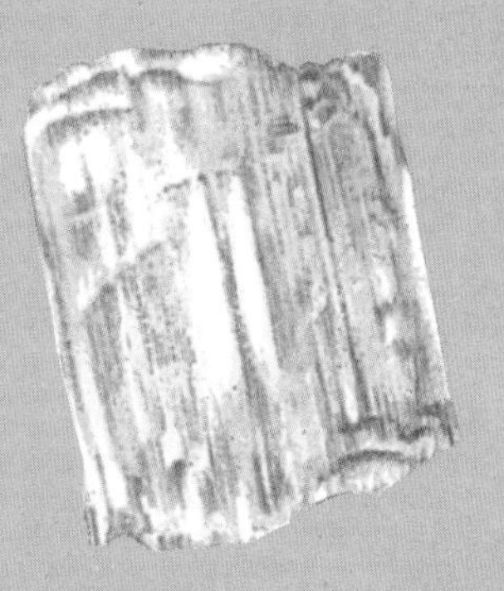

FOUND IT!

WHEN

DATE

WHERE

SPECIFIC PLACE AND SURROUNDINGS

NOTES

MINERALS

Actinolite

Silicates

CHEMICAL FORMULA $Ca_2(Mg,Fe)_5Si_8O_{22}(OH)_2$ (calcium, magnesium, iron silicate)

COLOR Green, gray green, black

CLEAVAGE Good

STREAK White

HARDNESS 5 to 6 on the Mohs scale

LUSTER Vitreous, silky

SPECIFIC GRAVITY 2.9 to 3.4

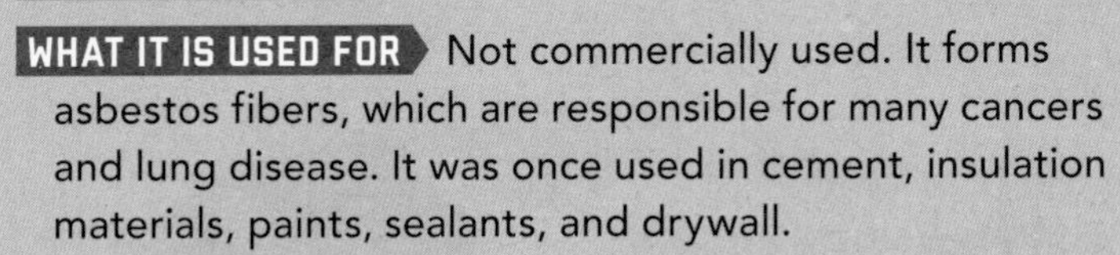

WHAT IT IS USED FOR Not commercially used. It forms asbestos fibers, which are responsible for many cancers and lung disease. It was once used in cement, insulation materials, paints, sealants, and drywall.

POINT OF FACT Tremolite and actinolite are very similar, but actinolite is less common and contains more iron than magnesium (tremolite is the opposite), which gives it a generally green color.

FOUND IT!

WHEN

DATE

WHERE

SPECIFIC PLACE AND SURROUNDINGS

NOTES

MINERALS

Biotite

Silicates

CHEMICAL FORMULA $K(Fe,Mg)_3(AlSi_3O_{10})(F,OH)_2$ (fluoro potassium, magnesium, iron, aluminum silicate)

COLOR Brown, black, dark green

CLEAVAGE Perfect

STREAK White or gray

HARDNESS 2 to 3 on the Mohs scale

LUSTER Vitreous

SPECIFIC GRAVITY 2.7 to 3.4

WHAT IT IS USED FOR Paint filler, rubber production, nonstick coating on roofing material. It is also used to determine age of rocks.

POINT OF FACT Biotite absorbs water and breaks apart, so it's hard to clean. The best way to clean it is with a dry electric toothbrush.

FOUND IT!

WHEN

DATE

WHERE

SPECIFIC PLACE AND SURROUNDINGS

NOTES

MINERALS

Chalcedony

Silicates

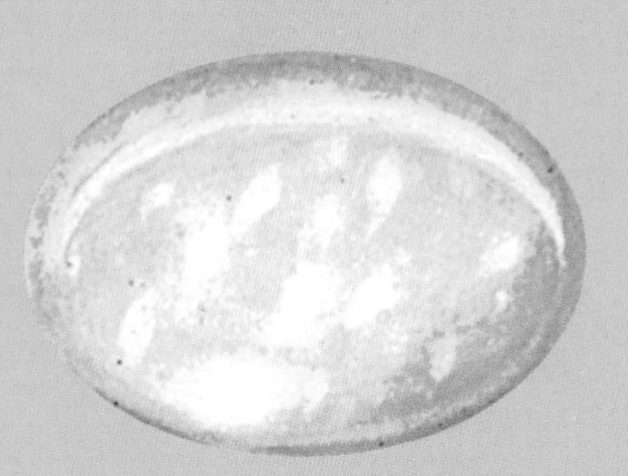

CHEMICAL FORMULA SiO_2 (silicon dioxide)

COLOR Colorless, yellow, purple, pink, red, black, brown, green, blue, orange

CLEAVAGE None

STREAK White

HARDNESS 7 on the Mohs scale

LUSTER Vitreous, waxy, or dull

SPECIFIC GRAVITY 2.7

WHAT IT IS USED FOR Ornamental stone, semiprecious gemstones such as carnelian, bloodstone, and sard

POINT OF FACT Chalcedony has crystals so fine that you cannot see them without a microscope.

CARNELIAN

BLOODSTONE

SARD

FOUND IT!

WHEN

DATE

WHERE

SPECIFIC PLACE AND SURROUNDINGS

NOTES

MINERALS

Hornblende

Silicates

CHEMICAL FORMULA $(Ca,Na)_{2\text{-}3}(Mg,Fe,Al)_5(Si,Al)_8O_{22}(OH,F)_2$

COLOR Green, brownish green to black

CLEAVAGE Perfect

STREAK White or gray

HARDNESS 5 to 6 on the Mohs scale

LUSTER Vitreous, submetallic, dull

SPECIFIC GRAVITY 3.1 to 3.3

WHAT IT IS USED FOR Not much on its own, but it gives igneous granite its black streaks and is abundant in metamorphic amphibolite, which is widely used in construction.

POINT OF FACT Hornblende is the name given to dark-colored amphibole minerals with similar compositions that can only be distinguished by a trained geologist.

FOUND IT!

WHEN

DATE

WHERE

SPECIFIC PLACE AND SURROUNDINGS

NOTES

MINERALS

Microcline

Silicates

CHEMICAL FORMULA $KAlSi_3O_8$ (potassium aluminum silicate)

COLOR Colorless, white, yellow, pale pink, green

CLEAVAGE Perfect

STREAK White

HARDNESS 6 to 6.5 on the Mohs scale

LUSTER Vitreous

SPECIFIC GRAVITY 2.6

WHAT IT IS USED FOR To manufacture porcelain and other ceramics, glass, abrasives

POINTS OF FACT

- Orthoclase and microcline are polymorphs, meaning their only difference is in their crystal structure, so sometimes you need an X-ray to tell one from the other.
- Amazonite, a type of microcline, is a brilliant blue green and prized as a gemstone.

FOUND IT!

WHEN

DATE

WHERE

SPECIFIC PLACE AND SURROUNDINGS

NOTES

MINERALS

Opal

Silicates

CHEMICAL FORMULA $SiO_2 \cdot nH_2O$ (silicon dioxide)

COLOR Colorless, white, yellow, red, orange, green, brown, black, blue

CLEAVAGE None

STREAK White

HARDNESS 5 to 6 on the Mohs scale

LUSTER Vitreous

SPECIFIC GRAVITY 1.9 to 2.3

WHAT IT IS USED FOR Precious gemstone

POINT OF FACT Opal has no set crystal structure, so it is not technically a mineral, but a mineraloid.

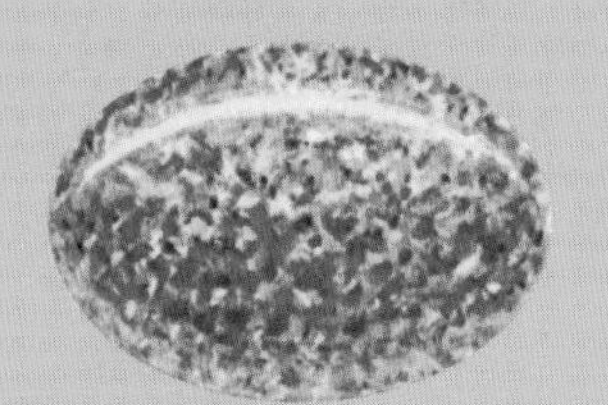

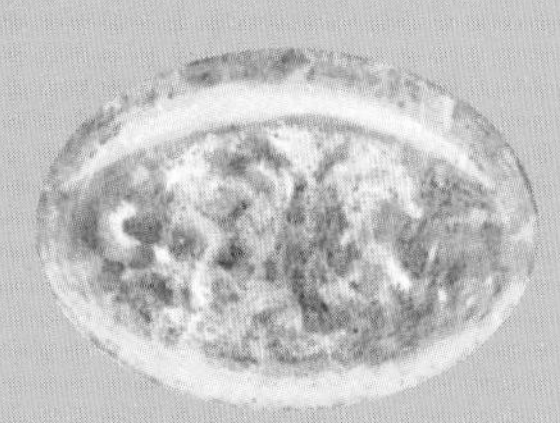

FOUND IT!

WHEN

DATE

WHERE

SPECIFIC PLACE AND SURROUNDINGS

NOTES

MINERALS

Orthoclase

Silicates

CHEMICAL FORMULA $KAlSi_3O_8$ (potassium aluminum silicate)

COLOR Colorless, white, light green, yellow, pink

CLEAVAGE Perfect

STREAK White

HARDNESS 6 to 6.5 on the Mohs scale

LUSTER Vitreous, pearly, resinous

SPECIFIC GRAVITY 2.5 to 2.6

WHAT IT IS USED FOR To manufacture porcelain and other ceramics, glass, abrasives

POINT OF FACT Moonstone gems are largely composed of orthoclase.

FOUND IT!

WHEN

DATE

WHERE

SPECIFIC PLACE AND SURROUNDINGS

NOTES

MINERALS

Pyrophyllite

Silicates

CHEMICAL FORMULA $Al_2Si_4O_{10}(OH)_2$
(hydrous aluminum silicate)

COLOR White, gray, pale blue, pale green, pale yellow, brownish green

CLEAVAGE Perfect

STREAK White

HARDNESS 1 to 2 on the Mohs scale

LUSTER Pearly

SPECIFIC GRAVITY 2.7 to 2.9

WHAT IT IS USED FOR Ceramics, paint, tailor's chalk, insecticides, rubber

POINT OF FACT Pyrophyllite gets its name from Greek *pyr*, "fire," and *phyllon*, "leaf," because it peels into thin layers when heated.

FOUND IT!

WHEN
DATE

WHERE
SPECIFIC PLACE AND SURROUNDINGS

NOTES

MINERALS

Quartz

Silicates

CHEMICAL FORMULA
SiO_2 (silicon dioxide)

COLOR Colorless, yellow, purple, pink, red, black, brown, green, blue, orange

CLEAVAGE None

STREAK White

HARDNESS 7 on the Mohs scale

LUSTER Vitreous

SPECIFIC GRAVITY 2.7

WHAT IT IS USED FOR Watches, clocks, radios, televisions, electronics, abrasives, glassmaking, and fracking

POINT OF FACT Quartz crystals are piezoelectric, which means they generate an electrical current when they are bent, stretched, or squeezed. And an electric current makes them bend, stretch, or compress. This means they can be made to vibrate at a specific frequency, which is handy for watches, radios, and all sorts of electronics.

FOUND IT!

WHEN
DATE

WHERE
SPECIFIC PLACE AND SURROUNDINGS

NOTES

QUARTZ also produces beautiful and valuable gemstones. Perhaps you've seen someone wearing one of these, or maybe you have one of these gems yourself.

There are many varieties of quartz, including gemstones and crystals.

PRASIOLITE

CARNELIAN

SMOKY QUARTZ

MILKY QUARTZ

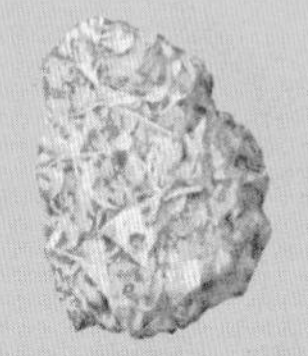
ROSE QUARTZ

TIGER'S EYE

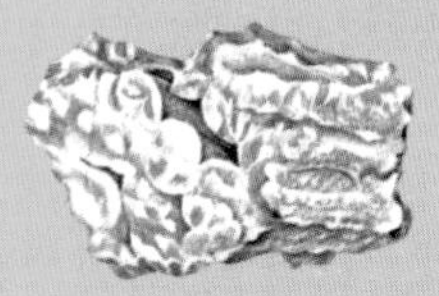
CHALCEDONY

CITRINE

BLUE QUARTZ

ONYX

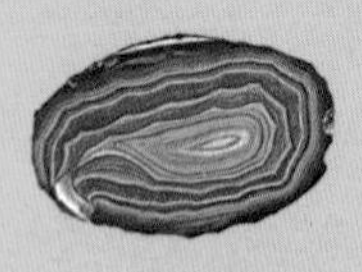
BANDED AGATE

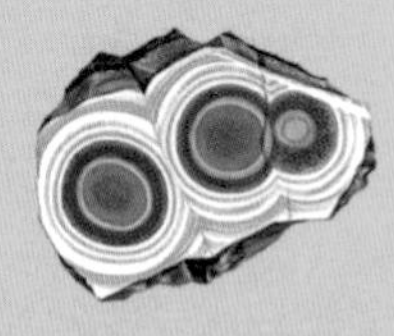
EYE AGATE

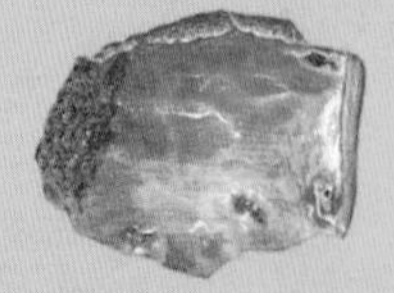
CHRYSOPRASE

RUTILATED QUARTZ

JASPER

AMETHYST

MINERALS

Serpentine

Silicates

CHEMICAL FORMULA Group of minerals with $(Mg,Fe,Ni,Al,Zn,Mn)_{2-3}(Si,Al,Fe)_2O_5(OH)_4$

COLOR Often green, but also white, yellow, gray, brown, black, purple

CLEAVAGE Perfect

STREAK White

HARDNESS 3.5 to 5.5 on the Mohs scale

LUSTER Greasy, waxy, silky

SPECIFIC GRAVITY 2.5 to 2.6

WHAT IT IS USED FOR Fire retardant and heat protection, asbestos production, ornamental and architectural stone, countertops, tiling, gemstones

POINT OF FACT The *mineral* serpentine is the official state *rock* of California. (The state's official *mineral*? Yep, gold. It is the Golden State after all.)

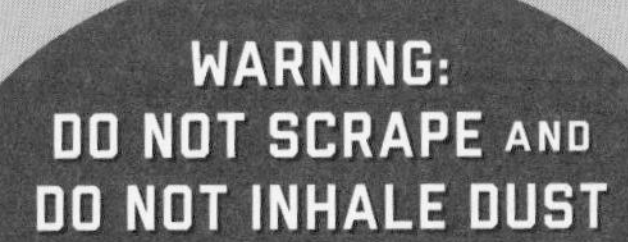

WARNING:
DO NOT SCRAPE AND
DO NOT INHALE DUST

Wear gloves while handling serpentine. It can be poisonous to humans.

FOUND IT!

WHEN

DATE

WHERE

SPECIFIC PLACE AND SURROUNDINGS

NOTES

MINERALS

Talc

Silicates

CHEMICAL FORMULA $Mg_3Si_4O_{10}(OH)_2$ (hydrous magnesium silicate)

COLOR White, beige, gray, yellow, brown, blue, green, rarely colorless

CLEAVAGE Perfect

STREAK White

HARDNESS 1 on the Mohs scale

LUSTER Greasy, waxy, pearly

SPECIFIC GRAVITY 2.8

WHAT IT IS USED FOR Plastics, ceramics, paint, papermaking, cosmetics, roofing, insecticide, rubber, ornamental carving stone

POINT OF FACT Ever used talcum powder to dry things up? Then you were using talc, because that is the primary ingredient.

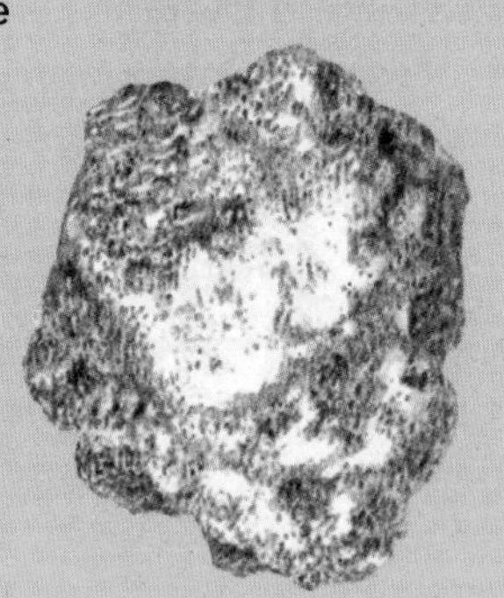

FOUND IT!

WHEN

DATE

WHERE

SPECIFIC PLACE AND SURROUNDINGS

NOTES

Tremolite

Silicates

CHEMICAL FORMULA $Ca_2(Mg,Fe)_5Si_8O_{22}(OH)_2$ (calcium, magnesium, iron silicate)

COLOR White, brown, colorless, gray, light green, green, light yellow, pink violet

CLEAVAGE Perfect

STREAK White

HARDNESS 5 to 6 on the Mohs scale

LUSTER Vitreous, silky

SPECIFIC GRAVITY 2.9 to 3.4

WHAT IT IS USED FOR No longer mined. It forms asbestos fibers, which are responsible for many cancers and lung disease. It was once used in paint, sealants, insulation, roofing, and plumbing materials.

POINT OF FACT Tremolite does not catch fire and is a good insulator.

WARNING: DO NOT SCRAPE AND DO NOT INHALE DUST
Wear gloves while handling tremolite. It is poisonous to humans.

FOUND IT!

WHEN
DATE

WHERE
SPECIFIC PLACE AND SURROUNDINGS

NOTES

MINERALS

Vermiculite

Silicates

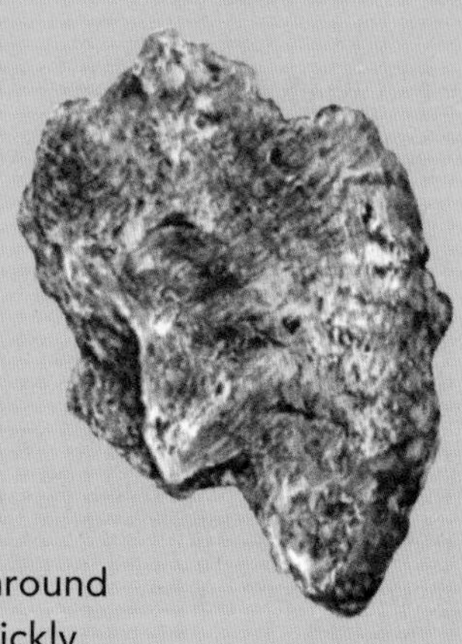

CHEMICAL FORMULA $Mg_{0.7}(Mg,Fe,Al)_6(Si,Al)_8O_{20}(OH)_4 \cdot 8H_2O$

COLOR Brown, bronze, yellow

CLEAVAGE Perfect

STREAK Colorless

HARDNESS 1 to 2 on the Mohs scale

LUSTER Dull to pearly

SPECIFIC GRAVITY 2.6

WHAT IT IS USED FOR It is added to soil around plants to keep them from drying out quickly.

POINT OF FACT When it's heated to very high temperatures, vermiculite expands into accordion-like "worms." This makes it spongy, allowing it to store water.

FOUND IT!

WHEN

DATE

WHERE

SPECIFIC PLACE AND SURROUNDINGS

NOTES

Agate

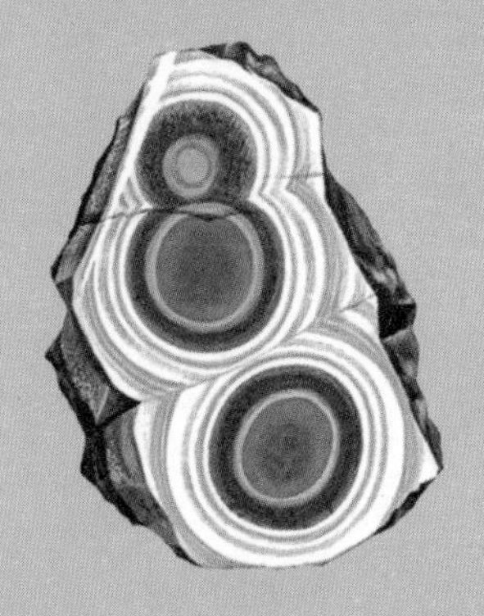

CHEMICAL FORMULA SiO_2 (silicon dioxide)

COLOR Any color due to trace elements, multicolored specimens not uncommon

CLEAVAGE None

STREAK White

HARDNESS 6.5 to 7 on the Mohs scale

LUSTER Waxy

SPECIFIC GRAVITY 2.6

WHAT IT IS USED FOR Gemstones, healing crystal

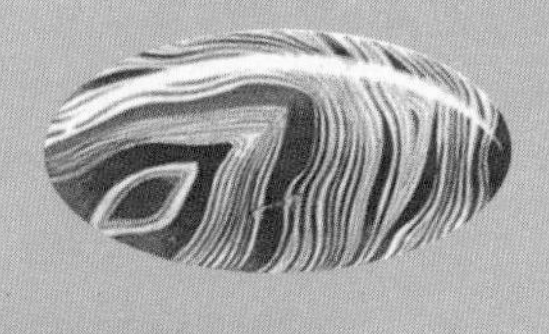

POINT OF FACT It's a banded form of quartz, which people have been using since the Stone Age.

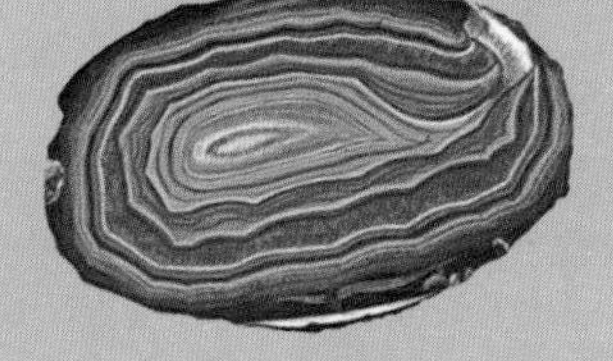

FOUND IT!

WHEN

DATE

WHERE

SPECIFIC PLACE AND SURROUNDINGS

NOTES

Apatite

CHEMICAL FORMULA $Ca_5(PO_4)_3(Cl,F,OH)$ (calcium fluoro-chloro-hydroxyl phosphate)

COLOR White, yellow, green, red, blue

CLEAVAGE Indistinct

STREAK White

HARDNESS 5 on the Mohs scale

LUSTER Vitreous

SPECIFIC GRAVITY 3.2

WHAT IT IS USED FOR Main source of phosphorous for fertilizers, chemicals, and drugs, also a gemstone

POINT OF FACT Apatite is the name of several related phosphate minerals, and the hydrogen-rich apatite found in moon rocks has proven to scientists that the moon does contain water.

FOUND IT!

WHEN

DATE

WHERE

SPECIFIC PLACE AND SURROUNDINGS

NOTES

Aquamarine (beryl)

CHEMICAL FORMULA $Be_3Al_2Si_6O_{18}$ (beryllium aluminum silicate)

COLOR Blue

CLEAVAGE Basal

STREAK White

HARDNESS 7.5 to 8 on the Mohs scale

LUSTER Vitreous

SPECIFIC GRAVITY 2.6 to 2.8

WHAT IT IS USED FOR Minor ore of beryllium, gemstones

POINT OF FACT It's the birthstone of people born in March, and the official state gemstone of Colorado.

FOUND IT!

WHEN

DATE

WHERE

SPECIFIC PLACE AND SURROUNDINGS

NOTES

Augite

CHEMICAL FORMULA $(Ca,Na)(Mg,Fe,Al)(Al,Si)_2O_6$ (calcium, sodium, magnesium, iron, aluminum silicate)

COLOR Yellowish green, green, brownish green, black

CLEAVAGE Perfect

STREAK Colorless

HARDNESS 6 on the Mohs scale

LUSTER Vitreous, dull

SPECIFIC GRAVITY 3.4 to 3.5

WHAT IT IS USED FOR Collectors' mineral, healing crystal

POINT OF FACT Although it is commonly found in rocks and can tell geologists about the earth's history, augite is one of the few minerals that has no commercial use.

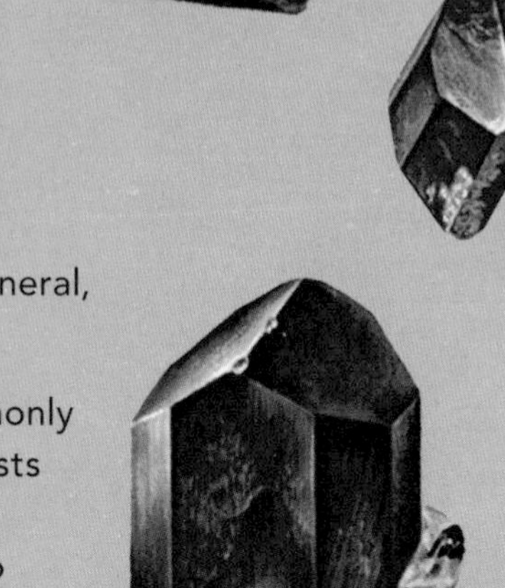

FOUND IT!

WHEN

DATE

WHERE

SPECIFIC PLACE AND SURROUNDINGS

NOTES

Bloodstone

CHEMICAL FORMULA SiO_2 (silicon dioxide)

COLOR Many shades of green with red splotches

CLEAVAGE None

STREAK Colorless

HARDNESS 6.5 to 7 on the Mohs scale

LUSTER Vitreous

SPECIFIC GRAVITY 2.6 to 2.7

WHAT IT IS USED FOR Powerful healing stone for many centuries

POINT OF FACT This form of chalcedony has red splotches that look like blood.

FOUND IT!

WHEN

DATE

WHERE

SPECIFIC PLACE AND SURROUNDINGS

NOTES

Chrysocolla

CHEMICAL FORMULA $(Cu,Al)_2(H_2Si_2O_5)(OH)_4 \cdot nH_2O$ (copper silicate)

COLOR Bright green, bluish green, sky blue, gray

CLEAVAGE None

STREAK Light green

HARDNESS 2.5 to 3.5 on the Mohs scale

LUSTER Vitreous

SPECIFIC GRAVITY 1.9 to 2.4

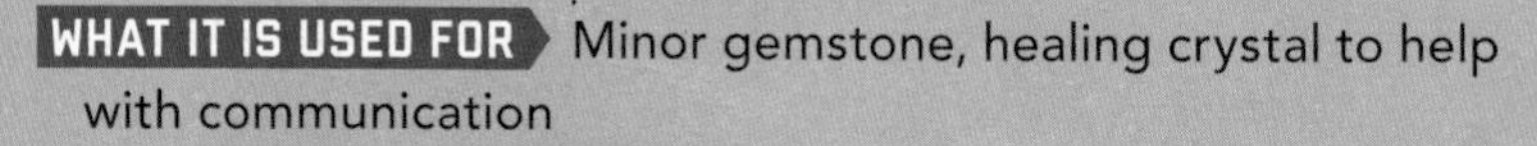

WHAT IT IS USED FOR Minor gemstone, healing crystal to help with communication

POINT OF FACT It is supposed to help you learn a new musical instrument easily.

FOUND IT!

WHEN

DATE

WHERE

SPECIFIC PLACE AND SURROUNDINGS

NOTES

Diamond

CHEMICAL FORMULA C

COLOR Colorless, white, yellow, brown, gray, black, rarely blue, green, red, orange, pink

CLEAVAGE Perfect

STREAK None

HARDNESS 10 on the Mohs scale

LUSTER Adamantine

SPECIFIC GRAVITY 3.5 to 3.53

WHAT IT IS USED FOR Gemstone, industrial cutting, grinding, drilling, and polishing

POINT OF FACT Some diamonds are billions of years old. More than a hundred million carats of diamonds are dug up every year.

FOUND IT!

WHEN
DATE

WHERE
SPECIFIC PLACE AND SURROUNDINGS

NOTES

Diopside

CHEMICAL FORMULA $CaMgSi_2O_6$

COLOR Grayish white, light blue to purple, light green to vivid green, brown, black

CLEAVAGE Distinct

STREAK White

HARDNESS 5.5 to 6.5 on the Mohs scale

LUSTER Vitreous, earthy

SPECIFIC GRAVITY 3.22 to 3.38

WHAT IT IS USED FOR Diamond prospecting, gemstones

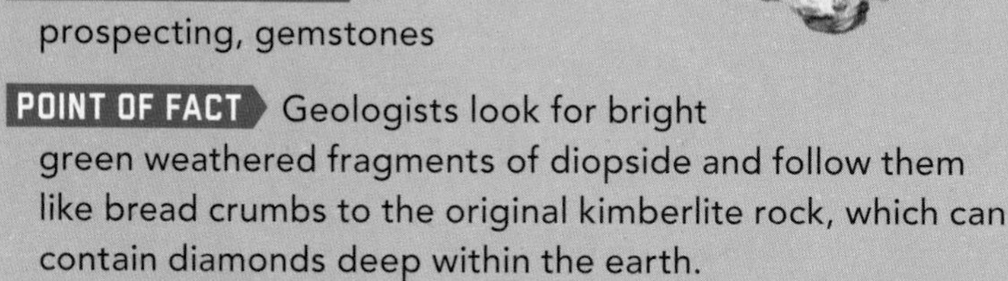

POINT OF FACT Geologists look for bright green weathered fragments of diopside and follow them like bread crumbs to the original kimberlite rock, which can contain diamonds deep within the earth.

FOUND IT!

WHEN

DATE

WHERE

SPECIFIC PLACE AND SURROUNDINGS

NOTES

Emerald (beryl)

CHEMICAL FORMULA $Be_3Al_2(Si_6O_{18})$

COLOR Rich, deep green

CLEAVAGE Imperfect

STREAK White

HARDNESS 7.5 to 8 on the Mohs scale

LUSTER Vitreous

SPECIFIC GRAVITY 2.6 to 2.9

WHAT IT IS USED FOR Minor ore of beryllium, gemstones

POINT OF FACT Emerald is a green gemstone variety of the mineral beryl. Beryl produces several gemstones of different colors. Blue is aquamarine; pink or rose is morganite; yellow is helidor; and light green is green beryl. Red beryl is one of world's rarest gems.

FOUND IT!

WHEN
DATE

WHERE
SPECIFIC PLACE AND SURROUNDINGS

NOTES

Epidote

CHEMICAL FORMULA $Ca_2(Al_2Fe)(SiO_4)(Si_2O_7)O(OH)$ (calcium aluminum iron silicate)

COLOR Yellowish green, green, brownish green, black

CLEAVAGE Perfect

STREAK Colorless

HARDNESS 6 on the Mohs scale

LUSTER Vitreous

SPECIFIC GRAVITY 3.4 to 3.5

WHAT IT IS USED FOR Collectors' mineral, minor gemstone, healing crystal

POINT OF FACT Epidote is sometimes mistaken for tourmaline.

FOUND IT!

WHEN
DATE

WHERE
SPECIFIC PLACE AND SURROUNDINGS

NOTES

Garnet (almandine)

CHEMICAL FORMULA $Fe_3Al_2(SiO_4)_3$ (iron aluminum silicate)

COLOR Deep red, brownish red, red violet, black

CLEAVAGE None

STREAK White

HARDNESS 7 to 7.5 on the Mohs scale

LUSTER Vitreous

SPECIFIC GRAVITY 4.32

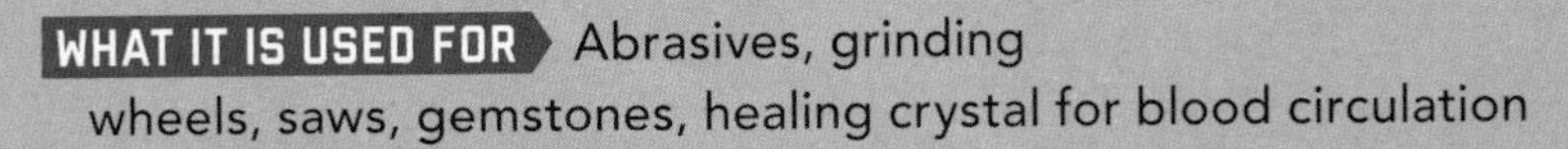

WHAT IT IS USED FOR Abrasives, grinding wheels, saws, gemstones, healing crystal for blood circulation

POINT OF FACT Almandine garnet is the official state mineral of Connecticut.

FOUND IT!

WHEN

DATE

WHERE

SPECIFIC PLACE AND SURROUNDINGS

NOTES

Garnet (grossular)

CHEMICAL FORMULA $Ca_3Al_2(SiO_4)_3$ (calcium aluminum silicate)

COLOR Brown, orange, red, yellow, green, white, colorless

CLEAVAGE None

STREAK White

HARDNESS 6.5 to 7.5 on the Mohs scale

LUSTER Vitreous

SPECIFIC GRAVITY 3.6

WHAT IT IS USED FOR Gemstone

POINT OF FACT Green grossular garnet was named after gooseberries, *Ribes grossularium*. It is the official state gem of Vermont.

FOUND IT!

WHEN
DATE

WHERE
SPECIFIC PLACE AND SURROUNDINGS

NOTES

Garnet (pyrope)

CHEMICAL FORMULA $Mg_3Al_2(SiO_4)_3$ (magnesium aluminum silicate)

COLOR Deep red to nearly black, rose red to purple

CLEAVAGE None

STREAK White

HARDNESS 7.5 on the Mohs scale

LUSTER Vitreous

SPECIFIC GRAVITY 3.58

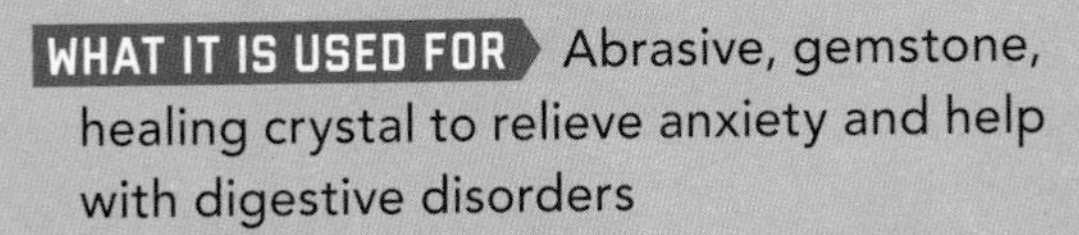

WHAT IT IS USED FOR Abrasive, gemstone, healing crystal to relieve anxiety and help with digestive disorders

POINT OF FACT Pyrope garnet is normally red, but when it is purple and in kimberlite rock, it's an indicator that diamonds may also be in the rock.

FOUND IT!

WHEN
DATE

WHERE
SPECIFIC PLACE AND SURROUNDINGS

NOTES

Hemimorphite

CHEMICAL FORMULA $Zn_4Si_2O_7(OH)_2 \cdot H_2O$ (hydrous zinc silicate)

COLOR Colorless, white, pale blue, pale green, gray, brown

CLEAVAGE Perfect

STREAK White

HARDNESS 4.5 to 5 on the Mohs scale

LUSTER Vitreous

SPECIFIC GRAVITY 3.48

WHAT IT IS USED FOR Zinc ore, collectors' mineral, gemstone

POINT OF FACT It was once called calamine, until a mineralogist discovered calamine actually was two zinc minerals, this zinc silicate and the zinc carbonate smithsonite.

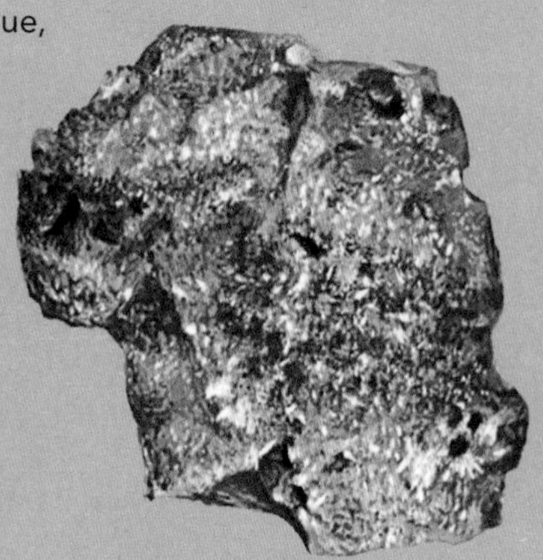

FOUND IT!

WHEN
DATE

WHERE
SPECIFIC PLACE AND SURROUNDINGS

NOTES

Jadeite

CHEMICAL FORMULA $Na(Al,Fe^3+)Si_2O_6$ (sodium aluminum silicate)

COLOR Apple green, greenish white, purplish blue, blue green, violet, white, black

CLEAVAGE Distinct

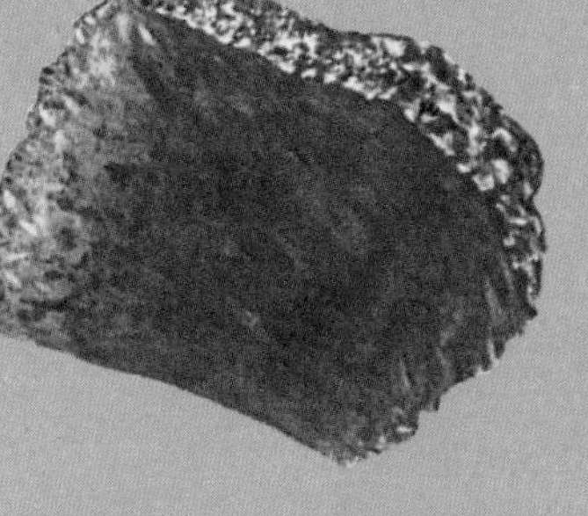

STREAK White

HARDNESS 4.5 to 5 on the Mohs scale

LUSTER Vitreous, waxy, greasy

SPECIFIC GRAVITY 14 to 19

WHAT IT IS USED FOR Jewelry, tools, sculpture, gemstones for over five thousand years

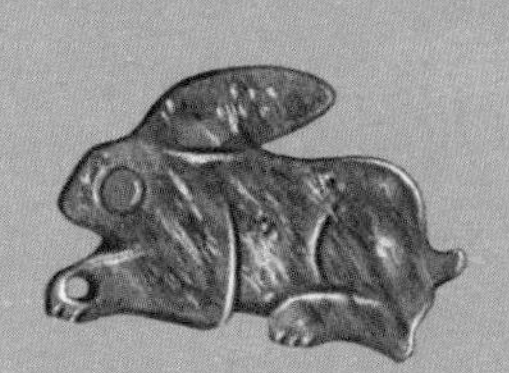

POINT OF FACT The more valuable of the two varieties of jade, jadeite is also known as imperial jade.

FOUND IT!

WHEN

DATE

WHERE

SPECIFIC PLACE AND SURROUNDINGS

NOTES

Kyanite

CHEMICAL FORMULA Al_2SiO_5 (aluminum silicate)

COLOR Blue, white, gray, green, colorless

CLEAVAGE Distinct

STREAK Colorless

HARDNESS 5.5 to 7 on the Mohs scale

LUSTER Vitreous, pearly

SPECIFIC GRAVITY 3.53 to 3.67

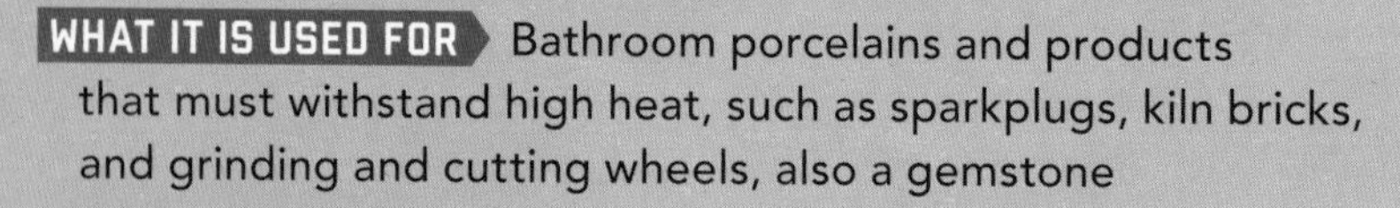

WHAT IT IS USED FOR Bathroom porcelains and products that must withstand high heat, such as sparkplugs, kiln bricks, and grinding and cutting wheels, also a gemstone

POINT OF FACT Kyanite can expand to twice its volume when heated.

FOUND IT!

WHEN
DATE

WHERE
SPECIFIC PLACE AND SURROUNDINGS

NOTES

Rhodonite

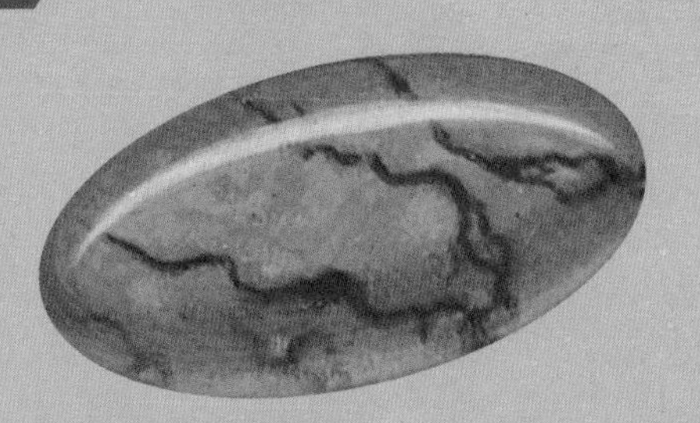

CHEMICAL FORMULA $Mn^{2+}SiO_3$ (manganese silicate)

COLOR Pink, red, brownish red to brown

CLEAVAGE Perfect

STREAK White

HARDNESS 5.5 to 6.5 on the Mohs scale

LUSTER Vitreous

SPECIFIC GRAVITY 3.57 to 3.76

WHAT IT IS USED FOR Gemstone, ornamental stone, healing crystal to balance emotions

POINT OF FACT This uncommon mineral is the state gem of Massachusetts.

FOUND IT!

WHEN

DATE

WHERE

SPECIFIC PLACE AND SURROUNDINGS

NOTES

Staurolite

CHEMICAL FORMULA $Fe^{2+}{}_2Al_9Si_4O_{23}(OH)$ (iron aluminum silicate)

COLOR Dark brown, brownish black, red brown

CLEAVAGE Good

STREAK White to grayish

HARDNESS 7 to 7.5 on the Mohs scale

LUSTER Resinous

SPECIFIC GRAVITY 14 to 19

WHAT IT IS USED FOR Collectors' mineral sometimes worn as jewelry. Geologists use it to identify the temperature and pressure conditions of a rock's metamorphosis.

POINT OF FACT Its name comes from Greek *stauros*, "cross," because its crystals commonly form a cross. It's the state mineral of Georgia.

FOUND IT!

WHEN
DATE

WHERE
SPECIFIC PLACE AND SURROUNDINGS

NOTES

Tourmaline

CHEMICAL FORMULA Complex boron silicates

COLOR Black, also blue, green, yellow, pink, red, orange, purple, brown, colorless

CLEAVAGE Poor

STREAK White or none

HARDNESS 7 to 7.5 on the Mohs scale

LUSTER Vitreous

SPECIFIC GRAVITY 2.9 to 3.3

WHAT IT IS USED FOR Gemstone, collectors' mineral, high-pressure gauges

POINT OF FACT Tourmaline is the state mineral of Maine.

FOUND IT!

WHEN

DATE

WHERE

SPECIFIC PLACE AND SURROUNDINGS

NOTES

Turquoise

CHEMICAL FORMULA $Cu(Al)_6(PO_4)_4(OH)_8 \cdot 4H_2O$ (hydrous copper aluminum phosphate)

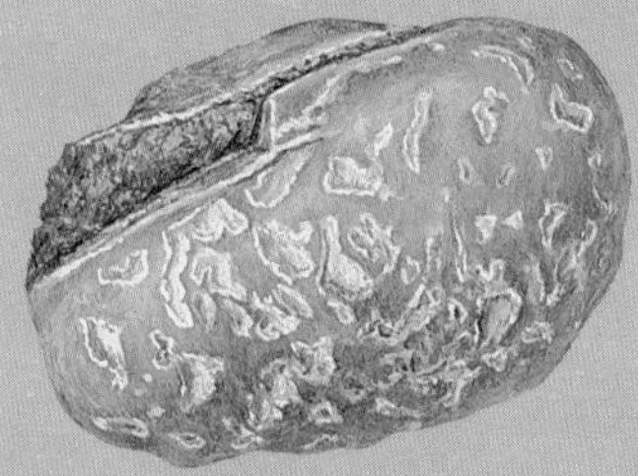

COLOR Sky blue, bluish green, apple green, greenish gray

CLEAVAGE Perfect

STREAK Pale greenish blue to white

HARDNESS 5 to 6 on the Mohs scale

LUSTER Waxy, dull

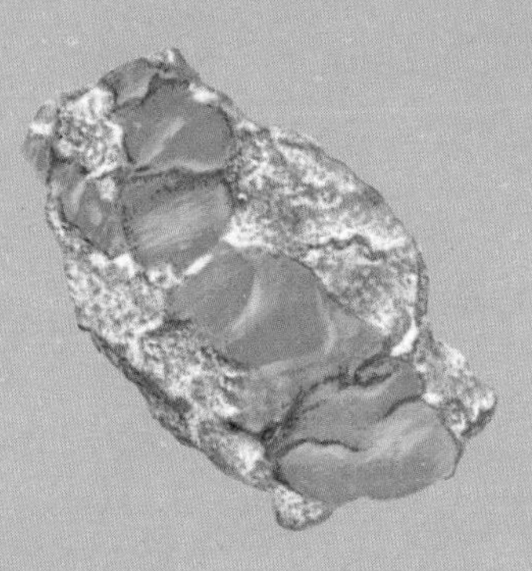

SPECIFIC GRAVITY 2.6 to 2.8

WHAT IT IS USED FOR Gemstone

POINT OF FACT Turquoise has been mined for its beauty since around 5000 BCE, and it is the state gem of Arizona.

WHEN

DATE

WHERE

SPECIFIC PLACE AND SURROUNDINGS

NOTES

Zircon

CHEMICAL FORMULA $ZrSiO_4$ (zirconium silicate)

COLOR Usually yellow, brown, red, also colorless, gray, blue, green

CLEAVAGE Basal

STREAK White

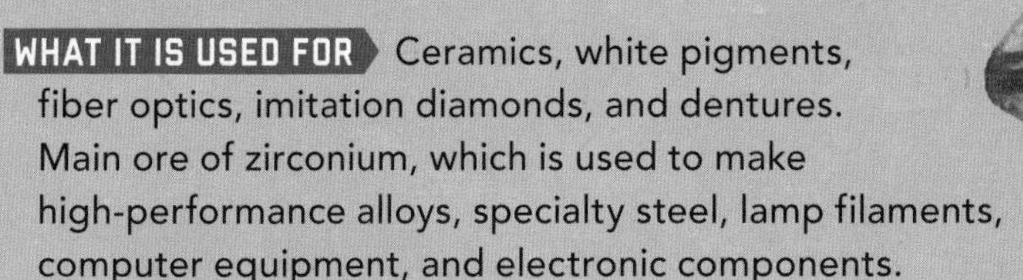

HARDNESS 7.5 on the Mohs scale

LUSTER Vitreous

SPECIFIC GRAVITY 14 to 19

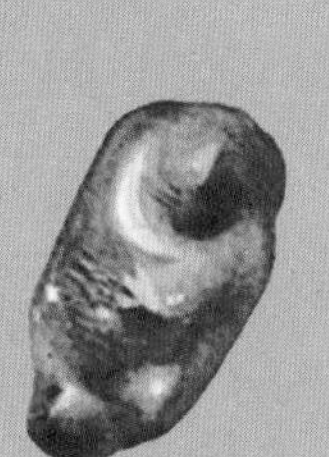

WHAT IT IS USED FOR Ceramics, white pigments, fiber optics, imitation diamonds, and dentures. Main ore of zirconium, which is used to make high-performance alloys, specialty steel, lamp filaments, computer equipment, and electronic components.

POINT OF FACT It has been mined from stream gravels for over two thousand years, mainly for use as a gemstone.

FOUND IT!

WHEN

DATE

WHERE

SPECIFIC PLACE AND SURROUNDINGS

NOTES

PART II

FOSSILS

What would YOU do?

Hefting your backpack filled with digging supplies onto your shoulders, you set out for the nearest stream. After all, that is where you can find sedimentary rocks, the *best* terrain for fossil hunting! As you walk along the stream, you keep your eyes peeled. Fossils are hard to spot. They can look like any regular, flat, smooth stone. The stream is filled with those types of rock. The continuous water running across them rubs off most of their rough edges. You pull out your sieve, fill it with rocks from the stream, and start sifting. A round one. Nope. A sharp one. Ouch! A rock that looks like a rectangle. Nothing special there.

Wait! What's that? A rock that's wide at one end and pointy at the other. You wipe it off for a closer look. That looks like a tooth! A very old one. It's all black and has weird looking lines on it. Could this be what you think it is? Did you happen to find a tooth from an ancient animal? A dinosaur? How do you know? How could you find out? What would you do?

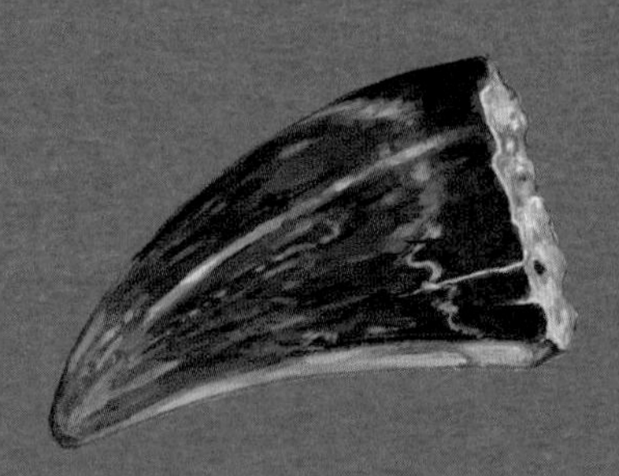

FOSSIL FINDING

NOTE As science advances, artistic renderings of fossils and dinosaurs often change. Please note that depictions are always evolving.

CHAPTER 8

Fossils & Where You Can Find Them

Fossils are preserved evidence of a plant or animal that lived in the past. Think of them as a snapshot in time of that particular plant or animal, one that is preserved forever for the future.

When you think of the word *fossil*, the first thing that pops into your head might be a dinosaur bone. Yes, dinosaur bones are fossils, but fossils can be made of anything: feathers, bones, shells, leaves, even footprints and poop. A fossil does not have to be the remains of a plant or animal. They can simply be traces or imprints of those organisms that are left behind in rocks. Rocks? Yes! Fossils are rocks! Even the bones and teeth. And like all rocks, it takes a looooong time for fossils to form. A fossil isn't generally considered a fossil until it's at least ten thousand years old.

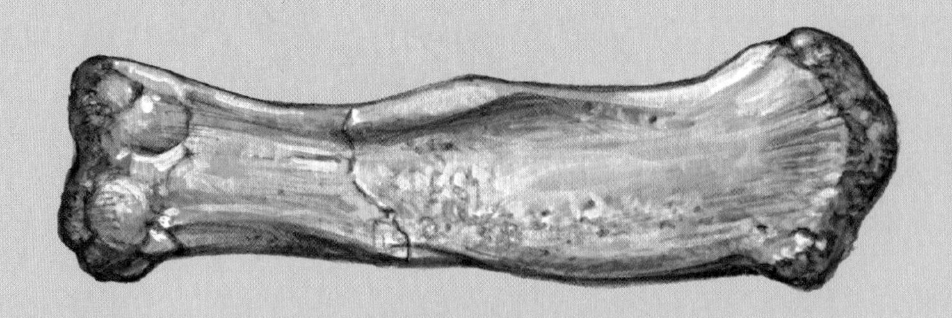

Fossil or Bone?

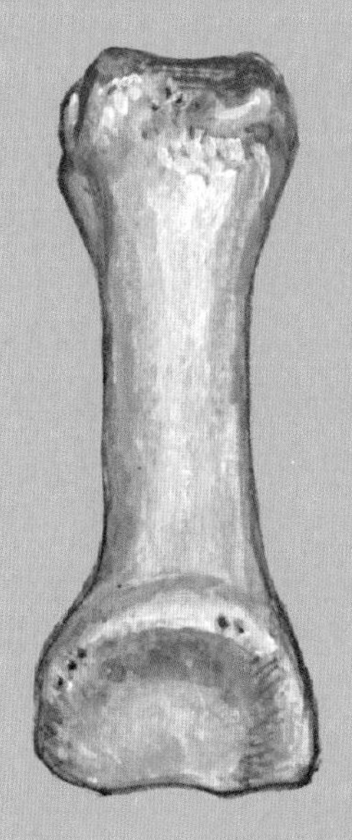

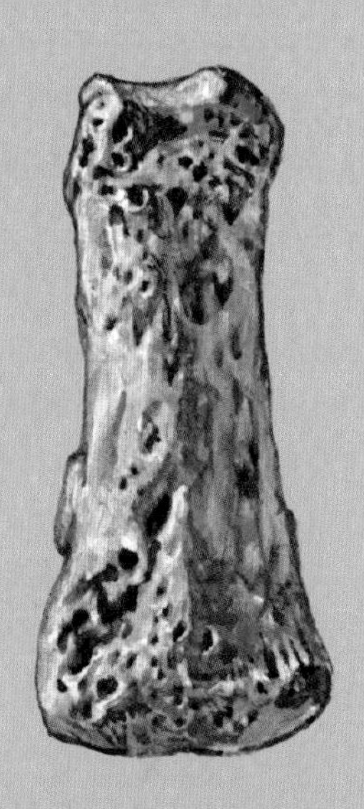

The main difference between the bones in your body and a bone fossil is that your bones are porous. A bone fossil is harder and denser than actual bone. It is also darker in color, because minerals have filled in the pores, or spaces, inside it. A fossilized bone will most likely be brown or black, or possibly even dark yellow or red or blue.

Permineralization

Fossils form in several different ways, but the most common method is through permineralization. That means that ten thousand or more years ago, a plant or animal died and started to decay. The organic matter that was left over from the decaying plant or animal was covered fairly quickly by sediment. The sediment cover protected the organic matter from weathering and erosion and slowed down the decay.

Over thousands of years, water seeped through the sediment, depositing dissolved minerals (most often calcite, pyrite, or silica) in the organic matter. These minerals crystallized and hardened. Bits of the original organism remain, but the added minerals essentially turn them into a rock that a scientist, or *you*, will hope to find in the future.

* Don't forget, *organic* means anything related to or produced by a living thing. So you are organic, and so is everything that comes out of you. (Yep, that means poop, pee, snot, toenail clippings.)

PERMINERALIZATION

The animal dies and starts to decay.

Layer after layer of sediment covers the organic matter, slowing the decay.

Water seeps through the sediment, depositing dissolved minerals into the decaying organic matter. The water evaporates and the minerals crystallize, forming—you guessed it—sedimentary rock!

Often water will continue to react with the permineralized fossil, dissolving every bit of organic matter away. This results in a progression of permineralization called replacement.

A replacement fossil.

You can see why fossils tend to form in and around watery environments. Tiny bits of sediment drop out easily from slow-moving water and quickly cover an organism. They attach to the organic matter of the organism and seal out oxygen (kind of like plastic wrap). As sediments build up on top of the organism, it is eventually buried under layers of mud. Safely inside the sediment, and without oxygen and moisture, what's left of the original organism decays very slowly, leaving bones, or even impressions from soft-bodied organisms like jellyfish, behind to form the fossil you will one day find.

Water is not the only place where fossils form. Other circumstances can take place that cover an organism quickly, sealing out oxygen and preventing decay. Volcanic eruptions spew out millions of tons of ash in a hurry, burying everything in their path. Sticky tree sap oozes down and coats the bones of the animal or plant, eventually hardening and preserving it in amber forever. Ice works well for preserving fossils, too. Sometimes if the entire animal freezes quickly, more of it is preserved.

Fossils of Different Organisms

Fossils are usually classified in the same categories as life-forms you would find today: invertebrates, vertebrates, and plants. An invertebrate is an animal without a backbone. Some major groups of invertebrates are arthropods, mollusks, annelids, and cnidarians. Invertebrates that you might know are insects, earthworms, sponges, centipedes, spiders, sea urchins, starfish, and jellyfish.

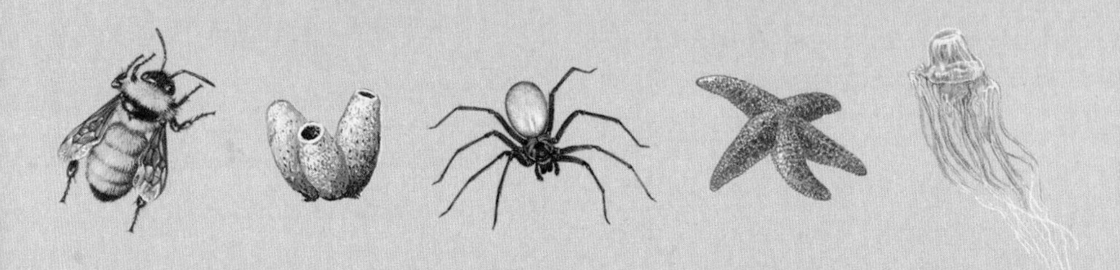

Vertebrates are animals that have a backbone (as you do). These include: reptiles, birds, fish, mammals, and amphibians. Some common vertebrates you might know are frogs, blue jays, sharks, elephants, lions, humans, snakes, and crocodiles.

Plants are trees, shrubs, and flowers, but also ferns and mosses. They are living things with roots, leaves, and stems that grow in the earth, or maybe in a pot in your house.

This piece of wood has fossilized around the edges, but inside, the wood is still soft and could give you a splinter if you ran your finger across it.

Does Everything Become a Fossil?

No. Only certain conditions allow an organism to be preserved as a fossil:

- The plant or animal must be covered by sediment soon after it dies. This keeps the organism safe from damage by scavengers, erosion, and weathering.
- The sediment creates an environment that is cold and dry and without oxygen. This prevents the microbes from breaking down the organism completely as they normally would.
- Organisms that have skeletons or other hard parts are not typically eaten and are naturally resistant to decay. Which is why many fossils are bones. Soft tissue, however, breaks down easily leaving nothing behind.

Body or Trace Fossil?

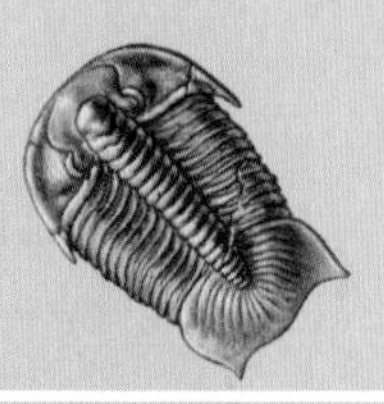

Fossils fall into two categories based on what kind of evidence of past life they record.

BODY FOSSILS Preserve or record parts of a plant or animal, such as teeth, claws, bones, leaves, stems, feathers, eggs, and shells. Rarely, a body fossil will be found of an entire organism. Body fossils give scientists an idea of what an ancient organism might have looked like—its size, shape, and structure.

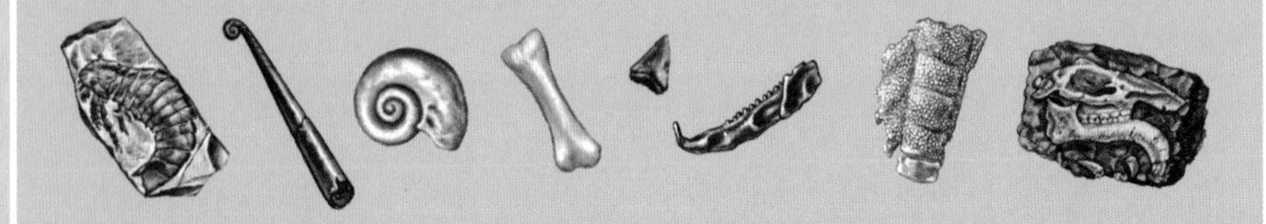

TRACE FOSSILS Show the trace of an ancient animal, not the actual animal itself. This can be in the form of movement, like a footprint, a track mark from talons or claws, or even a trail that an animal leaves. Or it could be an ancient nest, without any animal remains inside of it. Perhaps it is a burrow, where an animal once lived. Scientists love finding trace fossils because it shows them a lot about how an animal behaved during its lifetime.

Dinosaur footprints in sandstone

Molds and Casts

Casts or molds can be both body and trace fossils. They're formed when an imprint of an animal or plant is made in a rock. The imprint is created after the organism itself has been buried by sediment and decomposed. Over time, minerals seep through the rock and dissolve the hard shell or bones away. What is left is a three-dimensional impression of an organism's surface nooks and crannies. A mold is formed when the there is an empty space in the rock above the fossil imprint. Casts form when water deposits sediments in the cavity. The sediments fill in the imprint and form a cast, sort of like the plaster cast that might be made over a broken bone.

MOLD FOSSIL

CAST FOSSIL

Carbonization

All organic matter, dead or alive, plant or animal, contains the element carbon. (Yes, even you!) When an animal or plant dies and is first covered and then compressed by all of the sediment pushing down on it, the animal or plant gets crushed. (Imagine running over a chocolate bar with your car tire—Smoosh!) The crushed organism leaves a black carbon imprint on the rock. Over millions of years, the layers of sediment push the compressed organism deeper and deeper into the earth. At this depth, the temperatures are much higher within the earth. These high temperatures basically "cook" the organic matter in the organism. The result is a carbonized fossil.

Carbonized fossil of a fern

Whole Fossils

On rare occasions, an organism's whole body is preserved. That means every part of the body, even the soft tissues, such as skin, eyes, muscles, hair, or feathers. Amber does this on a small scale when it encases whole insects and other organisms in tree sap. Dehydration, or lack of water, can preserve whole bodies when organisms die in extremely dry climates and caves. Whole-body fossils have been found encased in ice, too. Scientists love to find this type of fossil because they can see what the actual animal looked like. Of course, keeping this fossil intact is difficult. If you thaw it out, the body will start to decompose. On the other hand, it's kind of tough to keep a giant woolly mammoth frozen. Takes up a lot of freezer space!

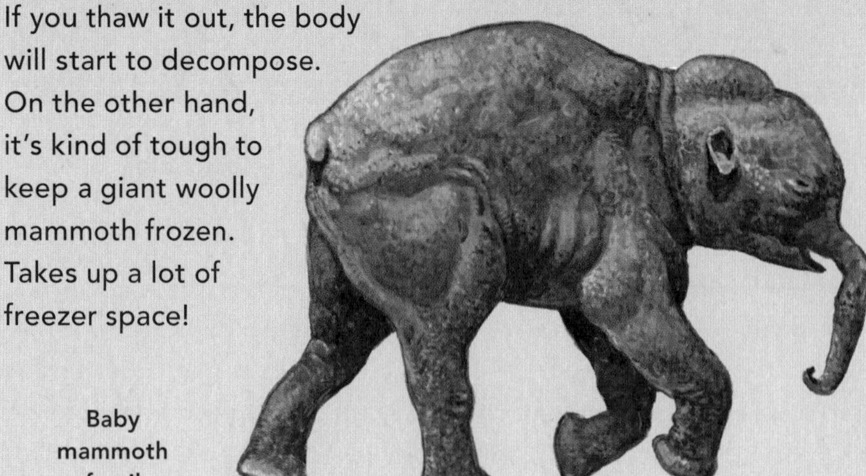
Baby mammoth fossil

Where Can You Find Fossils?

Despite all the requirements for their formation, fossils can be found anywhere, maybe even in your own backyard. Fossils have been known to turn up in the strangest places.

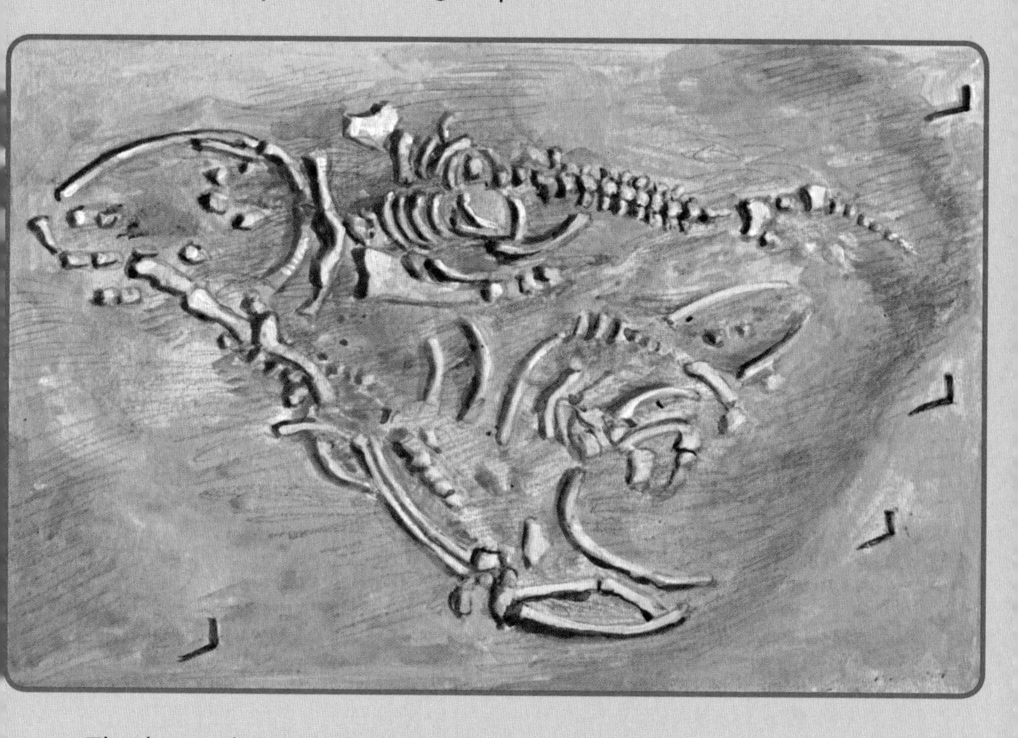

The best places to look for fossils are in and around deserts or near the edges of rivers and lakes. You can also find fossils along coasts, on the shore, in river valleys, inland cliffs, and bluffs. People have even found fossils along the side of a road, in a forest, or right outside their front door.

Want to know how a paleontologist, a scientist who studies fossils, searches for fossils? They take a look at rock formations. Remember that sedimentary rocks are a great place to find fossils. Try checking a geologic map for rock formations from a specific time period of the fossil you are looking for. Then pick out an area that appears to have a lot of hills and valleys, maybe some canyons or high outcrop rocks. Those are all great places to begin hunting for fossils!

You can also go on the internet to identify hunting grounds. Consult paleontology websites like myFossil and the Paleobiology Database for information and maps of just about every fossil ever documented on the planet.

The big question is, how do you know whether what you've found is an actual fossil?

What Do Fossils Look Like?

Unfortunately, most fossils that you will encounter probably won't look like something you will recognize right away.

Here are a few things to look for when you are hunting fossils:

- Fossils are found mostly in sedimentary rock. That means the rock might look like it has layers.
- Permineralized fossils feel smooth and soft, unlike most rocks, which are rough.
- Fossils are often brown or black in color. This is because they have taken on the colors of the minerals in the rocks around them.
- Rocks that contain fossils will often have an impression or outline of an animal or plant. This might look like a shell, a leaf, or bones of an organism. Something like this:

SHELL IMPRINT

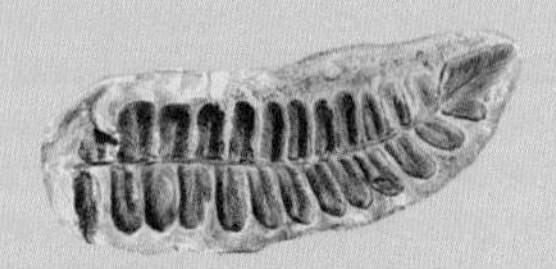

LEAF IMPRINT

FISH IMPRINT

→ Permineralized fossils have a specific shape. For example, a piece of leg bone is going to be more long and narrow. A shark's tooth will be shaped sort of like a triangle with wide base and a sharp, pointy end.

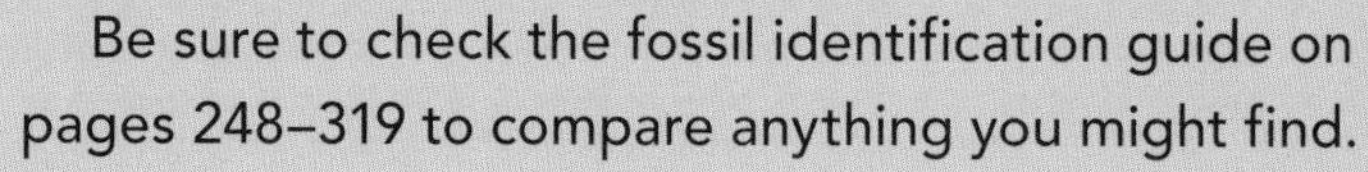

Be sure to check the fossil identification guide on pages 248–319 to compare anything you might find.

Is That a Real Bone or a Fake?

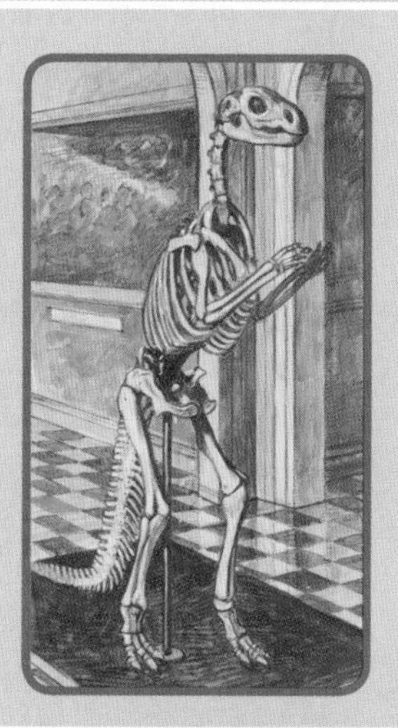

You might be surprised to learn that most fossils on display at museums are not the real ones. Instead many of them are casts or molds of the actual fossil. Using a mold for display keeps the real fossil safe and prevents it from being damaged by the strong lights in the display. Wonder whether you are looking at the real thing or a fake? Look at the card next to the display. It will tell you.

Before You Start Digging

Be aware of the rules that apply to the place you plan to dig *before* you remove any fossils.

→ If you are in your own backyard and your parents are okay with you digging it up, that's fine. If you are on someone else's property, you *must* get permission before you start digging. If you don't have permission to dig, then just look for fossils on the surface of the ground.

- → If you are going to a place that is known to have fossils, you must have permission to remove them. It is illegal to take fossils from some public property, particularly national parks, monuments, and any area managed by the Fish and Wildlife Service.

- → Be sure to look up the Bureau of Land Management (BLM) rules for an area before you decide to remove a fossil. According to the BLM, casual collection of fossils (meaning you don't plan to sell them), is fine on most lands if the fossil you take is a plant or invertebrate fossil. These include: stem and leaf impressions, traces of roots, and even organic material. For invertebrates you can take fossilized remains of animals such as snails, oysters, ammonites, corals, and shellfish. If these animals have left traces, tracks, or impressions in rocks, that is fine as well.

- → Note that casual collecting means that you are only taking a very small amount of fossils or rocks with you. These would then be used by you for your own collection, and not put on public display anywhere. Nor would you sell them to anyone.

- → Be aware of any posted signs on a property. If they specifically prohibit you from removing objects, follow those guidelines. When in doubt, do your research before you pick something up and take it home. Ask questions of the person who runs the area before taking anything. And remember, if you find something really cool, you'll probably want to call in a local paleontologist to check it out.

TRACK IT ↘

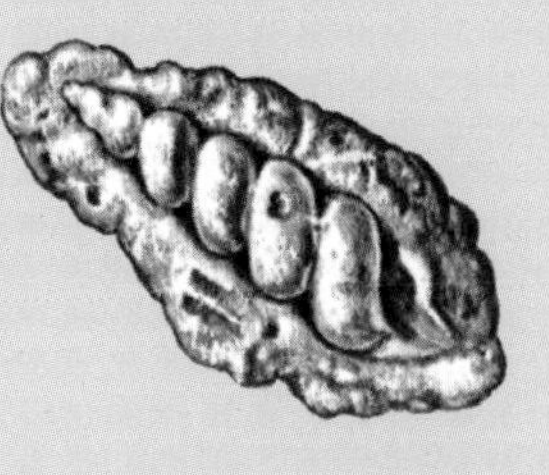

Explore Your Surroundings For Fossils

Hunting for fossils is a big job. Sometimes you find a fossil right away. Other times you can look for hours (or days) and not find anything. The thing to remember is that you should look everywhere.

WHAT YOU'LL NEED

- A pen or pencil and a piece of paper or this book

STEP 1 Pick a safe place to explore. It could be a local park, rocky trail, mountain, stream, lake, or even your own backyard. Research the most likely place to find fossils nearby. Find a geologic map, look for rock formations, and pick the most likely spot.

Look for these kinds of places:

- streams or rivers with sandbanks
- dry, sandy places (like a desert)
- sandy beaches (of oceans or lakes)
- mountains or outcrops that are made from sedimentary rock such as shale or sandstone

STEP 2 Before you start hunting, create or find a map of the area you plan to explore. Either draw one on the next page or print one out and tape it inside this book.

STEP 3 Now look at your map. Circle the kinds of places listed in step 1. Although fossils can be found anywhere, these areas will be the best place to start looking. Once you've figured out where to look, it's time to grab your gear and go!

Finding Fossils

WHAT YOU'LL NEED

➢ A dry day, a strong backpack, twelve bags or containers that close easily or an empty egg carton, a permanent marker and a roll of masking tape to make labels, a water bottle and a snack (fossil hunting can make you hungry!), a small hand shovel or trowel, gloves, safety goggles or glasses, safety hat, your fossil-finding map, a map and compass (even if you have a smartphone with GPS), camera, glue, a roll of paper towels or toilet paper (for wrapping your fossil), a bag of plaster of paris to create your plaster cast, a plastic bowl, a bottle of water (for your plaster), a small clean paintbrush (to brush dirt off fossils), a chisel and hammer, a magnifying glass, and a couple of small flags (you can make these out of a stick and a piece of cloth or paper).

Fossils can be found in many different places. Perhaps part of a fossil is peeking out from a pile of dirt or sand. Once you see signs of a fossil, assemble your tools and get ready to start quarrying, or working to remove the fossil from the rock. If the sand or soil is loose around your fossil, use your shovel or brush to clear as much of the area as you can. As you uncover the fossil, you may realize that part of it is stuck in a bigger piece of rock. Now you need to work a little more carefully. Taking a fossil out of a piece of rock is not so easy.

STEP 1 Put on your safety hat and gloves, and have your goggles handy. Use the map you created to help you figure out where to start. Walk around areas you circled on the map. Move slowly and look for oddly shaped rocks or ones with lines on them. Pick up a few and inspect them closely.

STEP 2 If you see something that might be a fossil (like a rock with a marking on it), pull on your goggles and then use your brush to remove the top soil, dirt, or mud from around it.

STEP 3 If you believe this is a fossil, take out your tools. First, find out if the fossil is attached to a piece of rock. If it is, go to step 4. If it's not attached to a rock, take a few pictures of it. You want to have a picture of it where you found it. Skip to step 8.

STEP 4 If your fossil is attached to a rock, you may want to protect it before you try to remove it from the rock. Use the glue you brought and squeeze it into the cracks of the fossil. Allow to dry. This will hopefully keep your fossil together as you remove it.

STEP 5 Cover the top of the fossil with several layers of paper towels or toilet paper.

STEP 6 Make your plaster of paris mold to create a protective shell over the fossil. This will keep the fossil safe as you excavate it from the rock.

Make sure you are wearing your goggles, then make the plaster of paris by mixing one part water to two parts plaster in the plastic bowl. Quickly pour the plaster over the paper-covered fossil and let it harden (about 30–45 minutes).

STEP 7 Take out your chisel and your hammer and carefully break up the rock around the fossil. Be sure to leave a little distance around the plaster and the rock. You don't want to damage the fossil. Work diligently. Chiseling fossils out of rock can take time. But it is well worth the effort if you are able to remove the fossil intact. Once it's free, move to step 8.

STEP 8 Before removing the fossil, note its position on your map or type it into your GPS. The most important thing about fossils is to know exactly where you found them, so stop here and record the fossil entry in the chart on page 227.

STEP 9 Gently pick up the fossil and wrap it in a paper towel or a few pieces of toilet paper. Place it into a container, and label it with a number. That way you know which fossil is which when you identify them later. Be careful when handling a fossil! Remember it could be hundreds of thousands or even millions of years old. It's fragile.

STEP 10 Before moving on, take another good look at what you've found. Does it look like it could be part of something? If it's a piece of an animal, maybe other parts of the skeleton or teeth are nearby. Continue digging and brushing. Sometimes you can find a bunch of fossils in one place.

What to Do If You Find Something BIG

If you happen to find a fossil that looks like it might be a bone, stop digging. Mark the area on your map. Call an adult who can come and look at what you've found and help you decide what to do next. If you think it is really a bone of an ancient animal, you will want to call a local paleontologist. Look up the number of the paleontology department in a nearby college, university, or museum. If you don't have access to any of those, you could call the town's historical society.

Be sure to provide the following information:

→ A picture of the fossil you found.

→ The fossil's location (GPS coordinates, a street address, specific trail in the park, etc.).

→ How you found the fossil: Did you dig it up? Was it lying on the ground? Under water?

→ Time and date you found the fossil.

→ Ask whether you should stay at the fossil's location until someone gets there. If that is not possible, carefully cover the area with dirt to keep it safe, and put one of your flags in the ground to mark its position. Make sure you have marked the location correctly on your map, so you can come back and find it, too.

TRACK IT ↘ Describe Your Fossil-Finding Field

Fill out the chart below with where you discovered your fossils by writing a few notes down about the area around them. Was it flat, mountainous, near a lake? Was it wet? Dry? Did you have to dig the fossil out? Was it found in a running stream or a still lake?

FOSSIL #	DESCRIBE THE AREA AROUND THE FOSSIL

You may need to go hunting many more times to find enough fossils to fill out this chart. But that's good. More time outside exploring!

I DID IT! DATE:

Trace, Body, or Rock?

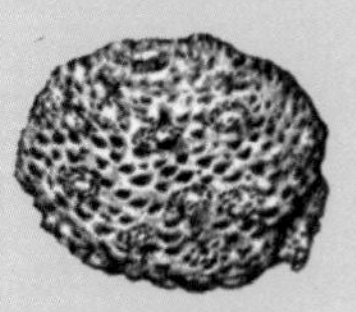

Time to decide whether your fossils are body or trace fossils, or yes, just rocks! Fill in the chart below.

FOSSIL #

HOW DID IT FOSSILIZE?

- ☐ TRACE
- ☐ BODY
- ☐ ROCK

FOSSIL #

HOW DID IT FOSSILIZE?

- ☐ TRACE
- ☐ BODY
- ☐ ROCK

FOSSIL #

HOW DID IT FOSSILIZE?

- ☐ TRACE
- ☐ BODY
- ☐ ROCK

FOSSIL #

HOW DID IT FOSSILIZE?

- [ ] TRACE
- [ ] BODY
- [ ] ROCK

FOSSIL #

HOW DID IT FOSSILIZE?

- [ ] TRACE
- [ ] BODY
- [ ] ROCK

FOSSIL #

HOW DID IT FOSSILIZE?

- [ ] TRACE
- [ ] BODY
- [ ] ROCK

➢ Are you unsure of which category to mark for your fossil? Perhaps your fossil doesn't have any marks on it that can help. For now, put an X in the rock column. And don't feel bad. There is such a thing as a pseudofossil. These are rocks that look like fossils but really aren't. They might be just a mineral deposit that was never part of an animal or plant. Pseudofossils can fool paleontologists, too.

TRY IT → Clean Up Your Collection

Before you go through your collection to see what you have, let's give those fossils you found a good scrub. Make sure to remove the plaster cast if you made one. This can be done by gently tapping the plaster with a hard object, like your hammer or chisel, and breaking off or brushing off the remaining pieces.

If your fossil is still surrounded by bits of rock, use a smaller chisel or a tiny hammer to remove what you can. Sometimes it's tough to determine what is fossil and what is rock, so pay close attention to what you are doing. You want to remove as much rock around the fossil as you can, but don't worry if there are still tiny pieces attached to the fossil. Paleontologists may leave some of this rock around the fossil, or use a chemical treatment if they aren't able to safely remove the remaining rock using tools.

WHAT YOU'LL NEED

- Your fossil collection, water (at least two gallons), vinegar (two tablespoons), two buckets, paper towels or a cloth towel that you can get dirty, and a toothbrush or small scrub brush.

STEP 1 Pour one gallon of water into one bucket and add two tablespoons of vinegar.

STEP 2 Pour a gallon of fresh water into the second bucket.

STEP 3 One at a time (you don't want to mix up which fossil goes with which number), use the brush to clean each of your fossils gently with the vinegar and water mixture.

STEP 4 Dunk each fossil into the bucket of fresh water to rinse it.

STEP 5 Gently pat the fossil dry with the paper towels or cloth towel. You want it to be clean and dry.

If you want to better preserve your fossil, you can paint it with resin. It doesn't affect the fossil itself, just makes it less fragile.

TAKE IT TO THE NEXT LEVEL

Rock or Fossil? Use the Lick Test!

After all your fossils are very clean, you will want to lick each one. Yes, you read that correctly. A very good test to tell whether you have a fossil or just a rock is to lick it. Paleontologists do this in the field all the time. However, if you are going to lick the rock, be sure to clean it well first! I know we said not to taste rocks earlier, but it is okay to lick one here if you're fairly certain it's a fossil and you cleaned it really well. Just to be safe, perhaps you'd better ask your parent or guardian first. And hey, maybe they will lick the rock, too. How can licking a fossil tell you that it's a fossil? Your tongue will stick slightly to a fossil. That is because fossilized bone is very dry and a little bit spongy. When your wet tongue encounters the spongy fossilized bone, it sticks, just a little. If that happens, cheer, because you have indeed found a fossil!

CHAPTER 9

Big Fossil Finds & Running an Excavation

It is every paleontologist and rock hunter's dream to find a really big fossil, like an entire dinosaur, or a big area with a lot of fossils in one place. Fortunately, there are many large fossil finds and dig sites around the world. The La Brea Tar Pits in Los Angeles, California, is one of the biggest. Paleontologists have found more than sixty species of mammals, about 140 species of birds, and hundreds of plants and insects all in one small area. They range in size from saber-toothed cats, mammoths, and dire wolves, to tiny microfossils of plants and insects. Apparently, it was once an ancient forest, then perhaps a savannah, where many different animals lived, ate, and interacted with one another. Eventually oil oozed up to the surface, creating lakes of sticky black tar that trapped unwary animals and whatever else happened to land on it. The animals would eventually die and then sink into the deep tar pit.

50,000 YEARS AGO

TODAY

More than a hundred different excavations have taken place at La Brea. Visit the pit today and see a recreation of a mammoth becoming trapped in the "tar."

TRY IT → Make Your Own Fossil Dig Site

Paleontologists look for fossils and then set up a dig site around what they find. They don't use a grid system, but allow the bones to guide where they need to dig. But if you aren't quite sure where to start, how do you set up an excavation, especially if there's nothing but just plain dirt? Try using a coordinate grid. This is what archaeologists, scientists who study ancient civilizations, do.

WHAT YOU'LL NEED

- A place to dig, small shovel or trowel, small unused paintbrush, containers or bags for collecting specimens, thirty sticks (bought or found), ball of string, scissors, paper and tape to make small flags, tape measure, pencil and marker, camera, and a roll of paper towels or toilet paper, plaster of paris, plastic bowl, bottle of water, hammer and chisel.

STEP 1 Find a place to dig. It might be in your backyard, a park, the woods, the mountains, or the beach. If you are in a public place, make sure you have permission before you start.

STEP 2 Decide how big to make your digging area. The best way to make this grid is to measure the whole space and divide it up into equal squares.

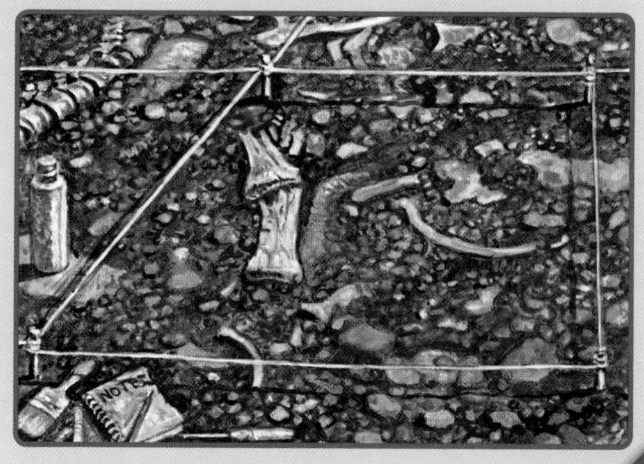

For example, if your area is two feet by two feet, then you will want to make four squares of about one foot by one foot each.

STEP 3 Place a stick in each corner of your digging area. Tie the string to the first stick and wind it around the sticks, creating a perimeter.

STEP 4 Lay your tape measure along each side of the square and place sticks at even intervals.

STEP 5 Measure and cut string long enough to stretch across your grid. Tie the end of one string to a perimeter stick and pull it across the square to its partner on the opposite side and tie it off. Do the same for the remaining pairs of perimeter sticks.

STEP 6 Take the paper or flags and place one on each stick in the grid. Number the flag in each square. That way you know which one you are working in.

STEP 7 Draw your grid below. Be sure to number all the squares the same as you have numbered the digging area. You will record anything you find on this grid.

STEP 8 Start digging! Pick a square. It doesn't have to be number one. You can start right in the middle if you want. Just remember you will need to be standing in a different grid from the one you are digging in. Start by brushing sand or dirt away with your brush. If you don't find something in a few minutes, give your shovel a try. But don't dig very deep. You don't want to damage a possible fossil with your shovel! When you shovel the dirt, it's best to move it off the grid completely.

STEP 9 If you find a possible fossil, put your shovel aside and start using your brush again. You will want to gently sweep the sand off the fossil so that you can see the whole thing. Once you can see it completely, don't move it! Instead, take a picture and later add it to the chart on the following pages. Make sure your picture includes the grid number.

STEP 10 Mark the fossil on the following pages. If the fossil stretches across two or more squares, be sure to note that in the picture you take as well as on the following pages. Place a pile of paper towels or toilet paper on top of your fossil.

STEP 11 Dig a trench around the fossil. Prepare your plaster by mixing one part water to two parts plaster in the plastic bowl. Quickly pour the plaster over the paper-covered fossil. Let it harden (about 30–45 minutes). Then dig around your mold and remove it from the ground.

STEP 12 If the fossil is embedded in rock, you will need to gently chisel it out with your hammer. Take your hammer and use the chisel to break apart the rock around the fossil.

STEP 13 Once the fossil is free, lift it out gently. Place it on some paper towels and wrap it up. Write the number of the grids on the paper towels and place it into a container.

I DID IT! DATE:

TRACK IT ↘ Excavated Fossils

Record the fossils you found on your dig on the chart below.

FOSSIL #

GRID #

PICTURE

NOTES POSITION, DEPTH, TYPE OF SOIL/SAND, ETC.

FOSSIL #

GRID #

PICTURE

NOTES POSITION, DEPTH, TYPE OF SOIL/SAND, ETC.

FOSSIL #

GRID #

NOTES POSITION, DEPTH, TYPE OF SOIL/SAND, ETC.

PICTURE

FOSSIL #

GRID #

NOTES POSITION, DEPTH, TYPE OF SOIL/SAND, ETC.

PICTURE

CHAPTER 10

Dating Your Fossils

Finding a fossil is awesome. Identifying it is great. But being able to date it is even better. This will tell you when the organism lived. Everyone should know their birth date, right?

Geologic Time Scale

Scientists have come up with a time line to describe the history of our planet called the geologic time scale. The scale divides time into chunks based on significant events in the earth's history. Eons are the biggest chunks, and they are divided into eras, then periods, epochs, and ages. The geologic time scale allows you to "jump through time" to see what type of life forms lived there, what the climate was like, and the geology of the planet. Were there continents? Huge oceans?

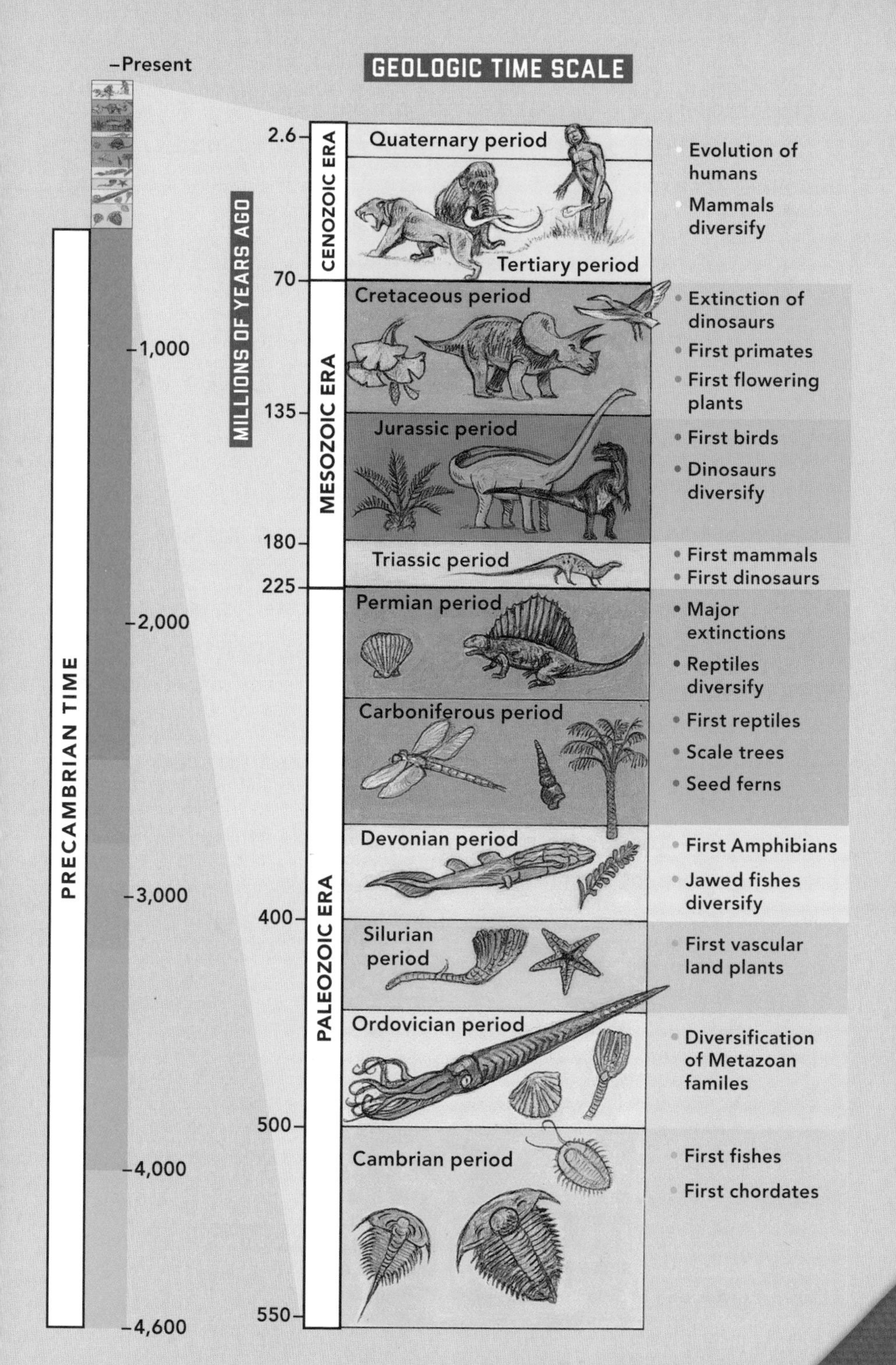
GEOLOGIC TIME SCALE
–Present
–1,000
–2,000
–3,000
–4,000
–4,600
PRECAMBRIAN TIME
MILLIONS OF YEARS AGO
2.6
70
135
180
225
400
500
550
CENOZOIC ERA
MESOZOIC ERA
PALEOZOIC ERA
Quaternary period
Tertiary period
Cretaceous period
Jurassic period
Triassic period
Permian period
Carboniferous period
Devonian period
Silurian period
Ordovician period
Cambrian period
Evolution of humans
Mammals diversify
Extinction of dinosaurs
First primates
First flowering plants
First birds
Dinosaurs diversify
First mammals
First dinosaurs
Major extinctions
Reptiles diversify
First reptiles
Scale trees
Seed ferns
First Amphibians
Jawed fishes diversify
First vascular land plants
Diversification of Metazoan familes
First fishes
First chordates

Take a look at the time scale. You can see that the Triassic period begins after the largest mass extinction in the earth's history. During this time, 85 to 90 percent of invertebrates in the oceans died out. Seventy percent of the land invertebrates did, too. The Triassic period ends with another mass extinction of sea life, and the Jurassic period begins.

Once scientists came up with the geologic time scale, they used it to create maps that are great for finding and dating rocks and fossils.

Reading a Geologic Map

Paleontologists use geologic maps to help them figure out where they might find a fossil. A geologic map shows the age and layers of the rocks in the area, fault lines and places where two tectonic plates might meet. Different colors on the map indicate types of rock and their age. Paleontologists look for rock strata, or layers, of certain ages when they are looking for fossils. That makes sense since the rock or soil must have been around about the time the organism lived. Because of this they try to focus on sedimentary rock or older layers of rock.

Every geologic map has a key, which shows the colors of each rock and where they fit into the geologic time scale.

GEOLOGIC MAP OF THE UNITED STATES

QUATERNARY Rocks and unconsolidated deposits of Pleistocene and Recent age

TERTIARY Rocks of Paleocene, Eocene, Oligocene, Miocene, and Pliocene age

MESOZOIC Rocks of Triassic, Jurassic, and Createaceous age

LATE PALEOZOIC Rocks of Devonian, Carboniferous, and Permian age

EARLY PALEOZOIC Rocks of Cambrian, Ordovician, and Silurian age

PRECAMBRIAN A variety of igneous, metamorphic, and sedimentary rocks (includes some metamorphosed Paleozoic)

EXTRUSIVE IGNEOUS ROCKS Chiefly lava flows of Tertiary and Quaternary age

INTRUSIVE IGNEOUS ROCKS (includes some metamorphic rocks) Granitoid rocks of various ages

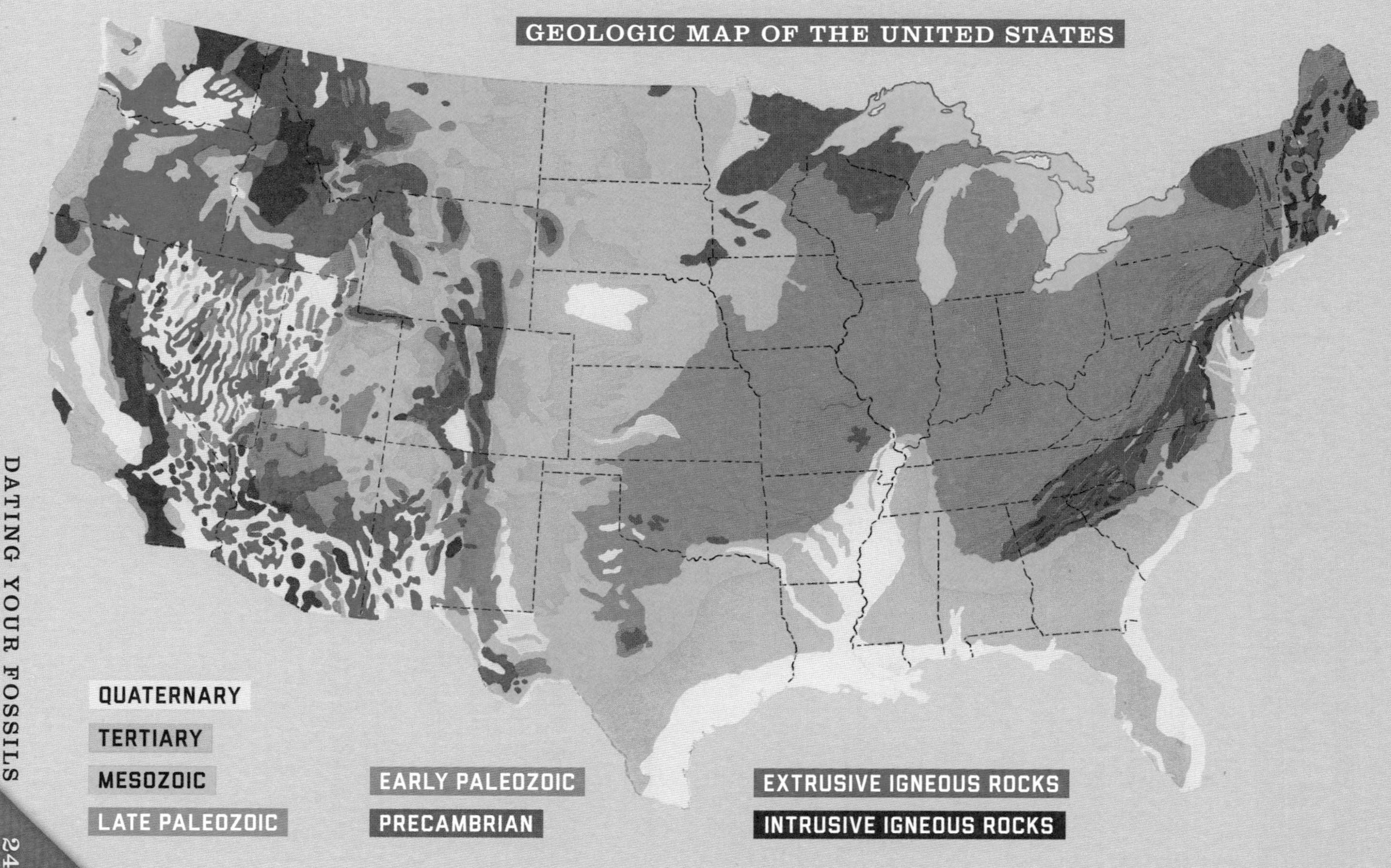
GEOLOGIC MAP OF THE UNITED STATES
QUATERNARY
TERTIARY
MESOZOIC
LATE PALEOZOIC
EARLY PALEOZOIC
PRECAMBRIAN
EXTRUSIVE IGNEOUS ROCKS
INTRUSIVE IGNEOUS ROCKS

TRY IT →

Using Geological Maps

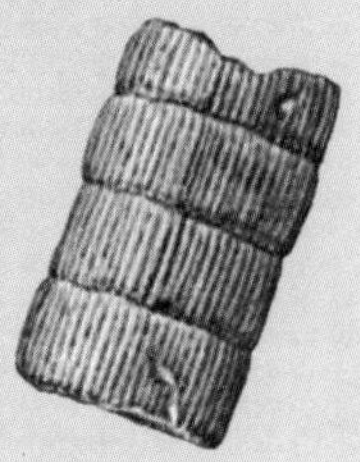

Look at the map on the previous page for fossils you're interested in finding, fossils that might be found near your home, or to learn more about the fossils you've collected.

STEP 1 Look at the key to the map. It lists the different eras of the geologic time scale. Pick a time scale of a fossil you would want to find.

STEP 2 Let's say you are looking for a calamite, a plant that existed in the Carboniferous period (more than 300 million years ago). You will need to search the map for the blue color of that period. Can you see it? If your plan is to find the calamite, that is where you would start.

STEP 3 Before the paleontologist goes to the site, they might look up that area on an internet mapping system like Google Maps. They want to see what the land actually looks like. They are looking for exposed rock that they can dig. Not a place where a lake or pond is found. You can do that with the area you have found, too.

PRO TIP Looking for a place to find fossils around you? Check out the National Geologic Map Database online.

TRY IT → Dating Your Fossils

Scientists look at the position of sedimentary rocks and use advanced techniques like measuring radioactive decay to determine the age of the fossils inside. You are going to use a more common way to date your fossils, by comparing each one to a known fossil that has already been dated. First, you'll have to determine what life-form the fossil preserves: plant, vertebrate, or invertebrate. Once you have identified the life-form, you will need to figure out the species of plant or animal. That is a bit more difficult. You will need to compare the size, structure, shape, and color of each part of your fossil with fossils that have already been identified. For that you will use the fossil identification guide in this book. But of course, not every fossil that has ever been discovered is in this guide. You might need to use additional resources for help with fossil identification.

To start, here are a few things to know and tools to use:

- Most fossils are invertebrates. Think worms, insects, clams, snails, and coral—just to name a few. Ninety-seven percent of all animals on earth today are invertebrates. Scientists believe there may have been even more invertebrates in the past.
- Study the map on page 241. This will give you an idea of what type of fossils are found where.
- See whether there have been any big fossil finds near where you found your fossil. If there have, it is possible that a paleontologist has already determined the era of this dig. Your fossil is likely the same age!

➢ Try fossil identification apps like the Digital Atlas of Ancient Life from the University of Kansas.

➢ Contact a paleontologist at a local college or university to see whether they will look at your fossil. They will most likely be familiar with the fossils typically found in your area.

Some fossils are easy to identify and date. Others take more time. Be patient. Keep hunting until you find the answer. And if no one knows what your fossil is, get excited. Maybe you discovered a new species!

This table shows when the different types of life-forms began to appear on earth. It will not give you an exact date for your fossil. But it can offer you a starting point to determine a fossil's age.

PERIOD
Quaternary
Tertiary
Cretaceous
Jurassic
Triassic
Permian
Carboniferous
Devonian
Silurian
Ordovician
Cambrian

ANIMALS
Animals with shells
Fishes
Amphibians
Reptiles
Mammals
Birds
Humans

PLANTS
Club mosses
Horsetail rushes
Ferns
Pines
Ginkos
Flowering Plants

TRACK IT ↘

What Did You Find?

Now comes the real test. Can you figure out exactly what type of fossil you found and how old it is? Do you know the plant or animal name? Get ready to work hard—this might take some real investigating!

FOSSIL #

ERA

HOW OLD IS IT?

NOTES

FOSSIL #

ERA

HOW OLD IS IT?

NOTES

FOSSIL #

ERA

HOW OLD IS IT?

NOTES

FOSSIL #

ERA

HOW OLD IS IT?

NOTES

FOSSIL #

ERA

HOW OLD IS IT?

NOTES

FOSSIL #

ERA

HOW OLD IS IT?

NOTES

FOSSIL #

ERA

HOW OLD IS IT?

NOTES

FOSSIL #

ERA

HOW OLD IS IT?

NOTES

I DID IT!

DATE:

FOSSIL IDENTIFICATION

Determining exactly what kind of fossil you've found can take time, research, and sometimes, honestly, a good guess. This fossil guide includes the most common fossils, and it's the first place you will want to look to identify your finds. Of course, there are still many fossils being discovered—hopefully you will find something even rarer than what's in these pages!

PLANT FOSSILS

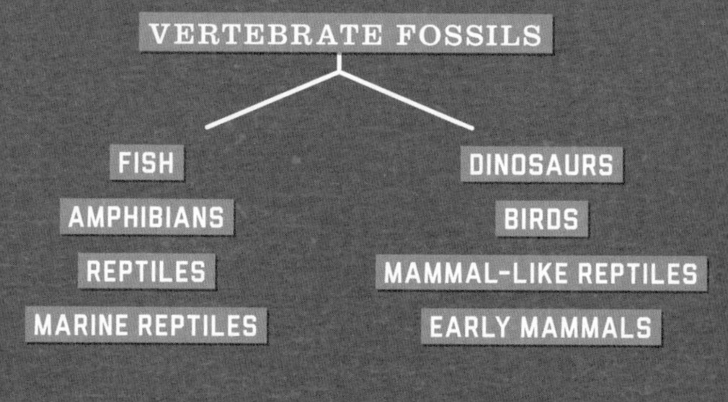

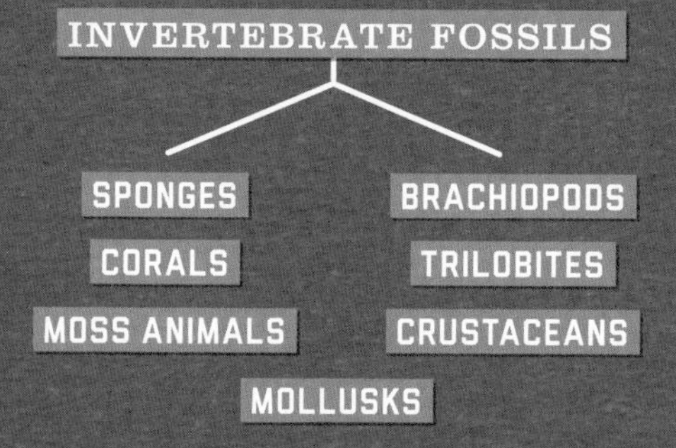

NOTE The sizes shown for the fossils are the average size of the fossils that have been found by scientists unless otherwise noted. You may also notice that some of the dates given for the time periods of these fossils are slightly different. All dates are based on the geographic time chart provided by the Geological Society of America. Scientists are as accurate as possible when determining the time period a fossil existed, but identifying a fossil is not an exact science, particularly given that a complete fossil may not be found.

Calamite

COMMON NAME Horsetail

SIZE 12 inches (30.5 cm)

HABITAT Sands by lakes and rivers

TIME PERIOD Carboniferous

DATE 300 million years ago

WHERE IT HAS BEEN FOUND Worldwide

POINT OF FACT These giant plants the size of trees once grew on the sides of swamps and marshland.

FOUND IT!

WHEN

DATE

WHERE

SPECIFIC PLACE AND SURROUNDINGS

NOTES

PLANTS

Sphenophyllum

COMMON NAME Climbing horsetail

SIZE 1.5 inches (4 cm)

HABITAT Edges of lakes and streams

TIME PERIOD Carboniferous

DATE 350–300 million years ago

WHERE IT HAS BEEN FOUND Worldwide

POINT OF FACT This plant was a climbing vine or shrub.

FOUND IT!

WHEN

DATE

WHERE

SPECIFIC PLACE AND SURROUNDINGS

NOTES

Trigonocarpus

COMMON NAME Medullosan

SIZE 4 inches (10 cm)

HABITAT Swamps

TIME PERIOD Carboniferous

DATE 350–300 million years ago

WHERE IT HAS BEEN FOUND Worldwide

POINT OF FACT The long ridges that run down this seed's length helps tell it apart from others.

FOUND IT!

WHEN

DATE

WHERE

SPECIFIC PLACE AND SURROUNDINGS

NOTES

PLANTS

Glossopteris

COMMON NAME Seed fern that looks as if it was from a tree

SIZE 4 inches (10 cm)

HABITAT Damp lowland areas

TIME PERIOD Permian to Triassic

DATE 300–200 million years ago

WHERE IT HAS BEEN FOUND Southern Hemisphere

POINT OF FACT This plant's leaves resemble banana leaves.

FOUND IT!

WHEN
DATE

WHERE
SPECIFIC PLACE AND SURROUNDINGS

NOTES

PLANTS

Lepidodendron

COMMON NAME Giant club moss

SIZE 10 inches (25 cm)

HABITAT Swamps

TIME PERIOD Carboniferous

DATE 360–300 million years ago

WHERE IT HAS BEEN FOUND Worldwide

POINT OF FACT Fossils can look like snakeskin imprints.

FOUND IT!

WHEN

DATE

WHERE

SPECIFIC PLACE AND SURROUNDINGS

NOTES

PLANTS

Stigmaria

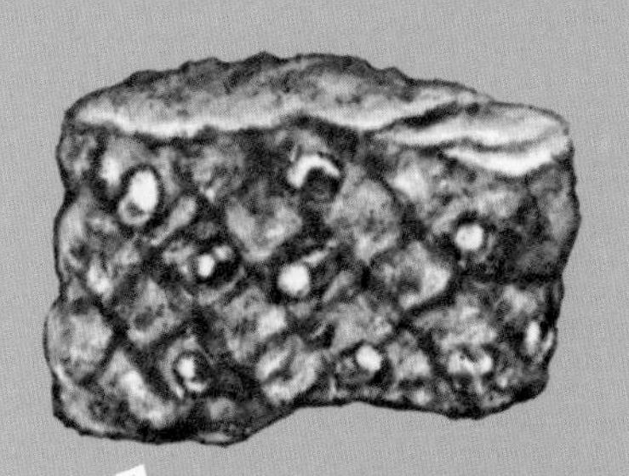

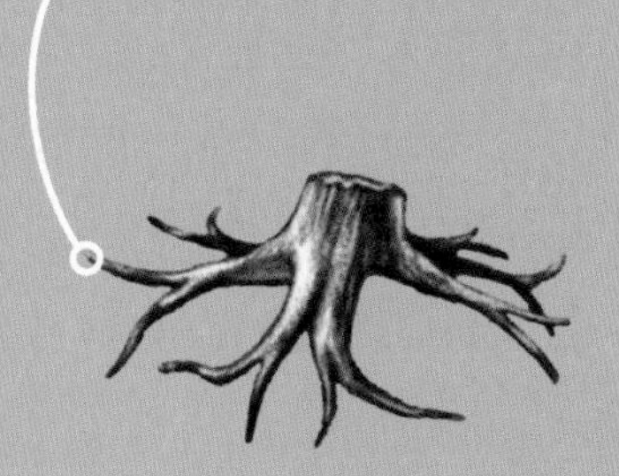

COMMON NAME Roots of the giant club moss

SIZE 10 inches (25 cm)

HABITAT Swamps

TIME PERIOD Late Carboniferous to Permian

DATE 330–250 million years ago

WHERE IT HAS BEEN FOUND North America, Europe, Asia, Australia

POINT OF FACT The roots of this plant belong to the earliest major group of plants.

FOUND IT!

WHEN
DATE

WHERE
SPECIFIC PLACE AND SURROUNDINGS

NOTES

Cycadeoidea

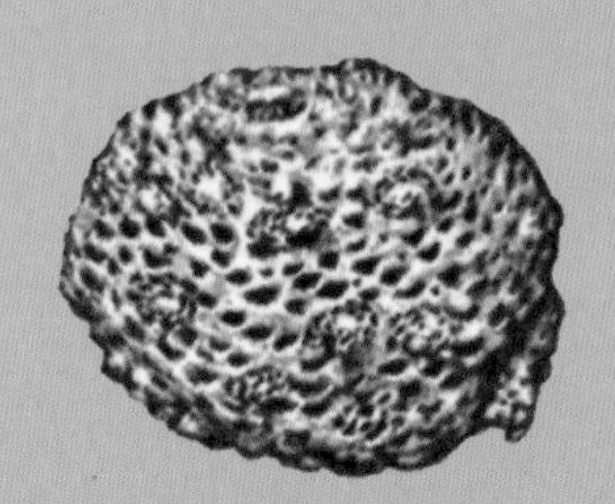

COMMON NAME Cycadeoid

SIZE 6 inches (15 cm)

HABITAT Dry uplands

TIME PERIOD Jurassic to Cretaceous

DATE 200–60 million years ago

WHERE IT HAS BEEN FOUND North America, Europe, Asia (India)

POINT OF FACT This fossil can look like a petrified pineapple.

FOUND IT!

WHEN

DATE

WHERE

SPECIFIC PLACE AND SURROUNDINGS

NOTES

PLANTS

Archaeopteris

COMMON NAME World's first tree

SIZE 8 inches (20.5 cm)

HABITAT Floodplains

TIME PERIOD Devonian

DATE 420–360 million years ago

WHERE IT HAS BEEN FOUND
Worldwide

POINT OF FACT This ancient plant formed the world's first forests.

FOUND IT!

WHEN
DATE

WHERE
SPECIFIC PLACE AND SURROUNDINGS

NOTES

PLANTS

Cordaite

COMMON NAME Ancestor of the conifer tree

SIZE 6 inches (15 cm)

HABITAT Swamps

TIME PERIOD Late Carboniferous to Early Permian

DATE 330–270 million years ago

WHERE IT HAS BEEN FOUND Worldwide

POINT OF FACT These were some of the tallest trees of the period.

FOUND IT!

WHEN
DATE

WHERE
SPECIFIC PLACE AND SURROUNDINGS

NOTES

PLANTS

Ginkgo

COMMON NAME Ginkgo

SIZE 2–3.5 inches (5-9 cm)

HABITAT Found in many different habitats

TIME PERIOD Late Triassic to today

DATE 235 million years ago to today

WHERE IT HAS BEEN FOUND Worldwide

POINT OF FACT The outer part of ginkgo seeds smell like vomit.

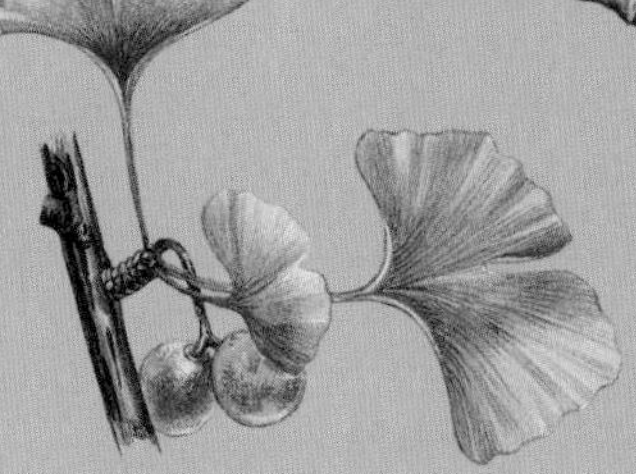

FOUND IT!

WHEN

DATE

WHERE

SPECIFIC PLACE AND SURROUNDINGS

NOTES

PLANTS

Araucaria

COMMON NAME Monkey puzzle tree

SIZE 2 inches (5 cm)

HABITAT Subtropical mountain forests

TIME PERIOD Triassic to today

DATE 250 million years ago to today

WHERE IT HAS BEEN FOUND Mostly Northern Hemisphere and India

POINT OF FACT This tree is part of Argentina's Cerro Cuadrado petrified forest, which was buried by a volcanic eruption 160 million years ago.

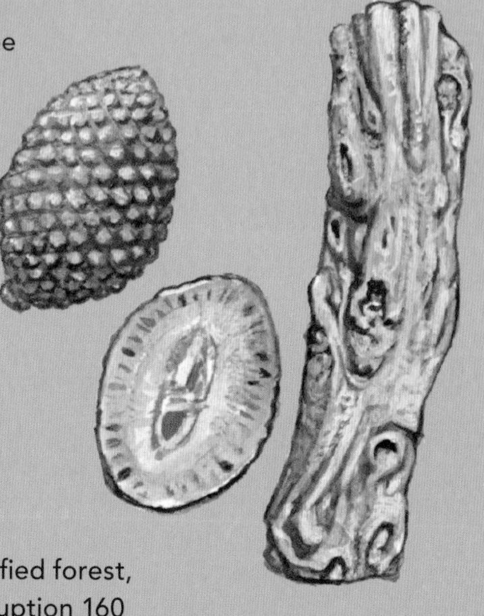

FOUND IT!

WHEN

DATE

WHERE

SPECIFIC PLACE AND SURROUNDINGS

NOTES

Sequoiadendron

COMMON NAME Sequoia

SIZE 2 inches (5 cm)

HABITAT Wet mountain slopes

TIME PERIOD Jurassic to today

DATE 200 million years ago to today

WHERE IT HAS BEEN FOUND Worldwide

POINT OF FACT Small spherical cones (aka pine cones) staggered on the branches are a trademark of this plant.

FOUND IT!

WHEN

DATE

WHERE

SPECIFIC PLACE AND SURROUNDINGS

NOTES

PLANTS

Metasequoia

COMMON NAME Dawn redwood

SIZE 2 inches (5 cm)

HABITAT Wet mountain slopes

TIME PERIOD Cretaceous to today

DATE 145 million years ago to today

WHERE IT HAS BEEN FOUND North America and Asia

POINT OF FACT The wood at the base of this tree grows vertically and is called its "knees."

FOUND IT!

WHEN
DATE

WHERE
SPECIFIC PLACE AND SURROUNDINGS

NOTES

PLANTS

Myrica

COMMON NAME Myrtle tree

SIZE 2.75 inches (7 cm)

HABITAT Woodland with mild temperatures

TIME PERIOD Oligocene to today

DATE 33 million years ago to today

WHERE IT HAS BEEN FOUND Northern Hemisphere

POINT OF FACT When they are alive, during the growing season, the leaves change from red to yellow to orange before dropping.

FOUND IT!

WHEN

DATE

WHERE

SPECIFIC PLACE AND SURROUNDINGS

NOTES

Sassafras

COMMON NAME Sassafras tree

SIZE 3.5 inches (9 cm)

HABITAT Woodland with mild temperatures

TIME PERIOD Late Cretaceous to today

DATE 100 million years ago to today

WHERE IT HAS BEEN FOUND North America, Germany, Japan

POINT OF FACT These trees are used to make root beer.

FOUND IT!

WHEN

DATE

WHERE

SPECIFIC PLACE AND SURROUNDINGS

NOTES

PLANTS

Liquidambar

COMMON NAME Sweetgum tree

SIZE 3.5 inches (9 cm)

HABITAT Woodland with mild temperatures

TIME PERIOD Early Cretaceous to today

DATE 145 million years ago to today

WHERE IT HAS BEEN FOUND Worldwide

POINT OF FACT These trees are used for herbs and medicine.

FOUND IT!

WHEN

DATE

WHERE

SPECIFIC PLACE AND SURROUNDINGS

NOTES

VERTEBRATES

Hybodus

Fish

COMMON NAME Humped tooth shark

SIZE (Tooth) 6.5 inches (16.5 cm)

HABITAT Oceans

TIME PERIOD Late Permian to Cretaceous

DATE 260–65 million years ago

WHERE IT HAS BEEN FOUND Worldwide

POINT OF FACT Most fossils of these sharks are of the spine and teeth.

FOUND IT!

WHEN

DATE

WHERE

SPECIFIC PLACE AND SURROUNDINGS

NOTES

VERTEBRATES

Ptychodus

Fish

COMMON NAME Folded-tooth shark

SIZE (Tooth) 0.2–0.4 inches (5–10 mm)

HABITAT Oceans

TIME PERIOD Cretaceous

DATE 145–65 million years ago

WHERE IT HAS BEEN FOUND North America, Brazil, Europe, Asia

POINT OF FACT This shark had teeth that were wide and flat, great for crushing shells.

FOUND IT!

WHEN

DATE

WHERE

SPECIFIC PLACE AND SURROUNDINGS

NOTES

VERTEBRATES

Coccoderma

Fish

COMMON NAME Lobe-finned fish

SIZE 12.5 inches (32 cm)

HABITAT Shallow marine lagoons

TIME PERIOD Late Jurassic

DATE 165–145 million years ago

WHERE IT HAS BEEN FOUND Europe

POINT OF FACT Relatives of these fish are some of the oldest "fossils" that are still living.

WHEN

DATE

WHERE

SPECIFIC PLACE AND SURROUNDINGS

NOTES

VERTEBRATES

Osteolepis

Fish

COMMON NAME Lobe-finned fish

SIZE 7 inches (18 cm)

HABITAT Shallow lakes and rivers

TIME PERIOD Middle to Late Devonian

DATE 390–360 million years ago

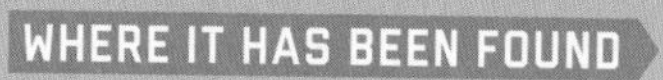

WHERE IT HAS BEEN FOUND Pennsylvania

POINT OF FACT This fish could breathe air as well as water through its gills.

FOUND IT!

WHEN

DATE

WHERE

SPECIFIC PLACE AND SURROUNDINGS

NOTES

VERTEBRATES

Dipterus

Fish

COMMON NAME Primitive lungfish

SIZE 8 inches (20.5 cm)

HABITAT Seas

TIME PERIOD Devonian

DATE 420–360 million years ago

WHERE IT HAS BEEN FOUND Europe, North America

POINT OF FACT This was one of the first fish to develop air-breathing lungs.

FOUND IT!

WHEN

DATE

WHERE

SPECIFIC PLACE AND SURROUNDINGS

NOTES

VERTEBRATES

Ceratodus

Fish

COMMON NAME Horned–tooth lungfish

SIZE 2.3 inches (5.5 cm)

HABITAT Shallow seas

TIME PERIOD Early Triassic to Eocene

DATE 250–34 million years ago

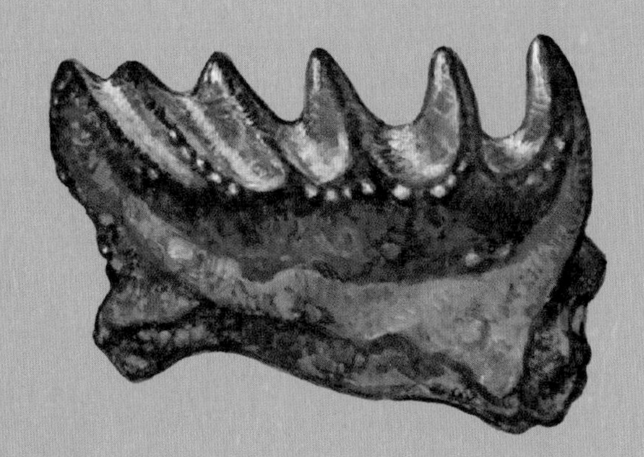

WHERE IT HAS BEEN FOUND Worldwide, especially Europe and Africa

POINT OF FACT This fish went extinct after living more than 180 million years.

FOUND IT!

WHEN
DATE

WHERE
SPECIFIC PLACE AND SURROUNDINGS

NOTES

VERTEBRATES

Cephalaspis

Fish

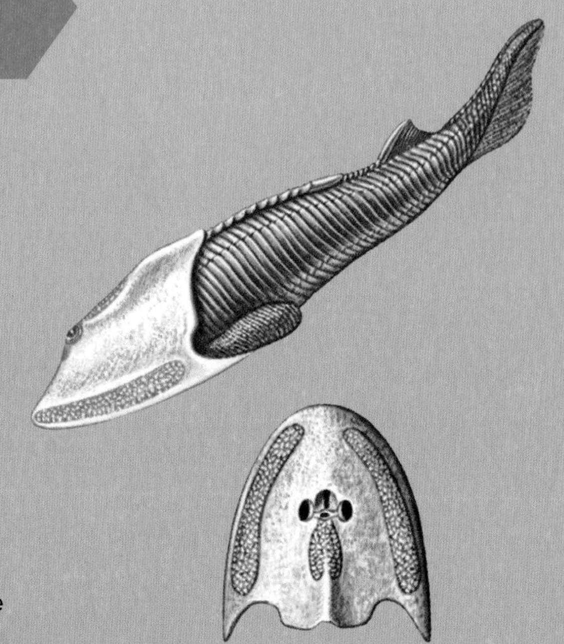

COMMON NAME
Armored jawless fish

SIZE 4.75 inches (12 cm)

HABITAT Shallow sea coasts, estuaries, rivers

TIME PERIOD Early Devonian

DATE 420–390 million years ago

WHERE IT HAS BEEN FOUND
North America and Europe

POINT OF FACT The earliest fish, like these, had no jaws. They are the ancestors of the hagfish and the lampreys of today.

FOUND IT!

WHEN
DATE

WHERE
SPECIFIC PLACE AND SURROUNDINGS

NOTES

VERTEBRATES

Palaeoniscus

Fish

COMMON NAME Predatory freshwater fish

SIZE 9.75 inches (25 cm)

HABITAT Fresh water

TIME PERIOD Permian to Late Triassic

DATE 290–260 million years ago

Europe, North America, South Africa

POINT OF FACT They are the ancestor of today's sturgeon.

FOUND IT!

WHEN

DATE

WHERE

SPECIFIC PLACE AND SURROUNDINGS

NOTES

VERTEBRATES

Lepidote

Fish

COMMON NAME Ray-finned fish

SIZE 10 inches (25 cm)

HABITAT Shallow coastal waters, lakes

TIME PERIOD Triassic to Cretaceous

DATE 250–65 million years ago

WHERE IT HAS BEEN FOUND Worldwide

POINT OF FACT Some scales from this fish have been found with the dinosaur Baryonyx, which makes scientists think that the dinosaurs may have scooped them up and held them to their chest before eating them.

FOUND IT!

WHEN

DATE

WHERE

SPECIFIC PLACE AND SURROUNDINGS

NOTES

VERTEBRATES

Leptolepis

Fish

COMMON NAME Ray–finned fish

SIZE 3.25 inches (8.5 cm)

HABITAT Warm coastal waters

TIME PERIOD Middle Triassic to Late Cretaceous

DATE 245–80 million years ago

WHERE IT HAS BEEN FOUND North America, Europe, Africa, Australia, Japan

POINT OF FACT Entire schools of these fish are usually fossilized together.

FOUND IT!

WHEN

DATE

WHERE

SPECIFIC PLACE AND SURROUNDINGS

NOTES

VERTEBRATES

Hylonomus

Reptiles

COMMON NAME First reptile lizard

SIZE 0.75 inches (2 cm)

HABITAT Swampy forests

TIME PERIOD Late Carboniferous

DATE 320–300 million years ago

WHERE IT HAS BEEN FOUND Nova Scotia, Czech Republic

POINT OF FACT These fossils were found near Sigillaria club mosses.

FOUND IT!

WHEN

DATE

WHERE

SPECIFIC PLACE AND SURROUNDINGS

NOTES

VERTEBRATES

Elginia

Reptiles

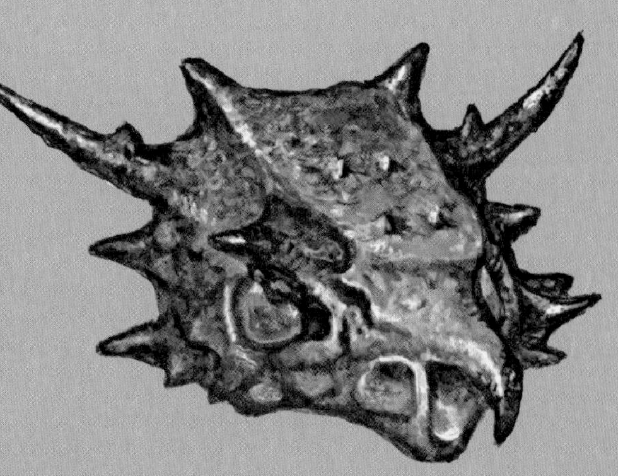

COMMON NAME Pareiasaur

SIZE (Head) 10 inches (25 cm)

HABITAT Small brush and around a lot of plants on land

TIME PERIOD Late Permian

DATE 270–250 million years ago

WHERE IT HAS BEEN FOUND Europe

POINT OF FACT These animals' triangular shaped skulls might have been used as a form of defense.

FOUND IT!

WHEN

DATE

WHERE

SPECIFIC PLACE AND SURROUNDINGS

NOTES

VERTEBRATES

Hyperodapedon

Reptiles

COMMON NAME Rhynchosaur

SIZE 8.5 inches (21.5 cm)

HABITAT Dry scrub (small bushes and grasses)

TIME PERIOD Late Triassic

DATE 227–206 million years ago

WHERE IT HAS BEEN FOUND Worldwide

POINT OF FACT They have a distinctive curved beak and can be found around fossils of Triassic plants, which they loved to eat.

WHEN

DATE

WHERE

SPECIFIC PLACE AND SURROUNDINGS

NOTES

VERTEBRATES

Emys

Reptiles

COMMON NAME Turtle

SIZE 0.75–1 inches (2–2.5 cm)

HABITAT Fresh water

TIME PERIOD Eocene

DATE 55–35 million years ago

WHERE IT HAS BEEN FOUND Worldwide

POINT OF FACT It is rare to find a full shell, but bits of shells are commonly found.

FOUND IT!

WHEN

DATE

WHERE

SPECIFIC PLACE AND SURROUNDINGS

NOTES

VERTEBRATES

Phytosaur

Reptiles

COMMON NAME Phytosaur

SIZE 1.75 inches (4.5 cm)

HABITAT Freshwater lakes, rivers, swamps

TIME PERIOD Late Triassic

DATE 235–200 million years ago

WHERE IT HAS BEEN FOUND Worldwide

POINT OF FACT These are the ancestors of today's crocodiles.

FOUND IT!

WHEN

DATE

WHERE

SPECIFIC PLACE AND SURROUNDINGS

NOTES

VERTEBRATES

Metriorhynchus

Reptiles

COMMON NAME Marine crocodile

SIZE 8.5 inches (21.5 cm)

HABITAT Shallow seas

TIME PERIOD Middle Jurassic to Early Cretaceous

DATE 175–100 million years ago

WHERE IT HAS BEEN FOUND South America, Mexico, Europe

POINT OF FACT This ancient crocodile-type animal had a fin on the end of its tail for propulsion.

WHEN

DATE

WHERE

SPECIFIC PLACE AND SURROUNDINGS

NOTES

VERTEBRATES

Ichthyosaurus

Marine Reptiles

COMMON NAME Ichthyosaur

SIZE 3.25 feet (1 m)

HABITAT Seas

TIME PERIOD
Jurassic

DATE 200–145 million years ago

WHERE IT HAS BEEN FOUND Europe, North America, Chile

POINT OF FACT This animal was shaped like a mix between a fish and a dolphin, with a long pointy nose.

WHEN
DATE

WHERE
SPECIFIC PLACE AND SURROUNDINGS

NOTES

VERTEBRATES

Pliosaur

Marine Reptiles

COMMON NAME Pliosaur

SIZE (Tooth) 4 inches (10 cm)

HABITAT Oceans

TIME PERIOD Mesozoic

DATE 250–65 million years ago

WHERE IT HAS BEEN FOUND
Europe and Tunisia

POINT OF FACT This animal may have been one of the fiercest predators in the sea.

FOUND IT!

WHEN
DATE

WHERE
SPECIFIC PLACE AND SURROUNDINGS

NOTES

Mosasaurus

Marine Reptiles

COMMON NAME Mosasaurus

SIZE (Jaw) 15 inches (38 cm)

HABITAT Seas

TIME PERIOD Late Cretaceous

DATE 100–65 million years ago

WHERE IT HAS BEEN FOUND Worldwide

POINT OF FACT These are ancient relatives of today's monitor lizard.

FOUND IT!

WHEN

DATE

WHERE

SPECIFIC PLACE AND SURROUNDINGS

NOTES

VERTEBRATES

Chirotherium

Dinosaurs

COMMON NAME Predinosaur

SIZE (Footprint) 15 inches (38 cm)

HABITAT Dry scrub (small bushes and grasses)

TIME PERIOD Triassic

DATE 250–200 million years ago

WHERE IT HAS BEEN FOUND North America, Europe, Africa, Asia

POINT OF FACT Only very rare footprints have been found.

WHEN

DATE

WHERE

SPECIFIC PLACE AND SURROUNDINGS

NOTES

VERTEBRATES

Diplodocus

Dinosaurs

COMMON NAME Sauropod

SIZE (Skull) 24 inches (61 cm)

HABITAT Woodlands and shrubs near freshwater

TIME PERIOD Late Jurassic

DATE 160–145 million years ago

WHERE IT HAS BEEN FOUND
North America

POINT OF FACT An adult may have weighed the same as two African Elephants.

FOUND IT!

WHEN
DATE

WHERE
SPECIFIC PLACE AND SURROUNDINGS

NOTES

VERTEBRATES

Carcharodontosaurus

Dinosaurs

COMMON NAME Carcharodontosaurus

SIZE (Tooth) 2.25 inches (5.5 cm)

HABITAT Marshes, swamps, floodplains

TIME PERIOD Early Cretaceous

DATE 110–100 million years ago

WHERE IT HAS BEEN FOUND Africa, Brazil

POINT OF FACT This animal was bigger than a T. rex.

FOUND IT!

WHEN

DATE

WHERE

SPECIFIC PLACE AND SURROUNDINGS

NOTES

VERTEBRATES

Dromaeosaurus

Dinosaurs

COMMON NAME Raptor

SIZE (Claw) 2 inches (5 cm)

HABITAT Woods and other land habitats

TIME PERIOD Cretaceous

DATE 110–65 million years ago

WHERE IT HAS BEEN FOUND North America, Siberia

POINT OF FACT This group includes the velociraptor, a fierce predator.

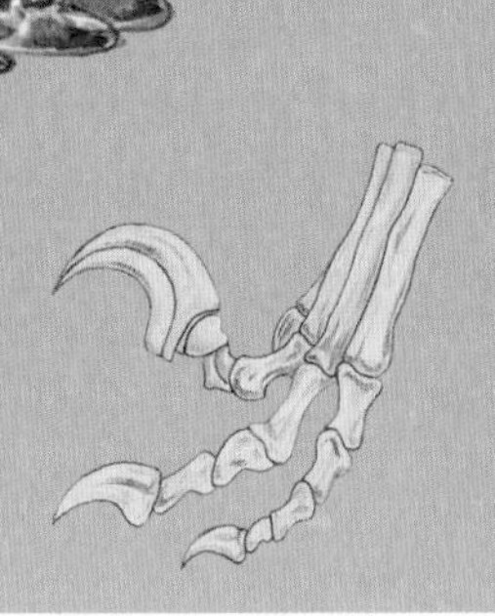

FOUND IT!

WHEN

DATE

WHERE

SPECIFIC PLACE AND SURROUNDINGS

NOTES

VERTEBRATES

Ornithomimus

Dinosaurs

COMMON NAME Ostrich dinosaur

SIZE (Foot/hand and claw) 4.5 inches (11.5 cm)

HABITAT Open land and scrub (small bushes and grasses)

TIME PERIOD Late Cretaceous

DATE 100–65 million years ago

WHERE IT HAS BEEN FOUND North America

POINT OF FACT This animal had a long beak, but no teeth. It ate seeds, insects, and worms.

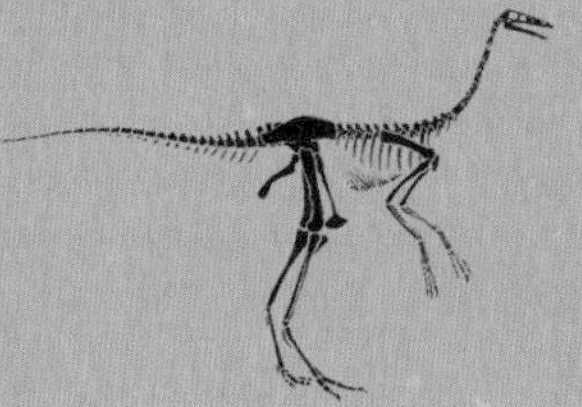

FOUND IT!

WHEN

DATE

WHERE

SPECIFIC PLACE AND SURROUNDINGS

NOTES

VERTEBRATES

Iguanodontid

Dinosaurs

COMMON NAME Iguanodon

SIZE (Single vertebrae) 2.75 inches (7 cm)

HABITAT Woods

TIME PERIOD
Early Cretaceous

DATE 145–100 million years ago

WHERE IT HAS BEEN FOUND
Europe, Texas, Sudan

POINT OF FACT It had a bony spike on its thumb that it used to jab at other predators.

FOUND IT!

WHEN
DATE

WHERE
SPECIFIC PLACE AND SURROUNDINGS

NOTES

Edmontosaurus

Dinosaurs

COMMON NAME Duck-billed dinosaur

SIZE (Tooth) 2.25 inches (5.5 cm)

HABITAT Woods, valleys, hills

TIME PERIOD Late Cretaceous

DATE 100–65 million years ago

WHERE IT HAS BEEN FOUND North America

POINT OF FACT Fossils of these dinosaurs are found in groups, which makes paleontologists think they traveled as herds.

FOUND IT!

WHEN

DATE

WHERE

SPECIFIC PLACE AND SURROUNDINGS

NOTES

VERTEBRATES

Triceratops

Dinosaurs

COMMON NAME Triceratops

SIZE (Tooth) 1.5 inches (4 cm)

HABITAT Woods and forests

TIME PERIOD Late Cretaceous

DATE 100–65 million years ago

WHERE IT HAS BEEN FOUND North America

POINT OF FACT A powerful beak helped break open plant stems.

WHEN

DATE

WHERE

SPECIFIC PLACE AND SURROUNDINGS

NOTES

VERTEBRATES

Pterosaur

Dinosaurs

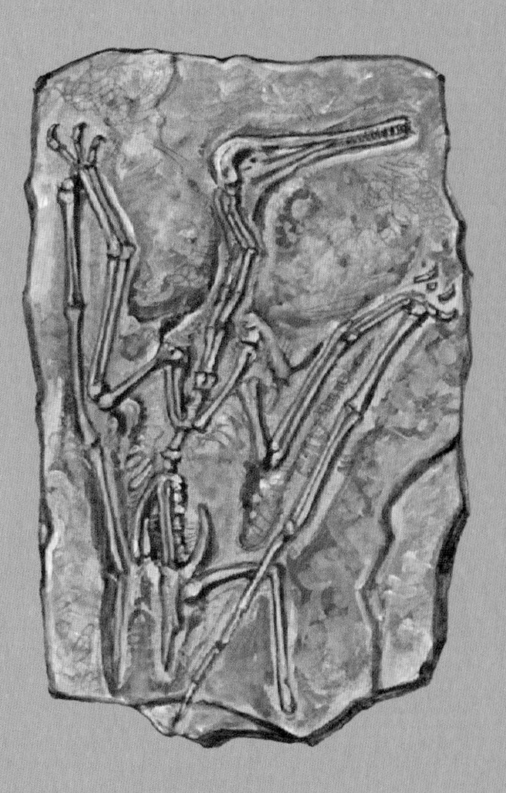

COMMON NAME Pterodactyl

SIZE (Fragment, tooth or jawbone) 1.5 inches (4 cm)

HABITAT Coastal areas

TIME PERIOD Mesozoic

DATE 250–65 million years ago

WHERE IT HAS BEEN FOUND Worldwide

POINT OF FACT This group of dinosaurs included some of the largest flying animals on the planet.

FOUND IT!

WHEN

DATE

WHERE

SPECIFIC PLACE AND SURROUNDINGS

NOTES

VERTEBRATES

Archaeopteryx

Birds

COMMON NAME First bird

SIZE 12 inches (30.5 cm)

HABITAT Woodlands, tropical islands

TIME PERIOD Late Jurassic

DATE 165–145 million years ago

WHERE IT HAS BEEN FOUND Germany and Spain

POINT OF FACT This is the earliest bird found, so its fossils are quite rare.

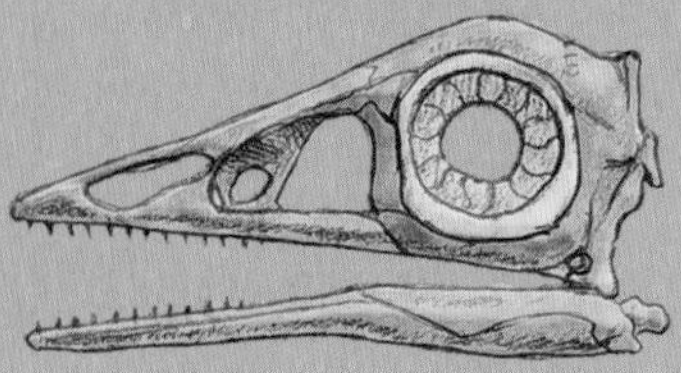

FOUND IT!

WHEN

DATE

WHERE

SPECIFIC PLACE AND SURROUNDINGS

NOTES

VERTEBRATES

Phalacrocorax

Birds

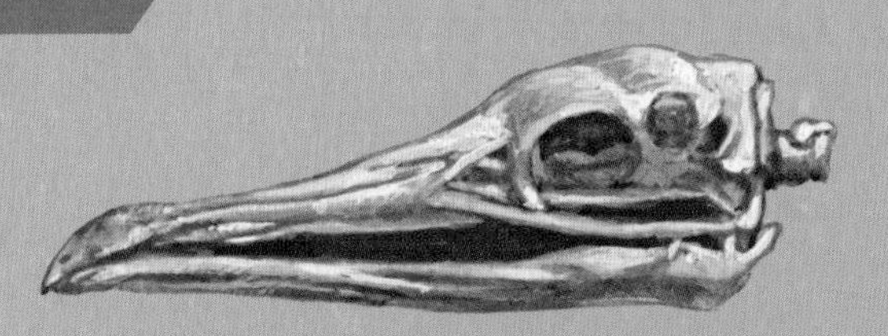

COMMON NAME Cormorant

SIZE (Skull) 24 inches (61 cm)

HABITAT Seashores and inland waterways

TIME PERIOD Pliocene

DATE 5–2.5 million years ago

WHERE IT HAS BEEN FOUND Worldwide

POINT OF FACT This is the ancestor of the modern cormorant.

FOUND IT!

WHEN

DATE

WHERE

SPECIFIC PLACE AND SURROUNDINGS

NOTES

VERTEBRATES

Dimetrodon

Mammal-Like Reptiles

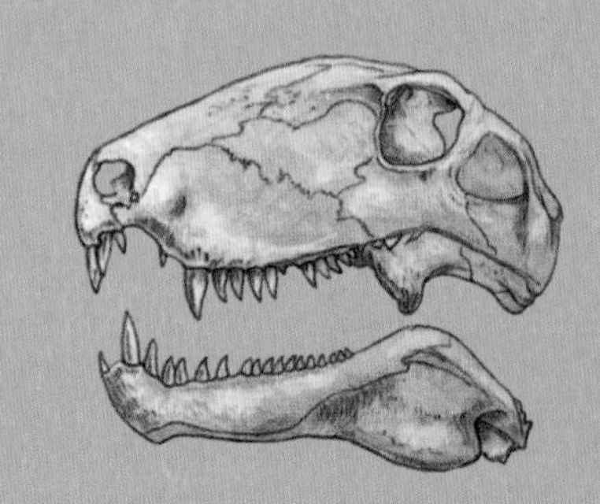

COMMON NAME Sail-back lizard

SIZE (Jawbone) 2 inches (5 cm)

HABITAT Swamps and scrub areas

TIME PERIOD Early Permian

DATE 300 million years ago

WHERE IT HAS BEEN FOUND
New Mexico, Texas, Oklahoma, Germany

POINT OF FACT Scientists believe the sail on the back of this creature was there to absorb heat from the sun to keep the animal warm.

FOUND IT!

WHEN
DATE

WHERE
SPECIFIC PLACE AND SURROUNDINGS

NOTES

Cynognathus

Mammal-Like Reptiles

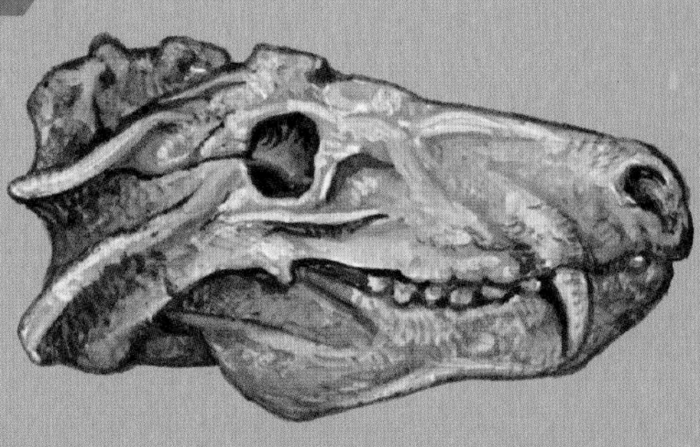

COMMON NAME Cynodont

SIZE (Skull) 16 inches (40.5 cm)

HABITAT Scrub (small bushes and grasses), semidesert

TIME PERIOD Early Triassic

DATE 250–245 million years ago

WHERE IT HAS BEEN FOUND Argentina, South Africa, Namibia, Zambia, Tanzania

POINT OF FACT This animal had very powerful jaws with three different types of teeth for ripping and chewing.

FOUND IT!

WHEN

DATE

WHERE

SPECIFIC PLACE AND SURROUNDINGS

NOTES

VERTEBRATES

Monotremata

Early Mammals

COMMON NAME Platypus

SIZE (Tooth) 0.5 inches (1.5 cm)

HABITAT Fresh water

TIME PERIOD Early Cretaceous

DATE 145–100 million years ago

WHERE IT HAS BEEN FOUND
Australia and Argentina

POINT OF FACT This is the ancestor of the platypus that is still around today.

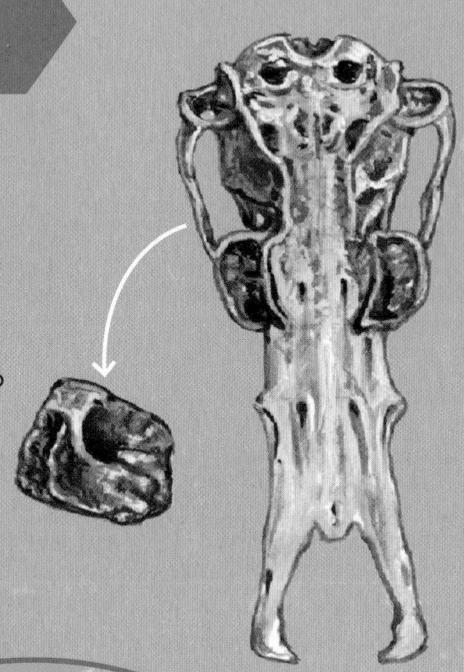

FOUND IT!

WHEN
DATE

WHERE
SPECIFIC PLACE AND SURROUNDINGS

NOTES

VERTEBRATES

Palaeolagus

Early Mammals

COMMON NAME Rabbit

SIZE (Skull) 1.5 inches (4 cm)

HABITAT Forests

TIME PERIOD Oligocene

DATE 30–25 million years ago

WHERE IT HAS BEEN FOUND
North America

POINT OF FACT The bones are so small and fragile that they are very rare to find.

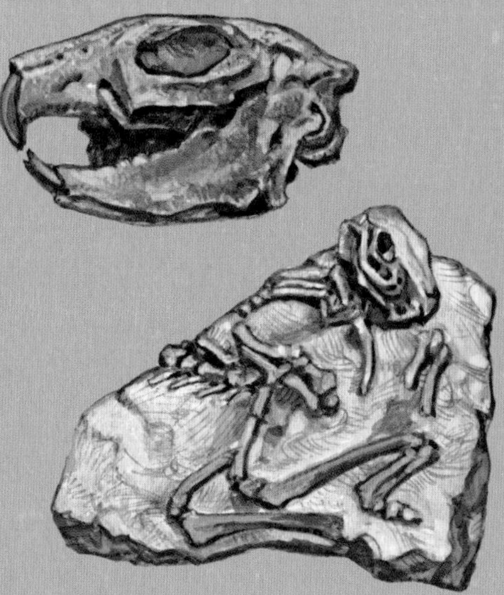

FOUND IT!

WHEN
DATE

WHERE
SPECIFIC PLACE AND SURROUNDINGS

NOTES

VERTEBRATES

Hyaenodon

Early Mammals

COMMON NAME Ancient hyena

SIZE (Skull) 6 inches (15 cm)

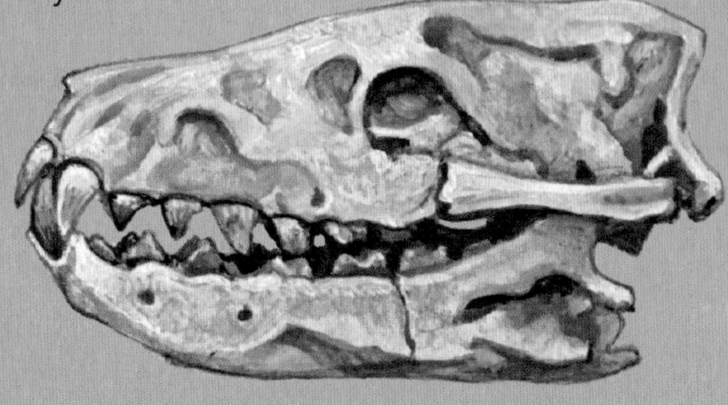

HABITAT Scrub (small bushes and grasses), wooded areas

TIME PERIOD Eocene to Miocene

DATE 55–2.5 million years ago

WHERE IT HAS BEEN FOUND North America, Europe, Africa, Asia

POINT OF FACT Some animals in this group were very small; others were as big as lions.

FOUND IT!

WHEN

DATE

WHERE

SPECIFIC PLACE AND SURROUNDINGS

NOTES

VERTEBRATES

Smilodon

Early Mammals

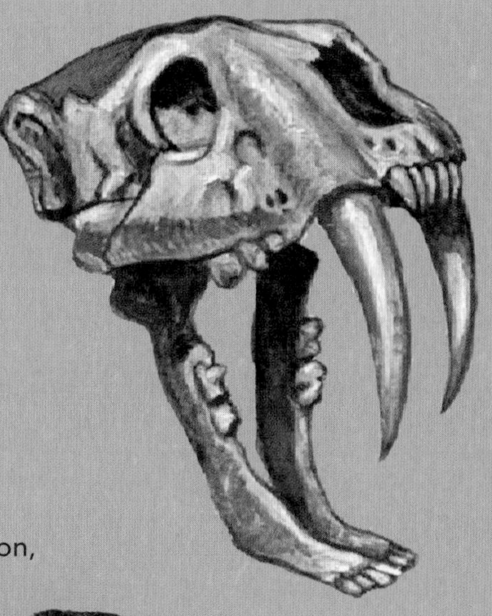

COMMON NAME Sabre-toothed cat

SIZE (Tooth) 6.5 inches (17 cm)

HABITAT All over since they roamed, mostly woods

TIME PERIOD Calabrian

DATE Up to 10,000 years ago

WHERE IT HAS BEEN FOUND North America, South America

POINT OF FACT Similar in size to a lion, this cat had long, curved canines for slashing prey.

FOUND IT!

WHEN

DATE

WHERE

SPECIFIC PLACE AND SURROUNDINGS

NOTES

VERTEBRATES

Ursus

Early Mammals

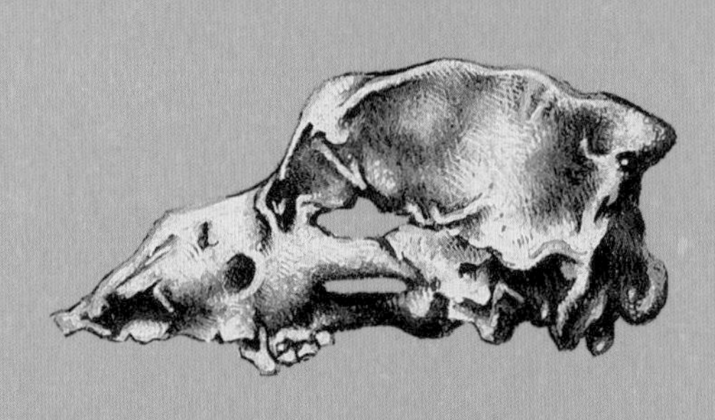

COMMON NAME Cave bear

SIZE (Skull) 20 inches (51 cm)

HABITAT All over since they roamed, mostly woods

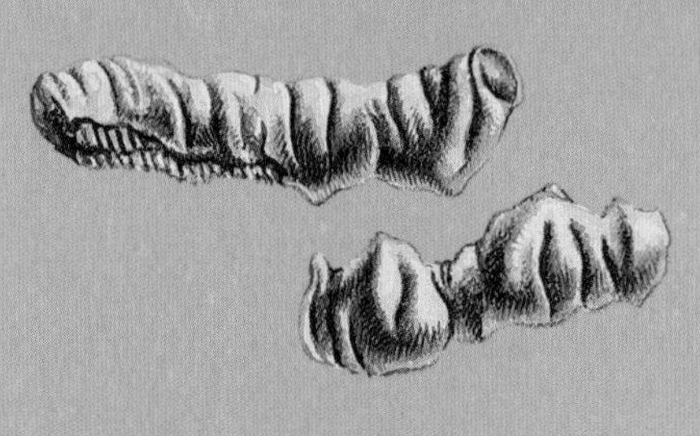

TIME PERIOD Pleistocene to today

DATE 2.5 million years ago to today

WHERE IT HAS BEEN FOUND Europe, North America, Asia

POINT OF FACT This bear was most likely alive when humans first appeared.

FOUND IT!

WHEN

DATE

WHERE

SPECIFIC PLACE AND SURROUNDINGS

NOTES

VERTEBRATES

Equus

Early Mammals

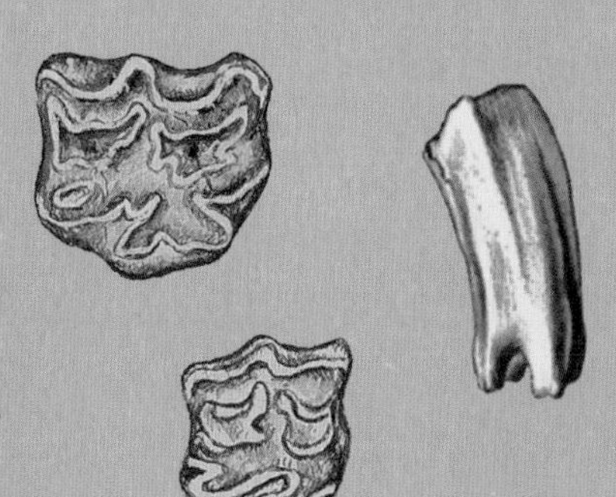

COMMON NAME Horse

SIZE (Tooth) 2 inches (5 cm)

HABITAT Grasslands and woods

TIME PERIOD Pliocene to today

DATE 5 million years ago to today

WHERE IT HAS BEEN FOUND Worldwide

POINT OF FACT These fossils include horses, zebras, and donkeys.

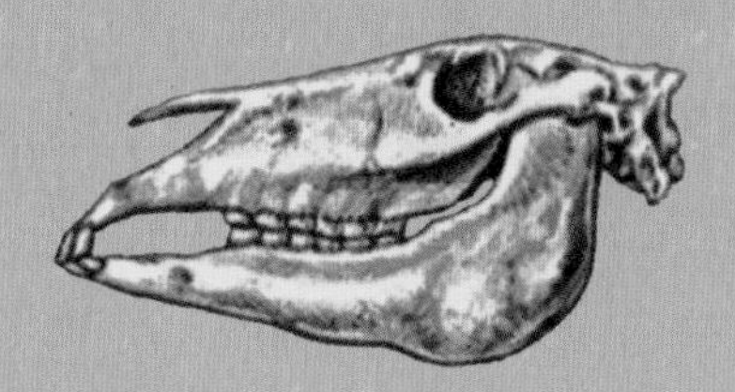

FOUND IT!

WHEN

DATE

WHERE

SPECIFIC PLACE AND SURROUNDINGS

NOTES

VERTEBRATES

Mammuthus

Early Mammals

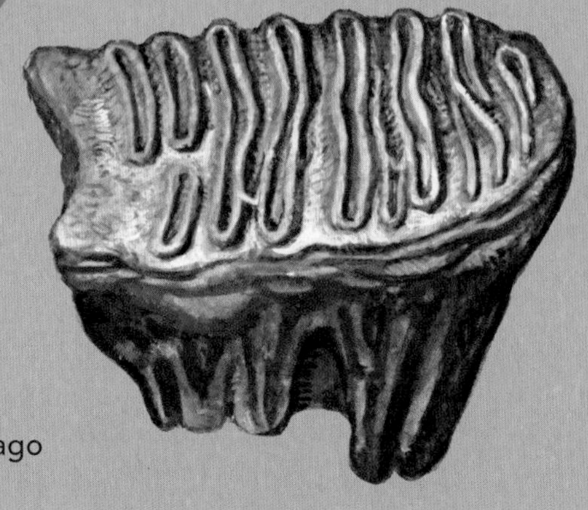

COMMON NAME
Woolly mammoth

SIZE (Tooth) 9.5 inches (24 cm)

HABITAT Tundra, open plains, lower mountains

TIME PERIOD Pleistocene

DATE 2.5 million–10,000 years ago

WHERE IT HAS BEEN FOUND
Northern Hemisphere

POINT OF FACT These animals were hunted by Neanderthals.

FOUND IT!

WHEN
DATE

WHERE
SPECIFIC PLACE AND SURROUNDINGS

NOTES

VERTEBRATES

Coelodonta

Early Mammals

COMMON NAME Woolly rhino

SIZE (Tooth) 2.5 inches (6.5 cm)

HABITAT Tundra, scrub, lower mountains

TIME PERIOD Miocene to Pleistocene

DATE 23–2.5 million years ago

WHERE IT HAS BEEN FOUND Asia and Europe

POINT OF FACT This woolly rhino had long, coarse hair to protect it from the cold.

FOUND IT!

WHEN

DATE

WHERE

SPECIFIC PLACE AND SURROUNDINGS

NOTES

VERTEBRATES

Bison

Early Mammals

COMMON NAME Bison

SIZE (Jaw) 8.25 inches (21 cm)

HABITAT Grasslands, scrubs (small bushes and grasses), woodlands

TIME PERIOD Quartenary to today

DATE 2 million years ago to today

WHERE IT HAS BEEN FOUND North America, Europe, Asia

POINT OF FACT These animals have bones that grow continuously.

FOUND IT!

WHEN

DATE

WHERE

SPECIFIC PLACE AND SURROUNDINGS

NOTES

INVERTEBRATES

Doryderma

Sponges

COMMON NAME
Doryderma sponge

SIZE 2.5 inches (6.5 cm)

HABITAT Seafloor

TIME PERIOD
Carboniferous to Late Cretaceous

DATE 360–85 million years ago

WHERE IT HAS BEEN FOUND
Europe

POINT OF FACT This creature forms beautiful but very fragile branches.

FOUND IT!

WHEN
DATE

WHERE
SPECIFIC PLACE AND SURROUNDINGS

NOTES

INVERTEBRATES

Spongia

Sponges

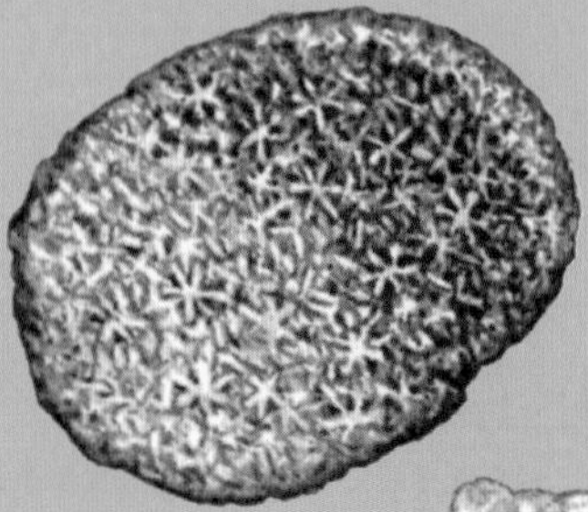

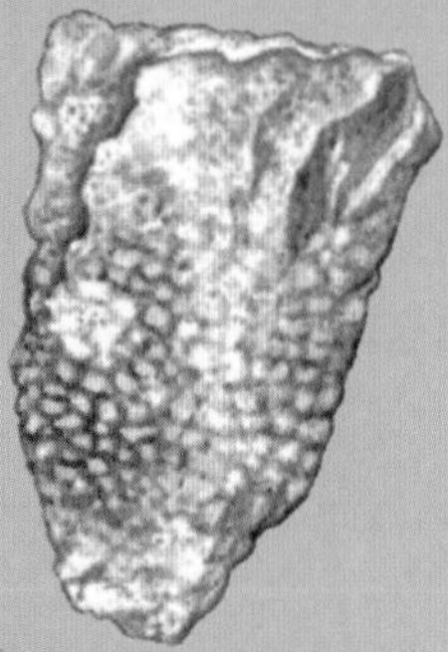

COMMON NAME Sponge

SIZE 3 inches (7.5 cm)

HABITAT Seafloor

TIME PERIOD Cambrian to today

DATE 540 million years ago to today

WHERE IT HAS BEEN FOUND Australia and North America

POINT OF FACT These sponges are actually used sometimes in the bath.

FOUND IT!

WHEN

DATE

WHERE

SPECIFIC PLACE AND SURROUNDINGS

NOTES

INVERTEBRATES

Raphidonema

Sponges

COMMON NAME
Spiny globe sponge

SIZE 2.5 inches (6.5 cm)

HABITAT
Warm, shallow seafloor

TIME PERIOD
Triassic to Cretaceous

DATE 250–65 million years ago

WHERE IT HAS BEEN FOUND
England, France, India

POINT OF FACT This sponge looks like a cup or a vase.

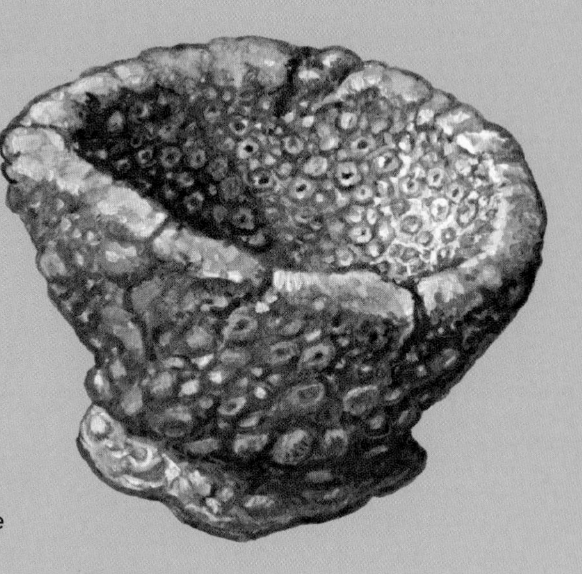

FOUND IT!

WHEN
DATE

WHERE
SPECIFIC PLACE AND SURROUNDINGS

NOTES

INVERTEBRATES

Favosite

Corals

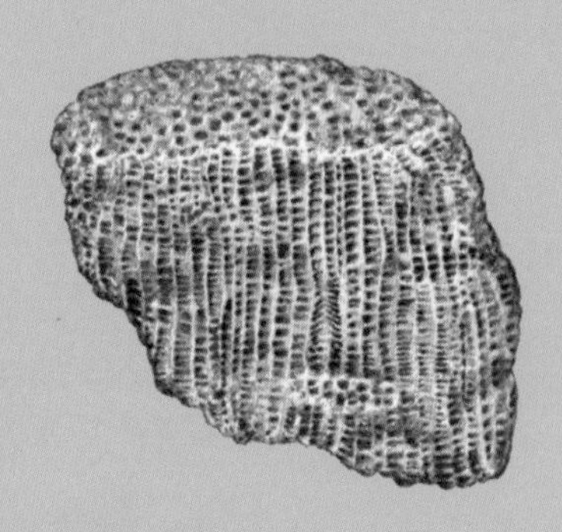

COMMON NAME Honeycomb coral

SIZE 2 inches (5 cm)

HABITAT Warm, shallow seafloors and reefs

TIME PERIOD Ordovician to Devonian

DATE 485–360 million years ago

WHERE IT HAS BEEN FOUND Worldwide

POINT OF FACT They formed colorful reefs in large colonies and are the most common fossil in Wisconsin

FOUND IT!

WHEN

DATE

WHERE

SPECIFIC PLACE AND SURROUNDINGS

NOTES

INVERTEBRATES

Halysite

Corals

COMMON NAME Chain coral

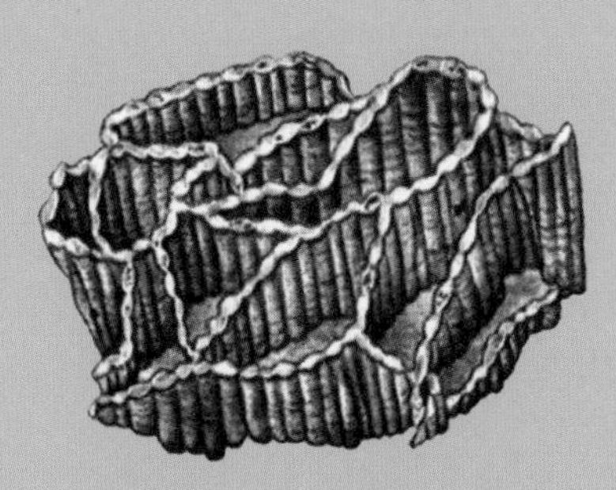

SIZE 2 inches (5 cm)

HABITAT Warm, shallow seafloors and reefs

TIME PERIOD Ordovian to Silurian

DATE 485–420 million years ago

WHERE IT HAS BEEN FOUND Worldwide

POINT OF FACT This fossil looks as if it is made of chains folded on top of each other.

FOUND IT!

WHEN

DATE

WHERE

SPECIFIC PLACE AND SURROUNDINGS

NOTES

INVERTEBRATES

Thamnasteria

Corals

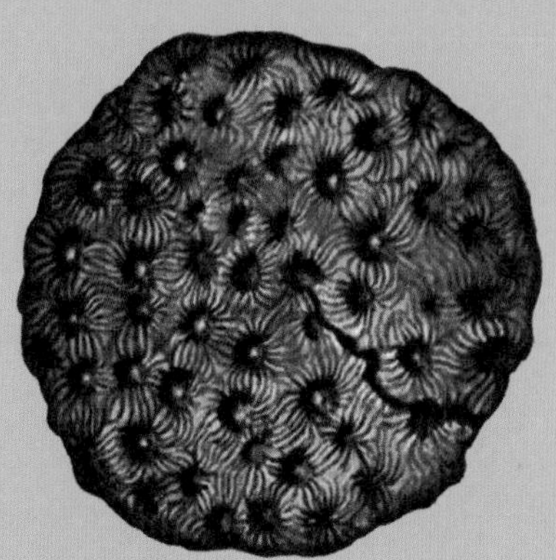

COMMON NAME Colonial coral

SIZE 2.5 inches (6.5 cm)

HABITAT Seafloor

TIME PERIOD Middle Triassic to Early Cretaceous

DATE 240–100 million years ago

WHERE IT HAS BEEN FOUND Worldwide

POINT OF FACT It's called a colonial coral because the polyp colonies are tough to tell apart. (Polyps are what make up coral.)

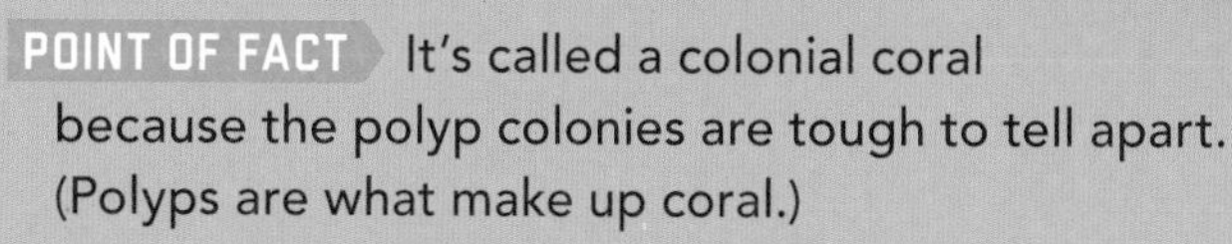

FOUND IT!

WHEN

DATE

WHERE

SPECIFIC PLACE AND SURROUNDINGS

NOTES

INVERTEBRATES

Archimedes

Moss Animals

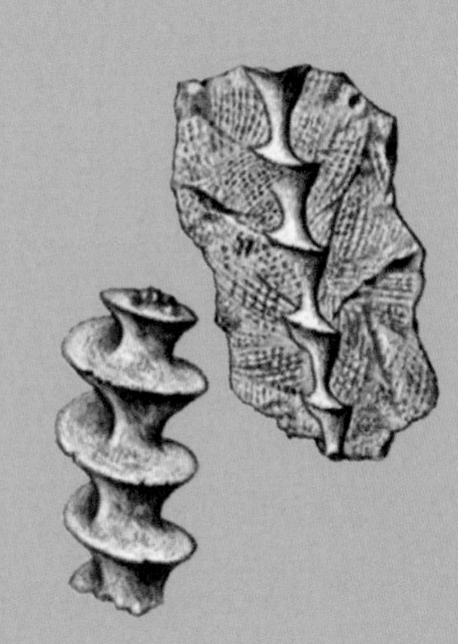

COMMON NAME Bryozoan screw

SIZE 1 inch (2.5 cm)

HABITAT
Sheltered marine ecosystem

TIME PERIOD
Carboniferous to Permian

DATE 360–250 million years ago

WHERE IT HAS BEEN FOUND
North America, Russia, Slovenia, Afghanistan

POINT OF FACT One of these branches can produce thousands of colonies, which may make it appear as if it's a small piece of coral.

FOUND IT!

WHEN
DATE

WHERE
SPECIFIC PLACE AND SURROUNDINGS

NOTES

INVERTEBRATES

Fenestella

Moss Animals

COMMON NAME Lace coral

SIZE 2 inches (5 cm)

HABITAT Seafloor

TIME PERIOD Silurian to Early Permian

DATE 440–270 million years ago

WHERE IT HAS BEEN FOUND Worldwide

POINT OF FACT It is called a lace coral because of its white pattern.

FOUND IT!

WHEN

DATE

WHERE

SPECIFIC PLACE AND SURROUNDINGS

NOTES

INVERTEBRATES

Spirifer

Brachiopods

COMMON NAME Lamp shell

SIZE 1.25 inches (3 cm)

HABITAT Seafloor

TIME PERIOD Ordovician to Permian

DATE 480–250 million years ago

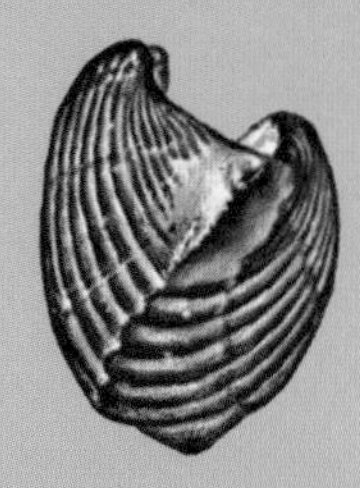

WHERE IT HAS BEEN FOUND Worldwide

POINT OF FACT These invertebrates lived by being attached to an object.

FOUND IT!

WHEN

DATE

WHERE

SPECIFIC PLACE AND SURROUNDINGS

NOTES

INVERTEBRATES

Calymene

Trilobites

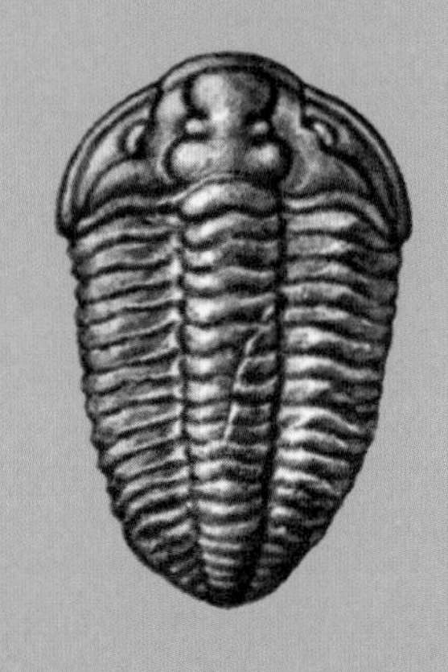

COMMON NAME Trilobite

SIZE 1.25 inches (3 cm)

HABITAT Lagoons or reefs

TIME PERIOD Silurian to Devonian

DATE 440–360 million years ago

WHERE IT HAS BEEN FOUND Worldwide

POINT OF FACT A fairly common fossil, this animal had a hard shell that protected it from predators.

FOUND IT!

WHEN

DATE

WHERE

SPECIFIC PLACE AND SURROUNDINGS

NOTES

INVERTEBRATES

Balanus

Crustaceans

COMMON NAME Acorn barnacle

SIZE 1.25–2.75 inches (3–7 cm)

HABITAT Shallow seafloors and rocky shores

TIME PERIOD Eocene to today

DATE 55–35 million years ago to today

WHERE IT HAS BEEN FOUND Worldwide

POINT OF FACT This type of barnacle grows on rocks all over the world.

FOUND IT!

WHEN

DATE

WHERE

SPECIFIC PLACE AND SURROUNDINGS

NOTES

INVERTEBRATES

Dentalium

Mollusks

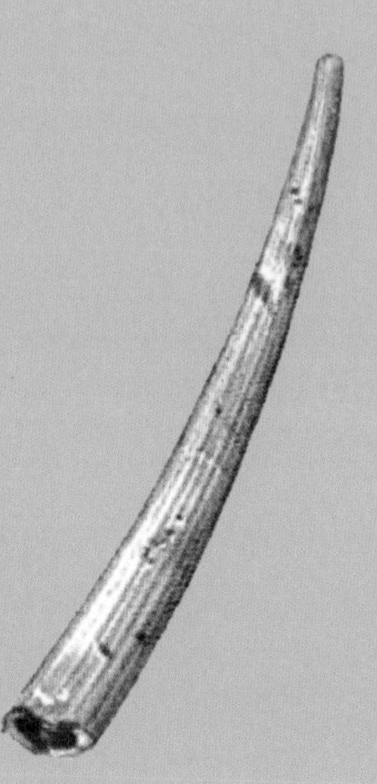

COMMON NAME Tusk shell

SIZE 4 inches (10 cm)

HABITAT Seafloor

TIME PERIOD Middle Triassic to today

DATE 245 million years ago to today

WHERE IT HAS BEEN FOUND Worldwide

POINT OF FACT This mollusk looks sort of like an elephant's tusk.

FOUND IT!

WHEN

DATE

WHERE

SPECIFIC PLACE AND SURROUNDINGS

NOTES

INVERTEBRATES

Neithea

Mollusks

COMMON NAME Scallop

SIZE 1 inch (2.5 cm)

HABITAT Seafloor

TIME PERIOD Cretaceous

DATE 145–65 million years ago

WHERE IT HAS BEEN FOUND Worldwide

POINT OF FACT These shells had gills with cilia (tiny hairs) that trapped food particles.

FOUND IT!

WHEN

DATE

WHERE

SPECIFIC PLACE AND SURROUNDINGS

NOTES

PART III

SHELLS

What would YOU do?

Sand. Can't you just feel it squishing through your bare toes as you walk along the beach making footprints? The ocean water laps against your ankles and causes you to sink just a tiny bit deeper into the sandy bottom. Being at the beach is the *best*! After all, there is sand, water, and . . . shells! Good thing you brought along your pail to carry the treasures that you find. Shells are everywhere at the beach. Many of them are tiny and a bit crunchy to walk on. Some are even broken pieces of bigger shells. But all were once homes to living creatures.

Hold on. Is that shell *walking*? You blink and rub your eyes. Is the sun getting to you? Perhaps the wave just flipped it over in a weird way. You watch some more. Now it appears to be skipping along the waves. That shell is *definitely* moving . . . and not by itself. It's probably *still* the home of a creature. But which one? How can you tell? What would you do?

SHELL SEEKING

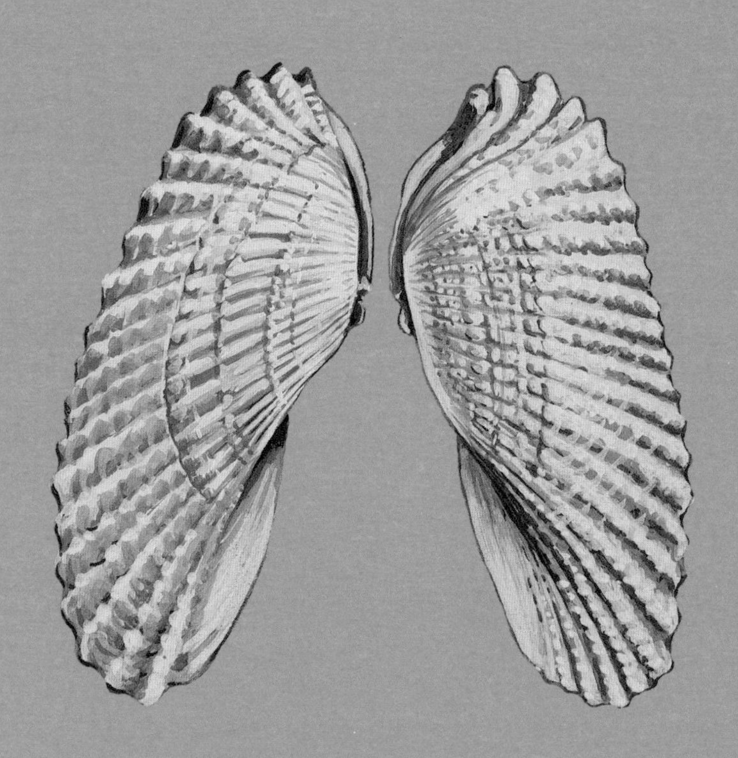

CHAPTER 11

Shells & Where You Can Find Them

You've seen them on the beach. You've probably stepped on tons of them as you played in the sand. But what exactly is a shell? A shell was once part of a living animal. Most are the hard exterior of an organism called a mollusk.

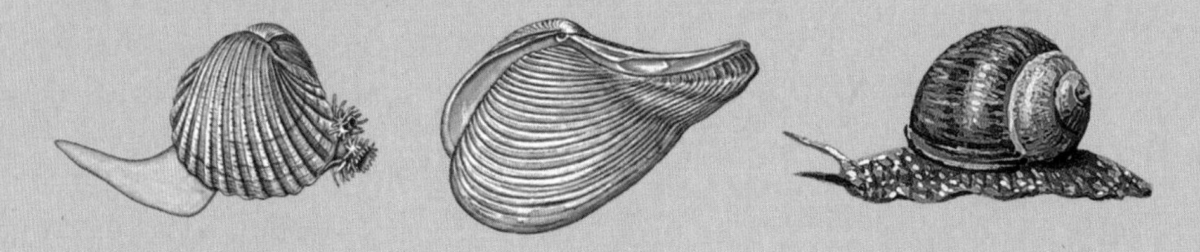

Mollusks

Mollusks are animals such as slugs, snails, clams, and oysters. They make up a large group of invertebrates. Mollusks don't have skeletons. Not inside anyway. Instead, most mollusks grow a shell for support. This external frame is called an exoskeleton. An exoskeleton is a hard structure located outside an organism's body that gives it support and protection. After all, mollusks are typically soft and quite tasty. They need protection from predators. The hard shell is tough to bite into, which can make a predator consider going somewhere else for their dinner.

Still, most of the shells you find on a beach are empty. What happened to the mollusks that lived inside them? They most likely died, maybe a long time ago. Some of the shells that wash up on the beach could be hundreds or even thousands of years old!

But there are so many shells! Did they all come from mollusks? Most of them, yes. But you may also find the hard skeletons of sea creatures such as sand dollars, sea urchins, or corals. Or maybe pieces of the exoskeletons from arthropods such as crabs and lobsters. (It is not easy to find an arthropod shell to collect, instead you might find it on your dinner plate!) For shell collecting, though, you'll want to focus on shells from mollusks.

How Are Shells Made?

Mollusks make their shells by secreting protein and calcium carbonate. (Sound familiar? Calcium carbonate is calcite and aragonite, the minerals that make up limestone and marble!) The protein acts like a mold for the calcium carbonate.

On the back of a mollusk is a layer of tissue called the mantle, which secretes the protein and calcium carbonate for the shell, typically in three layers:

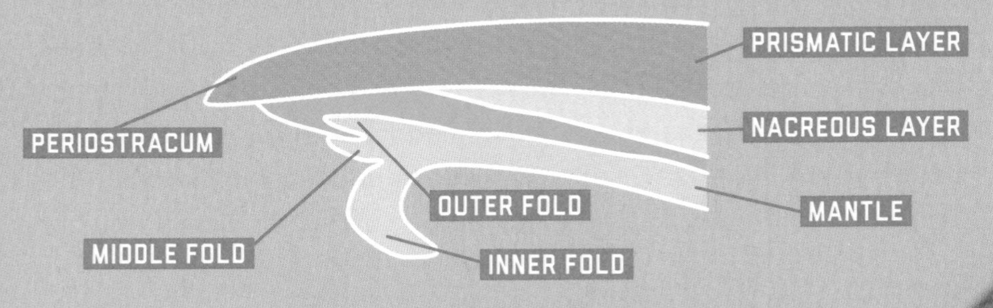

PERIOSTRACUM This layer forms first. It is made of protein and while initially flexible and leathery, it hardens into a solid. Secreted by the mantle, it creates the structure for the next layer.

PRISMATIC This layer contains calcium carbonate that forms the rigid inside of the shell. It's the thickest and strongest part of the shell and contains the pigments that make up the color and patterns on the outside.

NACRE This layer is secreted last. It contains calcium carbonate that form microscopic plates of aragonite. The plates are structured like bricks, so that they create a very strong structure of support for the shell. In several mollusks, this appears as an iridescent mother-of-pearl.

As a mollusk grows, the mantle extends beyond the edge of the opening and continues to secrete the protein and calcium carbonate bit by bit. This allows the shell "to grow" with the animal so that the mollusk is still within its protective shell.

Arthropods

Arthropods are another type of animal that have a hard, protective outer layer. A whopping 84 percent of all known animal species on earth are arthropods, which also includes spiders and insects.

Arthropods are different from mollusks in that their exoskeletons are made of a material called chitin. The animal secretes, or releases, chitin and protein from its skin. The protein and chitin hardens over time forming a solid protective covering. Unlike mollusk shells, the exoskeletons of arthropods do not grow with them. So to grow larger, the animal must shed its shell, or molt. They do this by secreting a new, soft exoskeleton under their old one. The arthropod then takes in water and air to "puff up" and crack the old exoskeleton. That releases the old exoskeleton from their body. To make a new exoskeleton, they "puff up" even more to get the size that is comfortable for them. Then they must wait for it to harden.

You may occasionally find an empty lobster or crab exoskeleton on the beach, but not very often. It's much easier to find mollusk shells on the shore since they are in huge abundance.

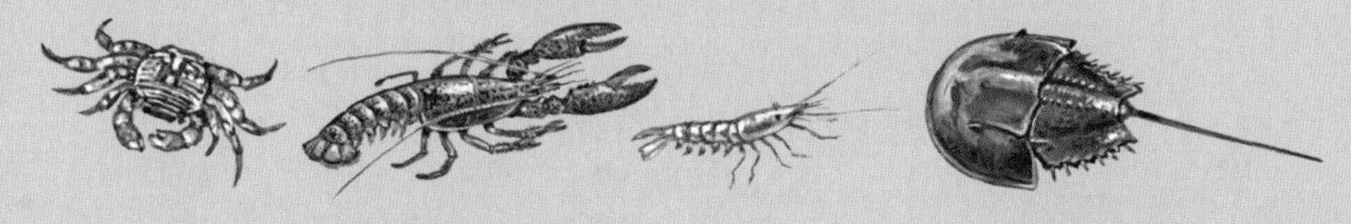

Hermit crabs are a special type of arthropod. They have an exoskeleton, but it is soft and doesn't provide much protection. Instead, hermit crabs must find an empty mollusk shell to live in. The problem? They grow but the mollusk shell doesn't. As hermit crabs get bigger, they must find new shells. (It makes sense: a shell needs to fit rather snugly around the animal to protect it, but too snug a fit and it can't completely hide from predators.) So, if you're a hermit crab and your shell is too tight, you know it's time to find another shell. Perhaps a smaller hermit crab will pick your old one up!

Where Do I Find Shells?

Now that you know more about shells, it's time to head outside and find them in their habitat. The best place to look for shells is by the ocean. Most mollusks live in salt water, and when they die, their shells wash up by the thousands along the sandy shore. Some mollusks, however, live in fresh water. So their shells can be found on the shores of a lake, river, stream, or creek.

So, where do you start? Let's take a look at this map. It divides North America into different regions where seashells can be found. Find the area closest to where you live and look for the shells in the identification guide on pages 366–424 to see what type of shells you might find there. Note that the areas that you find in the identification guide might be more specific than the ones listed here.

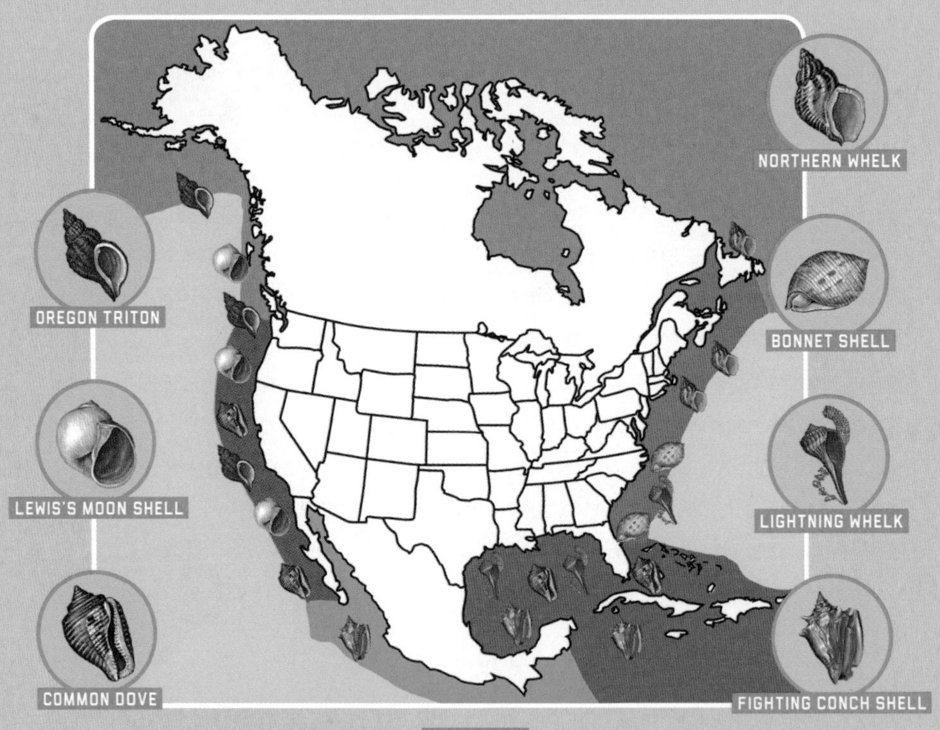

Do you live near a body of water? If so, then plan a visit for your first shell-hunting trip. If not, try your backyard—after all, you may just find shell there! It is unlikely, but if an ancient river flowed through your backyard, you might find evidence of it (and a fossil or two)!

BEFORE YOU HUNT FOR SHELLS, READ THIS!

It is usually okay to remove shells from the beach provided they are *not* still occupied! If there is an animal living in the shell, leave it alone. *Don't* take it with you. That animal needs to stay in its habitat. Plus, it can be costly to remove a live creature. Some beaches have fines for removing a live marine animal from the ocean.

How can you tell whether there's something living inside a shell?

- With a coiled shell, turn it over and look for a creature deep inside. Sometimes they curl up when the shell is picked up.
- If you see two halves of a shell closed tightly together, that means a mollusk is still alive inside.
- If you see two halves that are open at first but close when you touch them, the creature is still alive.
- If you go to pick up a sand dollar, be sure it is white and bald. If it is any other color and has hairs on it, it is still alive.
- If you see a starfish, squat down and look closely at its tiny tube feet. If they are moving, it's alive. If you aren't sure, gently touch them or put it in water to see whether they move. If you still aren't sure, leave it.

TRY IT → Checking Tide Cycles

There is one more thing that will make hunting for shells easier: knowing the cycle of the tides. Tides happen naturally as the level of the ocean or a tidal river rises and falls. Tides cycle throughout the day. The level of the ocean or a tidal river is constantly changing.

A TIDE CYCLE GOES LIKE THIS

- The water level begins to rise.
- *High tide* is reached when the water is at its highest level.
- The water level begins to fall.
- *Low tide* is reached when the water is at its lowest level.

HIGH TIDE

In most places around the world the cycle repeats twice a day.

The thing a good shell hunter needs to know is that low tide is the *best* time for shell hunting! Why? When the water is low, you can go farther out, and many shells that might normally be under water are now visible and ready to be snatched!

LOW TIDE

How can you check the tide levels in your area? Do an internet search for the National Oceanic and Atmospheric Administration (NOAA) and type in "tides in your area." NOAA keeps track of the tide cycles, which are important for boaters and people who fish as well as shell collectors. You can also check local news outlets near the beach you'll be heading to.

Before you go out shell hunting, check the tides and write them down here. It's different every day. So if you go out a couple of times, be sure to write down each date and the times. Not every river is tidal. Many don't have tide cycles. You can do a search on your local river to find that out, too. Write it all down here.

TRACK IT ↘

Make a Shell–Hunting Map

STEP 1 Pick a safe place to explore. It could be a stream, lake, along the ocean shore, or even your own backyard if you can't easily get to a natural water source.

WHAT YOU'LL NEED

- Colored pencils or pens and a piece of paper or this book.

STEP 2 Before you start the hunt, you'll need a map to mark where you find everything. You can draw your own map, trace your path on an existing map of a beach, lake, stream, or shore, or find one online using a site like Google Maps and print it out and paste it below. Note the basic area where you are walking. Include the shore, the waves, the color of the sea or river, etc.

I DID IT! DATE:

TRY IT → Searching for Shells

You are ready! Go get some shells!

WHAT YOU'LL NEED

- A dry day, a bucket or pail with a handle, twelve bags or containers that close easily or an empty egg carton, water bottle and a snack (shell hunting can make you hungry!), sunscreen, small shovel or trowel, a permanent marker and a roll of masking tape to make labels, map and compass (even if you have a smartphone with GPS), camera, sieve with a handle, small clean paintbrush or toothbrush (to brush sand off the shells), a couple of small plastic bags, towel (to wipe sand off your feet when you are done).

STEP 1 Grab your pail and walk along the beach looking for shells. You don't want to pick up every shell you see (your bucket will get very heavy), just the ones that catch your eye, or maybe the ones you dig up from under the sand. You'll want to pick up as many different kinds of shells as possible.

STEP 2 As you pick up a shell, take a good look at it. Tap it gently with your finger. And also refer to the directions on page 329 about live creatures. You need to make sure it's *really* empty. If you think that something might still be inside, place the shell in water to see if anything comes out to explore. Finally, smell it. If it smells like something died in there, most likely it did. And it might still be there.

> Cleaning out the former inhabitant of a shell is not always fun. Plus, bringing a smelly shell into your car might not be okay with everyone else. If you really want to take this shell with you, be sure to place it into a plastic bag right away. You may want to add a * or something so that you know you have to clean this shell really well when you get home.

STEP 3 If your shell passes the smell test (and all the others), place the shell in your bag or container and use your marker and masking tape to label it with a number. That way you know which shell is which when you identify them later.

STEP 4 Before you move on, note the shell by putting its number on your map. Or type it into your GPS. That way you'll know where you found each shell.

STEP 5 Once that shell is put away, keep moving. Don't just pick up the shells in front of you. Look down the beach, in the water, and by the dunes. Maybe you see one that sparkles or is really big. You may just find pieces of shells. Pick up a few of those. They can be fun to identify, too.

STEP 6 If you find a shell that is still inhabited, simply take a picture of it. You can still identify it later, even if you don't have the shell itself.

TAKE IT TO THE NEXT LEVEL ↗

Shell-Hunting Game

Hunt for shells with someone else and make it a game. See who can find the following:

- most colorful shell
- biggest shell
- tiniest shell
- starfish
- sand dollar
- hermit crab
- shark's tooth (They don't have to be fossils!)

PRO TIP If you find anything you can't keep, just take a picture of it and add it here. Then write up some observations!

I DID IT! DATE:

TAKE IT TO THE NEXT LEVEL ↗

Snorkeling for Shells

While you can find a bunch of shells on the beach, sometimes it's fun to get in the water to find them. The easiest way is to roll up your pant legs, wade in, and grab the shells you see on the bottom.

If you are an *experienced swimmer*, however, you may want to try snorkeling to find shells. Here are a few things you need to consider *before* you go snorkeling:

- Follow all posted signs and lifeguard regulations. If you are at a beach, check with the lifeguard to see whether there are rip currents present. If there are, *do not* go into the water.
- *Be careful* picking up shells underwater because they are more likely to have live animals in them. Some of these animals might bite, so wear gloves.
- *Do not* snorkel in rivers, because they have currents.
- *Do not* snorkel in a lake without wearing goggles.

WHAT YOU'LL NEED

- Mesh bag, snorkel, mask, swimsuit, waterproof diving gloves, an adult to supervise.

Once you are ready, wade out and begin snorkeling. Pick up any shells that look interesting and place them in your mesh bag. Do not pick up the moving ones. They could have creatures in them.

TRACK IT ↘

Describe Your Shells

After you have collected your shells, write them down and describe each one clearly. Make sure you note where you found the shell: in the water, by the shore, near the dunes, etc.

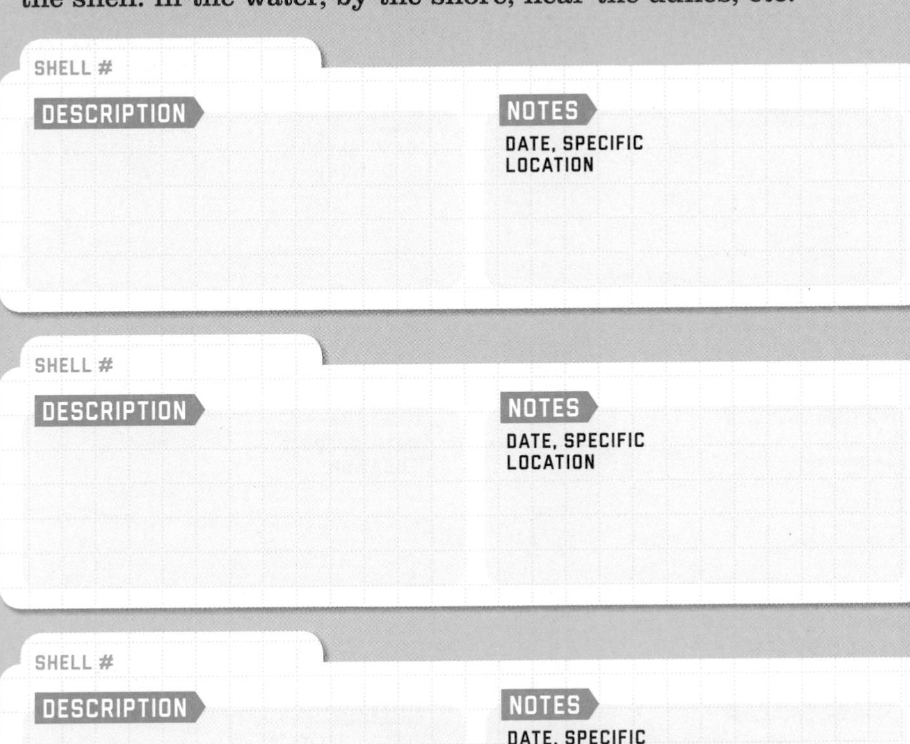
SHELL #

DESCRIPTION

NOTES

DATE, SPECIFIC LOCATION

SHELL #

DESCRIPTION

NOTES

DATE, SPECIFIC LOCATION

SHELL #

DESCRIPTION

NOTES

DATE, SPECIFIC LOCATION

SHELL #

DESCRIPTION

NOTES

DATE, SPECIFIC LOCATION

SHELL #

DESCRIPTION

NOTES

DATE, SPECIFIC LOCATION

SHELL #

DESCRIPTION

NOTES

DATE, SPECIFIC LOCATION

SHELL #

DESCRIPTION

NOTES

DATE, SPECIFIC LOCATION

SHELL #

DESCRIPTION

NOTES

DATE, SPECIFIC LOCATION

SHELL #

DESCRIPTION

NOTES

DATE, SPECIFIC LOCATION

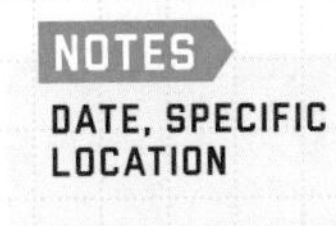

SHELL #

DESCRIPTION

NOTES

DATE, SPECIFIC LOCATION

SHELL #

DESCRIPTION

NOTES

DATE, SPECIFIC LOCATION

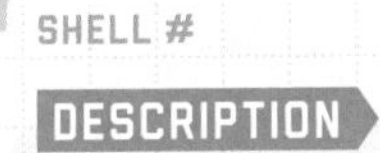

SHELL #

DESCRIPTION

NOTES

DATE, SPECIFIC LOCATION

If you collect more shells than this chart can hold, photocopy the page and extend your chart. Staple it inside this book to keep everything in one place!

TRY IT → Soak Your Shells

Once you return from your shell-hunting trip, it's best to clean the shells out right away as some might be a bit smelly.

WHAT YOU'LL NEED

- Small containers for each of your shells, fresh water, a place to let the containers sit for a week (it can be outside or inside, just somewhere where no one will mess with it).

STEP 1 One at a time, put each shell into a new container. Be sure to mark the number of the shell on the container (or keep the original bag or container next to the new one).

STEP 2 Pour fresh water into each container. You don't need to scrub or wipe the shell, just let it sit in the water.

STEP 3 Change the water every two days or so by removing your shell, dumping out the water, and refilling the container. Put the same shell back into the same container.

STEP 4 After a week, you will be ready to clean them (see page 349). For now, just let the water naturally soak your shells.

CHAPTER 12

Hunting for Different Types of Shells

While your shells are soaking, let's learn more about them! What kind of shells do you think you have? Most likely they are from mollusks. Why? Mollusk shells are stronger and last longer than arthropod shells. The real question is, What type of mollusk shell do you have?

Parts and Classes of Mollusks

All mollusks have three main parts: the mantle, visceral mass, and a muscular foot. The mantle makes the shell, if the mollusk has one, and wraps around the visceral mass as a sort of protection. The visceral mass is where the mollusk's vital organs are found—things like the stomach, intestines, reproductive organs, etc. Beneath the visceral mass is the muscular foot. Depending on the kind of mollusk, the foot is used for moving around, attaching to things, and capturing food.

There are several different classes of mollusks, and they are grouped according to how their body parts are arranged and function. These classes include: gastropods, bivalves, tusk shells, and chitons, which all make shells. There are other classes, but they either don't make shells or their shells are very rare and not included in this book. These include cephalopods (squid or octopus). Since they don't have shells, please don't pick up one of those and take it home.

Gastropods

Gastropods make up about 80 percent of all known mollusks. You know them as snails—and slugs, which don't have shells. Gastropods have a head, and the foot allows them to move around. They make a single shell that's often coiled. Gastropods are one of the few mollusks that can be found pretty much anywhere—from deep in the ocean to fresh water and inland salt water. These adaptable creatures can live on land, too.

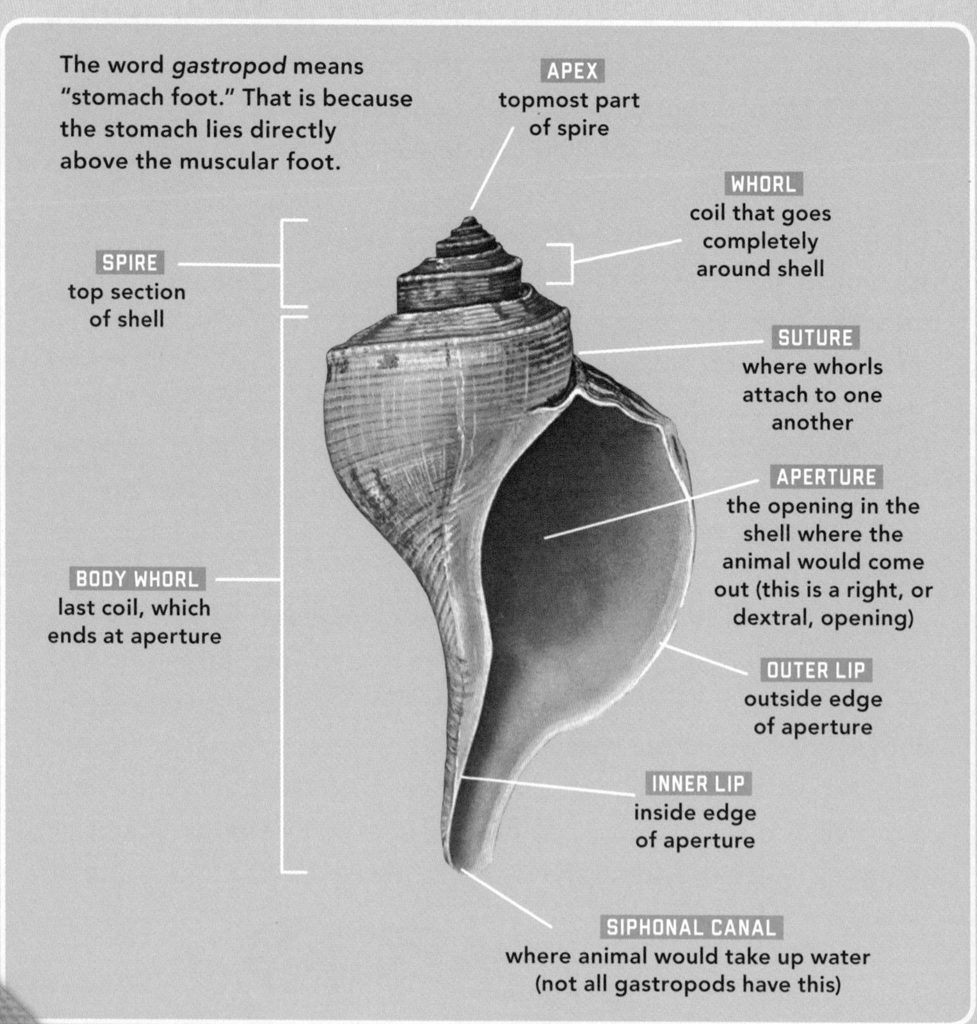

Gastropod shells take many different forms:

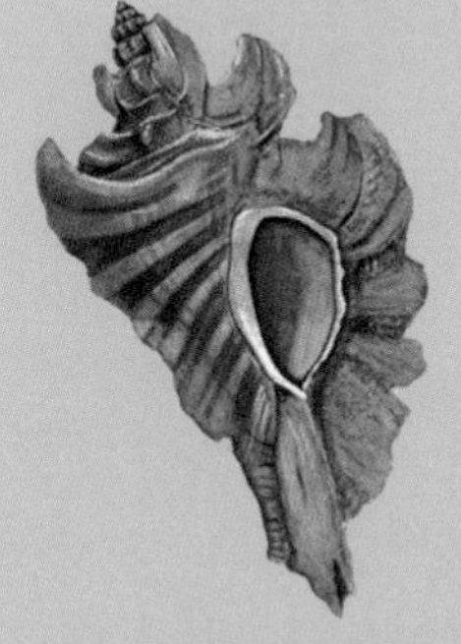

THREE WINGED MUREX

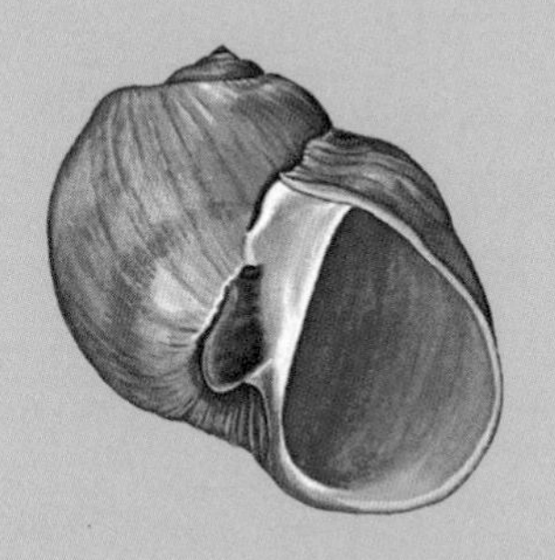

LEWIS'S MOON SNAIL

ABALONE

FLORIDA FIGHTING CONCH

TRUE LIMPET

COWRIE

ATLANTIC SLIPPER

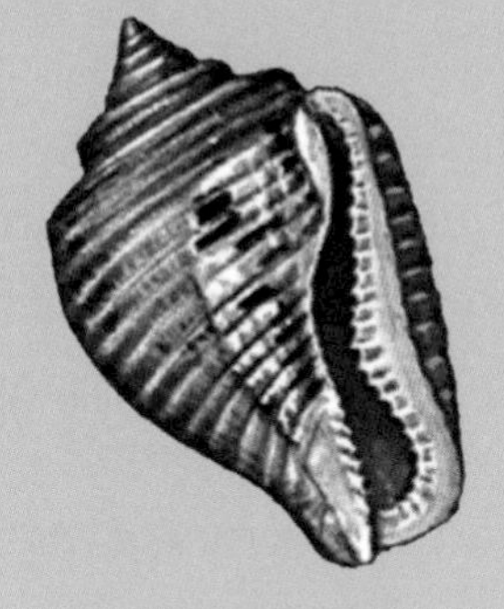

COMMON DOVE

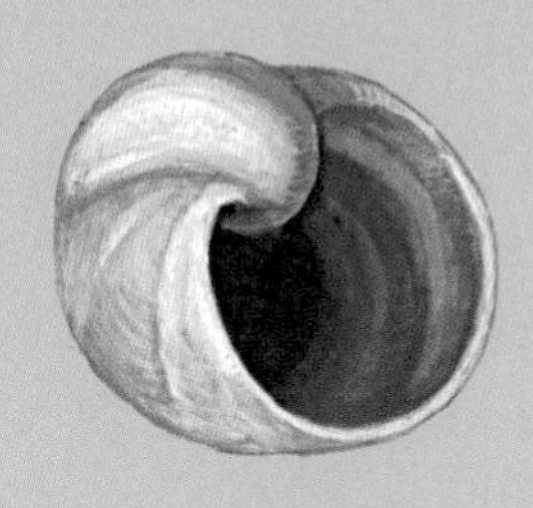

MOON SNAIL

Land Snails That Grow as Big as Your Hand (Really!)

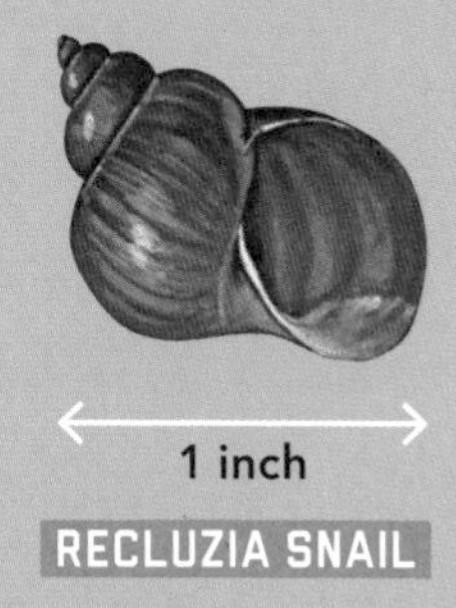

The sea snail shells that you may find on the beach are relatively small. Many will easily will fit into the palm of your hand. But if you happen to find a land snail, particularly an African land snail, you may be in for quite a surprise. These snails can grow as big as eight inches (20 cm) across. So you'd need both hands to pick it up. (But remember, we aren't keeping this shell if the snail is still in it!)

If you find this snail in any place but Africa, then it shouldn't be there. African snails belong in, well, Africa, particularly Kenya and Tanzania. They were most likely collected from Africa and brought to different continents, perhaps as a pet. If they got loose and reproduced, then you have African snails in other countries. This species can also carry the disease meningitis, so please don't touch it.

Bivalves

Bivalves are probably the mollusk you're most familiar with. They include clams, scallops, oysters, and mussels. A bivalve is made up of two half shells that are hinged together at one end, which allows the mollusk to open and close them as it filters water through its gills. This allows them to get oxygen and to remove food particles from the water to eat. Their muscular foot is used to anchor them to a particular object, like a rock or a reef or to dig into mud at the bottom of rivers, lakes, and oceans.

Bivalve shells take many different forms:

SUNRISE TELLIN

ANGEL WING

BLUE MUSSEL

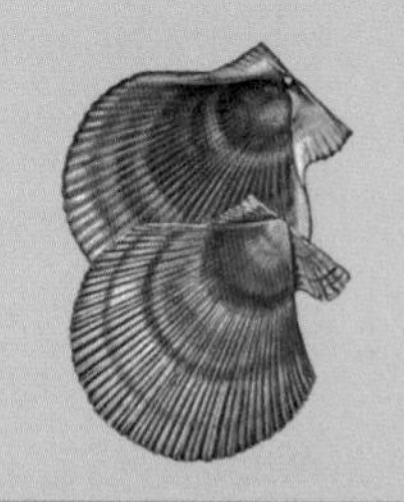
ICELAND SCALLOP

Tusk Shells

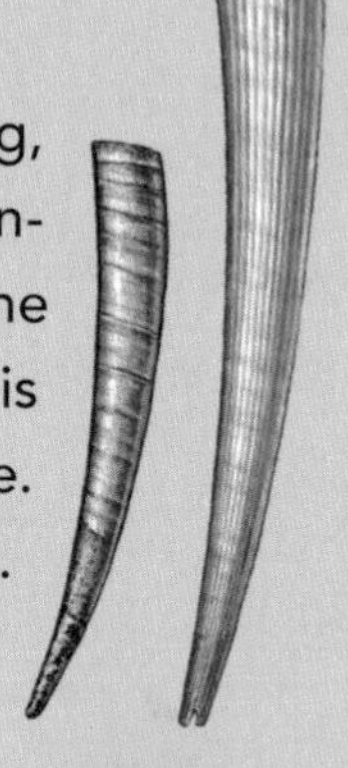

Tusk shells are easy to spot. Their shells look like long, thin tubes. They curve slightly and end in an open-ended point, sort of like an elephant's tusk. When the animal is inside the tube, its foot at the wide bottom is anchored in the sand or mud to keep the shell in place. There are about 350 different species of tusk shells. They are found mostly in sea water that is six feet (1.83 m) or deeper.

Chitons

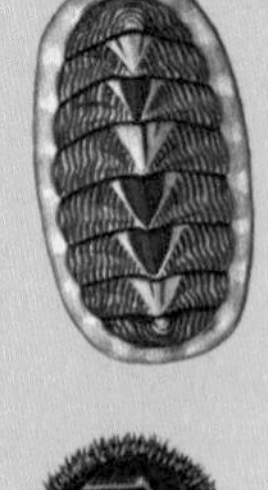

Chitons are sometimes described as looking a little like an armadillo. They have overlapping shell plates, usually eight of them. Chitons are found in seawater sometimes along coastal rocks or just beneath the surface of the water. But they can also live in very deep water (greater than 23,000 ft/7,010 m), too. They usually spend most of their life attached to rocks where they can eat the nearby seaweed.

Clam Shell or Oyster Shell?

If you were to look at a clam shell and an oyster shell, could you tell the difference? It might be more difficult than you think. They both have two shells that are attached at one end and can open at the other. They can be similar shades of brown, black, or gray. But oysters have a rough outer shell, while clams have smooth and usually shiny shells. Oysters also stay in one place and can't really move about. They are found in salty and brackish (somewhat salty) waters in bays and river estuaries worldwide. Clams have a foot and can move themselves around with it. They are found in freshwater lakes, ponds, and rivers, as well as in the ocean. Certain clams can also grow very large in size, unlike oysters. Both oysters and clams can form pearls, although it's more common in oysters.

Giant clams help keep coral reefs healthy by producing calcium carbonate, which is eventually absorbed as part of the reef.

Arthropods

Arthropods are a very diverse type of animal. They are more than a million different species, including both land- and sea-dwelling creatures. While it is unusual to find arthropod exoskeletons on the beach, it is not impossible. Why don't you find them? Most arthropods are either eaten by other animals or harvested as food for humans.

Arthropods can have the following characteristics:

JOINTED LIMBS Joints allow limbs to move more easily.

SEGMENTED BODY Body is separated into sections.

EXOSKELETON Supporting structure is on the outside of the body.

BILATERAL SYMMETRY The left and right sides of the body are the same.

COMPOUND EYES Which gives them great distance vision and the ability to see movement well (not all arthropods have these).

GILLS OR TRACHEAE Allows for the animal to breathe. If it lives in water, it has gills. If it lives on land, it has tracheae (tubes).

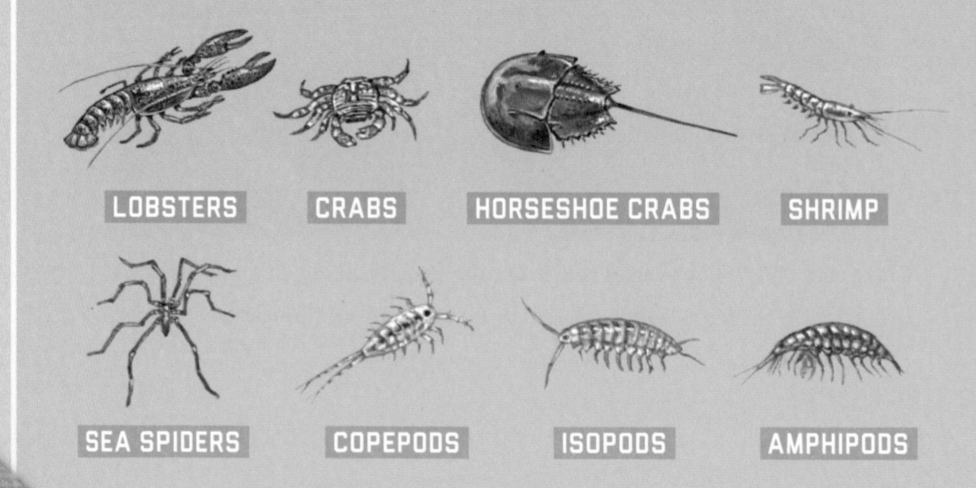

TRY IT → Cleaning Your Shells

If a week has gone by since you soaked your shells, it's time to finish cleaning them!

WHAT YOU'LL NEED

- A big towel, a covered area to lay out all your shells, a few small hand towels or a roll of paper towels, sandpaper, small bottle of mineral oil (optional, makes shells shine).

STEP 1 Find a big area where you can lay out your shells to dry. It needs to be protected from rain so your shells don't get wet again.

STEP 2 Spread the big towel on the floor.

STEP 3 One at a time, take each shell out, wipe it with a hand towel, and place it on the big towel to dry. Make sure that you note which shell is which by either putting a number on the inside with a marker, or putting it on top of its original container or bag with the number.

STEP 4 Leave your shells to dry overnight.

STEP 5 The next day take a piece of sandpaper and rub it across each shell. You want to remove any sand or debris that may still be sticking to it.

STEP 6 If you like the rough look of the shells, then you are done. However, if you want your shells to shine, get out the mineral oil. Pour a small amount onto a paper towel or small hand towel. Polish each shell with the towel. When you are done, set them back where you had them on the towel.

TRY IT → Organizing Your Collection

Are you ready to dig in and start organizing your shells? Let's do it!

WHAT YOU'LL NEED

- Bags or containers that close easily (if you need to change out the bag or container that you were originally using), marker, masking tape, pencil, ruler, vernier caliper (optional).

STEP 1 Pick up one shell at a time. Take a good look at it.

STEP 2 Note its color and shape on the next page.

STEP 3 Take the ruler and measure its length (the long side across it). Be aware that measurement with a ruler is only approximate because of the curvature of the shell. If you have a vernier caliper, use it instead. Place the shell's highest point on the lower "jaw" (the part that sticks out). And then push the lower jaw until the top point of the shell reaches the top jaw. Now read the measurement on the side of the caliper. Mark the size on the next page.

STEP 4 Place that shell back into the bag or container it came from.

STEP 5 Repeat this for each of your shells. Be sure to place your shells back into the original bag or container that they were in, or in a new one with the same number. You can then put your shells into a box like the one you made for your rocks if you wish. If your shells have vivid colors, you may want to keep them in a covered box or a dark bag to protect them from fading in the light.

SHELL #

COLOR

SIZE

SHAPE

NOTES

DATE, SPECIFIC LOCATION

SHELL #

COLOR

SIZE

SHAPE

NOTES

DATE, SPECIFIC LOCATION

SHELL #

COLOR

SIZE

SHAPE

NOTES

DATE, SPECIFIC LOCATION

SHELL #

COLOR

SIZE

SHAPE

NOTES

DATE, SPECIFIC LOCATION

SHELL #

COLOR

SIZE

SHAPE

NOTES
DATE, SPECIFIC LOCATION

SHELL #

COLOR

SIZE

SHAPE

NOTES
DATE, SPECIFIC LOCATION

SHELL #

COLOR

SIZE

SHAPE

NOTES
DATE, SPECIFIC LOCATION

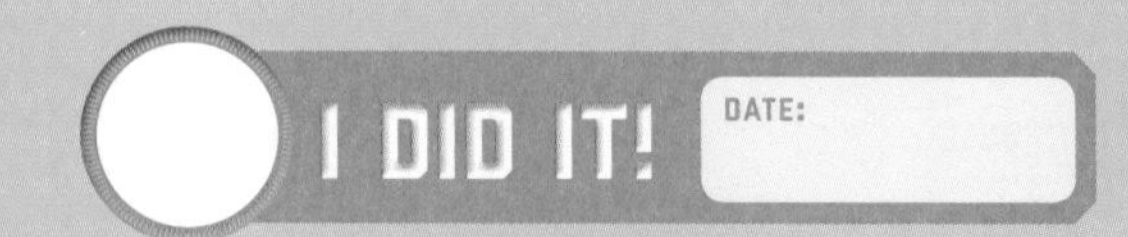

TAKE IT TO THE NEXT LEVEL ↗

Sorting Your Shells

If you really want to get into sorting your shell collection, you could do so by size, color, or even shape.

- If you sort them by color, you could put all the shells that are orangish in one section. Then put any with brown on them in another section. Gray ones over there, etc. . . .
- If you sort them by size, maybe you arrange your collection from small shells (or pieces of shells) to large. Or vice versa.
- If you sort them by shape, perhaps you put all the flat ones together. Then the ones with the swirls in one section. And the ones that are round or spiky in another section.

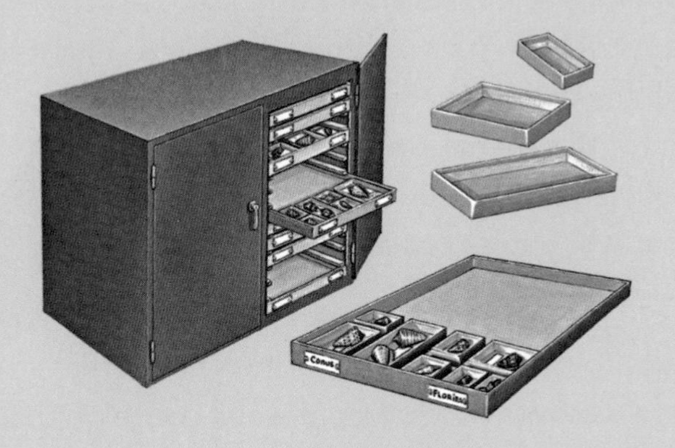

CHAPTER 13

Identifying Your Shell Collection

You have now collected, cleaned, and organized your shells. But what you really want to know is what type of shells you have found!

Here are a few tips as you start to identify your shells:

MOST GASTROPOD SHELLS OPEN TO THE RIGHT They are dextral, which means that if you hold the shell in your right hand, the opening will point toward your thumb. If by chance you find a shell that opens to the left, hang on to it and congratulate yourself! Shells that are sinistral, or open to the left, are not common. You may find this in a few snails, such as the lightning whelk, the left-handed whelk, the spindle shells, and the perverse turrid. Rarely, an individual snail makes a sinistral shell on its own.

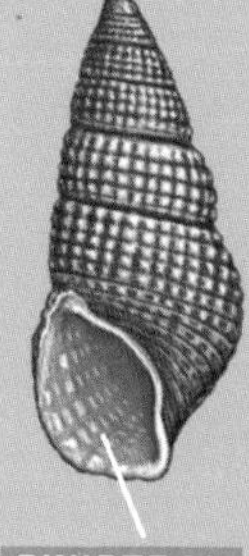

PATTERNS MATTER While scientists aren't quite sure exactly how a mollusk makes the pattern on its shell, they do believe that it has something to do with the environment it lives in. After all, these shells are protection for the animal. So, a hard, rough shell might mean the shell came from a deep part of the ocean, or an area that was subject to lots of waves.

SHAPE MAKES A DIFFERENCE Each shell has a shape that can be identified. Compare your shell to the ones in the identification guide to discover which type of shell you might have.

TRY IT → Identify Your Shells!

Go through your shells one at a time and mark off the characteristics below. Then compare your shell to the guide on pages 366–424 to help identify your shell!

WHAT YOU'LL NEED

- Your shells, a magnifying glass.

SHELL #

RIGHT OPEN ☐

LEFT OPEN ☐

TYPE OF SHELL

SIZE

SHAPE

COLOR

PATTERN

SHELL #

RIGHT OPEN ☐

LEFT OPEN ☐

TYPE OF SHELL

SIZE

SHAPE

COLOR

PATTERN

SHELL #

RIGHT OPEN ☐

LEFT OPEN ☐

TYPE OF SHELL

SIZE

SHAPE

COLOR

PATTERN

SHELL #

RIGHT OPEN ☐

LEFT OPEN ☐

TYPE OF SHELL

SIZE

SHAPE

COLOR

PATTERN

SHELL #

RIGHT OPEN ☐

LEFT OPEN ☐

TYPE OF SHELL

SIZE

SHAPE

COLOR

PATTERN

SHELL #

RIGHT OPEN ☐

LEFT OPEN ☐

TYPE OF SHELL

SIZE

SHAPE

COLOR

PATTERN

SHELL #

RIGHT OPEN ☐

LEFT OPEN ☐

TYPE OF SHELL

SIZE

SHAPE

COLOR

PATTERN

SHELL #

RIGHT OPEN ☐

LEFT OPEN ☐

TYPE OF SHELL

SIZE

SHAPE

COLOR

PATTERN

SHELL #

RIGHT OPEN ☐

LEFT OPEN ☐

TYPE OF SHELL

SIZE

SHAPE

COLOR

PATTERN

SHELL #

RIGHT OPEN ☐

LEFT OPEN ☐

TYPE OF SHELL

SIZE

SHAPE

COLOR

PATTERN

If you weren't able to match each of your shells, don't worry. Some shells look alike. If you need to, you can put down a couple different types of shells that you think it might be. This is what scientists do. They don't always know the answers, so they give good guesses based on everything they have learned.

TAKE IT TO THE NEXT LEVEL ↗

How Old Is Your Shell?

Many types of mollusks have visible rings on their shells. The number of these growth rings provides a clue to the mollusk's age. The more rings, the older the shell. Count each ring carefully using a magnifying glass. Sometimes the rings are really pressed together.

It might take a while, but you are a shell hunter and scientist and you love to gather data!

WHAT YOU'LL NEED

- Your shells, a magnifying glass.

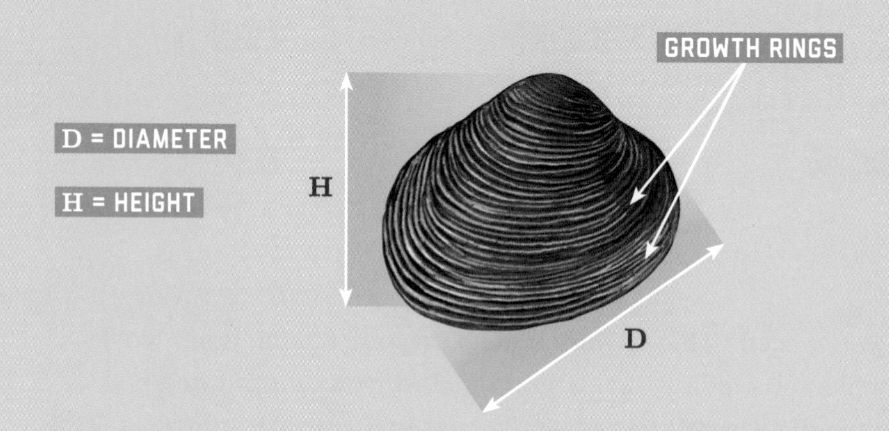

PRO-TIP If it is too difficult to count all the rings in a shell at once, then try counting a group of them say, one hundred rings at a time and estimating using this number.

1. Measure that distance with your ruler:

100 ridges = ______ inches (______ cm) = A

2. Now measure the diameter of your shell (or take it from the chart on pages 355–357):

Diameter = ______

3. Divide the diameter by A: Diameter ÷ A = B ______

4. Multiply B by 100: B x 100 = ______ rings on your shell

HERE'S AN EXAMPLE

Shell #1 has:

100 rings = **0.5 cm** = A

➢ Now measure the diameter of your shell (or take it from the chart on pages 355–357):

Diameter = **8 cm**

➢ Divide the diameter by A: Diameter ÷ A = B **16**

➢ Multiply B by 100: B x 100 = **1,600** rings on Shell #1.

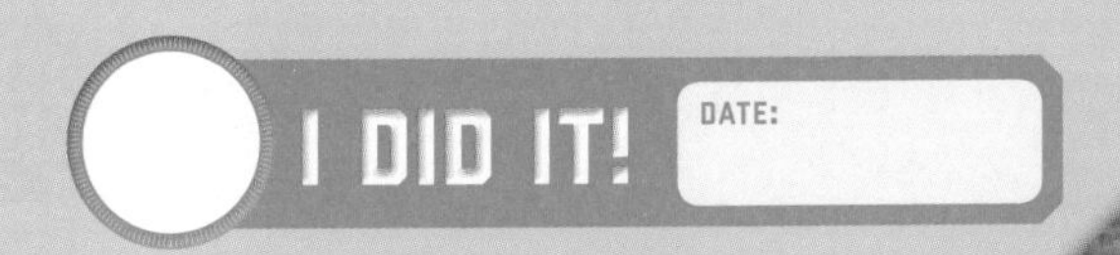

CHAPTER 14

Expanding Your Shell Collection

Did you have so much fun hunting, sorting, and identifying shells that you want to collect more? Awesome! Let's go on another hunt!

Try new places each time you go shell hunting. If you went to a sandy ocean beach before, try looking for shells in an estuary or a tide pool or a lake. You'll find different kinds of shells depending on where you go.

Where the Mississippi River meets the Gulf of Mexico is a good example of an estuary.

ESTUARY The area where one or more rivers widen and meet the ocean, mixing fresh water with salt water.

TIDE POOL A pool of water that is left behind on rocks and sand during low tide.

TRACK IT ↘ Map Your New Shell-Hunting Area!

Before you go, use a map to look for a different water ecosystem near you that's safe to explore. Note any tides, and study the area. Is it a marsh? An estuary? Will there be tide pools? Write down some of the area's features.

WHAT YOU'LL NEED

- Colored pencils or pens and a piece of paper or this book.

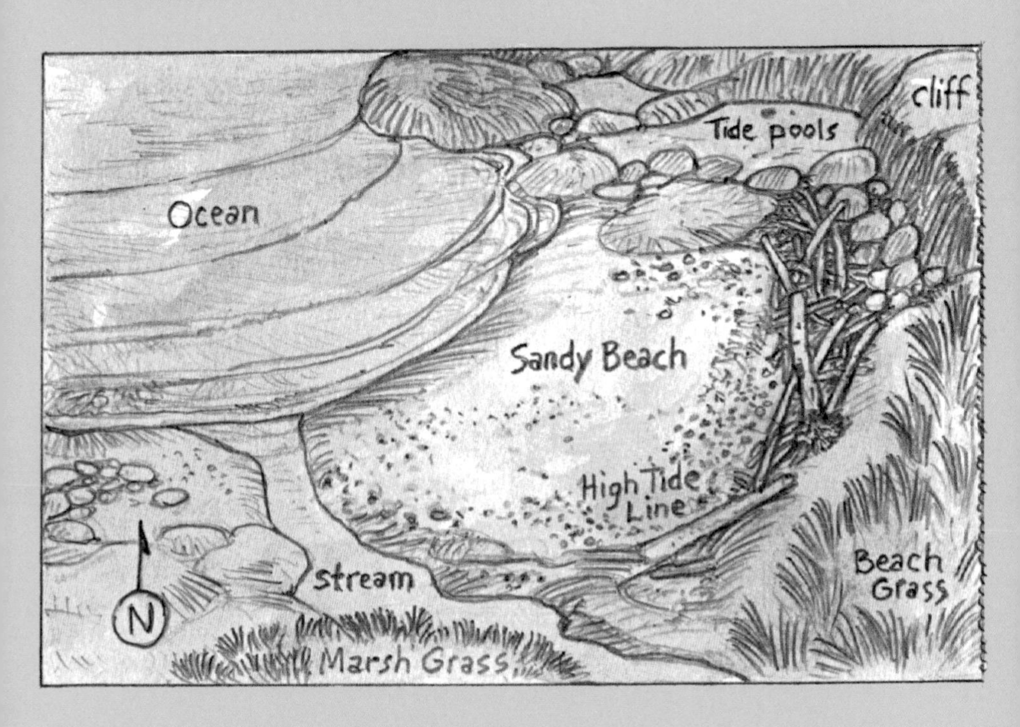

STEP 1 Before you start exploring, you'll need a map to mark where you find everything. Draw your own map or paste and trace your path on an existing map on the next page. Note the basic area where you are walking. Include the shore, the waves, the color of the sea or river, etc.

I DID IT!
DATE:

TRY IT → New Shell Hunt!

Let's go hunting! You are going to follow the same directions as you did on your first shell hunt. Refer back to pages 333–334.

Gather your shells, soak them for a week as instructed on page 340, and then categorize them here:

SHELLS IN THIS CHART WERE COLLECTED FROM

SHELL #

RIGHT OPEN ☐

LEFT OPEN ☐

TYPE OF SHELL

SIZE

SHAPE

COLOR

PATTERN

SHELL #

RIGHT OPEN ☐

LEFT OPEN ☐

TYPE OF SHELL

SIZE

SHAPE

COLOR

PATTERN

SHELL #

RIGHT OPEN ☐

LEFT OPEN ☐

TYPE OF SHELL

SIZE

SHAPE

COLOR

PATTERN

SHELL #

RIGHT OPEN ☐

LEFT OPEN ☐

TYPE OF SHELL

SIZE

SHAPE

COLOR

PATTERN

SHELL #

RIGHT OPEN ☐

LEFT OPEN ☐

TYPE OF SHELL

SIZE

SHAPE

COLOR

PATTERN

Compare these shells to the ones from your first shell-hunting expedition. Do they look different because they were found in different ecosystems? Are some the same? How do you think similar shells ended up in two different places?

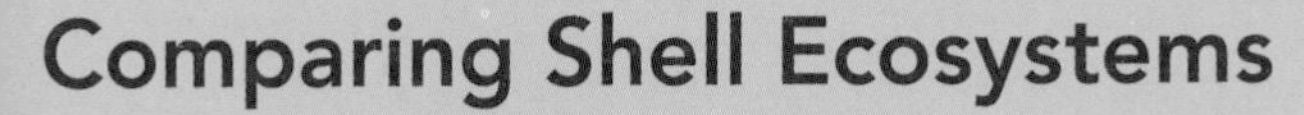

Comparing Shell Ecosystems

As you compare shells, make some observations and some notes below:

If you don't want to keep all the shells that you've collected (or rocks and fossils, for that matter), you can always take them back to the places where you found them. After all, shells are eventually crushed up naturally, and the bits of calcium carbonate will fall to the ocean floor or become part of a reef. The planet is very good at recycling itself.

SHELL IDENTIFICATION

Determining exactly what kind of shell you've discovered can take time, research, and sometimes, a good guess. This guide includes the most common shells, so it's the first place you will want to look to identify what you collect. It might be easiest to look at the images first and compare, then go from there. Be aware! Shells can look alike, so be sure to compare the image against your shell very carefully.

NOTE Remember to follow the guidelines outlined in "Before You Hunt for Shells, Read This!" on page 329.

GASTROPODS

Abalone

SHELL FAMILY Haliotidae

SIZE 10 inches (25 cm)

COLOR Red, blue, green, pearl, pink

HABITAT Offshore rocks in warm seas

WHERE IT CAN BE FOUND Worldwide

POINT OF FACT Shells have a row of holes that allow the animal to excrete waste.

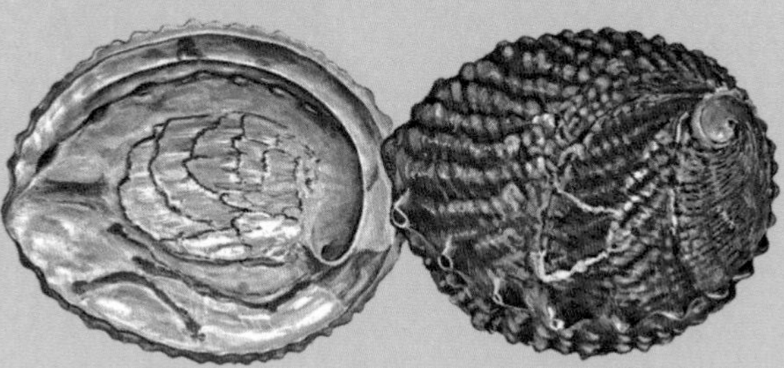

FOUND IT!

WHEN

DATE

WHERE

SPECIFIC PLACE AND SURROUNDINGS

NOTES

True Limpet

SHELL FAMILY Patellidae

SIZE 2 inches (5 cm)

COLOR Light brown, gray, white, pink

HABITAT Rocky shores among algae and lichens

WHERE IT CAN BE FOUND Worldwide

POINT OF FACT Limpets leave a slime trail as they graze, which attracts new algae, which provides food for the snail to eat eventually.

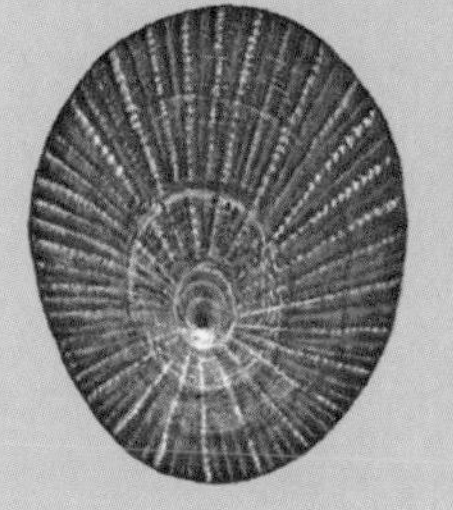

FOUND IT!

WHEN

DATE

WHERE

SPECIFIC PLACE AND SURROUNDINGS

NOTES

Painted Top Shell

SHELL FAMILY Trochidae

SIZE 1 inch (2.5 cm)

COLOR Yellow, red, pink, or white

HABITAT Rocky shores

WHERE IT CAN BE FOUND Worldwide

POINT OF FACT Sea stars eat these animals.

FOUND IT!

WHEN
DATE

WHERE
SPECIFIC PLACE AND SURROUNDINGS

NOTES

Commercial Top Shell

SHELL FAMILY Trochidae

SIZE 4.5 inches (11.5 cm)

COLOR White or pink with brown streaks

HABITAT Near coral reefs

WHERE IT CAN BE FOUND Indian and West Pacific Oceans, the Atlantic Ocean

POINT OF FACT Fishermen collect the snails for their meat and sell the shells for their nacre, the mother of pearl layer, which is used to make pearl buttons.

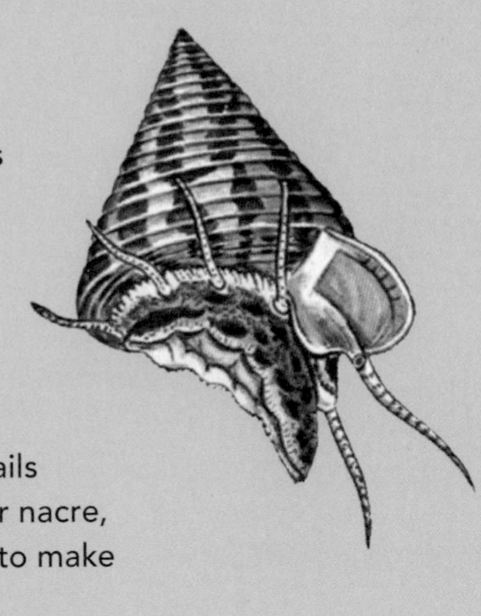

FOUND IT!

WHEN

DATE

WHERE

SPECIFIC PLACE AND SURROUNDINGS

NOTES

GASTROPODS

Bleeding Tooth

SHELL FAMILY Neritidae

SIZE 1.25 inches (3 cm)

COLOR Yellow, red, or white, with brown or black streaks

HABITAT Rocks near the shore

WHERE IT CAN BE FOUND Gulf of Mexico, Caribbean

POINT OF FACT The opening of these shells has a bloodred-colored blotch with one to three teeth.

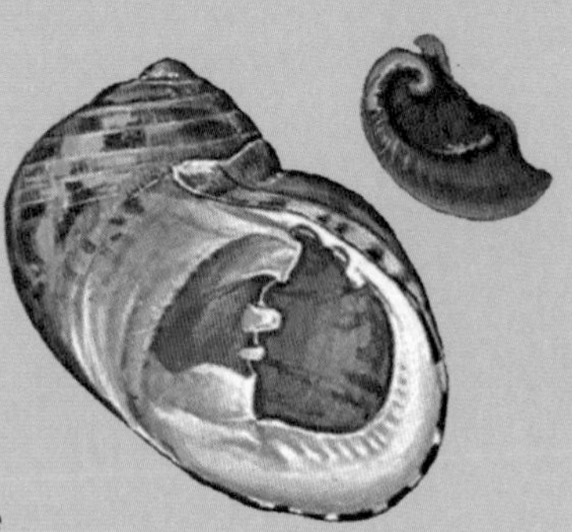

FOUND IT!

WHEN

DATE

WHERE

SPECIFIC PLACE AND SURROUNDINGS

NOTES

Periwinkle

SHELL FAMILY Littorinidae

SIZE 1.25 inches (3 cm)

COLOR Dark brown or gray with dark bands of black

HABITAT Rocks in tidal pools

WHERE IT CAN BE FOUND Worldwide

POINT OF FACT There are more than twenty different species of this shell.

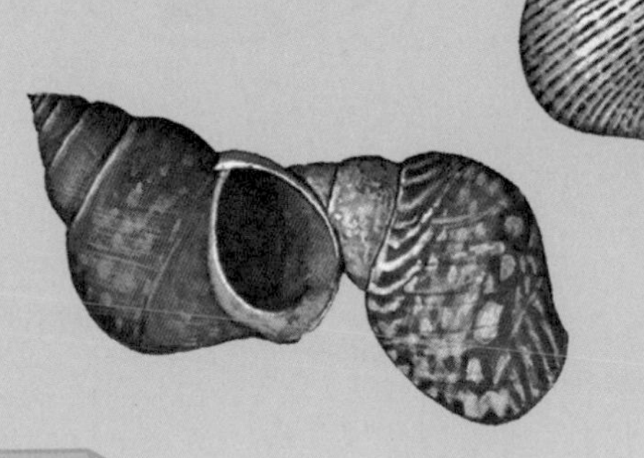

FOUND IT!

WHEN
DATE

WHERE
SPECIFIC PLACE AND SURROUNDINGS

NOTES

Atlantic Slipper Shell

SHELL FAMILY Calyptraeidae

SIZE 1.5 inches (4 cm)

COLOR White, yellow, brown with reddish brown streaks

HABITAT Shallow water

WHERE IT CAN BE FOUND Atlantic shores of North America, including Gulf of Mexico, Caribbean; introduced to Pacific Northwest and Western Europe

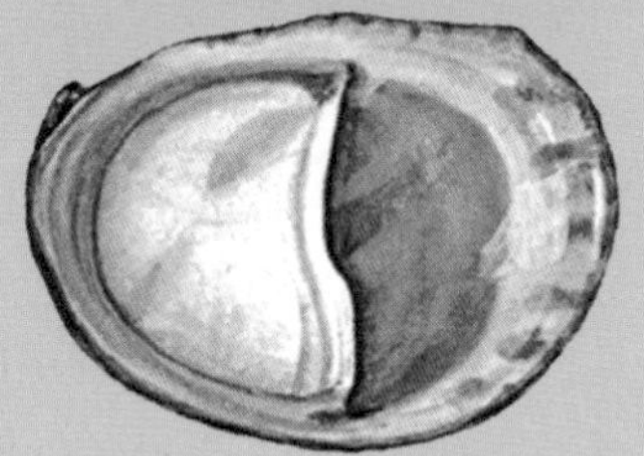

POINT OF FACT The male snails turn into females when they are two or three years old.

FOUND IT!

WHEN

DATE

WHERE

SPECIFIC PLACE AND SURROUNDINGS

NOTES

Florida Fighting Conch

SHELL FAMILY Strombidae

SIZE 3 inches (7.5 cm)

COLOR Pale brown, yellowish

HABITAT Ocean floor

WHERE IT CAN BE FOUND North Carolina to Florida, Gulf of Mexico, Caribbean

POINT OF FACT They are called fighting conchs because the males battle over territory.

FOUND IT!

WHEN

DATE

WHERE

SPECIFIC PLACE AND SURROUNDINGS

NOTES

Queen Conch

SHELL FAMILY Strombidae

SIZE 12 inches (30.5 cm)

COLOR Pale yellow, pink inside

HABITAT Ocean floor

WHERE IT CAN BE FOUND North Carolina to Florida, Gulf of Mexico, Caribbean

POINT OF FACT These were once used as blowing horns in the Native and Mesoamerican cultures.

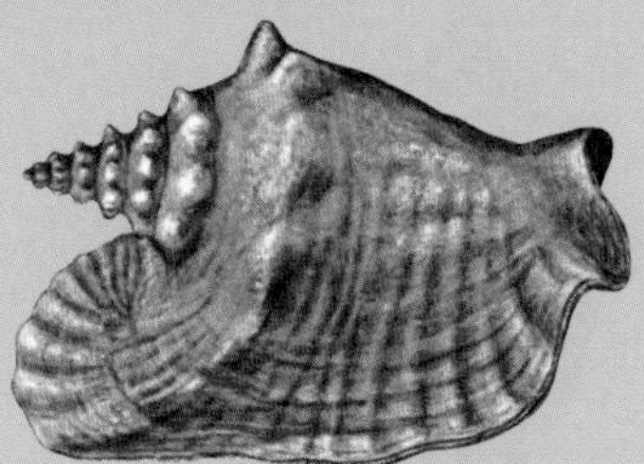

WARNING:
It might be illegal to take this shell home with you. Please check before removing this shell from its environment.

FOUND IT!

WHEN

DATE

WHERE

SPECIFIC PLACE AND SURROUNDINGS

NOTES

Cowrie

SHELL FAMILY Cypraeidae

SIZE 3 inches (7.5 cm)

COLOR Shiny brown with white or gold splotches

HABITAT Under rocks

WHERE IT CAN BE FOUND Warm waters worldwide

POINT OF FACT There are more than 150 species of this shell.

FOUND IT!

WHEN

DATE

WHERE

SPECIFIC PLACE AND SURROUNDINGS

NOTES

GASTROPODS

Lewis's Moon Snail

SHELL FAMILY Naticidae

SIZE 3.5 inches (9 cm)

COLOR Brown or grayish brown with white

HABITAT Silt and sand in shallow water

WHERE IT CAN BE FOUND Alaska to California, Japan

POINT OF FACT The largest species of moon snails.

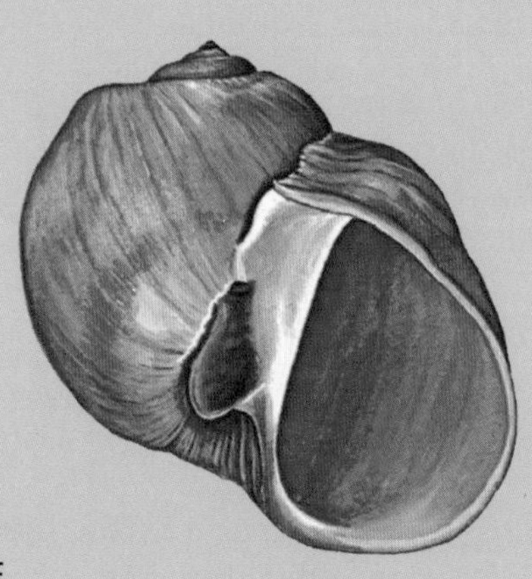

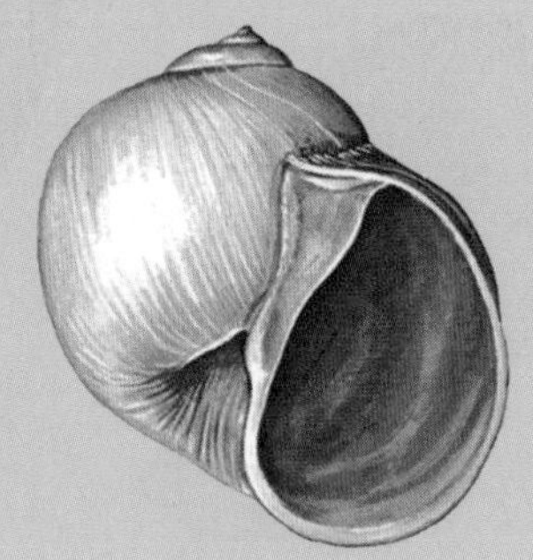

FOUND IT!

WHEN

DATE

WHERE

SPECIFIC PLACE AND SURROUNDINGS

NOTES

Moon Snail

SHELL FAMILY Naticidae

SIZE 2 inches (5 cm)

COLOR Brown with purplish grooves

HABITAT Shallow water

WHERE IT CAN BE FOUND Worldwide

POINT OF FACT Moon snails are carnivorous and drill a hole into the shells of their prey.

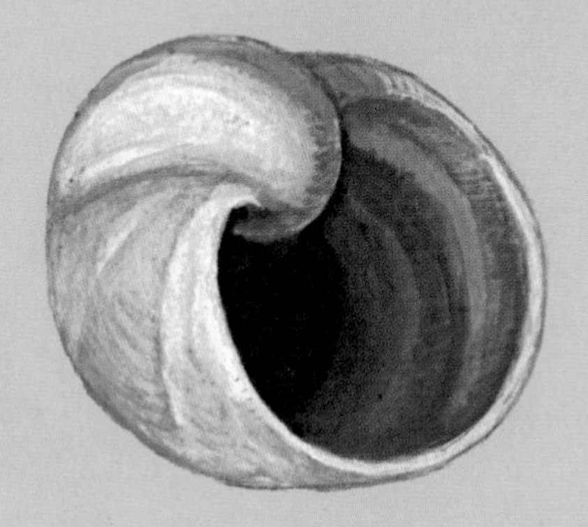

FOUND IT!

WHEN
DATE

WHERE
SPECIFIC PLACE AND SURROUNDINGS

NOTES

Bonnet Shell

SHELL FAMILY Cassidae

SIZE 4–5 inches (10-12.5 cm)

COLOR Cream with spotches of light brown that make it look like a plaid pattern

HABITAT Warm tropical waters around depths of 50–150 feet (15–45m).

WHERE IT CAN BE FOUND North Carolina to Texas shorelines and Brazil

POINT OF FACT The scotch bonnet shell is the state shell of North Carolina

FOUND IT!

WHEN

DATE

WHERE

SPECIFIC PLACE AND SURROUNDINGS

NOTES

King Helmet Shell

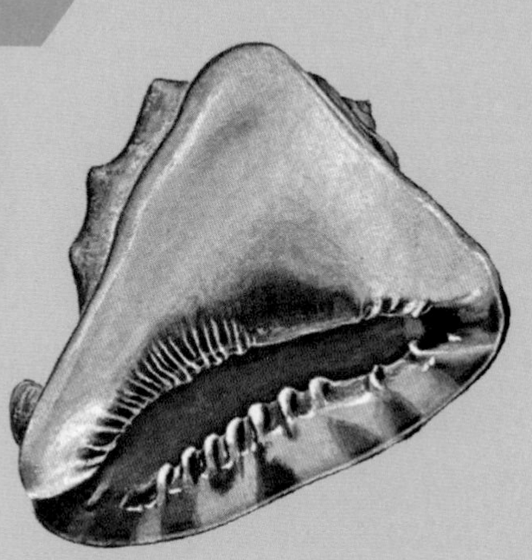

SHELL FAMILY Cassidae

SIZE 7 inches (18 cm)

COLOR Brown or grayish brown with white

HABITAT Sandy bottoms of tropical and temperate seas

WHERE IT CAN BE FOUND Caribbean

POINT OF FACT Helmet shells have a thick, flat shield next to their opening that helps them glide over and burrow into sand.

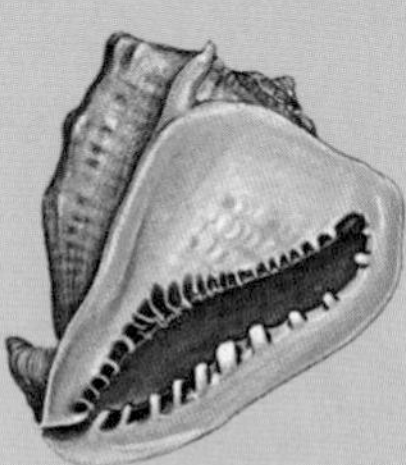

FOUND IT!

WHEN

DATE

WHERE

SPECIFIC PLACE AND SURROUNDINGS

NOTES

GASTROPODS

Giant Tun

SHELL FAMILY Tonnidae

SIZE 6 inches (15 cm)

COLOR Brown with purplish grooves

HABITAT Offshore coral reefs, deep warm water

WHERE IT CAN BE FOUND Atlantic, Caribbean, Gulf of Mexico, Mediterranean, West Africa, South Africa

POINT OF FACT This snail has very acidic saliva that it will spit at other creatures when it is threatened.

FOUND IT!

WHEN

DATE

WHERE

SPECIFIC PLACE AND SURROUNDINGS

NOTES

Oregon Triton

SHELL FAMILY Ranellidae

SIZE 4.5 inches (11.5 cm)

COLOR Light brown and white with yellow highlights

HABITAT Rocky shores

WHERE IT CAN BE FOUND Pacific Ocean, Alaska to California, and Japan

POINT OF FACT These shells have bristly hair growing out of them.

FOUND IT!

WHEN
DATE

WHERE
SPECIFIC PLACE AND SURROUNDINGS

NOTES

Angular Triton

SHELL FAMILY Ranellidae

SIZE 5 inches (12.5 cm)

COLOR Reddish brown with white inside

HABITAT Shallow water

WHERE IT CAN BE FOUND Gulf of Mexico, Caribbean, Florida south to Brazil

POINT OF FACT These shells have large ribs with smaller ridges in between.

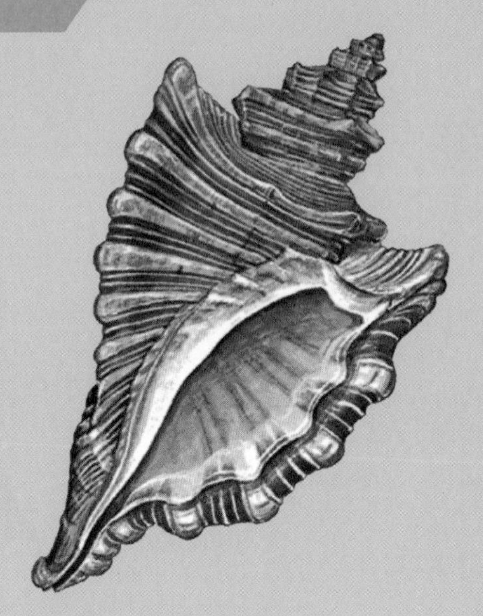

FOUND IT!

WHEN

DATE

WHERE

SPECIFIC PLACE AND SURROUNDINGS

NOTES

Neapolitan Triton

SHELL FAMILY Cymatiidae

SIZE 4 inches (10 cm)

COLOR Light to dark brown with multi-colored splotches

HABITAT Reefs, rocky shores, coastal estuaries where rivers meet the sea

WHERE IT CAN BE FOUND
Warm seas worldwide

POINT OF FACT Triton shells are often called trumpet shells because larger ones can be made into musical horns.

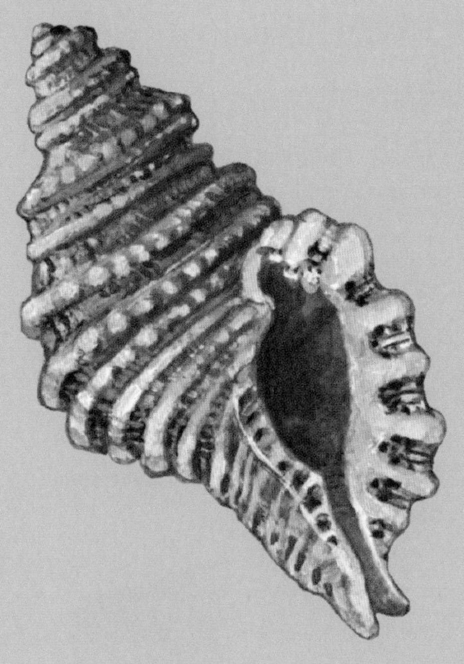

FOUND IT!

WHEN
DATE

WHERE
SPECIFIC PLACE AND SURROUNDINGS

NOTES

California Frog Snail

SHELL FAMILY Bursidae

SIZE 4 inches (10 cm)

COLOR Yellowish brown with small brown lines across it

HABITAT Rocks offshore

WHERE IT CAN BE FOUND Central California south to Mexico

POINT OF FACT This shell has bumps on it that make it feel sort of like a frog, which is how it got its name.

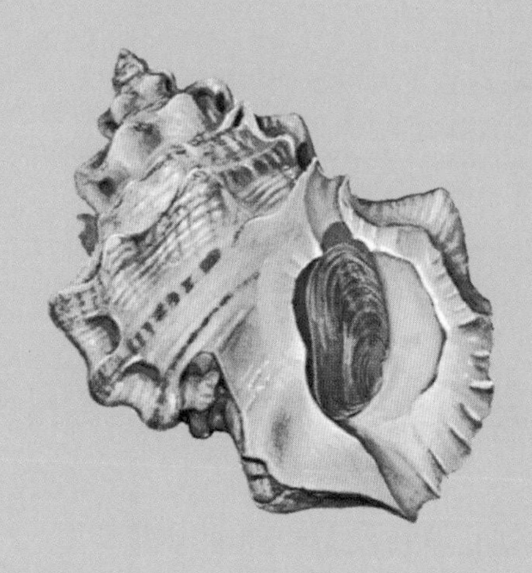

FOUND IT!

WHEN

DATE

WHERE

SPECIFIC PLACE AND SURROUNDINGS

NOTES

Three-Winged Murex

SHELL FAMILY Muricidae

SIZE 2.5 inches (6.5 cm)

COLOR Yellowish white with small brown lines

HABITAT Rocks offshore

WHERE IT CAN BE FOUND California to Mexico

POINT OF FACT These creatures eat bivalve mollusks.

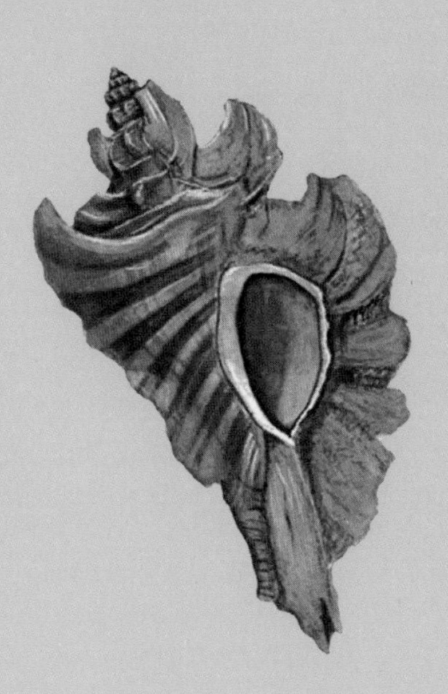

FOUND IT!

WHEN

DATE

WHERE

SPECIFIC PLACE AND SURROUNDINGS

NOTES

Apple Murex

SHELL FAMILY Muricidae

SIZE 3 inches (7.5 cm)

COLOR Yellow to dark brown

HABITAT Offshore on rocks and sands, coral reefs, mangroves

WHERE IT CAN BE FOUND Gulf of Mexico, Caribbean

POINT OF FACT These creatures eat oysters by making holes in the shells and sucking them out.

FOUND IT!

WHEN

DATE

WHERE

SPECIFIC PLACE AND SURROUNDINGS

NOTES

Lace Murex

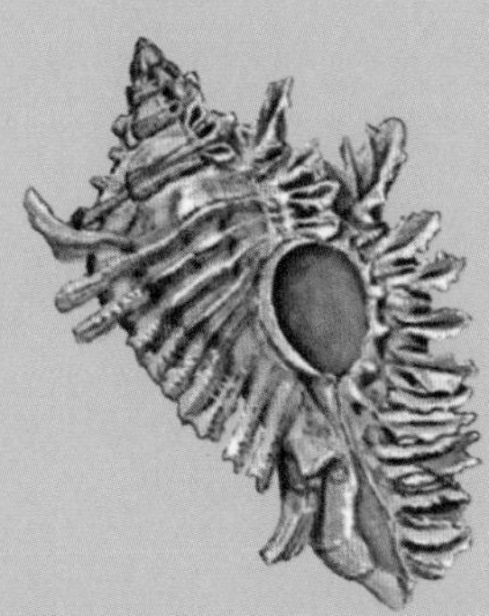

SHELL FAMILY Muricidae

SIZE 2 inches (5 cm)

COLOR Cream and yellow

HABITAT Offshore on rocks and sands, coral reefs, mangroves

WHERE IT CAN BE FOUND Gulf of Mexico, Florida

POINT OF FACT A common species in the Gulf of Mexico, although it's tough to find them on the shore intact.

FOUND IT!

WHEN

DATE

WHERE

SPECIFIC PLACE AND SURROUNDINGS

NOTES

Dog Whelk

SHELL FAMILY Muricidae

SIZE 3 inches (7 cm)

COLOR White, yellow, or brown, and rarely colors like purple, blue, and pink

HABITAT Rocky shores and estuaries

WHERE IT CAN BE FOUND
Arctic, North Atlantic coasts of Europe, North America

POINT OF FACT These shells are easier to find during low tide. They also may look different depending on their exposure to waves.

FOUND IT!

WHEN
DATE

WHERE
SPECIFIC PLACE AND SURROUNDINGS

NOTES

Common Dove Shell

SHELL FAMILY Columbellidae

SIZE 0.75 inches (2 cm)

COLOR Brown, orange, white, or pink

HABITAT Shallow waters

WHERE IT CAN BE FOUND Gulf of Mexico, Caribbean, south to Brazil

POINT OF FACT The shell patterns help camouflage these snails in algae.

FOUND IT!

WHEN
DATE

WHERE
SPECIFIC PLACE AND SURROUNDINGS

NOTES

Stromboid Dove Shell

SHELL FAMILY Columbellidae

SIZE 1.75 inches (4.5 cm)

COLOR Reddish brown with white splotches

HABITAT Shallow tidal waters

WHERE IT CAN BE FOUND Southern California to Peru

POINT OF FACT These shells have large teeth at the lips of the mouth.

FOUND IT!

WHEN
DATE

WHERE
SPECIFIC PLACE AND SURROUNDINGS

NOTES

Common Northern Whelk

SHELL FAMILY Buccinidae

SIZE 3 inches (7.5 cm)

COLOR Brown or cream, with darker brown bands

HABITAT Hard and sandy bottoms of cold seas

WHERE IT CAN BE FOUND Arctic, North Atlantic coasts of Europe and North America

POINT OF FACT The females get together to lay their eggs in a group.

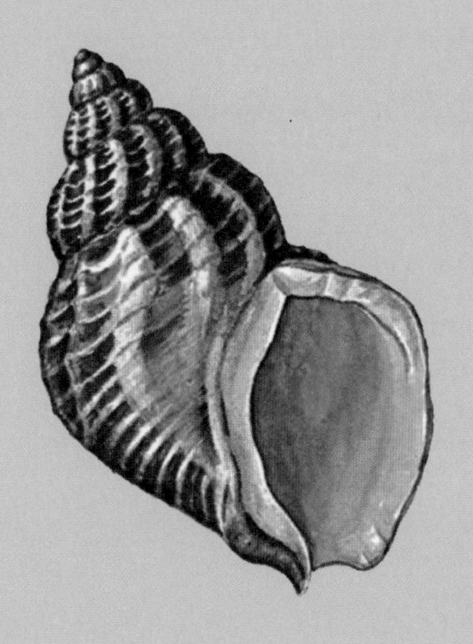

FOUND IT!

WHEN

DATE

WHERE

SPECIFIC PLACE AND SURROUNDINGS

NOTES

Kellet's Whelk

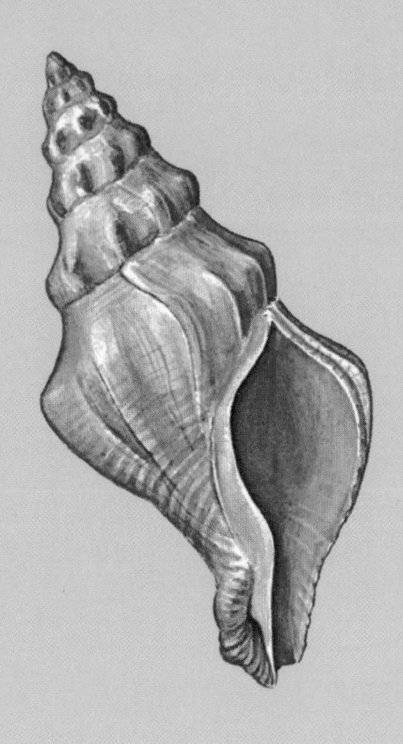

SHELL FAMILY Buccinidae

SIZE 4.5 inches (11.5 cm)

COLOR Yellowish white

HABITAT Kelp beds on soft and rocky ocean bottoms

WHERE IT CAN BE FOUND Central California south to Mexico

POINT OF FACT These animals are scavengers and eat anything that is dead on the ocean floor.

FOUND IT!

WHEN

DATE

WHERE

SPECIFIC PLACE AND SURROUNDINGS

NOTES

Lightning Whelk

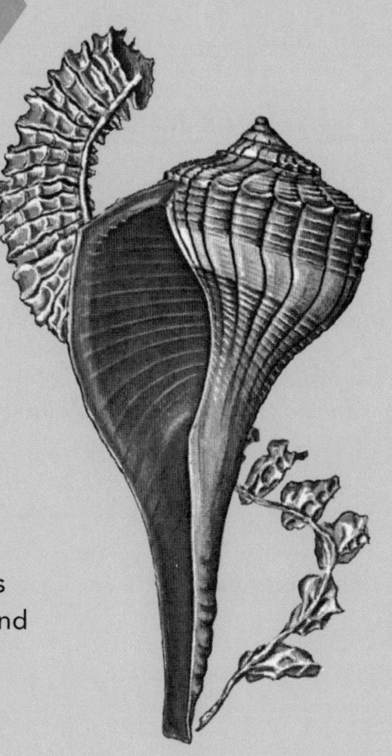

SHELL FAMILY Melongenidae

SIZE 6 inches (15 cm)

COLOR White with brown vertical stripes

HABITAT Sandy bottoms of shallow water

WHERE IT CAN BE FOUND Southeastern United States, Gulf of Mexico

POINT OF FACT Two-million-year-old fossils of these left-handed shells have been found in Florida.

FOUND IT!

WHEN

DATE

WHERE

SPECIFIC PLACE AND SURROUNDINGS

NOTES

GASTROPODS

Pear Conch Whelk

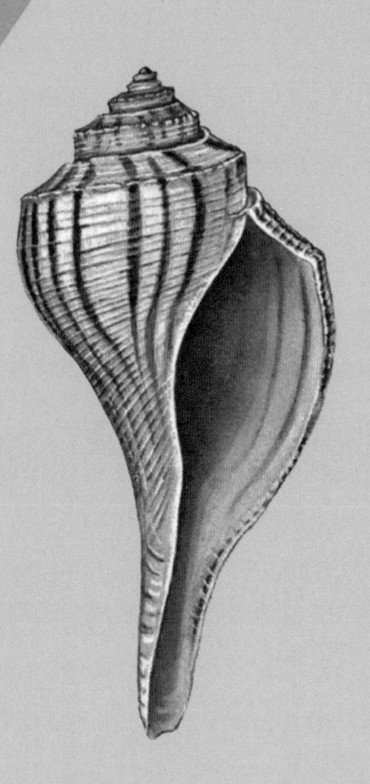

SHELL FAMILY Melongenidae

SIZE 4 inches (10 cm)

COLOR Cream with brown stripes

HABITAT Shallow water

WHERE IT CAN BE FOUND Southeastern United States, Gulf of Mexico, Caribbean

POINT OF FACT Whelks are edible, and quite tasty to people who live in Northern Europe.

FOUND IT!

WHEN

DATE

WHERE

SPECIFIC PLACE AND SURROUNDINGS

NOTES

Three-Line Mud Snail

SHELL FAMILY Nassariidae

SIZE 0.75 inches (2 cm)

COLOR Yellow with red stripes

HABITAT Shallow water

WHERE IT CAN BE FOUND Atlantic coast of North America

POINT OF FACT These shells have tiny bumps that look like beads.

FOUND IT!

WHEN

DATE

WHERE

SPECIFIC PLACE AND SURROUNDINGS

NOTES

New Zealand Mud Snail

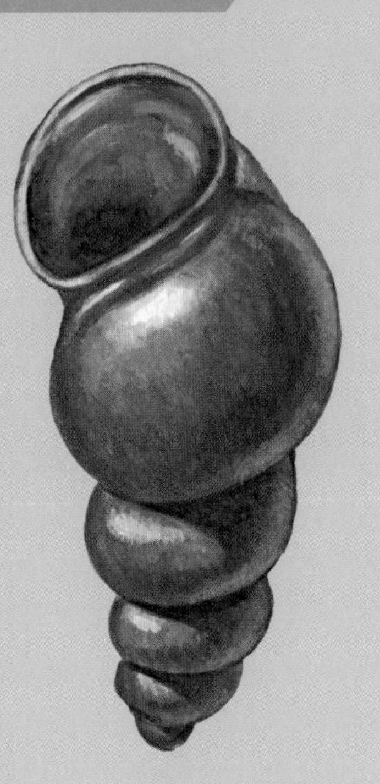

SHELL FAMILY Hydrobiidae

SIZE 0.2 inches (6-7 mm)

COLOR Gray, light to dark brown

HABITAT Lakes and rivers

WHERE IT CAN BE FOUND West coast, Great Lakes, and Chesapeake Bay. Also Europe, North America, Australia, Iraq, Turkey, and Japan.

POINT OF FACT This shell is considered an invasive species in the United States, as it is native to New Zealand.

FOUND IT!

WHEN

DATE

WHERE

SPECIFIC PLACE AND SURROUNDINGS

NOTES

GASTROPODS

Giant Western Nassa

SHELL FAMILY Nassariidae

SIZE 1.5 inches (4 cm)

COLOR Brown

HABITAT Intertidal areas with mud and sand

WHERE IT CAN BE FOUND Pacific coast of North America

POINT OF FACT These creatures can crawl very fast with their one foot.

FOUND IT!

WHEN
DATE

WHERE
SPECIFIC PLACE AND SURROUNDINGS

NOTES

GASTROPODS

True Tulip

SHELL FAMILY Fasciolariidae

SIZE 5 inches (12.5 cm)

COLOR Pink or white with brown splotches, or bright orange

HABITAT Shallow water

WHERE IT CAN BE FOUND West Atlantic, North Carolina to Gulf of Mexico, Caribbean

POINT OF FACT These shells are often taken over by hermit crabs.

FOUND IT!

WHEN
DATE

WHERE
SPECIFIC PLACE AND SURROUNDINGS

NOTES

GASTROPODS

Banded Tulip

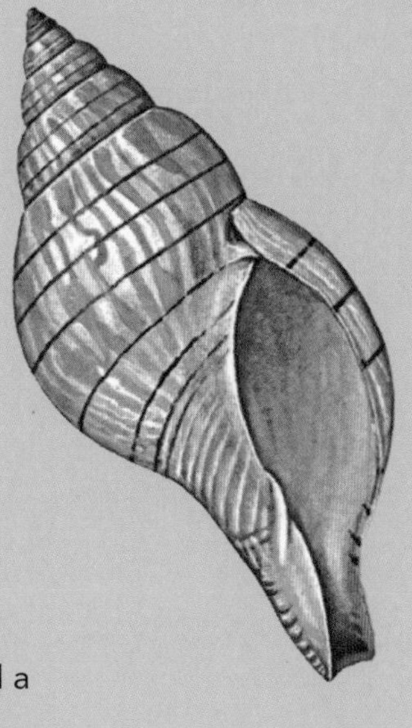

SHELL FAMILY Fasciolariidae

SIZE 3.5 inches (9 cm)

COLOR Yellow with gray streaks and brown lines that go around the shell

HABITAT Shallow grassy bays

WHERE IT CAN BE FOUND West Atlantic, North Carolina to Gulf of Mexico, Caribbean

POINT OF FACT Tulip shells are home to black snails, which can hide from predators inside their shells safe behind a lid-like plate on their foot.

FOUND IT!

WHEN

DATE

WHERE

SPECIFIC PLACE AND SURROUNDINGS

NOTES

GASTROPODS

Trochlear Latirus

SHELL FAMILY Fasciolariidae

SIZE 2 inches (5 cm)

COLOR Cream with light brown splotches

HABITAT Rocky beaches, coral reefs

WHERE IT CAN BE FOUND Caribbean

POINT OF FACT These shells are on a postage stamp in Belize.

FOUND IT!

WHEN
DATE

WHERE
SPECIFIC PLACE AND SURROUNDINGS

NOTES

Brown-Lined Latirus

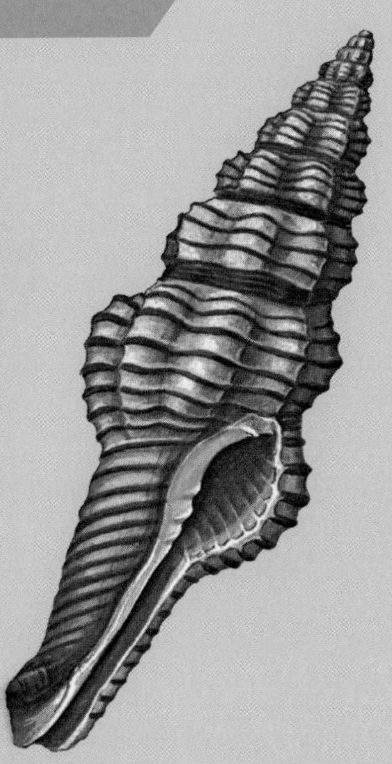

SHELL FAMILY Fasciolariidae

SIZE 3 inches (7.5 cm)

COLOR Light brown

HABITAT Shallow water

WHERE IT CAN BE FOUND Gulf of Mexico, Caribbean

POINT OF FACT These shells have blunt teeth around the opening.

FOUND IT!

WHEN

DATE

WHERE

SPECIFIC PLACE AND SURROUNDINGS

NOTES

Caribbean Vase

SHELL FAMILY Vasidae

SIZE 3 inches (7.5 cm)

COLOR Brown, cream

HABITAT Shallow seabeds, coral reefs

WHERE IT CAN BE FOUND Gulf of Mexico, Caribbean Sea, West Atlantic, Florida to Brazil

POINT OF FACT These animals like to eat bivalves and worms and are often found in pairs.

FOUND IT!

WHEN

DATE

WHERE

SPECIFIC PLACE AND SURROUNDINGS

NOTES

GASTROPODS

Common Nutmeg

SHELL FAMILY Cancellariidae

SIZE 1.5 inches (4 cm)

COLOR Cream or yellow in color with brown splotches

HABITAT Soft seabeds in shallow water offshore

WHERE IT CAN BE FOUND Gulf of Mexico, West Atlantic, North Carolina to Brazil

POINT OF FACT Scientists think this species is carnivorous because of the shape of its tonguelike feeding structure.

FOUND IT!

WHEN

DATE

WHERE

SPECIFIC PLACE AND SURROUNDINGS

NOTES

Hooked Cavoline

SHELL FAMILY Cavoliniidae

SIZE 0.5 inches (1.5 cm)

COLOR Light brown or amber

HABITAT Warm seas

WHERE IT CAN BE FOUND West Atlantic, West Central Pacific, Mediterranean

POINT OF FACT These snails are also called sea butterflies. Their foot is specially adapted to flap like wings in the water.

FOUND IT!

WHEN
DATE

WHERE
SPECIFIC PLACE AND SURROUNDINGS

NOTES

Three-Toothed Cavoline

SHELL FAMILY Cavoliniidae

SIZE 0.75 inches (2 cm)

COLOR Light brown or amber

HABITAT Warm seas

WHERE IT CAN BE FOUND
West Atlantic, Mediterranean, Pacific Ocean

POINT OF FACT These swimming snails form mucus webs to trap their food and then eat the food and web together, excreting whatever they can't digest.

FOUND IT!

WHEN
DATE

WHERE
SPECIFIC PLACE AND SURROUNDINGS

NOTES

Ancylid

SHELL FAMILY Ancylidae

SIZE 0.8–3 inches (2–8 cm)

COLOR Brown to light tan

HABITAT Lakes, ponds, and slow-moving rivers

WHERE IT CAN BE FOUND Worldwide

POINT OF FACT Sometimes they can be found clinging to cattails.

FOUND IT!

WHEN

DATE

WHERE

SPECIFIC PLACE AND SURROUNDINGS

NOTES

Pond Snail

SHELL FAMILY Lymnaeidae

SIZE Up to 1.9 inches (5 cm)

COLOR Dark to light brown

HABITAT Lakes, swamps, and even some ditches if they have water from a spring, usually in the mud or attached to plants

WHERE IT CAN BE FOUND Northern United States and Canada

POINT OF FACT This shell is dextral, which means its opening is to the right.

FOUND IT!

WHEN
DATE

WHERE
SPECIFIC PLACE AND SURROUNDINGS

NOTES

Acuta Bladder Snail

SHELL FAMILY Physidae

SIZE 0.75 inches (2 cm)

COLOR Light yellowish-brown or tan

HABITAT Mountain streams, ponds, swamps

WHERE IT CAN BE FOUND
Bodies of water below 10,500 feet (3,200 m) elevation

POINT OF FACT Because these shells are so common, they are called the "pigeons of fresh water."

FOUND IT!

WHEN
DATE

WHERE
SPECIFIC PLACE AND SURROUNDINGS

NOTES

Marsh Rams-Horn

SHELL FAMILY Planorbidae

SIZE 0.8 inches (2 cm)

COLOR Light yellowish-brown

HABITAT Shallow waters in lakes, rivers, and ditches

WHERE IT CAN BE FOUND
Central, southern, northeastern, and northwestern United States

POINT OF FACT These shells are about the size of a dime.

FOUND IT!

WHEN
DATE

WHERE
SPECIFIC PLACE AND SURROUNDINGS

NOTES

Mud Amnicola

SHELL FAMILY Physidae

SIZE 0.2 inches (0.5 cm)

COLOR Light brown

HABITAT Slow-moving shallow creeks with a muddy bottom

WHERE IT CAN BE FOUND Eastern United States from Canada to Florida

POINT OF FACT These pond snails graze on algae.

FOUND IT!

WHEN
DATE

WHERE
SPECIFIC PLACE AND SURROUNDINGS

NOTES

GASTROPODS

Perverse Turrid

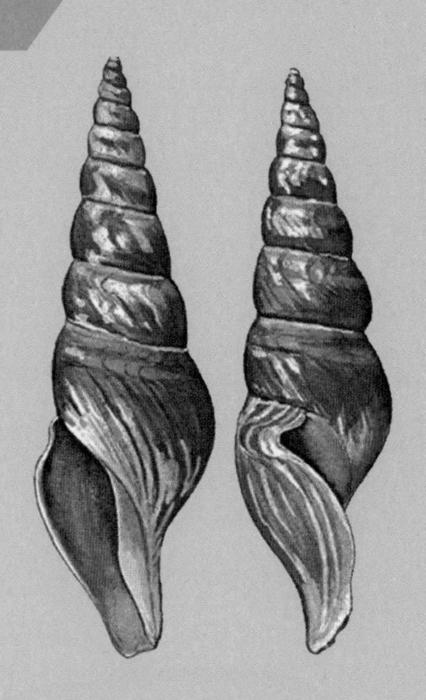

SHELL FAMILY Turridae

SIZE 2 inches (5 cm)

COLOR Whitish-brown

HABITAT Offshore in ocean water from 30–300 feet (9–90 m) deep

WHERE IT CAN BE FOUND Alaska to Southern California

POINT OF FACT The Turridae class of shells has been around for 100 million years.

FOUND IT!

WHEN

DATE

WHERE

SPECIFIC PLACE AND SURROUNDINGS

NOTES

Common Blue Mussel

SHELL FAMILY Mytilidae

SIZE 3 inches (7.5 cm)

COLOR Blue

HABITAT Intertidal rocks

WHERE IT CAN BE FOUND Worldwide

POINT OF FACT This snail is fished commercially and grown in aquaculture (like agriculture but in water), where marine animals are grown for food.

FOUND IT!

WHEN

DATE

WHERE

SPECIFIC PLACE AND SURROUNDINGS

NOTES

Iceland Scallop

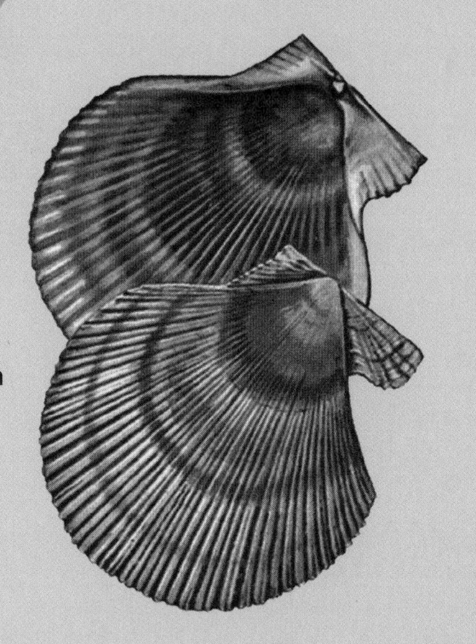

SHELL FAMILY Pectinidae

SIZE 3.5 inches (9 cm)

COLOR White or reddish pink

HABITAT Both shallow and deep water on the seafloor

WHERE IT CAN BE FOUND Arctic, North Atlantic, and North Pacific Oceans

POINT OF FACT This animal is known for its beautiful fan-shaped shell.

FOUND IT!

WHEN
DATE

WHERE
SPECIFIC PLACE AND SURROUNDINGS

NOTES

Lion's Paw

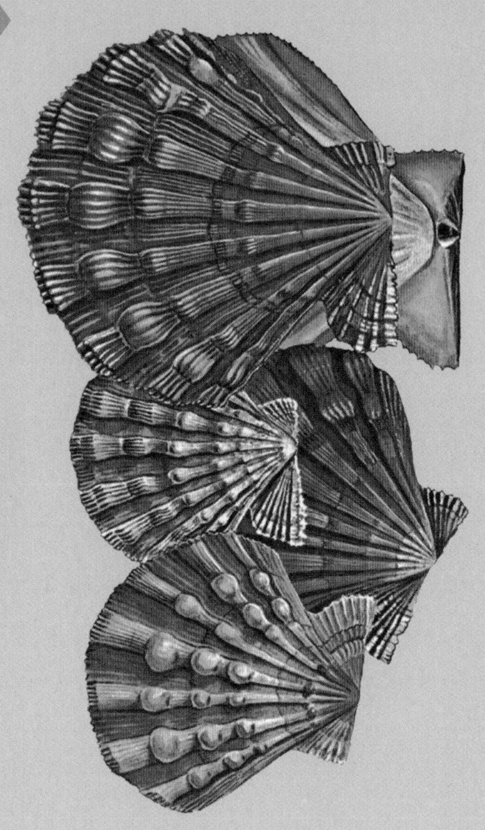

SHELL FAMILY Pectinidae

SIZE 4 inches (10 cm)

COLOR Dark orange to red with brownish stripes

HABITAT Offshore

WHERE IT CAN BE FOUND Gulf of Mexico, Caribbean, West Atlantic, southeastern United States to Brazil

POINT OF FACT These shells are popular for use in crafts and jewelry making.

FOUND IT!

WHEN

DATE

WHERE

SPECIFIC PLACE AND SURROUNDINGS

NOTES

Sulcate Astarte Clam

SHELL FAMILY Astartidae

SIZE 1 inch (2.5 cm)

COLOR Brownish white

HABITAT Offshore buried in mud and sand in cold water

WHERE IT CAN BE FOUND North Atlantic, Nova Scotia to New Jersey, Norway to United Kingdom, Mediterranean

POINT OF FACT This species is a hundred million years old.

FOUND IT!

WHEN
DATE

WHERE
SPECIFIC PLACE AND SURROUNDINGS

NOTES

Atlantic Giant Cockle

SHELL FAMILY Cardiidae

SIZE 5 inches (12.5 cm)

COLOR Cream, with brown splotches

HABITAT Shallow waters and the coast of beaches, bays, and estuaries.

WHERE IT CAN BE FOUND North Carolina to Florida and the Gulf of Mexico.

POINT OF FACT Different kinds of cockles can be found in both salt and fresh water. Some are more than 65 million years old.

FOUND IT!

WHEN
DATE

WHERE
SPECIFIC PLACE AND SURROUNDINGS

NOTES

Sunrise Tellin

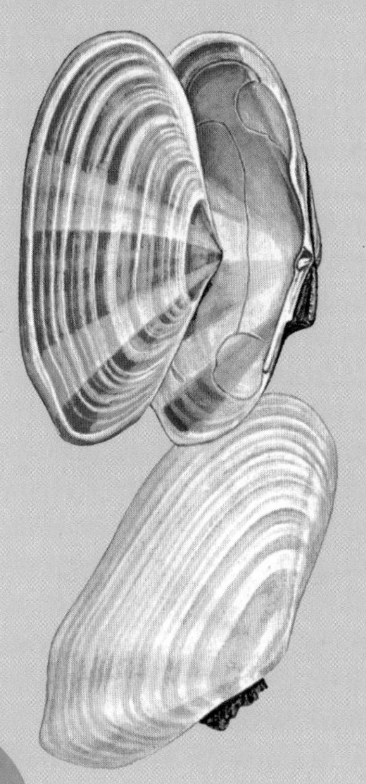

SHELL FAMILY Tellinidae

SIZE 3 inches (7.5 cm)

COLOR White with pink, yellow, or red highlights

HABITAT Offshore buried in mud

WHERE IT CAN BE FOUND Gulf of Mexico, Caribbean, West Atlantic, southeastern United States to Brazil

POINT OF FACT These animals are found on a lot of beaches, where they burrow under the sand.

WARNING:
It might be illegal to take this shell home with you. Please check before removing this shell from its environment.

FOUND IT!

WHEN
DATE

WHERE
SPECIFIC PLACE AND SURROUNDINGS

NOTES

Speckled Tellin

SHELL FAMILY Tellinidae

SIZE 3 inches (7.5 cm)

COLOR White with purplish and brown highlights

HABITAT Offshore buried in sand

WHERE IT CAN BE FOUND Gulf of Mexico, Caribbean, West Atlantic, North Carolina to Brazil

POINT OF FACT Tellin snails eat tiny organisms that crawl on the sand, which is why they bury themselves with their posterior siphon pointing up.

FOUND IT!

WHEN

DATE

WHERE

SPECIFIC PLACE AND SURROUNDINGS

NOTES

Soft-Shelled Clam

SHELL FAMILY Myidae

SIZE 4 inches (10 cm)

COLOR White with brown lines

HABITAT Intertidal muddy areas

WHERE IT CAN BE FOUND Arctic, Atlantic and Pacific, northern coasts of North America, Europe, Asia

POINT OF FACT Soft-shelled clams are prized by humans as a delicious meal.

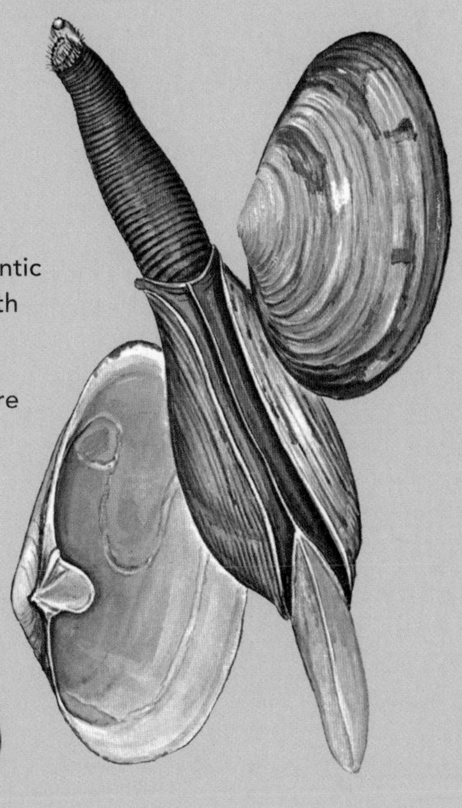

FOUND IT!

WHEN
DATE

WHERE
SPECIFIC PLACE AND SURROUNDINGS

NOTES

Angel Wing

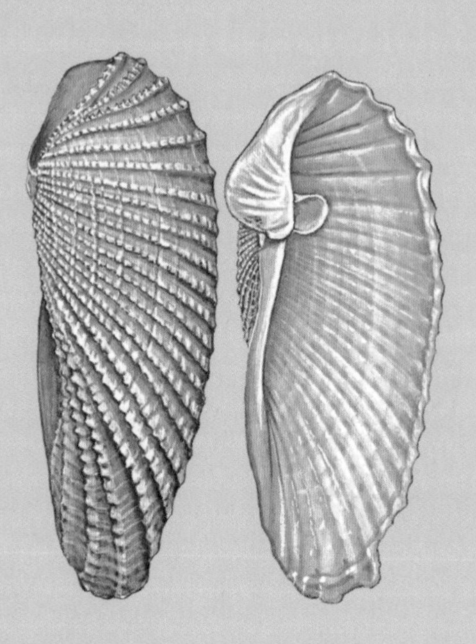

SHELL FAMILY Pholadidae

SIZE 5 inches (12.5 cm)

COLOR White

HABITAT Shallow muddy areas

WHERE IT CAN BE FOUND Gulf of Mexico, Caribbean, West Atlantic, southeastern United States to Brazil

POINT OF FACT This creature can bore through rocks such as gneiss and shale.

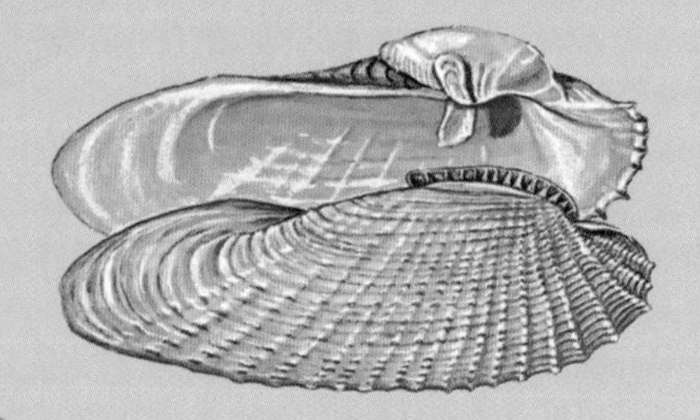

FOUND IT!

WHEN

DATE

WHERE

SPECIFIC PLACE AND SURROUNDINGS

NOTES

California Lyonsia

SHELL FAMILY Lyonsidae

SIZE 1 inch (2.5 cm)

COLOR White

HABITAT Mud and sand offshore

WHERE IT CAN BE FOUND Pacific coast of North America

POINT OF FACT This creature can live inside a sponge or sea squirt.

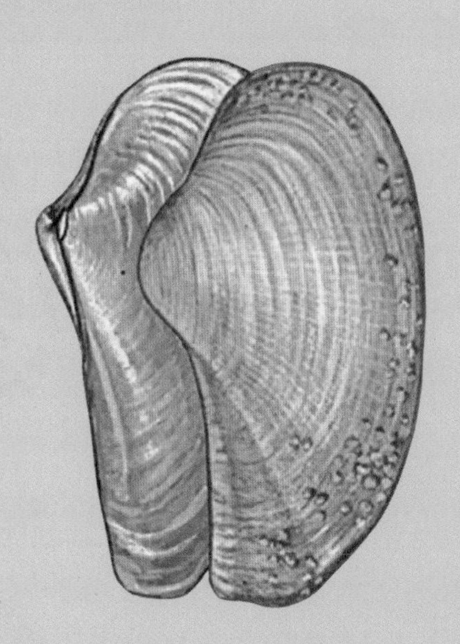

FOUND IT!

WHEN
DATE

WHERE
SPECIFIC PLACE AND SURROUNDINGS

NOTES

Incongruous Ark

SHELL FAMILY Anadara

SIZE 1–2 inches (2.5–5 cm)

COLOR Red, blue, green, pearl, pink, yellow, and white

HABITAT Offshore rocks in warm seas

WHERE IT CAN BE FOUND North Carolina to Brazil

POINT OF FACT Arks have a unique "figure eight–shaped" opening in their mantle, which they use to eat plankton.

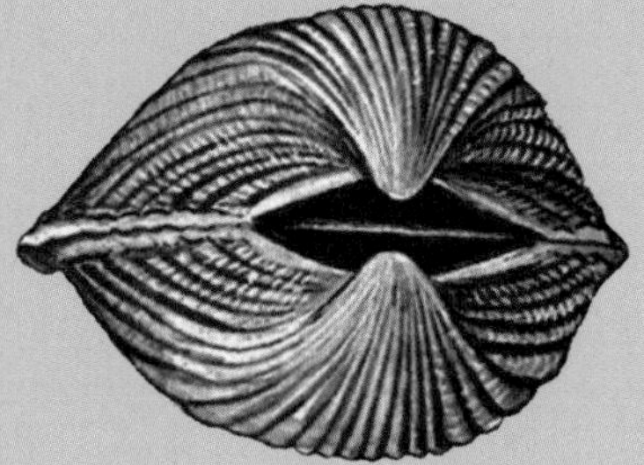

FOUND IT!

WHEN
DATE

WHERE
SPECIFIC PLACE AND SURROUNDINGS

NOTES

101 ACHIEVEMENTS

INDEX

101 OUTDOOR SCHOOL
ROCK, FOSSIL, AND SHELL HUNTING
ACHIEVEMENTS

The outdoors are calling—and this is the list of everything they have to offer. Track everything you master, experience, and collect on your adventures by checking off your achievements below. See if you can complete all 101!

- 1 Made a rock-hunting map
- 2 Learned to use a compass
- 3 Went on my first rock hunt
- 4 Excavated a rock with a hammer and chisel
- 5 Waded for treasure with a sieve
- 6 Collected my first ten rocks
- 7 Opened up a rock to see what's inside
- 8 Discovered a geode
- 9 Built a rock collection display case
- 10 Polished my rocks to make them shine
- 11 Collected a rock smaller than a dime
- 12 Collected a rock bigger than my hand
- 13 Collected five igneous rocks
- 14 Collected an intrusive rock
- 15 Collected an extrusive rock
- 16 Collected five sedimentary rocks
- 17 Collected a clastic rock
- 18 Collected a chemical rock
- 19 Collected five metamorphic rocks
- 20 Collected a foliated rock
- 21 Collected a nonfoliated rock
- 22 Hunted for rocks on a riverbank
- 23 Hunted for rocks in a stream or creek

- 24 Hunted for rocks on a mountain
- 25 Hunted for rocks on the ocean shore
- 26 Hunted for rocks in a valley
- 27 Hunted for rocks in a meadow or prairie
- 28 Identified rocks from my local area
- 29 Collected a rock in an unexpected environment
- 30 Tested rocks for hardness, streak, and cleavage
- 31 Smashed a rock!
- 32 Found the density and specific gravity of a rock
- 33 Completed a rock acid test
- 34 Completed a rock magnetic test
- 35 Discovered a meteorite or other space rock
- 36 Identified the rocks in my collection
- 37 Collected granite
- 38 Collected limestone
- 39 Collected coal
- 40 Collected shale
- 41 Collected sandstone
- 42 Collected marble
- 43 Collected quartz
- 44 Collected a rare mineral
- 45 Collected copper
- 46 Collected gold
- 47 Collected silver
- 48 Collected iron
- 49 Collected a diamond
- 50 Collected a gemstone
- 51 Made a fossil-hunting map
- 52 Went on my first fossil hunt
- 53 Hunted for fossils on a riverbank
- 54 Hunted for fossils in a stream or creek
- 55 Hunted for fossils in a desert or beach
- 56 Discovered my first fossil
- 57 Made a plaster of paris cast to excavate a fossil
- 58 Completed the lick test
- 59 Read a geological map to find or date a fossil
- 60 Discovered the age of a fossil
- 61 Identified a fossil in my collection

- 62 Went to a fossil dig site
- 63 Made my own fossil dig site
- 64 Discovered a permineralized fossil
- 65 Discovered a body fossil
- 66 Discovered a trace fossil
- 67 Discovered a mold fossil
- 68 Discovered a cast fossil
- 69 Discovered a carbonized fossil
- 70 Discovered a whole fossil
- 71 Discovered a plant fossil
- 72 Discovered an animal fossil
- 73 Discovered petrified wood
- 74 Learned to check tide levels
- 75 Made a shell-hunting map
- 76 Went on my first shell hunt
- 77 Dug for shells in the sand
- 78 Waded for shells in the shore
- 79 Snorkeled for shells
- 80 Collected five gastropod shells
- 81 Collected gastropod shells of different shapes and sizes
- 82 Collected five mollusk shells
- 83 Collected mollusk shells of different shapes and sizes
- 84 Collected an abalone shell
- 85 Collected a cowrie shell
- 86 Collected a periwinkle shell
- 87 Collected a whelk shell
- 88 Collected a blue mussel shell
- 89 Collected a sand dollar
- 90 Collected a shark tooth
- 91 Collected a star fish
- 92 Collected a shell smaller than a dime
- 93 Collected a shell bigger than my hand
- 94 Identified the shells in my collection
- 95 Discovered the age of my shells
- 96 Collected shells by an ocean
- 97 Collected shells by a lake
- 98 Collected shells by a river
- 99 Collected shells by an estuary
- 100 Collected shells by a tide pool
- 101 Filled my collection with over 100 rocks, fossils, and shells

INDEX

JENNIFER SWANSON is the award-winning author of over forty-five books for kids, mostly about science. Her books have received a Parents' Choice Gold Award, a *Kirkus* Best Books award, and many NSTA Best STEM Book awards. When she isn't writing, you can find Jennifer hunting for rocks on her travels or walking along the beach looking for shells.

JENNIFERSWANSONBOOKS.COM

JOHN D. DAWSON has created art spanning over four decades, from early years in advertising art to freelance work for the US Postal Service, National Park Service, United Nations, National Wildlife Federation, National Geographic Society, National Audubon Society, and the Golden Guide books. He and his wife, Kathleen, have lived on the Big Island of Hawaii since 1989.